After

Published by
Soho Press Inc.
853 Broadway
New York, NY 10003

Library of Congress Cataloging-in-Publication Data

Naylor, Phyllis Reynolds.
After / Phyllis Reynolds Naylor.
p. cm.
ISBN 1-56947-354-4 (alk. paper)
1. Widowers—Fiction. 2. Loss (Psychology)—Fiction.
3. Grief—Fiction. I. Title.
PS3564.A9A69 2003
813'.54—dc21 2003050695

10 9 8 7 6 5 4 3 2 1

To the memory of two old friends, G.W. and I.O.

After

ONE

The Daughter

THE DAY AFTER his wife's funeral, in the spring of his fifty-sixth year, three things happened to Harry Gill that were unsettling—four, actually, but he didn't discover that until later: He phoned work only to be told he should be mourning; he found a hand-delivered condolence card slipped under his door, inviting him to dinner the following Saturday, with the added notation that a lovely woman about his age would be present; and his daughter called to say that her husband had disappeared.

Hearing this, Harry sat down heavily on a kitchen chair with its faded green cushion, his deep-set eyes fixed unblinking on the Sierra Club calendar hanging just off-center above the microwave.

"Elaine, for once in your life, talk sense," he said. "What do you mean, 'disappeared'?"

"As in 'off the face of the earth,'" she replied.

"When?"

"About an hour after we got back from your place yesterday. I heard the Chevie drive off, and haven't seen him since."

"Don didn't come home at all last night?"

"It's what I'm telling you!"

"He ever do this before?"

"No. He didn't show up at work, either. They called. I debated all day whether or not to tell you, because . . . well, this on top of Mother. . . ." Elaine's voice suddenly rose in pitch and her nose sounded clogged. "What am I going to do, Dad?"

There was a distinct whine coming from his daughter, like the drone of a mosquito, that had irritated Harry when she was eighteen months old, eighteen years old, and annoyed him now. It had appeared at intervals throughout her twenty-nine years and, just when Harry thought it was banished forever, there it was again, buzzing in his ear. The boys never had this problem.

"Elaine, I just—"

"Oh, this is so like him! This is so utterly, completely like him! And all because I said he's never done anything wild and unpredictable in his life."

The genesis of that escaped him, and Harry decided not to ask. "So he did something wild."

"Don't you see? All you have to do is tell Don Wheeler he's so damned predictable and he'll promptly do something he thinks you wouldn't expect which is just the kind of thing you'd expect him to do after you told him he was predictable." A door slammed in the background. "Jodie just came in, Dad. I'll talk to you later." Elaine hung up.

Harry loved his children. He loved so fiercely that he'd often wished on them some near calamity when they were small so that he could risk his life to save them—Elaine falling into an icy river, Jack fear-frozen at the approach of a grizzly, Claude being snatched by a child molester at the mall. Harry would plunge amid the ice floes, hurl himself between the bear and Jack, tackle the child molester and bring him to his knees.

Then he would hold his trembling son or daughter, feel the small arms around his neck, and be assured that the child would never forget this father's love. It was what you did, what you imagined doing, when it was not you but your mate who had brought an original life into the world, and you, the helpless observer, were merely the enabler.

But children grew tall and restless, by turns sweet and surly, and then they were adults, and what did you do with all this backed-up love? How to express it then? When their tender child-skin had grown thick with experience and disappointment, how did you help? And what did you say to a daughter who had probably driven her husband from their bed, if not half out of his mind?

Harry placed one hand on each knee—hands as thick as bread boards—and a deep sigh came from his chest, the weight of it filling the room. The one person who would know how to deal with this, who would know exactly what to do, in fact, was gone. He continued to stare at the calendar. Beneath a brilliant orange photograph of Arches National Park, the small squares of April days seemed identical. Yet in one of those benign-looking squares his wife had died, and in another his son-in-law had run off. Sort of made you want to cross out the rest from now till Christmas. Nip them in the bud.

He leaned back, resting his head against the wall. His wife hadn't even been buried yet. Harry didn't know if he only imagined it but Fred Fletcher had seemed a bit peeved over the whole business. He'd been Harry's friend for many years, Fred had reminded him, and with Beth so loved by everyone he had naturally assumed that she'd be laid out proper where folks could pay their respects. He could do cremations of course, but somehow it just didn't seem right for Beth.

"Well, that's what she wanted," Harry had said, handing Fred the large green ceramic jar with the black and purple flowers painted on one side and a stem forming the handle of the lid. Beth had bought it at an antique store in Kensington. She had wanted her ashes in the jar and the jar sitting right up there in front at the funeral service. Later, she had instructed, her remains were to be scattered on the Chesapeake Bay, where she and Harry had spent their honeymoon. The jar was to go to Elaine.

"And what am I supposed to do with it after *she's* been in it?" Elaine had sobbed, grieving for her mother.

But in the end they had got Beth as far as the jar and the jar up in front of the sanctuary in a tangle of forsythia branches, artfully arranged. If Fletcher hadn't gone around shooting off his mouth, Harry mused, nobody would have known Beth was up there. As it was, the minister preached from one corner but all eyes focused on the jar in the other.

Fred Fletcher wasn't the only one who had been upset, however. The organist was put out because Harry wanted a recording of Brahm's *Third Symphony* as postlude.

"I don't much see the need for me if you're going to have an orchestra playing," she'd sniffed.

"Only the third movement," Harry had repeated, trying to be reasonable.

What happened was that Miss Emory got up and left when her part was over, whereas Harry, who should have been the first to exit when the postlude began, stayed in the pew to hear Brahms. This meant that Jack, Elaine, and Claude felt obliged to stay seated with their father, hence the whole congregation. When everyone stood up to leave at last, the music had stopped.

Harry sat immobile now, eyes half hidden by brows as ragged as an untrimmed hedge. His mouth, with no lips to speak of, formed a straight line bisecting the lower half of his square face. The thick, graying hair above his weathered forehead rose straight up like the bristles on a scrub brush before collapsing backward in a rolling wave.

"Oh, Beth," he said, remembering the way they sat across from each other in summer when dinner was over, Beth's legs stretched out beneath their round oak table, bare feet resting on the edge of Harry's chair, where he was sitting now. The way he caressed them, gently probing between her toes while recounting the oddities that had gone on at work that day. Those early years of marriage, when each of them occupied the other's thoughts. What else was there?

He'd always liked the look of her, even as she aged. Liked the way one strap of her sun dress slipped down off her freckled shoulder; Beth holding up her long brown hair in back, fanning her neck with it. She smiled with her eyes, talked with her eyes, and they always said the same thing: *I'm here.* Sometimes the caresses took them to bed, and other times Beth and Harry lay outside in the hammock, looking up through the limbs of the beech tree, branches splayed against the sky, trying to remember how high it had been when they'd bought the house.

"Let's don't ever sell this place," Beth had told him. "When we're eighty, we're still going to come out here to this hammock."

She lied. He was suddenly as tired as an old mop. A button, he noticed, was missing off the cuff of his flannel shirt—had been for some time. Harry wasn't even sure whether the hands resting on those wrinkled Dockers were his, the fingers curled stiffly over the edge of his kneecaps. It was as though he were watching some other man sitting in his kitchen, staring at where the white and yellow linoleum was getting dingy. His wife wouldn't have stood for that. The funeral, the floor, the button, the son-in-law. . . .

Beth would have handled things differently, Harry was sure. But his own goal was simple: to survive the first year and show his grown children how it was done. You carried on, that's all there was to it. He had taught them to tie their own shoes, ride a two-wheeler, parallel park, and file a 1040. This would be the most difficult lesson by far.

THE REFRIGERATOR CHURNED and gave him a sense of purpose; Harry snapped to attention. It had been making ominous noises for several days. They started out low and straining, escalating to labored groans. Then the pains would stop, the patient would rest, before the motor kicked on and the process repeated.

Something like this Harry could deal with. He'd had no control over the tubes and monitors that had pinned Beth to her bed each time she went in the hospital, but an appliance you could make whole again by unscrewing one part and replacing it with another.

He went to the pantry and looked in the black and white speckled file box marked "Instructions," where his wife had kept dozens of five-by-eight cards, service manuals and warranties. Searching the Rs, Harry paused. RAPE, read a card, telling how one could fend it off and, if unsuccessful, what to do immediately afterward.

Following RAPE was RASPBERRIES, HOW TO GROW; then RATS, EXTERMINATING; and finally REFRIGERATOR, followed by ROSES and RUG CARE. Harry thumbed backward and forward at random. There were instructions for cleaning a typewriter; a booklet titled *Five Things Every Wife Should Know about the Prostate,* and even a pamphlet, *How to Reason with a Cat*. Blinking, Harry sought out REFRIGERATOR once again.

Squatting down before the opened door of the GE, with the *Use and Care Guide*, Harry found himself face to face with an assortment of dishes he did not recognize—quivering gelatin salads, a plate of white and yellow cheese, and cellophane-wrapped breads tied with yarn. The plastic lid on a container of meat loaf rose up in one corner as though secretly pried from inside. There were ceramic saucers and cut-glass platters filled with foods that had somehow come unbidden into his house. He felt as though he had mistakenly opened the door of the guest room to find people he did not know perched on beds and chairs. It was enough to give any refrigerator a belly ache.

Harry had never understood why *funeral* equaled *food*—why the first idea in anyone's mind was to gather at the home of the bereaved and cover every available surface with deviled eggs. He himself had not been hungry for three days. He had not truly relished a meal for months. Occasionally his stomach rumbled and he felt washed-out, but he just had no appetite, and merely grazed a little at meal times.

Still squatting before the open door of the fridge, he turned his attention to the problem at hand, rocking back on his heels, and instantly a brash cry filled the air, bringing him quickly to a standing position.

Zeke, the nine year-old cat, gave him a reproachful glance as he scurried under the table and sat licking his injured paw.

Harry's heart was still pounding. "Sorry," he said. "I didn't know you were there." The cat studied him disdainfully.

The large tabby with the yellow eyes was an unnerving presence in the house with Beth gone. Harry was almost surprised to see him, as though he'd expected the cat to follow his wife no matter what. When had he last fed the cat? Had he fed the cat at all? Harry reached into the refrigerator for a plate of roast beef, took off the cellophane, and set it on the floor. Then, feeling the need to connect with someone other than a cat, he decided to touch base at work. When he picked up the phone, however, he was startled to discover he had forgotten the number.

Slowly he placed it back in the cradle. Was it 469-5 . . . 236? Or was it 469-3265? Was it even 469 at all? Harry reached for the Yellow Pages and looked up his own ad: *Gill's Garden Center; Flowers, Shrubs, and Trees; Stone Casting and Restorations. Open Year Round.*

It was reassuring to see that his business was still intact. Since his wife's illness, he had found himself reading the obituaries each morning, his eye stopping involuntarily at the Gs. He dialed the number and Wanda answered.

"Gill's Garden Center. How may I help you?"

"That truckload of mulch come in?"

"Harry Gill, don't you worry your head about mulch!" Harry could almost see the large, elegant woman leaning against the counter, receiver tucked under one ear as she counted out a customer's change. "I told you it won't hurt to let things slide for a while. You shouldn't come in until you feel like it."

"Well, I feel like it, and I'll be there in twenty minutes," Harry said, and felt better already.

In his Ford Lariat, he turned the radio to National Public Radio and got a symphony, he didn't know whose. He rested his arm on the open window as he rolled along Old Forest Road from Rockville, and thought what a relief it was to be going to work again, the landscape pregnant with spring. If you followed the road north you would parallel the Potomac all the way to White's Ferry. If you followed it south, as Harry was doing, you would eventually reach the DC line, but that was farther than he needed to go. At a traffic light, he glanced down into the Volvo alongside to see a woman studying him, her eyes scanning the tools and grass seed piled in the back of his pickup, her ears taking in the violins and horns. Harry gave her a polite smile. The woman looked away.

Harry Gill had known this neighborhood all his life, yet lately he had begun to feel he did not know it at all. It used to be, when he drove the two-lane stretch from his father's quarry to the garden center, trees formed a canopy over the pavement. He would pass a small farm, a Roy Rogers restaurant, or a cluster of two-bedroom houses, each with its chain-link fence to protect it from its neighbors.

In the past decade, however, Old Forest Road had gone from two lanes to six. The small farms and gas stations sold to developers who saw in the bucolic, Maryland countryside a setting for custom homes. In the last few years, in fact, small French restaurants and women's boutiques in colonial grays and blues replaced Radio Shack and Dunkin' Doughnuts. The one supermarket turned gourmet: a tank of live trout moved in, and baskets of quail eggs adorned the dairy case. Homes and businesses on the edge of Rockville petitioned to designate their zip codes North Bethesda or North Potomac, names with a more upscale sound than *Rock*ville.

Harry passed a bank of trees and then the last remaining box-like houses defiantly lining the road, refusing to leave. *No solicitors* read a sign that dangled from one chain-link fence, and another warned,

Beware of Dog. No North Potomac address needed here, they seemed to say. He drove one mile more and turned in at the garden center.

"THE ANGEL GABRIEL," Wanda told him, pointing to a wrapped bundle on the floor. "Church of the Annunciation says his wings are chipped. I told them there were two shepherd girls, a Madonna, a Chinese lady, and the Apostle Paul ahead of him. They said they could wait."

Wanda Sims, a handsome, large-boned woman of fifty with almond-shaped eyes, turned her full attention to Harry. "How are you feeling?"

"Doing okay, actually." Except for the fact that he had no appetite and his house was dirty, that was the surprising truth.

"We draped you in black the day of the funeral," Tracy said soberly from behind the cash register.

Harry turned to see one of his part-time workers, a parochial student in plaid skirt and navy sweater, pulling her books out from under the counter and preparing to leave. "What?" Harry said.

"We took that black crepe from Halloween and hung it over the ends of the garden center sign," Wanda explained, hugging his arm maternally. "A lot of people asked about you, Harry." She handed him a memo pad. "Here are the messages from the last three days. I crossed out the ones I could answer."

"Oh. Right." He thrust it in his shirt pocket. Harry had no doubt that if she had to, Wanda could run the place indefinitely, with the help of Steve and Bill.

Rose Kribbs came in from the storeroom and, seeing Harry, immediately began the soft tongue clicking that reminded him of dolphins in distress. It was a multi-purpose kind of click that she used to express sympathy, disdain, surprise, or merely fatigue. There was no mistaking the emotion today, however. Smoothing the front of her flowered smock, she clasped her hands at waist level.

"Mr. Gill, I am so, so, so, sorry!" she said, and with each *so,* her head bobbed forward a centimeter or two. "It just must be *awful!*"

"Thank you," Harry said. "Yes, it's been rough."

Rose took a step backward then, having recited her lines. Mid-forties, married and childless, she wore clothes with a sweetheart neckline, dirndl skirts, and often a ribbon at the back of the head, like a 50s prom queen wanna-be. No jewelry but the thin gold band on her ring finger and two pairs of dangling earrings that she wore on alternate weeks.

Harry studied the elfin-faced woman whose faint mustache betrayed her frizzy bleached hair. The first time he'd seen her, when Wanda hired her six months ago, she'd reminded him of hairy mouse-ear chickweed, with the delicate line above her upper lip, the down on her forearms, and—for the white petals of the flower—her halo of blond hair.

Feeling the awkwardness of these condolences, he wondered if some other comment on his part was called for. "It wasn't entirely unexpected," he said finally. "Beth was sick for a long time, you know." He looked at the floor thoughtfully for another moment or two and then, the official moment of silence dispensed with, he slapped his thigh with one hand, turned to Wanda and asked, "Who's working the lot today?"

"Bill's watering the hanging baskets, the herd's out there unloading mulch, and Steve's on deliveries," she said.

There were nineteen employees in season, only seven in fall and winter. Spring brought out "the herd," as Wanda called them—young men who wanted fast money to spend on summer weekends at the beach.

Harry walked over to the covered statue, bent his knees, and slowly picked it up, keeping his back straight. He carried it out the side door of the garden center, into the grape arbor, past the tables of flowering plants, through the covered walkway lined with clay pots, and into an old greenhouse, thick with plaster dust. Not a green or growing thing inside.

It was here, away from the generic music Wanda played in the store—"treacle" Harry called it—that he cast new statues from old. If a much-loved saint was missing a nose, or if a second bird bath with a seashell motif was wanted, it was usually Harry Gill people turned to.

He cut the twine and removed the cardboard from around the statue, examining two chips on one wing, five on the other, plus half the angel's big toe. He would repair the damage with plasticine, make a mold by covering the original with layers of liquid rubber, then plaster, and finally he would cast a new piece in concrete. It was as close to creation, he imagined, as he would get.

It had been a long climb from water boy in his father's quarry to the Angel Gabriel—working his way up to grunt, truck driver, loader, splitter, and blaster; then eight years as a tool and die maker over in Virginia, coming back home to start a new business down the road from his father's. He took the details of a master sculptor and duplicated them, but he could not make the original. There was always this lack.

Harry took the memo pad from his pocket and read the first message: *Mrs. Grittinger says she's sorry for her choice of flowers so soon after Beth's passing, but she really does want lilies.*

"Dad."

He turned to see Elaine in the doorway. She wore loafers and blue tights, and a long, loose shirt on top. Her short dark hair was in a pixie cut, with wisps of bangs hiding her forehead. Elaine was attractive, slightly less pretty than Beth at the age of twenty-nine, however, and decidedly less beautiful when she was upset, which was now.

"Where's Jodie?" Harry began with his granddaughter, knowing that Elaine would work up to Don soon enough.

"Back in the store with Wanda. Dad, I still haven't heard from Don, and it's been almost twenty-four hours."

"Hmmm." Harry leaned against his workbench, studiously examining the floor and the imprints their shoes had made in the plaster dust.

"I called Jack and said I was thinking of filing a missing-persons report, but he says that doesn't work for adults—not unless you suspect foul play. Do you think I should call the police?"

Harry wished with all his heart that Beth was here at this moment. It had not occurred to him before, but he wondered if there wasn't a pamphlet in the file box marked, HUSBAND, MISSING.

"Well?"

He startled. Harry hated it when Elaine's voice took on that cawing sound.

"You want to tell me what happened between you and Don after you left my place yesterday?" he asked, glad to have thought of something.

Elaine sighed impatiently, but came over to sit on a high dusty stool, one foot on the rung, the other just touching the floor. "I was in a foul mood, I'll admit it. I had a headache from crying. I was hungry, but when we were at your place, I didn't feel like eating. By the time we got home I was starved. Don, though—he'd eat at a funeral supper if it was *me* in the coffin!—he even went back for seconds, and when we got home, he was eating peanuts he'd put in his pocket. I'm sitting at the table too hungry to sleep, too tired to cook, and he's standing in the doorway eating peanuts."

"Where was Jodie?"

"A neighbor took her for the night. Anyway, Don's standing there watching me, and do you know what he said?" Elaine's eyes glowered. "He said, 'Why don't you open a can of soup?'" She waited, and when Harry didn't react, told him, "Not, 'Would you like me to fix you some soup?' or even 'You look as though you could use some soup.' Just, 'Why don't you open a can of soup?' That is so *typical!*"

"Soup?"

"No! The way he never *sees* anything; never *senses* anything! He wouldn't think of opening a can himself because he never has. Would never think of cooking for me even when I'm mourning my mother! He's the most predictable person on the face of this earth."

"Just because. . . ?"

"Dad, he eats the same thing every morning for breakfast, goes to the same diner for lunch, listens to the same newscast in the evening, wears the same old crummy T-shirt and shorts to bed."

Harry listened without comment, waiting for some grievous sin to be exposed. Don Wheeler was not, to be sure, a spontaneous person. Everything about him seemed premeditated. His remarks at family dinners, even, sounded rehearsed. But lack of spontaneity was hardly a felony.

"The story of our marriage, that's for sure. I could tell you everything he does in bed before he does it."

"Elaine . . . "

Her voice rose. "Who do I tell if I can't tell you? He makes love according to *Robert's Rules of Order*! Not a pass out of place. Name a part of the body. *Any* part."

"Now, look."

"Go on!"

"Elaine!"

"Thighs? They come after breasts and buttocks, but never buttocks and breasts. He always starts with breasts. Name another part."

"Listen, honey—"

"Navel? Let's try that one. Only in his oral mood. Then it's nipple . . . nipple . . . navel. . . ."

"Elaine!"

She stopped for breath.

"You told him all this?"

Elaine nodded and let her knobby shoulders slump. She hugged herself with her arms, bent over as though her stomach were aching now from hunger of a different sort. When she dropped her head that way, so that all Harry could see was her hair, she reminded him of the teenager she'd been some fifteen years before, going around in those same kind of oversized clothes. She sounded as though she were on the verge of tears.

"I just screamed at him. Sat there screaming, I was so tired and hungry and disgusted. I asked if it ever occurred to him that *he* might cook for *me*. I told him he was so predictable I could set my watch by when he goes to the bathroom, and asked him if he ever considered, just once in his life, doing something really wild and unpredictable. And when he didn't answer, I screamed, 'Hit me, Don! Go on! I dare you!' I just kept screaming it."

"Good God!" Harry tried to imagine Don, as large and gentle a man as he had ever seen, hitting his daughter. "Did he?"

"No. He went upstairs. I lay down on the couch and about a half hour later, heard him come down, pick up his car keys, and go out. Heard the car drive off. Do you know, I actually thought he might be going to get me a sandwich or something, but when he didn't come back. . . ." Elaine hugged herself even tighter. "I don't know what to tell Jodie. She keeps asking."

"Did he take anything with him?"

"His underwear. Some of his clothes. I'm not sure how many."

"Suitcase?"

"Duffel bag."

"Checkbook?"

"No, but he wrote out a check for cash for $500. I saw it on the stub."

"No note?"

She shook her head. And then, in a voice that had become small and tremulous, asked once more, "What am I going to do?"

"I guess you're going to have to wait and see what happens, and that's going to be one of the hardest things you ever did."

Elaine was quiet awhile. At last she said, "Jack says if Don had intended staying away more than a few days—if he was planning to leave us—he would have taken a lot more than $500."

"Probably so."

With the toe of one shoe, she made small overlapping indentations in the plaster dust. This time, when she asked a question, Harry could hardly hear her. "What if he doesn't come back at all? I'm only teaching half days this year." And when Harry didn't answer, she looked up, eyes angry and moist: "Damn it, why couldn't we have done something wild and unpredictable together?"

"*Both* of you run off?"

"Not that." Elaine got up finally and slipped the strap of her purse over her shoulder. "Part of me wants another chance and the other part wants to kill him. I'm sorry, Dad. Dragging all this in here just after Mom died."

"It's okay."

They exchanged a quick hug and Harry followed her out through the covered walkway, past the tables of impatiens under their trellised roof, back through the grape arbor and the picnic table beneath, to the side entrance where four year-old Jodie was spinning the wings on a wooden duck. It sat in a row of seven, waiting to desecrate someone's yard. In deference to his upwardly mobile neighbors, Harry had insisted that lawn ornaments be kept to a minimum, but some people still asked for them, so there was always a row of "uglies," as he dubbed them, near the back of the store.

"Give Gramps a hug, Jodie. We're going," said Elaine.

The small gray-eyed girl reached up as Harry leaned down and clasped him dutifully around the neck. The veins showed blue under the thin skin over her temples. She had the fragile look of a cream pitcher.

"Don't be sad, Grandpa," she said soberly. "Nana's with the angels."

"Don't bet on it," Harry mumbled.

"Dad!" Elaine's voice.

"Maybe so," he corrected. He watched them get in Elaine's Honda, noticing how Jodie was careful to keep her funereal countenance as long as he was looking.

It was truly amazing the way people tried to alter the world of the bereaved, Harry thought, Jodie giving him a sad little wave. From the time it became obvious that Beth was dying, nothing pleasant ever seemed to happen to any of their friends. No one had good tidings of any sort, but told Harry and Beth only the worst things that had befallen them—a talisman, he guessed, against envy. Even those who came to visit Beth in the hospital came bearing tales of how difficult it had been to find a parking space, or how badly their lunch had agreed with them. *You won't be missing a thing,* they seemed to say. Just when she had needed something beautiful around her, her dearest and closest friends offered only their long faces and sour stomachs.

And, of course, the cures. Every third visitor suggested a doctor Beth should try. A miracle food that had worked for a cousin or neighbor. Massive doses of vitamin C, old Laurel and Hardy films, daily incantations.

Finally the visitors stopped coming at all, and Beth was left to the patronizing ministrations of nursing attendants. "How about a nice shampoo this morning, hon? Get you all sweet-smelling again—make you pretty."

There was something about standing here at the back of the garden center's parking lot that seemed out of place to Harry. He had walked over this asphalt every day for the last twenty-eight years, but suddenly nothing looked the way he remembered it.

He turned slowly, studying the bags of landscape stone next to the fence, the clay pots and wire frames, each in separate bins. Life was the same and not. His daughter and granddaughter were going home to an empty house. He himself was going back to a house without Beth.

The sad relief Harry felt at the long ordeal being over gave way to the desolate reality that she was truly gone. It was as incomprehensible to believe he would never see his wife again as it had been for him, as a boy, to imagine eternal life, knowing that if you make it to heaven, buddy, it's long white robes forever. That depressed him then and was no comfort now. And suddenly Harry needed to be home, to be in the place she had last spoken and sighed, as though he might still breathe her aura if he got there in time.

A thirty-something woman, with legs so long she looked like a giant spider, almost collided with him as he wheeled around and started toward his pickup. She was holding a bouquet of daffodils, and stared after him as he continued his robot walk.

Nothing in Harry's body seemed to bend. It was as though a steel rod held the separate parts of him together, shafting through his skull, filling his throat with its sharp metallic taste, extending on down his neck and backbone, holding his vertebrae rigid. At the same time, his chest seemed to be swelling, his lungs ballooning with air he could not expel. He did not know if he were suffering something physical or whether the grief he had felt before was mere prelude, and he was getting a taste now of the real thing.

"You all right, Mr. G.?" Bill called, hose in hand.

Still clutching the memo pad, Harry kept walking. The steel rod in his throat would allow no sound to escape. It took all his determination to move his feet forward, first one, then another, conscious of each step.

He saw Wanda standing in the doorway of the garden center, staring after him. Saw several customers turn. With great effort, he opened the door of the Lariat, climbed in, and thrust the key in the ignition.

He turned on the radio and heard the announcer introduce a Brandenberg concerto. There was something about that frenzied pace, note falling upon note, up the scale and down again, tumbling headlong into the next measure and the next, that helped dispel the hollowness. Saved by Bach.

Harry sat for a few moments, taking deep breaths, waiting for his pulse to subside. Then he backed from his parking space and moved out onto Old Forest Road. Maybe this was what mourning was all about—searing stabs now and then that took you unawares. That knocked you off balance momentarily. The trick, it seemed, was to stay busy, so what was he doing going home? Nothing made any sense today.

He relaxed his foot on the gas pedal, letting the evening rush-hour traffic careen around him, not caring whether he made the lights. It was four years ago, while sitting in a Midas Muffler shop, that he'd picked up a paperback someone had left called *Learning to Love the Music You Hate: A Beginner's Guide to the Classics*. The only magazines not taken were New Woman and Parenting, so he read the first few pages of the book.

Do you ever wonder if people who go to symphony concerts actually enjoy themselves? Why other people seem able to distinguish Bach from Beethoven, when they both sound the same to you? When they sound, in fact, like so much noise?

Yes, yes, and yes.

Harry had been hooked for reasons he had not understood, but he liked the idea of an experiment. Liked the thought of learning something out of school. So that very day he'd dropped by a music store and purchased Brahms' *Third*, as suggested. He played it every day for two weeks—the first and second movements driving to work each morning, the third and fourth going home.

Harry remembered the exact moment the music "took". He had been delivering rhododendrons to Gaithersburg when he found himself humming a melody he didn't know he knew. Surprisingly, he could anticipate what was coming next. So he had played Brahms each day for a month, and each time he discovered something new. Melodies that had begun in the first movement came back again in different disguises, and haunted him even when there was no music playing at all.

As he turned onto his street and drove under the leafy branches of the linden trees that arched overhead, Harry found the windows of his house dark in the early evening. It was this hour before nightfall that objects took on an almost surreal clarity—they appeared in such sharp focus that they almost seemed too close. Still, he wished he had left the porch light on to illuminate the stone front which he and Beth had installed soon after they'd bought the two-story. Any light at all to say that this was home.

He was not halfway up the porch steps when he heard a car pull up, and Jack climbed out of his Lexus. At thirty-two, the oldest of the Gill offspring, he more closely resembled Harry's brother Wade, though Wade was tall and large, whereas Jack was tall and lean. Both had receding hairlines. Jack and his father had the same sort of nose, however—a ridge down each side that gave it a square appearance. Same sort of smile that sagged at the corners.

"Thought you might like some company for dinner," Jack called cheerfully, coming up the walk. He studied Harry's face.

"Sure. Help me eat all those leftovers." Harry opened the door and Jack followed him inside. They would not let him be alone, he realized. Elaine would stop by his shop at the garden center. Jack would drop in at mealtimes. There was even a message from Claude, the youngest, on the answering machine: "Hi, Dad. Just wanted to call and see how you're doing. Sue and I thought it was a beautiful service yesterday; Mom would have loved it. If you want to go out for dinner or see a movie or anything, just let us know." Who was the teacher here, and who the pupil?

While Jack walked through the rooms turning on lights, Harry ran through the rest of the messages: "It's Marge, Harry. I'm just across the street, remember." *Beep*. "Ginny and I are just as sorry as can be, Harry. We know it's tough. Keep your chin up." *Beep*. "Harry? Wade. Want anything from the store?" *Beep*. "Mr. Gill, it's Miss Emory. Just so there's no misunderstanding about my fee, it's the same whether I played the postlude or not." *Beep*.

Harry watched color return to the living room as Jack went from lamp to lamp. Beth's gold chair next to the fireplace; Harry's recliner in brown tweed; the olive-green couch with stripes of cream and bronze. Across the hall, his lonely bedroom beckoned, but Harry ignored it. Up the stairs with its familiar worn banister sat the three deserted rooms of the children once raised in this house. Harry and Beth could well have moved to Potomac proper years before, but by the time they could afford a more affluent neighborhood, they didn't want it. They had planted an oak tree here, then their children, and finally a bit of themselves. The roots ran deep.

Harry was glad now that Jack had come, if only for the companionship. As he pressed the rewind button, he realized he was feeling hungry, and this was definitely a good sign.

"Son of a bitch! What's this?"

Harry turned to where Jack was gingerly lifting his foot up off the carpet. "When did he start doing *this*, Dad?"

"Who?"

"Zeke. Didn't even have the decency to put it on the linoleum."

Harry stared blankly at the carpet between living and dining room where Zeke had done his business. And once again he was surprised to discover he had a cat. If there was going to be any thought of supper, this had to be disposed of first, but his mind did not seem to be in gear. He remembered picking up Claude once as a two year-old and holding him over the toilet, but it obviously didn't apply to a cat.

In the dining room, Zeke watched the proceedings from beneath a chair.

"I'll take care of it," Jack said quickly, and as Harry scanned his mail, he heard a toilet flush beyond his bedroom. "Zeke, you clod," Jack was saying as he came back out again.

The phone rang.

"Yes?" said Harry.

"Oh, Harry. . . ." Wanda's voice. "Just wanted to check about the brick. Did you order glazed or sand finish?"

She already knew that. "Glazed, Wanda."

"Good. Just checking. Anything we can do for you, Mr. Gill?"

"I'm fine, Wanda."

"Really?"

"Jack's here. We're going to have dinner."

"Wonderful!" Relief in her voice. "See you whenever. Don't come in till you're ready."

When were you ever ready? Harry wondered. The world had changed in the last three days, and he had no instruction book for what lay ahead.

THEY WORKED TOGETHER in the kitchen, Harry taking things out of the refrigerator one by one and placing them on the table, Jack peering tentatively under the tinfoil, giving his consent or refusal.

Harry had no favorites among his children, but he felt most comfortable with Jack. His older son was all surface, but what Harry saw and admired was drive—the pure joy of getting up in the morning and getting *at* things. Jack seemed to have been born with dual engines, and being in the same room with him was both exhilarating and exhausting. It was Jack's business ventures that were a worry.

The conversation at the moment focused on Harry.

"You know what they say," Jack told him. "If you make it through the first day, you'll make the first week; if you make the first week, you'll make the first month; and if you make the first month, you'll make the first year. After that, it's all downhill."

Downhill didn't sound quite as jolly as Jack intended. "I suppose," Harry said. "Listen, Elaine says she talked to you about Don disappearing."

"Yeah." Jack put a plate of food in the microwave. "Just what you needed, huh?"

"Well. . . ."

"Trouble with Elaine," Jack continued, "is she shoots off her mouth first and thinks later. Even good old Don has his limits. You know, I have to admire the guy. All the years he's been taking it from her. . . ."

"The real problem right now is Jodie—what to tell her."

"The truth, I guess. That Daddy went away a few days to think things over. Unless of course the real truth is that Daddy flew the coop. Oh, man! Problems everywhere you look." The microwave dinged, Jack took out one plate and put in another. He set the first in front of his father and opened a beer.

"So what's new at the laundry?" Harry asked.

"I've sort of let things slide since Mom got sick," Jack told him. "But I've got some renovations in mind. Changed the name, for one. 'Suds' just doesn't do it anymore. It's short and classy, but it only says 'laundry,' you know? Somehow I have to sell people on the idea that it's more than a place to wash their clothes."

"So?"

"Suds and Spuds." Jack grinned. "Like it? I'm going to sell baked potatoes along with the pizza—five different toppings. I'm aiming for a classier crowd—white-collar singles." The microwave dinged again and Jack removed his own plate.

Harry had already voiced his misgivings about buying the laundry, but Jack had got the business cheap, sure he could make it work. Laundries as rendezvous for singles had gone out twenty years ago along with the do-it-yourself picture frame shops, Harry had tried to tell him. The upwardly-mobile white-collar singles all had washing machines in their apartment buildings. As even Jack had observed, if they wanted to meet someone they went to sports centers or night clubs. But he hadn't the money to buy either, so settled on a self-service laundry.

"You ever have doubts when you started the garden center?" Jack asked, probably more out of politeness than interest.

"Couple times a day for the first five years."

Jack sat back down and something clunked under the table. "Jesus Christ, now what?" He leaned down to look. "Dad, did you know there's a plate of roast beef under here? What's left of it, anyway?"

VERY LITTLE ESCAPED Harry's attention that evening: the way Jack removed the plate from under the table, as though putting it there was to be expected of the bereaved; his casual mention of Marge Decker and the kindness of neighbors, should Harry need anything; his turning on the TV before he left, so the house would be filled with sound. As soon as Jack got back to his apartment, he'd be on the phone to Elaine and Claude: *You'll never guess what I found under the table at Dad's. . . .* Part of the crazies, that's what they'd say.

That's what happened to Liz Bowen after Max died, only that was a year ago, and the crazies were still going on. The last time Harry had seen her, in fact, all she did was cry.

He'd known Max before he knew Beth. They used to do the clubs together, drive downtown and take in some jazz. Even after Max became one of Washington's top Realtors and switched to pin-striped suits, he'd take a night off, put on his scruffies, and he and Liz and Harry and Beth would seek out the summer concerts—go to Wolf Trap with a picnic supper. Now Max was gone, Liz was nuts, and Harry had lost his Beth. Life sure had a way of turning on you.

Wade called again. "Anything you want me to pick up at the store?" he asked. His brother had been asking it daily for the past two or three weeks, and sometimes, just to give him something to do, Harry had him pick up some paper towels or a can of creamed corn.

"I'm okay, Wade, thanks," he said.

It was just after eight when the fourth unsettling thing happened to Harry Gill. He remembered the messages Wanda had given him. The memo pad was still in the truck, and he ambled outside in his stocking feet to retrieve it.

The sky was a deep purple but the street lights cast a warm glow at regular intervals as far as Harry could see. It was an eclectic neighborhood of one-of-a-kind houses—bungalows, Victorians, redwood moderns—scattered on their quarter-acre lots, with an air more of comfort and convenience than style. The trees were large and plentiful, the sidewalks well used but crumbling in places—the kind of neighborhood where it was still permissible, though not encouraged, to own a pickup.

He made his way along the flagstone path to the Lariat, but came to an abrupt halt when he noticed a large dark puddle on the blue hood. It looked like blood. He stared at it curiously, then took a few more steps and stared some more, first at the truck, then at an empty aluminum can in the grass. His face crinkled in astonishment, and he leaned over to sniff. His truck had been christened with Progresso tomato sauce.

It was then he discovered a folded sheet of paper beneath one windshield wiper. He pulled it out, opened the door of the pickup and slid onto the seat beneath the overhead light.

In a heavy scrawl, someone had written: *You like Italian? Here's Italian.*

TWO

The Truck

HE COULD TELL by the angle of sunlight between blind and window that it was later than eight o'clock. There was an immediate decision to be made: either leap out of bed and try to get to the garden center at a still respectable hour, or lie perfectly motionless and hold onto the modicum of peace he was feeling at the moment. Harry chose peace.

And then his mind returned to the tomato sauce. He would have dismissed it as a prank except for the note, and couldn't begin to guess what he was supposed to deduce from that. Was sauce on the hood of his pickup more weird than having a son-in-law disappear? More extraordinary than having a wife die? More peculiar than an inconsolable cat? Not only was Zeke being incontinent, but some time in the night Harry had wakened to the sound of a creature in anguish. Rising up on one elbow, he had just been able to make out the form of Zeke, sitting in the hallway and flooding the night with wave after wave of despair.

"We all miss her," Harry had said aloud.

Now, closing his eyes again, he sifted through the chores he could tend to if he stayed home, and realized he was putting each to the test: Would it make him feel better or worse? Sending in the last of Beth's insurance forms: worse. Paying her doctor bills: worse. Clearing out her closet: impossible. Acknowledging the flowers, cards, letters, food. . . .

What he needed right now was for the phone to ring—Elaine to call and say that Don had come home last night, and everything was fine. All right, don't ask for fine. He'd be satisfied if she just said that the quiet man with the large belly had come home. Was that so much to ask?

The doorbell chimed instead, a pleasant little bing-bong. Harry had almost decided to stay put when he wondered if it might be his son-in-law. He threw off his blanket, swung his legs over the side of the bed, and reached for his cotton robe.

A neighbor stood at the door in a kimono—what there was of it. Paula Hamilton had not pulled it quite together in front under its sash, revealing a peach-colored gown with a lace bodice, through which Harry could make out a nipple and the darkened circle of an areola. He quickly shifted his eyes. Harry had no idea how old she was because she was well-preserved. About his age, he guessed.

"I just came out to get my paper and decided to walk yours up to the door," she told him. Harry saw that she was wearing mascara and lip gloss. "How are you doing, Harry?"

"Doing okay, actually," he lied, half covering his fetid-tasting mouth with one hand.

"Have you had your coffee?"

Heaven intervened, and kept him from saying, No, have you? "I think I'll wait. Thanks for the paper, Paula," he told her, and moved back away from the screen.

"Is there anything I can do?" she asked gently.

"Well, not at the moment, but I appreciate your asking."

As he watched her carefully cross the wet grass to the house next door, holding her kimono up to mid-calf, the phone rang. When he answered, he heard laughter in a woman's voice. Marge Decker, across the street, had been watching.

"Paula Hamilton's always been dressed by seven before," she said. "When a man's being chased as hard as you are, Harry, I figure he ought to be warned."

Harry knew it was meant as a joke, and that a chuckle of some sort was called for, but he had none at the ready. So he just said, "Right."

"When you've been widowed as long as I have, you've seen it all," Marge went on. "You just have to be firm, Harry."

"Well . . . thank you," he told her, not knowing what else was appropriate. "Thank you very much." And he hung up.

It was times like this Harry felt that a drama was going on around him. He was one of the actors, but didn't know his lines. He didn't even understand the plot. The mascara and lace, perhaps, but what about the cat and the tomato sauce? The only way to get through the next scene and the next was to follow his old routine. He had got out of bed. Now what? *Take a shower, stupid.*

It was when he was putting on his shoes that Harry realized there were places in the house he did not go. Things he did not do. He did not go in his wife's closet. It was hard enough going into his own, which Beth had stocked with enough pants and shirts to last forty years, all purchased after she'd found out her cancer was terminal. Harry did not open her side of the medicine cabinet, either, or remove her slippers from under their bed. The routine wouldn't hold still for that. He followed the path he'd made on the rug, from bed to shower to dresser to door. Detours invited disaster.

Zeke was waiting for him in the hall, watching as Harry walked to the kitchen in a striped shirt and chinos, then rubbed against his legs, more out of reproach than affection. He was a large cat, eleven pounds, with only a part of his balls. The vet always left a little something, he'd said, so the cat wouldn't miss them.

"How's the eunuch?" Harry greeted, and put a scoop full of greasy-looking pellets in a dish on the floor.

THINGS NEEDED ATTENTION. Harry turned the calendar to May, and realized the checkbook hadn't balanced since January. The next woman who asked if there was anything she could do would get the checkbook. What called for Harry's immediate scrutiny were the medical bills. Coffee in hand, he walked to his desk in the living room and began.

"I'm calling about my wife's hospital statement. . . . Gill. G-I-L-L. . . . Beth. . . . No, *Beth*. B as in boy, E as in elephant, T as in truck, H as in. . . ." He could envision two upright poles with a bar between, but somehow could not think of a single word in the English language that began with H.

"Hell," said Harry, forgetting his own name.

There was silence from the other end of the line. Then, "What seems to be the problem?"

The problem was that Beth was dead and all the offers of help in the world could not bring her back. The problem was that there was an invisible wound in Harry's chest that never healed. He was now a lifetime member of Achers Anonymous. *My name is Harry Gill, and I have this wound. . . .*

"Sir?"

Harry stared at the papers before him. "There are a couple of items here I don't understand," he said. "There's a bone scan listed on February third, but my wife wasn't in the hospital then. She came home the middle of January."

"You'll have to check with radiology."

"On whether or not my wife was home?"

"On why they have a bone scan listed for that day."

"And according to this bill, she had a testicular biopsy on the twelfth," Harry said.

"She wasn't in the hospital on the twelfth?"

"My wife was a woman!"

"I'll check into that, sir."

"I already did."

Harry stayed with the bills till eleven fifteen, then decided he'd had enough. The irony was, Beth was supposed to be doing this for him. He hadn't wanted to leave behind a wife ignorant of financial matters. And so, when she inherited some money at her parents' death, and later earned a salary for seventeen years as a school secretary, Harry had told her, "That's yours. Invest it, spend it—do what you like." They had filed separate returns so she could learn to do her own taxes, and for a long time—until Wanda took over at the garden center—Beth had sent out the monthly bills so she could get an understanding of the business. Wife, mother, housekeeper, secretary—she could do everything. Now she was gone, and all Harry had taught went with her. It was Harry who was left with the problems, questions, the to-do lists, the whole shebang.

What to do with Beth's money, that was next on the agenda. Harry opened the left-hand drawer of the desk, Beth's drawer, and idly examined her checkbook. Balance of forty-three thousand dollars. He paused. Jodie's education was the first thing that came to mind. He wished that he and Beth had talked more about what he should do with her money. Up until the last six weeks, however, they hoped and reassured and comforted until there was no comfort left—only the relief that morphine could give.

But . . . forty-three *thousand?* In checking? She had a few stocks, of course. A couple of CDs. A money market account. He thumbed back through the pages of the checkbook, scanning the entries—dress shops, The Shoe Palace, Sierra Club, the Red Cross. . . . He stopped once again and studied a cash withdrawal only a year ago of four thousand dollars. He tried to remember what she might have bought for cash, and gave a quick perusal of the living room. Beth wasn't much of a shopper.

Harry leaned back in his chair and turned the pages more methodically now, one by one. His thumb paused again. Eight months ago: a cash withdrawal of two thousand five hundred. He suddenly pulled the drawer open wide and took out all the checkbook stubs he could find. Fifteen years worth. Starting with the oldest, he went through each one. The first significant cash withdrawal was for three thousand ten years back. Two months later, another for nine-hundred. As he moved through the books, he found one for a thousand. Then eight hundred. Then fifty-seven hundred.

With a determined sweep of the hand, he returned all the stubs to the drawer. There were enough mysteries on his plate at the moment to occupy him for the next two years. It had been Beth's money to do with as she'd pleased, and it was the problems of the living that concerned him now.

He looked at the clock, saw that it was noon, and he needed to eat lunch, hungry or not. Harry got up and ambled to the refrigerator. When he opened the door, a plate of blueberry muffins slid off a cellophane-wrapped loaf of bread, and the muffins rolled across the linoleum like tennis balls. He poked around, rearranging as he went: macaroni salad, veal stew, pound cake, Jello. Most bore stickers, denoting the neighbor or friend who had brought them. Why hadn't he told Jack to take some home with him? What was he, nuts?

The amount and variety of food was staggering, choices impossible, so Harry did the only sensible thing he could think of: he went out. Got a barbecued chicken leg and potato salad at the Giant, ate a few bites, and threw the rest away.

He was probably still in shock, he decided, which meant he was right on target. Liz Bowen had copied *The Six Stages of Grief* from an old *Reader's Digest* and mailed them to him. Shock was first on the list, followed by Panic, Anger, Despair, Apathy and Recovery. *Think SPADAR*, she had written at the bottom. The list did not say, however, how long this business of grieving would last, or when he could expect to move from Shock to Panic, or just where on the calendar he should pencil in Despair.

He decided to go some place he could do no harm, and settled on the barbershop for the haircut he should have had for Beth's funeral service. There were still a few particles of tomato he had overlooked on the windshield, and Harry pondered the mystery once again as he drove to the other side of Rockville.

It seemed more like a case of mistaken identity than anything else. They had simply targeted the wrong address. Yet they had come up the driveway, onto his property with their can of Progresso, and deliberately planted the note beneath his wiper. No, this was not a drive-by tomato throwing.

Another thought: Harry had not looked for the artist's signature when he unwrapped the statue of the Angel Gabriel, but he guessed it was cast in Italy in the 1930's. Maybe someone decided it was better for Gabriel to go the rest of his days with chipped wings and a missing toe than to be recast by a non-practicing Irish-Protestant who had never even been to Italy.

He shook his head. Who would have known or cared that the statue was waiting for him there at the garden center? As far as he could tell, he had no local rivals in the restoration business. The few who dabbled in stone casting were more interested in producing originals, and usually referred their customers to Harry when a foot or a nose was needed.

Yet someone was angry: *You like Italian? Here's Italian.*

ONLY ONE BARBER worked at Swann's, Jim Swann himself. The little shop next to a deli in Rockville had seen the town change, grow around it, but it stayed the same, except that the worn linoleum at the entrance was so thin now that the floorboards showed through the holes. There was a card table by the window where Leroy Schneider ate his lunch, a half dozen plastic chairs along the wall. A box of fifty-cent combs sat collecting dust by the cash register, along with a small American flag and, above them all, a Norman Rockwell print of a kid getting his first haircut. That and the Mona Lisa.

"Well, Harry! Good to see you, friend!" Jim's voice was as warm and welcoming as Southern Comfort on the tongue. He had been married twice, his second wife with more money than sense. But he kept his shop because it gave him something to do and he liked the companionship, he said—old friends coming by to chew the fat.

He was a small man, slight of build, with curly hair above his glasses, more gray than red. His skin was tanned and deeply lined, like that of a sailor's, and he smiled with his lips pressed together. Standing next to a customer in the barber chair, he wore a nylon shirt with vents at the sides, and Harry could never understand why the heck he chose nylon, because the armpits smelled. Still, he'd known that man and those armpits for almost twenty-five years, and you know someone that long, you almost get to liking the smell after a time—the familiarity of it.

"Harry, how you doing?" The pudgy, balding man at the card table put down the sandwich he was eating and stood up, shaking Harry's hand with his right and holding Harry's elbow with his left.

"Well . . . hanging in there, Leroy."

Leroy Schneider kept pumping his hand. The features of his face were crowded together in the center, framed by a wide expanse of flesh. "You've got to keep doing things like you did before. I'm telling you this so you'll know. Step by step, day by day, it'll get you through."

"That's what I'm thinking, so I came to get a haircut," Harry said.

"It's on the house, Harry," Jim told him. "Sit down. Have a Pepsi or something. Be with you in a minute."

Both Leroy and Jim were older than Harry, Jim by only a few years, Leroy by nine. The customer in the chair, leaning forward while Jim brushed off the nape of his neck, could not have been more than thirty. Hardly dry behind the ears, Harry thought somewhat enviously, and was glad when the man paid and left. Glad they could reclaim the shop for themselves.

Jim shook out his barber cloth and motioned Harry to the seat. "Leroy just came by with his lunch. Your turn." He tucked the cloth solicitously under Harry's chin. "Beautiful service the other day. Really beautiful. Beth would have been pleased."

Leroy took his seat again by the window and picked up his sandwich. He held it out in front of him, studying it from various angles as he chewed, and every so often his head darted forward to bite off another chunk. His right knee bobbed up and down while he ate. "After Edith died," he said, wiping one hand on his trouser leg, "I wondered sometimes if I'd make it. If you'd asked me, I would have said no."

"First year's the hardest," Jim went on. "You're going through everything alone for the first time, you know? Holidays . . . anniversaries. . . . Jeez, you go nuts. But after that. . . ." He ran the back of his hand over Harry's cheek. "You didn't shave. Let me give you a shave too."

"You're the doctor."

Harry liked the feeling that all he had to do was sit and the chair would turn, the scissors would cut, and he did not have to take responsibility for a thing. For once, there was nothing he could do, and it was okay.

"Oh, yes," Leroy said again, putting the last bite of bread in his mouth and swallowing. "The days aren't so bad. It's the nights that really get you."

Jim said, "For me it was both. After Barbara died, I didn't go out of the house for a month." He snipped around Harry's ears.

"A month!" exclaimed Leroy. "Who bought your groceries? A month I don't believe!"

"I'm telling you, I closed down for a month. My sister took over the house. I was a mess."

"You kept it to yourself, all right," said Leroy. "I don't remember you locking yourself up in your house for a month."

Jim grunted. "It happens to someone else, it's like a week. It happens to you, it's a year. Every day is sixty hours long. I'm not kidding."

"It happens to you, it's like you've dug yourself a hole and can't get out," Leroy added. "Nobody can reach down there and help. I tell you, it's awful, only you know this yourself, Harry. It suddenly hits you: They're not fooling! There is this thing called death, and it happened to your wife. And it's not supposed to be that way, 'cause the man's supposed to go first. Right?"

"Right," said Jim. "And here we are. Living proof it's bullshit."

Feeling the warmth of Jim's fingers against his neck, the cushioned softness of the chair, their words rolled right over him and broke farther on. Harry was safe. Taking in the Tidewater calendar on the wall and the barber pole in the window, he had a sudden vision of stopping by the barbershop every day. Bringing his lunch to eat with Jim and Leroy at the card table by the window. A step back in time. A fellowship of brothers. Friends who understood.

The fingers moved on around his head—first the comb, then the scissors. The quiet *snip, snip* of the blades.

Leroy Schneider wadded up his paper sack, aimed at the trash basket across the room, and missed. "Here's what you have to remember, Harry. When you're missing your wife and you think how if she was there you'd have her in your arms, here's the thing: you probably wouldn't."

Harry's eyes followed Leroy across the room to the trash basket where he bent to retrieve the wadded-up sack. His blue sleeveless sweater was stretched wide over the stomach, the lens of his glasses almost as thick as the soles on his Nubuck shoes. His worn gray trousers started out wide at the waist and hips, dwindling down to nothing at the ankles.

"You'd probably be sitting in front of the TV or working in the basement, and Beth would be at the sewing machine," Leroy said, retreating a step or two, and tossing again.

"That's right," said Jim. "When you're apart, you think about being together. But when the both of you are together, you're doing things apart. Anything you're going through, though, you can tell us because we've been there. Whatever happens to you, we've seen it all."

"I don't think so," said Harry.

Leroy went back to his chair and his knee bobbed up and down. "Try us," he said.

"Tomato sauce," said Harry.

Jim lifted the comb and paused. Both men stared at him without speaking.

"On the hood of my pickup," Harry told them.

"When did that happen?" asked Jim.

"Last night. I went out to get something I'd left in my truck, and there was a twenty-ounce can of tomato sauce all over the hood."

"They get your Cadillac too?" asked Jim, beginning to cut again.

"No, just the truck."

Leroy scratched his head, his lips creeping up at the corners. "Well, you've got me there. Sure never had anything like that happen. How do you know what it was?"

"Can was there in the yard. Then I see this note under the windshield, and it says, 'You like Italian? Here's Italian.'"

Jim looked dumbfounded. "Seems to me they got the wrong address. Doesn't make sense."

"No, it doesn't," said Harry. He was lying back in the chair now, and Jim in his nylon shirt was leaning over him, lathering his face. Harry could see the hairs in his nostrils as he scraped away on one cheek.

Jim shook his head. "That's a strange one, all right. Be glad it wasn't egg. Egg's the worst. You going to report it?"

"What the hell am I going to say? 'Officer, there's tomato sauce on my pickup?'"

The three of them chuckled.

"I think it's connected with work," said Leroy. "You got a Balducci or a Spumoni on the payroll?"

"There's a thought!" said Jim. "Somebody get a raise that nobody else got?"

Harry tried to think. He wasn't sure who was on the payroll, to tell the truth. Steve hired 'the herd' each spring, and Wanda put in her two cents when she thought someone was out of line. But as for their names. . . . Most of them were here one summer, gone the next.

"I'll look into that," he said.

Jim made two more long strokes with the blade, then wiped off Harry's face and splashed on some after-shave. He was grinning now. "Next time they bring over the tomato sauce, you get out the spaghetti," he said.

"Yeah," Leroy chortled. "Tell 'em to throw in some bread."

They laughed together as Jim cranked the chair forward and Harry sat up. Laughed together just like old times, and it felt remarkably good.

He decided to put in a few hours at the garden center, get back into the familiar routine. Leroy had a point: the most obvious source of contention was some sort of favoritism going on at work. He'd check it out with Steve and Wanda.

Driving along Old Forest Road and passing the line of hold-out houses, Harry brought his pickup to a stop as the light turned red. He surveyed the corner house, awed, as always, by the majestic ugliness of it. Perched off-center above the original was an addition with a single gable. The gable, in turn, had a small round window, like an eye. It was as though some misshapen toad had hopped upon the roof of this unassuming little bungalow and attached itself to the frame. And there it sat, keeping a lookout to the south, lest some larger creature try to come along and dislodge it. An architectural embarrassment.

Harry studied this house each time he was stopped at the light. He rarely saw anyone on the property at this hour, yet there was evidence of human activity all over the place. But it was the yard that captured Harry's attention, for it appeared to be moving. Not flowers or plants, season to season, but the soil itself.

He had driven by once to see a huge mound of dirt dumped just inside the fence, with children's trucks and shovels scattered about the base. The next time he came by, it had been transferred to the center of the barren yard where it had sat for a month or two, and finally had been shaped into terraces around one corner of the house, each layer held in place with green plastic edging.

Yet enthusiasm for the project seemed to have died out, for nothing was ever planted in that hard clay soil. Bit by bit the rain took its toll, the edging fell off, and the movable mud became a formless heap once again. Paper cups and soda bottles lay about, and rusty folding chairs were strewn helter skelter, back to back, like relatives no longer speaking.

Bunch of gypsies, Harry thought, smiling, and moved his truck forward as the light turned green again.

Each time he drove in at the garden center, there was something new to admire—a marvelous spring wreath of fresh flowers on the door, perhaps, or a huge arrangement of forsythia on the counter inside. It was all Wanda's doing, and he was grateful, for along with the housewives and office workers who shopped at the garden center for a pot of African violets, there were now sleek women in shimmering leotards and headbands studying the orange begonias. Men in Gucci loafers came to Harry's for a dozen roses, sometimes two. They seemed to look upon the garden center and the old Gill quarry as anachronisms that gave the area flavor. Wanda, however, had as much style as the best of them, for she was a stately presence, with near-perfect posture, her large bosom riding high beneath the folds of her rayon blouse, dark hair shiny-black above her forehead, nails polished and shaped.

Harry enjoyed being back at work, and vowed he would keep regular hours from now on. He didn't like the way Rose Kribbs scurried about among the urns and planters, casting sorrowful glances his way, and he was tired of the sad lilt in Tracy's voice, as though each word was a bead on a rosary. But Wanda was affectionately cheerful.

"Good to have you back," she said. "Spring just isn't spring without you here."

"Thanks, Wanda," he told her. And then, "When you can snag Steve, could the three of us talk a few minutes in my office?"

"Sure, Mr. G.," she told him.

The office was no more than eight by ten and, except for the window, every bit of wall space shoulder height or below was blocked by something—desk, file cabinets, storage bins. Harry went inside and pulled out the metal chair, sitting down at an angle as though unwilling to fully commit himself to the mountain of mail that had accumulated during the past two weeks. He had written only three checks for bills overdue when Steve appeared in the doorway.

Lean as a runner, he was nevertheless the strongest man on the lot. Both his sweatshirt and jeans, though laundered, were so embedded with stains of rust and clay and grass that they seemed a part of the fabric. His brown eyes, the identical shade of his hair, fixed themselves on Harry.

"What's up?" he asked.

Wanda came in after him, nudging him forward in order to shut the door behind them.

Harry pushed away from the desk, legs sprawled out in front of him. "I was just wondering," he began, twirling his pen around from finger to finger, "who we've got on the payroll right now."

"Well, we have five guys for spring and summer besides Bill and me. You want names?" Steve asked.

"Sure."

"There's Kenny . . . George . . . Tony. . . ."

"Last names too," said Harry.

"Let me look," said Wanda. She squeezed past Steve to open a file drawer, and her long nails caught at each folder, pulling it forward until she found what she wanted. Then, sitting down in the chair opposite Harry, she began reading off names:

"George Lyons, Mike Zapata. . . ."

"He Italian?" Harry asked.

Wanda looked up.

"Latino," said Steve.

"Who else?" said Harry.

Wanda continued. "Carl Zorn, Kenny Haines, and Tony Berto."

"Tony's Italian?" asked Harry.

"I . . . think so," said Steve. He and Wanda exchanged glances.

"These men all paid the same, are they?" asked Harry.

"All but Kenny. This is his second season with us, so he gets a little more."

"And do these guys all get along?"

"Harry, what's going on?" Wanda asked, folding her hands over the file in her lap.

"A piece of nonsense is what it is," Harry said. "But last night I found tomato sauce all over the hood of my truck."

"*Tomato* sauce?" Wanda's eyes opened wide with either surprise or merriment, Harry couldn't tell.

"And you think one of our guys did it?" asked Steve.

"All I know is there was a note stuck under one wiper blade. It said, 'You like Italian? Here's Italian.'" Harry was getting tired of repeating the stupid thing. "An empty can of Progresso was on the grass."

"I don't get it," said Steve.

"It's acidic!" said Wanda. "Bad for the paint."

"So I'm grasping at straws here, wondering if we had an Italian working for us, getting a better deal than the other men," said Harry.

Steve shook his head. "Tony's getting the same as the rest. They all do the same work."

"Well, that's about what I figured. But somebody's obviously pissed off about something."

"That's for sure," said Wanda. "Wasted a good can of Progresso." She covered her mouth with one hand.

"Look. I don't want this to get any further than the three of us. If it was one of the boys out there, I don't want to encourage him by getting steamed. And if it wasn't—if it was someone else—I don't want to spook Rose and Tracy. Just keep your eye on things. Let me know if somebody's disgruntled."

"Sure, boss," said Steve.

As Wanda rose to leave, she gave Harry a mischievous smile. "Tony Berto's handsome as anything, you know. If I was thirty years younger and it was my truck, I'd put a note under the wiper myself. I'd say, 'Next time, just skip the tomato sauce and leave the Italian.'"

"Get outta here," Harry growled, waving them off, and they were still laughing when they closed the door.

WHEN HE REACHED home that day, Harry paused at the door of the dining room. It looked unnaturally large and empty without the rental bed. This room had become their hospital for a time, and the bed, for Beth, her universe.

It did not seem possible that in this room with the ivory wallpaper, where birthdays and anniversaries had been celebrated, his wife had died. And the dying was not like anything Harry had imagined.

In the past, whenever he had thought fleetingly of death, his or his wife's, he'd imagined them holding hands, a kiss on the forehead, a long goodbye with assurances of love and joy in things remembered. And for a while it was that. She liked him to look through old photo albums with her, relive the past since there would be no future. She would take his hand as he sat by the bed and snuggle up against it as though it were a stuffed animal, straining his back. He lay behind her, spoon-shaped, on the hospital bed, letting her hold his arm while he wrapped himself around her.

He had not factored in pain, the times Beth—angry at life—would rail at him over some neglected chore. The evenings he would come to her and she would turn her face to the wall, too nauseated to talk. He had not reckoned with the boring predictability of her complaints and requests, his resentment that she couldn't leave this world in a better humor. Yet one by one she had been forced to give up the things she loved—walks in the neighborhood, tandem showers, chocolate eclairs—until only people were left, most precious of all. And she knew she would have to give up those as well.

Harry inhaled, then let his breath out slowly until there was no trace of a sound from his lips. His eyes moved from corner to corner, mentally cementing each object back in place to certify this space as a dining room once again. On the wide ledge of the bay window where they had put the bouquets friends sent when she was alive, there now sat the large ceramic jar with the black and purple flowers on the side. Harry had not touched it since the funeral service and, turning abruptly now, he headed for the kitchen.

There was flour all over the floor. He turned on the light and stared. One of the lower cupboard doors stood ajar, and a bag of flour was emptying its contents from a ragged, wet-looking hole at the bottom. Small white paw prints led under the table.

"Zeke!"

Harry dived forward and turned the flour sack on its side. Squatting down, hands on his knees, he could see Zeke's yellow eyes looking at him guiltily from as far under the table as he could get.

"What *is* this?" Harry demanded. Since when did cats eat flour? "*Damn* you, Zeke!" he exploded. The cat didn't move. Was this some kind of fixation? Neurosis? Zeke, he was sure, lived his life on the edge of a nervous breakdown.

Harry got the broom and dustpan, but even after he swept, a white film covered the floor.

"Okay, buddy," he said at last, feeling more charitable. "We're in this together, aren't we?" He reached under the table and scratched the cat's ears. During the last month of Beth's life, when Harry had tried to imagine what life would be like without her, he had somehow failed to include Zeke among the survivors.

When Harry opened the refrigerator, however, he got his second shock. He reached across the alien bowls and pans for the milk, and the carton was warm. *Oh, my God.*

He shut the door and opened the freezer section. Everything was coated with moisture. There was no sound from the refrigerator except a clicking at intervals, and a faint drip, drip of water from beneath. He turned all the controls to high. Nothing happened. Bit by bit, it seemed, the house was giving up the ghost.

He dialed Elaine and got no answer. Dialed Jack and got his answering machine. Dialed Claude and Sue.

"Make room in your freezer," he said. "I'm coming over."

When he ran outside to get a box from the trash, he waved to Paula in the side yard where she was weeding. "I need your help," he called, and almost before the words were out of his mouth, she was there. The sight of all this activity brought Marge Decker as well, and soon both women were in his kitchen, equipped with trays.

Harry stood by the opened refrigerator like a captain at the lifeboats, handing out bowls and platters.

"That's my casserole!" said Marge, reaching for her meat loaf, and then, taking a peek, "Harry! You haven't even touched it!" She handed the next item to Paula. "Your muffins," she said, with evident satisfaction.

"That's Effie Black's bowl," said Paula as another dish came forward. It had a slightly unsavory smell. The silence in the kitchen grew heavier still. The women accepted the food stoically, and finally, when they were down to half-used bottles of soy sauce and a molding jar of mayonnaise, they left. Harry had scarcely piled all that remained in the box when the phone rang. Marge.

"Harry, of *course* you don't have any appetite! What man wants to eat alone? Come over for dinner. Come have a home-cooked meal—pot roast and pie. How does that sound?"

"Marge, thanks so much, but I'm eating at my son's tonight," Harry told her, and hurried the box out to the pickup.

HE HEADED FOR the small house in Glen Echo where Claude was living with Sue, or Sue was living with Claude. Harry had no idea who was paying for what. Modern relationships were an enigma. Claude himself was an enigma.

It occurred to him that he should have called a repairman before he left and set up an appointment. No, too late in the day. How did you pay a repairman, cash or check? He wasn't even sure. Beth had handled that. Then he thought of her bank stubs, those cash withdrawals, and once again pushed it off the edge of his mind.

He followed MacArthur Boulevard to the turn-off beyond the fire station. The little town near the C&O Canal was born in the late eighteen hundreds as the area's Chautauqua, and had streets named Radcliffe and Yale. He parked in front of the bungalow and carried his box up the steps.

"Well, what have we here?" Sue asked, holding the door open wide so Harry could get by. She had been reading, evidently, and studied Harry over the rims of her glasses which had slipped down off the bridge of her nose. She was a lawyer for a conservative company in McLean, and Harry had no doubt that whatever he had interrupted was important.

Sue was neither pretty nor plain, fat nor slim, the type of woman, he guessed, that Beth would have filed under *MISCELLANEOUS*. She wore a shirt and slacks the color of putty, and her shoulder-length hair was curled under at the ends.

Harry took the food to the kitchen and plunked it on the table. Soggy cartons of green beans, a Sara Lee pound cake, packaged waffles, frozen corn. . . .

"Hey, Dad," Claude joked, coming in from the other room. "We'll feed you, don't worry."

"Damned refrigerator," Harry said.

Claude moved from table to freezer in his Birkenstock sandals. His shirt and shorts did not stand out in either color or design, but he wore them meticulously, shirt tucked in, shorts belted. The only thing that gave him a distinctive note was the thin mustache above his lip that was precisely tapered at either end. Together Claude and Sue seemed to have advanced to a sort of premature middle age.

"As soon as I heard you were coming, I made a spinach salad," Sue told him. "We'll eat on the patio. If it's too chilly, I've got sweaters."

They sat around a redwood table, each with a large glass bowl of spinach leaves, sliced egg, bacon and croutons.

Harry looked down at the dark green leaves. He liked his eggs scrambled, his bacon hot, his croutons in soup, and his spinach cooked. He saw no merit in mixing things together cold like this. Not to mention that he had no appetite to speak of.

Sue noticed. "We're going to keep up our strength, aren't we?" she said pleasantly. Ever since Beth became ill, Sue had addressed Harry in the plural.

"I slept in this morning and had a late breakfast and lunch," he told her. And then, to Claude, "Have you talked with Elaine recently?"

"Yeah. Don didn't show up at work again today."

Harry shook his head. "It's a funny business, Don walking out like that."

Claude agreed. "I don't know what to make of it. The same week that Mom died. . . . And Jodie's all upset."

"We're going to keep the conversation pleasant, aren't we?" said Sue briskly, smiling around the table. "Harry doesn't need any sad talk here."

Forks clinked politely against the sides of the bowls, and Harry gave himself the mental task of trying to figure out how Sue and Claude made love. Sue on top of Claude? She was a large-boned woman, and the picture in Harry's mind more closely resembled a wrestling match. Claude over Sue?

"So how goes it?" Claude asked.

Harry snapped to. "Taking it one day at a time," he said. He was so tired of that phrase, as though there were men who did not—

people who lived whole weeks at once, galloping through their lives at twice the pace. He thought of telling Claude and Sue about the tomato sauce incident, but when he thought how Sue would respond he thought better of it. "How's work?" he asked.

He tried to remember the name of the company where Claude worked. New Age Novelties came to mind, but he was horrible at remembering things about his children. When Elaine was expecting, Harry kept forgetting that his daughter was pregnant. He could not remember the phone number of Jack's apartment. Not only would Beth have been able to tell you all this, but she could have recited their shoe sizes as well.

"Actually, we're taking a new direction," Claude told him. "Look at the gift wrap in any store. Ninety percent is targeted for a specific event, and only ten percent for the all-occasion market."

Harry couldn't remember buying gift wrap in his life. He didn't even know where you would go to get it.

"If you buy two sheets of marbleized paper—say, mauve and gray and blue—you've got paper for Mother's Day, birthdays, anniversaries, you name it. We're not doing duck decoys or roses at all anymore. Only one percent clowns and puppies." Claude's voice was low and flat.

"But if the same paper can be used for any occasion, people won't buy as much," Harry suggested. Was he the only one in this family with an ounce of business sense?

"That could be a problem, I suppose, but we're doing each pattern in seventeen different colors," Claude told him. "When people see a pattern they like, they'll want it in every color. Or so the theory goes."

"It's certainly a novel approach," said Harry. "Are you doing any painting at all?"

"Thought you'd never ask," Claude told him, brightening, and there was an immediate change in his voice. "Let me show you what I did last month." He went inside the house.

"He hates his job, you know," Sue said in his absence, collecting the dishes. "We've talked about his painting full-time, but we probably couldn't meet the mortgage payments."

"He have any shows lately?"

"Just the shopping mall circuit."

The back door banged again, and Claude flopped down the steps carrying four framed canvasses. He propped them against the patio furniture at odd angles, then stood back with his arms folded.

This was the part Harry hated—the Thinking of Something to Say. He wondered if there was a book called *Learning to Love the Paintings You Hate*. The thing was, Claude seemed to take all the color he had drained out of his life and put it on canvas. There was the silhouette of a sailboat on a sea at sunset. The sky looked like tomato soup, with blue and black and purple and gold around the edges. The reflection on the water was dazzling. Harry could accept that somewhere, perhaps, since the birth of the solar system, there might have been such a sunset, but it was beyond anything he had ever imagined.

"Well, ...!" He slowly turned his attention to painting number two. It was the same sunset, same sky and water, but this time the sailboat was facing the opposite direction.

"In case you want to hang it at the other end of the room," Claude told him.

"Oh," said Harry.

The third was better, a snow-capped mountain beyond a lake. The proportions were good, the reflection in the water competently done. Harry wondered if he hadn't seen some version of this scene before—if Claude wasn't painting the same subjects over and over.

"Hmmm," Harry said, and swiveled his head to look at the last canvas resting against Sue's leg. This was a rural landscape of a barn, an old plow rusting off to the left. The barn was red, the sky was blue, and there were yellow and purple flowers in the meadow. What was wrong with these paintings? Harry surveyed them all again. They looked as though. . . .as though they belonged on Hallmark greeting cards! That was it! Nice, but nothing that would draw you in for a deeper look. What you saw was all there was—a description rather than an expression.

"Has your company ever thought of doing both gift wrap and greeting cards?" he asked.

"I don't want to do greeting cards, Dad, I want my own show," said Claude, an edge to his voice. "What do you think? Do you like them or not?"

"Of course!"

"But do you *like* them? Really, I mean?"

At what age do you stop lying to your children? Beth wouldn't even call it lying. Supporting, she'd say.

"You get better with each one, Claude," Harry said, and was rewarded with Claude's smile. *Thank you, thank you*, Harry said silently to the invisible God of Speech, but a gentle sadness swept over him. There were different kinds of hell, he decided. One was losing your wife. Another was not liking what you *could* do, and wanting what you couldn't. Harry ached for the blond-haired boy Claude used to be, so intent with his water colors, his papers spread out over the kitchen table. Ached for what was always, it seemed, beyond his grasp.

"Choose one," Claude said. "You can have it."

"I didn't mean—"

"Sure, go ahead, Dad."

"Claude, I've already got so many of your paintings. I hate to deprive you of sales."

"He wants you to have it," said Sue emphatically.

Which would he tire of the least? Harry wondered. The red, red barn? Sailboat listing right? Sailboat listing left?

"This one," he said, choosing the barn.

Claude looked puzzled. "Really? Why?"

Harry spluttered and held out his hands, palms up. "There's no accounting for taste," he said, and picked up the painting. "Kids, it's time to head home. Thanks for the meal."

Sue suddenly latched onto his arm and walked him out to his

truck. "We have to start getting out more, don't we? We need to have other people in our lives, Harry, or we're going to grow old alone."

"Oh, I don't think you need to worry about that," he said. "You and Claude have years ahead of you yet."

HE PULLED IN his driveway and slowly got out of the truck. The screen door was ajar, and Harry knew without looking that there was food wedged behind it. A glass bowl full of macaroni and cheese, and he with no fridge. He took it indoors, ladled out a scoop full for Zeke, then sat listlessly watching the cat eat. Zeke snapped at each piece, turning his head sideways and making little jerking motions while he chewed.

When Harry looked at the clock again, it was seven thirty-three. Wanda would be working till nine tonight, going about closing up shop. In a few more hours the first two days of mourning would be over, but still he waited for that horrific thing called Grief to ambush him once again.

On the other hand, maybe he was one of those lucky people who grieved and got it over with. Beth had been sick for so long. . . . Maybe that sinking sensation he'd had at the garden center his first day back was the worst it was going to get. As if to test himself, he walked deliberately into their bedroom where there had been quarrels and making up. Where there had been both passionate comings together and humdrum sex. Nights he had been as potent and energetic as a rooster, and nights he had been content to hold his wife and stroke her hair.

Her hair. To please him, Beth had worn it long and loose about the shoulders. Twice she had explained that she'd reached an age where long hair had the effect of pulling her face down. But Harry wouldn't hear of it shorter, and so she'd humored him. Harry loved the feel of it in his face when she bent over him making love.

He walked to the closet and opened the folding louvered doors on the left—the doors behind which Beth's shirts and dresses had hung undisturbed for the last four months, replaced by a hospital gown.

Longing fluttered in his chest, warning him away. Harry pushed a clump of hangers aside, skirts dangling tenuously from their hangers, and looked at Beth's robe at the back of the closet—a rayon robe with lavender shafts of bamboo that he had given her one Christmas. He had always loved the way rayon clung to her, swung from her hips when she tied the sash.

His fingers closed around the material, pulling it off the hook, and drew it toward him. *He could do this!* He sniffed at the robe. Sniffed again. Then, more desperately, bunched up the silky rayon and, holding it against his face, inhaled. He grappled with it, searching for the sleeves, the underarms, the pocket over the breast, taking deeper and deeper breaths.

Harry sank down on the edge of the bed, the robe in his hands, his eyes a blur. He'd waited too long; only the faintest trace of her scent remained. Eyes squeezed shut, he exhaled shakily, then picked up Beth's pillow and held it to his face.

He lay on the living room couch as the evening dribbled away. The phone rang but he did not answer. The room darkened as night came on, but he turned on no lights. Once in a while, he heard a voice leaving a message on the answering machine in the hall, but he did not stir.

"Dad, it's Jack. I tried you earlier. I'll call again around ten."

Beep.

"Wade, Harry. Need anything from the store?"

Beep.

"It's me, Dad. Could I leave Jodie with you for a few hours next Wednesday? I've got an interview at the Board of Education to see about teaching full time in the fall."

Beep.

"Jim here. Listen, I'm going to pick up a bushel of crabs Saturday. First of the season! Why don't you come over?"

More beeps as people dialed and hung up, an inaudible message from AMVETS. And then, about nine-twenty, a call from Liz Bowen:

"Harry? Are you there? . . . I saw Max! I'm sure of it! I was shopping at White Flint and he was walking toward Bloomingdale's. That's just where he'd be going, because he always liked their socks. . . ."

THREE

The Crazies

BECAUSE HE DIDN'T return her call, Liz phoned Harry at the garden center the next day.

"It was Max, Harry."

He was at the back of the lot separating the load of maple saplings, and hoped they had the right tags or a customer expecting a red-leafed October Sunset might find a tree aflame with yellow come fall. Harry wished he had turned off his cell phone.

"Did you . . . say anything to him, Liz?" He steadied the trunk of the largest sapling and watched it list again to the left when he removed his hand.

"What do you think? Wouldn't I be wild with joy if I'd brought him home with me? I lost him somewhere in the shoe department. All I can figure is that he went back into a stock room somewhere."

"Maybe he works there. Maybe it was a Max-Bowen look-alike."

"Harry, it was his walk, his height, his weight. . . ."

"I understand, Liz. I know what grief can do." He tried to imagine Liz as he remembered her--the dark hair, the perfectly shaped brows, the way she used to lean against Max when they sat together. Imagined her listing now, like this tree, without even a ball of earth to support her.

"You don't believe me," she said accusingly. "I know what I saw."

"How do you explain it?"

"Sometimes, Harry, there's this . . . Well, they linger. They don't want to go yet, so they hang around their favorite places. I've been reading this book called *The Reluctant Dead*. . . ."

"I've got another call, Liz."

"I'm going to haunt Bloomingdales, Harry. I'm going to go there every day at the same time and just wait. I'll get a job in the men's sock department if I have to, and wait for him to come by."

"It was good talking to you, Liz. Keep in touch," Harry said, and pressed the Off button with his thumb. Slipping the cell phone in his pocket, he tipped his head back and closed his eyes. He too felt the tilt.

Was the world more crazy since he'd lost his wife? Harry wondered, or did it just seem that way? He suddenly felt the need for contact with a member of his own planet. Pulling out his cell phone again, he punched in Jim's number.

"What time you picking up those crabs Saturday?" he asked. "I think I'd like to come."

IT HELPED TO have something to look forward to, and Harry was feeling upbeat on Saturday as he loaded the last of the azaleas the nursing home had ordered and sent Bill out with the truck.

Around noon, he spent an hour in his office to go over some invoices. His window, opening into the grape arbor, brought in the heady scent of the herb tables beyond—basil and mint. The fragrance of sweet peas. Even the spicy salami of a submarine sandwich.

Tracy and Rose were eating their lunch at the picnic table. The grapevines overhead shaded Harry's window in summer, died back in winter, offering the sun.

". . . arsenic. Just a little at a time," he heard Rose say.

Harry looked up.

"Every pay day, she takes a few dollars from his pocket and puts a pinch of arsenic in his supper. She's been doing it for six months."

"She'd actually *kill* him?" Tracy gasped, her mouth full of sandwich.

"It's all she can think of to do, she's so desperate. But now her little boy eats some of the cake, and she's terrified he's going to die. She rushes him to the hospital, and this doctor. . . . You should *see* this doctor, Tracy. Look. He's on the cover. . . ."

Laughter. "Wow!" Tracy's voice. "He's *hot!*"

"She's crying, and she tells the doctor *every*thing. That's how they meet, and they fall in love. You should read it. The beginning's a little slow—all the years she's been putting money away so she can leave her husband—but once she meets this doctor. . . ."

"I can't take on any more till I've finished *To Kill a Mockingbird*. Big test coming up."

"Murder mystery?"

"Not exactly."

Harry shook his head and went back to the invoices. What *did* arsenic taste like, anyway? And how dense could a man be?

There was a steady stream of customers in the afternoon, and Harry gave them his full attention, knowing he would be leaving early. Some, he suspected, had stopped by to offer their condolences, but all, it seemed, walked out with at least something in their arms, and more than one told him they were planting this or that in his wife's memory.

"Much appreciated," Harry told them.

Wanda Sims was pleased he'd be having dinner with friends. "That's what I like to hear, Harry," she told him, picking a piece of fern off his shirt.

Each outward manifestation that he was alive brought out the cheering section, Harry discovered. He picked up a few six-packs on his way home, then went inside to shower and change. The red light on his answering machine was flashing and he listened to a message from Liz Bowen, The Crazie: "Whenever you feel like it, Harry, we could get together and talk about Max and Beth."

Harry did not intend to reply.

Yet as he drove to the Swanns', Mozart was on the radio and Beth was on his mind. She'd been eight months older than Harry, but seemed like a young girl to him—small-boned, a lightweight with a girlish voice and a shy smile. Harry had tried to interest her in classical music, in playing a CD when she busied herself with projects around the house—sewing, refinishing old furniture—but it never took. He never heard her hum the melodies that meant so much to him, and once, he found her listening to a talk show on a small radio beside her sewing machine while Liszt waltzed back in the living room.

His arm on the open window, Harry found that you could play classical music with your windows down in a Cadillac DeVille and women would not give you the puzzled stares. On the other hand, women—young women, anyway—would scarcely look at you at all. If you drove a DeVille and your hair was turning gray, other drivers prepared to cut you off when the light changed, certain that if there was any drink in your cup holder, it was Ensure.

Harry didn't mind. He liked the comfortable ride, especially on a May evening like this that put shame to summer—fresh and warm, with a breeze like a woman running her hands through your hair. The azaleas that hadn't bloomed yet were thinking about it, and all the people in the Washington area who didn't grow them already were on their way to buy.

The thing was, Harry didn't care all that much for flowers. Cultivated flowers, that is, grown in circular beds or alternating rows on terraced hillsides, like chorus girls on stage. He liked his trees and flowers unpruned—a rural landscape dotted here and there with white dogwood, a ramble of wild roses. Liked rounding a bend on a country road and finding himself face to face with a field of buttercups, or violets at the edge of a woods.

Why was it that things seemed better in the daytime? Right now, he felt strong enough to deal with the hard-shelled, sharp-clawed, soul-sucking sadness that plagued him sometimes at night. Yet he knew it would come scratching at the window once again, or sliding in under the door, filling first the room, then his chest with an overpowering emptiness. For now there were friends waiting for him, and Harry was surprised to find that he was not only hungry, but ravenous.

The Swanns' house, a rambler, had additions on both sides. When Jim married again, he'd allowed Virginia to change what she liked, and the only thing that remained untouched was the wide screened porch at the back. It was here, as Harry made his way around the lilac bushes at the side, that Jim had covered a redwood picnic table with newspaper.

"Hey, hey, hey!" Leroy Schneider called out as Harry opened the screen and set the beer on the table.

Fred Fletcher took his pipe from his mouth and extended his hand. "How you doing, Harry?" A genteel mustached man in his late sixties, Fred had lost his wife over a decade ago. Harry glanced around. This was a charity supper, then? Jim and Ginny throwing a little crab feast for three old geezers who had lost their wives, and hadn't the looks or the fortunes to remarry? But he was feeling too good to be offended, too grateful to be included, and smiled as Virginia stepped out on the porch in her cotton slacks and V-necked sweater.

"Harry, sweetheart!" She placed a basket of wooden mallets on the table, then walked over and gave him a squeeze, her soft bosom burrowing into his chest before she pulled away. She was a good-looking woman with bad skin—luminous eyes and thick chestnut-colored hair—but skin that had aged prematurely from long summers spent on the beach. Her face was etched all over like an old china plate, and there were small lines spreading outward from the lips. Even now, she had told him once, she loved the sun, wrinkles be dammed. Beth never cared that much for it, never seemed to tan, in fact. Whenever Harry thought of his wife at the beach, he envisioned her wearing a hat of some kind, a towel thrown over her shoulders.

Virginia's voice was husky. Grabbing Harry next by both arms, she looked directly into his eyes. "How are you, Harry? Really?"

"Hungry, actually!," he said.

"Well!" She smiled again, then let her hands drop. "Good sign."

"Hey, hey, hey!" Leroy called again as Jim's car, the trunk lid raised over a bushel basket, pulled into the driveway. Harry held the screen open for him as he carried in the steaming crabs, a thin stream of pungent brown liquid dripping from beneath, their spicy, ocean-bottom scent enveloping the porch.

"Aren't those honeys?" Jim said, grinning down at the coral-colored crabs piled on top of each other. "Come on, folks. Dig in! We got the beer, we got the vinegar, we're all set."

Harry stepped over the picnic bench and took a place near the end of the table where Jim was dumping large clutches of crabs. He reached for a big one, turned it belly up, lifted the tab of its breastplate, and within seconds was extracting the succulent meat. Here he was, a normal man having a crab dinner at the home of friends.

He had wondered if he could socialize like this only a week since Beth had died. If he would be a drag, unable to talk of anything of interest. But after two beers it seemed the natural thing to do, and after three, he even forgave Virginia for leaning her elbows on the table in such a way that it deepened her cleavage.

The conversation was all about food—low murmurs of approval, a grunt or a nod to pass along the roll of paper towels. Six-packs slid down the table and back."If there's a better way to spend a Saturday, I don't know what it is," said Fred, who had arrived inexplicably in his undertaker's suit and had long since discarded the jacket and tie.

Virginia wasn't eating much. As often as she picked up a crab and wrestled with it, she put it down again, content to crack only the claws and see if she could pull out the meat in one try. Now and then Jim or Harry gave her a particularly good piece, but she didn't seem to relish it the way Beth would have. She did, however, when Harry fed her a bite, hold onto his hand for a moment as it grazed her lips.

Harry reached for his beer again, but his eyes returned furtively to the slender brown arms Virginia had brought back from Florida not long ago, and he thought of Beth and a time the whole family had gone to the beach, back when Elaine was nine. He was remembering one particular morning when he'd awakened in the cottage they'd rented at Rehoboth to find that he was alone in the bedroom and the sun was high. He'd gone to the window to see Beth and the kids heading for the ocean with their buckets, looking for sand crabs and shells, and it suddenly seemed to him that this was the way life should be. The air smelled of salt—he imagined he could taste it on his lips—and feeling invigorated, he had decided to put on his jogging shoes and go for a half hour run on the road. He loved his life at that moment—his wife, his children. He had never, in fact, felt more fit.

But when he arrived at last back at the cottage, ready to shower and enjoy a good breakfast, he'd found his family waiting sullenly on the steps.

"Where *were* you?" they chorused in unison.

"You *knew* we were going to the Pancake House for breakfast!" Jack had said.

Harry remembered no such thing.

"Then why didn't you wake me?" he'd asked.

"Because you were tired and we wanted to let you sleep," he was told.

"And when you woke up, you went jogging instead, and we were *waiting!*" wailed Elaine, while Jack looked on stoically, his twelve year-old stomach rumbling.

"Then why didn't you go to the Pancake House without me?" Harry had asked.

"Because we wanted you to go with us," said Claude.

"Well, as soon as I shower, I will."

Too late, they said. It was almost lunch time and he'd ruined it for everyone. And so it went. Once again he was out of step, out of tune, marching not only to a different drummer, but down the wrong street entirely.

Yet his wife never made this error. Beth, the electronic sensor, heard and understood every innuendo. She knew what her children wanted before they did, anticipated their every need. How did women *do* this? How did they *know*? Telepathy, that's what it was.

"How you doin' down there, Harry?" Jim asked.

"Just getting started." Harry grinned. "Boy, Beth would have loved this. She could pick crab with the best of them." He realized suddenly that, to this point, no one else had said that four letter word: B-E-T-H.

"She sure could," said Leroy.

"One fine woman," said Fletcher.

"She was a little dear," said Virginia, smiling at Harry again. A crab leg dangled between the long red nails of her thumb and finger, and her lipstick was smeared, so that her mouth had a lopsided look.

Harry tore off a paper towel and wiped his hands. "What I miss," he continued, conscious of the way his words came rolling out, no censor on duty, "was how she . . . she knew what to *do* about things, you know?" He leaned his arms on the table. "The kids come to me with a problem, what am I supposed to tell them? Beth always had an answer ready."

Virginia was looking at him pityingly. Virginia, Harry concluded, also had one of those files in the pantry, with alphabetical solutions to any problem: SECOND MARRIAGES, WHAT TO EXPECT; CRABS, HOW TO AVOID; WIDOWERS, HOW TO ENTICE. . . .

"Never be another like Beth," said Leroy.

"True blue," said Jim.

"You take Elaine and Don," Harry told them. "I mean, who would have thought? Elaine asks me and what do I tell her?" Virginia, who had risen to throw out a heap of crab carcasses, stopped with her hands in mid-air.

"Something happen?" asked Jim.

And Harry heard his voice telling the story—his head telling him to shut up. These were his friends. People who understood. Old shirt-off-my-back Jim. Same with Leroy and Fred.

". . . and she hasn't heard from him since," Harry finished.

Silence.

Virginia wiped her hands and went over to sit in the wicker rocking chair, one foot resting beside Harry on the picnic bench, her painted toenails showing through the sandals.

"Harry," she said, "a man just doesn't walk out on his wife without somewhere to go."

"Of course he's staying *some*where," he told her.

"I mean some*one*. I'll bet he's got a girl."

Harry shook his head. "Elaine was goading him! It was a spur of the moment thing."

"If it hadn't been that it would have been something else. Take it from me; that's what my first husband did. Packed his bag and was in this woman's apartment an hour later. Don was probably just looking for an excuse."

Was it possible?

"Where does he work? What do they say there?" Fred asked.

"He was a car mechanic. Peugots, I think." Harry shook his head. "Hasn't shown up there either."

Leroy gave a low whistle, and the crab picking went on in silence for a while, broken only by the creak of the rocking chair.

"You know," said Jim, "some problems just have to work themselves out. Not a damn thing you can do about them, so you might as well put them on a back burner."

"That's about the way I figure," Harry said, a certain mellowness overtaking him.

"When you're feeling low, I always say, get a haircut," Jim continued. "If that doesn't help, drink a beer. And if that doesn't help . . ."

"Eat crab!" said Fred, and the others laughed.

"I feel better already," Harry said.

He smiled genially around the table, satisfied to stop eating and enjoy the conversation. But whether the beer or the fact that Virginia was idly but deliberately caressing his thigh with her toe, he was beginning to tire, and eventually stood up and said his goodbyes.

More claps on the shoulder, another slap on the back, a squeeze on the arm from Ginny as she said, "You can stop here for dinner anytime, Harry."

And then he was driving slowly off down the street as dusk closed in, his fingers smelling sweetly of vinegar and crab. Maybe they'd do this again, start a tradition. Four old friends, and. . . . Well, maybe Virginia could go to her sister's or something.

Along with the satisfaction of an evening well-spent, however, came a prickle of uneasiness that he could not decipher. It was what Virginia had said about Don having a girl somewhere. Not impossible, Harry decided, but highly improbable. He just wasn't the type. But then, who would have expected a man like Don to walk out? And what exactly was the type to cheat?

The prickle gave way to the knowledge that it was not Don who had brought it on, but a memory of long ago, when Claude was twelve, maybe. Elaine was in high school, Jack off doing who knows what. The garden center was expanding; Beth was involved in projects with the kids.

Her name was Stefanie Morrison, the woman who ran the store in the garden center before Wanda. Even her name seemed out of place now, as though she had crawled unbidden into the front seat beside Harry.

It wasn't that she had been such a knockout. Her features were somewhat irregular, the jaw a little too prominent, but she had great legs. It was a certain receptivity about her that acted as lure.

She never made seductive gestures, but the way her eyes met his glances, and the slow movements of her limbs transformed her body into a question mark, and Harry craved an answer.

He began going to work early to be there when Stefanie arrived, and was the last to leave for those few minutes they might have alone. There was only a touch now and then, but the air was so charged with possibility that once on a Saturday, Harry drove home and made love to Beth in the middle of the day. Then he felt sheepish and peeved when she burst into tears.

There was no need for that, was there? He was married, Stefanie was married, so this meant nothing would happen, right? He could enjoy the playful banter between them that heated up his body, but it was not "an affair."

He repeated it now aloud: "It was *not* an affair!" That settled, he let his mind play back the conversation at the Swanns' that evening, and wished his wife had been there. He could almost see her sitting at the table after the meal was over, extracting crab meat for salad the next day while the others finished their beer. See her laugh with the others, her long hair clipped up in back with a comb, exposing her neck. She had a great neck. He just longed to see her sitting there in her jeans again. Beth in an old shirt. Beth barefoot. Just Beth.

It was the natural order of things, he supposed, to appreciate someone more after she was gone. Regret, someone had told him, was part of the grieving process. It would be the same for his children after he was gone and his children's children. His faults would become fond eccentricities and his cautions obeyed. Yet were he to miraculously rise from the dead and seat himself at the table, his jokes would once again wear thin and his taste in ties and socks deemed abominable.

As he drove down Old Forest Road, he discovered he was perspiring, and rolled the window down. He hadn't had more than four beers all evening, but he couldn't drink like he used to. Made him lethargic, and he needed a steady hand in the shop. By the time he realized he was heading for the garden center instead of home, he was right by the house with the movable yard. If he had not heard music as he approached the corner, he might have driven on by, but the light was green and on sudden impulse he made a turn in front of the house. He stared to see a yard full of people, caught the fragrant smell of cooking meat, heard the sound of rock music from a boom box on the hood of a car up on blocks. He went down the street, turned around, and came back to park on the other side.

What captured his attention was the difference in ages, from an infant held loosely over a shoulder to an elderly woman sprawled on the front steps, her skirt forming a hammock between her knees. Toddlers clambered up and down beside her, hanging on to steady themselves. Three bare-chested men drank under the one tree in a corner, while the remainder of the clan spilled into the side yard and on around in back where smoke rose from the make-shift grill.

Laughter and squabbling, teasing, calling, along with the crying-whine of a child who was refused his share of attention. Two pubescent boys were wrestling on the ground near a table where others were eating.

Relishing life. This is the way it should be lived, Harry thought, as his eyes drifted. The past is gone, tomorrow only a maybe, so live in the *now.* Laugh and love and wrestle.

He didn't know just when he became aware of it, but all at once he discovered the elderly woman looking at him. All around the yard, people were staring in his direction—the girls, the men, the boys on the grass. . . . Someone leaned over and turned off the radio, eyes on Harry all the while.

Swallowing, Harry gave them a polite nod, turned the key in the ignition, and was relieved to see that the traffic light ahead of him was green. The Cadillac lurched forward, rounded the corner, and Harry didn't look back.

HE COULD HEAR the phone ringing as soon as he got out of the truck. Harry sprinted up the walk, jabbed the key in the lock, and picked up the handset before the answering machine cut in.

"Harry!" A woman's voice, gently scolding. "Where in the world have you been?"

Jesus, now what?

"We're so disappointed."

His mind ticked off a list of possibilities. Definitely a woman he knew, but who? Marge? Paula? The Crazie, even?

"We *waited*, Harry, but finally went ahead and ate without you." Rita Mitchell's voice.

"Rita, what are you talking about?"

"The dinner invitation! I slipped it under your door last week and asked you to call if you couldn't come. Remember? I have the loveliest woman here—I've known her for ages. You two would have hit it off so well."

"Jesus," said Harry again. No other word seemed appropriate.

"Windy wants to talk to you," said Rita.

A man's voice next. "Harry, how you doing? We missed you."

"I forgot," Harry said simply.

"Oh, no problem, really." Windy lowered his voice. "You know how it is with women. They plan these things. You missed a real looker, though, I'll tell you that. I must say, Rita can pick 'em. Sales rep for some New York outfit."

"Maybe another time."

"She's going back tomorrow."

"Ah, well," Harry said.

HE DID NOT go upstairs more than a couple of times a week, but tonight Harry stood in front of Jack's old chest of drawers, a maple bureau with one of the handles missing, the scratches and nicks of childhood on the front and sides.

Swallowing, he stooped and pulled open the bottom drawer. It was crammed with school notebooks. Algebra tests, theme papers—"The Changing Face of China"—a layer of comic books, and then, near the bottom, a *Playboy* of the 80s when Jack was just a kid. Still there.

Guiltily Harry pulled it out, first checking to see if there were more, then took it down to the bath adjoining his bedroom. He had come across it when Jack was away at college and Harry was looking for the road atlas he'd loaned him the year before. He remembered going through the magazine then, smiling at the cover of a young woman in a thin bikini, bra, and long white stockings held up by a garter belt. She was holding a rose. He remembered checking out the centerfold too, and finding that someone—Jack, probably—had drawn arrows to crucial spots on the model, and in boyish script had scrawled beside them, *First base, Second base, Third base, Home run!!!*

He checked the centerfold now. The arrows were still there. Harry ran water in the tub, took off his clothes and climbed in. Folding a towel behind his head, he propped the magazine on his stomach.

There was something quaintly innocent about the cover photo—the girl's panties covering all her bottom except for the lower inch or so of one buttock. Her skin had a rosy glow, the patina bestowed only by a photographer's filter and the developer's skill.

The bath water reached Harry's chest, lifting the hair so that it floated a half inch or so above his body, and the corners of the magazine were beginning to curl. Harry lifted one foot and turned the handle. Water sloshed against the overflow outlet.

He lay very still, eyes taking in the full swelling of the young woman's breast, the curve of her back, the slight protrusion of her lower lip in a seductive pout, the long dark hair.

Saliva gathered in Harry's throat and he swallowed again, turning to the inside pictures. Fresh-faced girls with bouncy hair and bouncy bottoms; long-legged blondes in posed ecstasy, fingers cupping their naked breasts; girls in high heels bending over chairs, with animal lust in their eyes.

Something was not quite right, but Harry didn't know what. The faces were a little too . . . vacant, perhaps. Untested. It was too much like looking at your own daughter. Harry liked his women to look slightly more . . . well, used.

Nonetheless something poked up beyond the pages of the magazine and wove drunkenly about. Harry slowly lowered the *Playboy* and observed. It reminded him of those plastic roly-poly dolls his children had as babies, with weights at the bottom.

Curiously, he reached down and gave his penis a little push. It bobbed to the left and back again. He pushed it to the right. It made a wide semi-circle and rose once more.

This way, that way, and the crazy thing was that there were tears in Harry's eyes. It was as though his penis were giddily waiting for Beth, and didn't realize she would never come.

The phone.

Harry closed his eyes and lay motionless against the back of the tub, hands on his thighs. Three rings. Four. He heard his own voice out in the hall advising callers to leave a message.

"Dad? Dad?" Elaine's voice, loudly calling. "Come on, Dad. Are you there? Well, anyway, Don got fired. His boss called and said that Don has been on unauthorized leave for a week. I asked if Jodie and I had any benefits coming, and he said to talk to a lawyer."

Harry sighed. He stayed in the water another few minutes. When he opened his eyes, his buddy lay on its side. Harry reached down and gently massaged it to life again. Then he pulled out the towel from behind his head and slowly got to his feet. On the floor lay the girl in the white garter belt and stockings, studying him still. And this time, Harry knew, she was laughing.

ON SUNDAYS, GILL'S Garden Center didn't open till noon, and morning was his favorite time to work in the shop. When he'd gone to church at all, it was because Beth had sung in the choir and liked an audience, but Harry never understood the Holy Ghost. He never understood Grace. And the more Reverend Fuller tried to explain it to him, the less sense it made.

Nor had Harry ever tried to make a deal with God. If the Lord of the Universe was all He was cracked up to be, He did not need to be wheedled and coaxed and flattered to allow Beth to live. No, Harry felt most reverent when he worked at making a mold in the greenhouse on Sunday mornings, his quiet disturbed only by the chirpings and rustlings of nature outside the open door. Like a member of an orchestra taking the music of a genius and bringing it to life again in the playing, Harry kept statues alive by repairing their flaws.

And so on this Sunday, a week after the funeral, Harry pulled into the drive at work, past the "closed" sign and the large concrete goose at the entrance to the store. She had been clad for the month of April in a yellow raincoat and boots that probably cost more than a slicker for Jodie, and now she was resplendent in a gardening apron and straw hat. *Barbie*, the employees dubbed her in derision because of her many outfits, yet women who disdained to put a pink flamingo on their lawns would line up to purchase the heavy goose for their porch or steps, then come back regularly to add to her wardrobe.

Harry drove around to the greenhouse and sat awhile before getting out. This property was the last on the commercial stretch to keep some trees, making Harry's five-acre lot an oasis amid the bustle of traffic on Old Forest Road. Each year it seemed that the leaves came out when he wasn't looking. One day there were bare branches, and the next there were leaves, the greenest of greens. Yet they'd been out now for a month. He closed his eyes. Green was Beth's favorite color. He would go the rest of his life, he knew, with the weight of this particular spring on his heart.

Inside the greenhouse, the new foliage was merely a blur beyond the frosted glass. With the door propped open, though, Harry could hear the mockingbird that went through its repertoire from a telephone pole at the front of the lot.

On Sunday mornings he tried to park his truck unobtrusively behind the greenhouse, but occasionally people saw it there and, if they had their minds set on a Japanese maple or a row of yews, Harry would sometimes stop what he was doing and write up the sale. Today the mockingbird sang to him alone.

He was working on the Apostle Paul. The cheekbone, the fingers, and a broken foot had been made whole again with plasticine, awaiting a new mold. The Chinese lady off to one side had only her fin to be sanded, that thin line where the halves of the mold had come together. The shepherd girls needed micro-surgery, and the Madonna had not been started yet.

Harry liked his work, liked moving around in baggy pants, an old shirt tied around his waist to wipe his hands on. When a T.G.I. Fridays had opened a mile down the road, theirs was not a philosophy he understood.

He scrutinized Saint Paul as he prepared it for its ordeal, deciding where the two pieces of his mold would come together over the statue, the place they could most easily pull apart. He put on a pair of surgical gloves and brushed on a thin coat of urethane elastomer, careful to reach every small indentation, leaving no air bubbles if he could manage.

There would be three coats in all before the mother mold of plaster topped it off, and shims of thin aluminum placed along the parting line would separate the halves when needed. It was painstaking and slow, but that didn't bother Harry.

Wade had tried casting for a few months, but proved allergic to silica, so he went back to working the quarry and took it over when their father died. A man of few words, his brother. Couldn't exactly call them a close-knit family. Wade had come to Beth's funeral service, but—never having married, or perhaps because he and Beth hadn't seen eye to eye on almost everything—he did not stand up and make any tribute to his sister-in-law.

Harry put his mind on the project at hand, knowing work had made him happy once, and hoped it would do so again. The trick was to concentrate on turning a statue inside out in his mind. When he looked down into a newly created mold he was seeing not the outside, as the world would see it, but that part visible only to the sculptor's eye. And now, it was his life that was turned inside out.

As the morning wore on, the first coat dried and Harry applied a second, thicker one. He was working on Paul, listening to Beethoven, and thinking of sex. Oddly, he was remembering Virginia Swann's cleavage across the table when they were eating crab. He was thinking specifically that if he had, say, thirty years left—twenty, anyway, and who knows for how many of those years he'd be potent—then, grief or not, he had to start the whole caboodle over again if he wanted female companionship—the search, the approach, the courtship, the misunderstandings, compromises, quarrels, reconciliations. Oh, God! He felt tired already.

It had been easy with Beth, because he hadn't even noticed her at first. He'd been dating another woman he couldn't seem to please: Bring her roses, she'd want champagne; bring champagne, she'd want shoes.

"Shoes?" Harry had asked.

"Max bought Liz a pair of sling-backs," the woman told him.

Their crowd got together at a favorite place in Silver Spring to dance, and on this particular night, Harry had gone to the bar to get her the Alexander she'd requested, and came back to find her dancing in the arms of another man. He stalked out, knowing that if he'd bought her shoes, they would be the wrong color, and even if they weren't, this woman could not be satisfied in a million years. And there was Beth, sitting on the hood of a car, hugging herself against the evening chill.

"Hi," she'd said, and smiled. Harry had been hungry for a smile.

"You too?" he had joked.

"What?"

"You just walk out on somebody?"

She'd laughed. "No. I came with a girlfriend. Too smoky in there. Every so often I need to breathe."

They talked—she had an on-again, off-again boyfriend, Joe Wyman, but she didn't think she loved him, she'd said. So Harry had driven her home, then called her the next day. And no matter what he brought her, or whether he brought anything at all, she never stopped smiling.

Harry's eyes wandered to the door of the shop and he inhaled deeply of the fragrant May air, as though to keep himself afloat. In that brief interlude, he saw an ancient Pontiac Grand Am pull alongside his pickup, and watched as a woman got out. Even if she'd missed the sign, she should be able to tell by the empty lot that the garden center was closed, Harry thought. He went back to applying the last of the mixture to the apostle's feet.

The woman, however, yanked at the strap on her shoulder bag, and stood with hands on her hips, looking around. Long locks of brown hair, a bit straggly, blew about her face. The wide sleeves of her loose jacket flapped in the breeze.

She'll leave, Harry told himself.

But then she walked on around the car, taking a step or two toward the greenhouse, and Harry recognized the Spider Lady he'd seen a time or two before. She was wearing tight jeans and had two of the longest legs he had ever seen on a woman. On the skinny side, definitely skinny, she continued walking in his direction.

Harry put down his brush and moved to the open door.

"Help you? Actually, we're closed."

She stopped about six feet away and studied his face. Hers was thin, with heavy lidded eyes—a little too close together, perhaps—full lips, and a shiny nose that turned up abruptly at the end.

"I *thought* it was you!" she said.

"Beg your pardon?"

"The robber."

"What?"

"Casing the joint," she went on.

He stared.

"That's what we figured you were, sitting out there in your car like that, staring at our house."

Oh, my God. "Look, I'm sorry. I was just driving by, and was attracted by the music and people. I was turning around, actually."

"That's what I told them after you left. I said it's the man at the garden center, just lost his wife. But you sure upset my grandmother. She said if you ever park in front of our house like that again, she'll shoot you."

The woman smiled, and Harry could see that her top teeth protruded slightly. He wouldn't call her pretty. Appealing, maybe. Thirty-six, thirty-seven, he guessed.

"Tell your grandmother to save her ammunition. I won't frighten her again," Harry said, managing a smile himself. He pulled off the surgical gloves and realized that even those made him suspect. "Did you need anything? As I said, we're closed Sunday mornings, but—"

"No. I come here sometimes to buy flowers. I don't know what it is, I just like being in the same room with them, you know? I bought one of those wooden ducks once, the wings go round? It wasn't in the yard a week before my cousin's kid broke it."

"Oh, those."

"Not worth diddly," she told him.

"No, they're not."

"Then why do you sell them?"

"Because people ask. People without kids, I suppose. Anyway, I'm sorry I scared your grandmother." The woman made no move to leave, and Harry figured he owed her something. Casing her house, the wooden duck, the grandmother. "Could I get you a Coke?"

"Sure."

He went through the covered walkway and the grape arbor to the machine at the back of the store. Retrieving some change from his pocket, he returned with the can. As he handed it to her, he nodded toward the greenhouse. "There's a stool inside, if you'd like to sit down. But you'll have to wipe off the plaster dust."

She yanked at the recalcitrant purse again, keeping one shoulder hunched to hold it on, preceded him into the greenhouse and sat down on the high stool, dust and all. Taking several large swallows of the drink, she dropped the shoulder bag on the floor beside her with a thunk, pushed up the sleeves of her jacket, right foot propped over her left knee.

She seemed to Harry a woman at odds with her clothes. The jeans were so tight he did not know how she sat without splitting them. The tag on her jacket stuck straight up like a flag at the nape of her neck. A button was missing, the heels of her loafers were worn down almost to the soles, and she sat pulling at a thread that hung from the cuff of one sleeve.

"This is what you do back here, huh?"

He nodded. "Stone-casting, we call it."

She looked about at the Chinese lady and the soulful Madonna. "You must be some kind of sculptor."

"No. Other people design them. I just make copies."

She took another swallow. "Isn't that . . . you know . . . illegal?"

"No. Statues get chipped, broken. I patch them up and cast copies in cement." He picked up his brush again. "What kind of work do you do?"

"I'm between jobs. I clerked in a video store, but they lost their lease. You hiring?"

"I'm afraid not. I'm pretty well covered. Harry Gill, by the way."

"Iris Shaw," she said, and sighed, resting the Coke can on her knee as she watched him work.

"Ever done anything besides clerk?"

"Manicurist. Doesn't pay much, though. I *knew* I should have finished college."

"How many more years do you have to go?"

"Three and a half. To go to college you have to have money. To have money, you have to have a job. To get a job, you have to go to college." She grimaced.

"Well, some people work part-time at anything they can get, and take evening classes."

She idly rubbed one arm. "You ever try studying in a house full of people, don't even have your own room?"

"You live there, then? That house?"

"Me and thirteen others, four of them under the age of eight."

"Have children?"

"No, I'm not married. Not at the moment, anyway." This time she yanked at the thread on her cuff so hard that the material puckered. Then she slouched over, arms resting on her knees, staring sideways out the door. "My sister's car," she said, nodding toward the parking lot.

There was something about the dejected slump of her body, the long hair hanging down each side of her face, baring the back of her neck, the bony shoulders, the droop of her hands.

Harry suddenly heard himself saying: "Well, I can't give you a job, but I've got an extra room you could use, if it would help. Rattling around in a big old house by myself." *Had he said that?*

She turned to face him again, looking puzzled.

"It's upstairs, I'm down," he said quickly. "I wouldn't bother you or anything, it's just a suggestion. I don't need any rent."

"Why?"

Because he was totally out of his mind. He shrugged. "You need a room, I have a room, that's all."

She finished her Coke and set the can on the floor. "You know, you're a really nice man, Mr. Gill. But I couldn't. Gram would kill me. Anyway. . . ." She slid off the stool. "Thanks for the Coke." She dusted off the seat of her jeans and took a step toward the door, then stopped again. "I like her best," she said, pointing to the Chinese lady.

And then she went out, her long legs taking her back to the Pontiac, battling her shoulder bag all the way. Harry leaned against the wall. He didn't know if he was relieved or disappointed. Beth had been dead exactly six days, and he was half crazy.

FOUR

The Madonna

THE REFRIGERATOR REPAIRMAN could not come until Wednesday, and since Harry had promised to care for Jodie that afternoon, he took the entire day off. It started out well enough, with Harry remembering to feed the cat and Zeke staying out of the way. No hairballs to clean up on the rug. Breakfast would be coffee and toast and a shriveled apple that had been sitting in a bowl since . . . when? March?

He did not *want* this widower stuff—the image of himself as this pathetic man silently spreading his marmalade. It felt as though, if he just got mad enough, raged long enough, Fate would hear and bring her back. Sorry, bud. Got the wrong guy.

The doorbell rang and the GE man stopped whistling when Harry answered.

"Refrigerator?" he said and, at Harry's nod, took his tool box to the kitchen. Zeke cautiously came out of hiding and sniffed the box, and the man reached down to scratch his ears. Harry watched from the doorway. Zeke looked like a cat pleading to be rescued from this mortuary of a place to where there were living people.

"Well, let's see what we have here," the repairman said, and opened the refrigerator door. The gray tell-tale sign of mold was beginning on the walls, exuding a musty odor. Harry picked up his coffee and toast and took them into the living room, making a pretense of reading the paper. The man went on whistling, an occasional clunk of a tool his only accompaniment.

Harry was missing his wife especially that morning. Whether it was the marmalade or the cat or the fact that Jodie was coming, Harry simply felt adrift. Each week, each month, he knew, would bring fresh reminders of all he had lost, and that did not seem fair. Everyone missed her, but not as much as he did. *One fine woman,* Fletcher had said. *A little dear:* Virginia. *Never be another like Beth. True blue.* His feelings exactly, but so much more.

Ten minutes later the repairman was standing over Harry with a clipboard. "The news isn't good," he said, and Harry remembered when he'd heard that before, a man in a white coat standing before him with a lab report. "You've got old hardened rubber in the compressor mounts, but the compressor itself is shot, and that's going to cost plenty. Now we're talking about an eleven year-old appliance here, so I'd recommend . . ."

"Fix it," said Harry.

"Excuse me?"

"Fix it." What kind of world was this, anyway, where you threw things away when they were old and sick?

"Like me to tally it up and see what it will cost?"

"Just do what you have to do," said Harry. "I want to keep this refrigerator."

The repairman went back to the kitchen with his cell phone and called his supervisor. There was a muted one-way conversation beyond the doorway, like doctors huddled together: "I did, but he says he wants to keep it. . . . He didn't want to know the cost. . . . I *told* him it would be plenty. . . . I don't know. Something else could give way next week."

The refrigerator took up most of the morning. The repairman had to go back to the shop for another part, and Harry wondered if this was a mistake. There was something disquieting about the way the man swore under his breath, or sighed and grunted as he worked. It seemed certain that some new defect had been discovered of disastrous proportions, yet five minutes later he might be whistling again.

"Four hundred eighty-seven dollars and fourteen cents," the repairman said at last. "Give 'er another hour and she'll be cool."

"Thank you," said Harry. "Thank you very much," and reached for his checkbook.

BY THE TIME Elaine arrived with Jodie, he felt much better and had some Sprite cooling in the refrigerator. Harry was not used to seeing his daughter in a dress, small-heeled sandals on her feet. Why would Don want to leave such a shapely woman? he was thinking as he watched them traipse in, Jodie dragging a drawstring bag of treasures with her. How could he leave a four year-old daughter?

"You're taking care of me this afternoon," Jodie announced as she walked over to the coffee table and withdrew from the bag a troop of plastic ponies with bouffant manes. The voice was in sharp contrast to so pale a face, the skin translucent around the eyes. Her silky brown hair was brushed back away from her forehead and held in place with a small barrette, and her denim pants with the elastic waist rested low on her hips.

"Oh, darn! I forgot about your refrigerator. I meant to pick up some lunch for you and Jodie," Elaine said.

"It's working now, no problem," Harry told her. "And I've been keeping a few things in a cooler."

"Are you sure this is okay, Dad?"

"Take all the time you need."

Elaine bent to give Jodie a quick kiss on the cheek, and was out the door again. The small girl stood with arms dangling at her sides. "What are we having for lunch?" she asked.

"Peanut butter sandwiches and Sprite," Harry said.

Jodie scooped up her ponies and followed him to the kitchen, climbing up on a chair, eyes on him all the while. "Are you still sad?" she asked after a while.

"Yes. Now and then. Off and on."

"When we see Grandma, I'm going to . . . ." Jodie stopped. "We can't see Grandma ever again, can we?"

"No. That's why I'm sad."

"Not even once? To show her my ponies?"

He didn't answer.

Jodie silently began lining up her animals in a row on the table. She sang to herself as Harry fixed their sandwiches. "I can sing you a song," she offered.

"Okay."

She was perched on her knees, and accented each beat with a tiny bounce of her butt:

"*The it-sy-bit-sy spi* . . . No! *The een-sie-ween-sie spi-der went up the spout. . . .* No! *The een-sie-ween-sie spi-der went up the water spout. . . .*"

Jodie kept moving the last horse to the front of the line as she sang, so that the entire troop progressed across the table. She stopped her singing when Harry put the sandwich in front of her.

"*That's* not the way you make it, Grandpa!" She put her hands on her small hips in exasperation.

"No?"

"No! You have to put raisins on it!" She lifted the top slices off both halves, placed them on the table, and pushed the bottom halves of the bread together to form one piece. "Grandma always makes a raisin face on it for me." She handed the plate back.

Somewhere in Beth's file box, Harry was sure, under "S" for

sandwich or "J" for Jodie, there were instructions for making a sandwich. For now, Harry would have to wing it. He found the raisins, pressed two into the peanut butter for eyes, and five or six in a straight row along the bottom for the mouth. Then he set the plate on the table again.

"Not *that* way!" Jodie insisted, her voice shrill. "It's got to be smiling."

"Eat it," said Harry, and sat down across from her with a Sprite.

She ate soberly, eyes on her plate. When a few minutes had passed, Harry said, "Did you go to day-care yesterday?"

She nodded.

"What did you do there?"

She shrugged her shoulders.

"Nothing? Sounds boring."

"I took the paint brush away from Mickey and had to go on time-out. Miss Anna gave me a sad face." As proof, she held out the back of one hand, displaying a faint, sad ink-stamped face. Then, more happily, "I know how babies are born."

"You do?"

"Rosalind told me." Grinning, Jodie put down her bread and took the lead pony from the line-up, stuffing it up under her T-shirt. "I've got a baby in my stomach!" she whooped, digging at one nostril with her finger, leaving a faint smudge of peanut butter on her cheek.

Harry smiled.

"Do you know how it gets out?" Her eyes were mischievous. "Rosalind told me. It comes out your belly button!" Jodie leaned forward, pulling at the bottom of her shirt, so that the pony fell to the floor. "I had a baby!" she shrieked.

"Rosalind is a wellspring of knowledge," said Harry.

It occurred to him that this was probably the first time he had been in a house alone with a four year-old, when he was expected to be the sole source of entertainment. What did you discuss with a pre-schooler? He never remembered Beth having to ask. When did the conversation end? Jodie seemed to babble on and on, no connection between one thing and another. He tried to remember Elaine at that age. He had bounced her on one foot, carried her on his shoulders, swung her by her heels. But he couldn't remember a prolonged conversation.

The kitchen was suddenly quiet and Harry looked up to see Jodie leaning back against her chair, a wisp of hair hanging down in front of her eyes, toying absently with the crusts of her sandwich. He didn't know if she was aware he was looking at her, but he suddenly saw in that face such sadness that his heart leapt to her defense.

"You done, sweetheart?"

She looked over at him, nodding.

"Then let's go sit in the living room."

She got down from the chair and took his hand, and when they reached the sofa, he pulled her up on his lap. She gave off a smell of peanut butter, Dove soap, and little-girl perspiration.

"Now," Harry said, "we can just sit here and hug, or we can talk. Which do you want to do?"

She leaned back against him and toyed with his fingers, which were clasped over her stomach—lifting first one, then the next and the next, and watching grimly as they flopped back down again. "Hug *and* talk," she said finally.

"Okay."

"You first," she told him.

He felt her body suck in a deep breath and let it out again. Her head seemed exceptionally warm against his chest. "Well," he told her, placing one cheek against her hair. "I'm very sad that Grandma died. I miss her."

"I know." Her voice was small and bird-like. "I feel sad too. About Grandma and about my dad."

"Uh huh."

She was lifting his fingers again, and this time bent each one back sharply so that he had to brace them against her onslaught.

"I guess I won't ever see him again either, will I?"

"What makes you think that?"

"You know. He's gone, like Grandma."

"He didn't die, honey."

"Then where is he?"

"I don't know. He just went off to be by himself."

"Why?"

"I don't know the reason."

Jodie sniffled. "Everything's going wrong."

"Not everything. Just some things." Harry patted her stomach. "There are nice things too. We have each other, don't we, you and me?"

She nodded, and grew quiet.

A WEEK BEFORE Mother's Day. Every tree, shrub, and plant at the garden center was being coaxed into bloom. Wanda Sims leaned low over recalcitrant buds, whispering encouragement. Every man who had promised his wife azaleas for years past seemed to have decided to keep his word this time. Every son who had forgotten his mother, every woman who was missing hers—they all showed up at Gill's Garden Center the second week of May.

It was all right with Harry. He wanted to be busy from the time he opened his eyes in the morning until he opened his front door at night, so tired that he had only energy enough to feed the cat and fall into bed. Some nights he fell *over* the cat, with predictable results. Then he would go to the kitchen and give Zeke the first thing he could put his hands on from the refrigerator. Zeke grew fatter by the day and his breath stank.

It was the small day-to-day things that were getting Harry down. While he could organize an unloading or a spring planting, he couldn't seem to get his toast on the table along with his eggs, or his clothes properly sorted for the washing machine.

Yet there was both the reality and the relief to face. There was nothing that said he *had* to eat toast along with his eggs. If the bread popped up too late, he could eat it with coffee. If he ran out of clean underwear, he could buy more. Life did not have to proceed in the orderly fashion Beth had deemed not only necessary but imperative. It was all a matter of balance—a setting of priorities, and some days he was better at it than others.

Mother's Day itself was harder on his grown kids. Claude told him he and Sue were planting a salmon-colored azalea in their side yard in memory of Beth. Jack called the garden center to see if Harry wanted to go out to dinner, but he was too busy even to come to the phone. Harry did, however, feel it necessary to call Elaine after he got home that night.

"You and Jodie do anything special?"

"She made a card for me at day-care, and we went to McDonald's."

"We've got some nice-looking dogwoods," Harry said. "I could bring one over and plant it for you."

"Thanks, but I'm not even sure Jodie and I can afford to stay here, Dad, if that teaching job doesn't come through. I won't know until August. But of course I can't sell without Don's signature." She gave a sardonic laugh. "Mom used to tell me that whenever I felt restless in my marriage, I should 'change the house, but not the heart.' Looks like I'm about to do both."

"You could always rent it out and move back here for a while, Elaine. Until you know the score, I mean."

"And have all the neighbors pity me? Give Don Wheeler, wherever he is, that bastard, the satisfaction of seeing me move back home? No, thank you."

After Harry hung up, he decided he did not like his daughter. He loved Elaine, but that was something else. You loved a child because she was yours, but that did not mean you enjoyed being in the same room with her. In the past, Harry had always thought twice before calling her on the phone. It was an admission he could make without guilt. Now that he had a grandchild, however, it finally gave them something to talk about.

It was the day *after* Mother's Day that the garden center got really crazy. Mothers and grandmothers from all over the greater Washington area drove to Gill's in their station wagons to return azaleas which were the wrong color, or to buy the peat moss their husbands had overlooked.

Harry let Wanda handle the returns and exchanges, and while Rose manned the cash register, Harry set himself the task of arranging pots of red and yellow tulips on wooden risers along the far wall of the parking lot. It was the first thing the eye would see as you rounded the bend on Old Forest Road—alternate rows of red and yellow—like choir boys dressed for Easter.

And there he was, bending over the tulips when a shoe appeared on the concrete beside him. Then two shoes, side by side, a couple of inches apart.

Harry stared at the shoes, shiny black patent leather wing-tips, overhung by the cuffs of gray pin-striped trousers. The skin on Harry's arms turned to gooseflesh. Those were Max Bowen's shoes, Max Bowen's trousers. Max had been dead for a year.

Harry braced one hand on his knee in the act of straightening up and found himself looking into the hazel eyes of a woman in a gray fedora.

"Liz!" he said, astounded, and stared, for she was dressed head to toe in the clothes of her late husband.

One thing you could say about Liz was she aged well. Only a few strands of silver in her dark hair. Good skin. She had wonderful skin. Her jaw was fuller, but the only wrinkles on her face were laugh lines. Except she wasn't laughing. She used to laugh. Harry remembered when he had found Liz Bowen's throaty chuckle a special delight.

"I had them altered," Liz said in reply to his unspoken question. Max had always been on the portly side. Liz was no nymph, but she was a size or two smaller. The only thing she had not altered was his tie, and she was wearing one of those too. "He's alive, Harry. As long as I wear his clothes, he's alive. I made the tailor promise he wouldn't have them dry-cleaned first; I want to keep the scent of Max's cologne."

"Ah, yes," said Harry. He understood about scent. "So . . . how did it go at Bloomingdale's?"

"I went back every day for a week and didn't see him again. So I asked about a job in men's hosiery, but they only had openings in housewares. When I told them why it had to be men's socks or nothing, they suddenly had no openings for me at all." Her eyes teared up.

Oh, God. Don't! Harry prayed.

Liz blew her nose. "I'm looking for a tree for Max. A flowering pear, maybe."

"For the cemetery?"

"Max is in the back yard, remember?"

"Oh. Sorry."

Max too had ended up in a jar, only Liz had the decency to bury it. She did not have it sitting in her dining room window.

"Let's walk up to the back lot and you can pick out the one you want," Harry said, and led her up the mulched path toward the ornamentals.

Liz clutched at Harry's arm. "So how does it feel?" she asked.

"About Beth, you mean?"

She nodded.

"Numb."

"Be grateful. Be grateful for as long as that lasts. I didn't cry for a whole month after Max died, and than I couldn't stop. At home, at the store whenever I passed his favorite coffee. . . ." Her voice broke again, and Harry waited it out. "I feel as though my skin is burned all over—as if I can't let anyone get near me." She dropped her hand and dug in the pocket of Max's suit for another tissue.

Harry steeled himself. Pointing, he said, "There are the pear trees. You want to look them over?"

She wandered away from him, blowing her nose, and gave a cursory glance at the saplings. Then, waving a hand toward one and waiting while he tagged it, she went on wandering aimlessly through the arbor until the path curved and brought her back again. Together they returned to the lot below, two old friends with nothing safe enough to say.

"Hat looks good on you," Harry ventured at last. "You picked the right suit to alter, too." He lied. Altering Max's suits was akin to altering Max himself.

"I'm restoring them all," Liz replied.

Harry stared back. "All of them?"

"Every last one. The whole closet. It's cost me eleven-hundred dollars so far. No one dressed like him. *No* one. And it just makes me feel better—grounded."

Poor Liz, thought Harry as he rang up the sale.

HE WORKED LATE that evening, and it was eight-thirty before he left in his truck. Mozart played again on the radio, the *Piano Concerto in D Major*, the announcer said. Harry did not know a concerto from a fugue or a sonata, but the beauty was, he didn't have to. Needed only to enjoy it and, failing that, he could turn the radio off.

The thing about music, Harry had discovered—this kind of music—was that an overture or even the first movement to a piece was a preview of what was to come. A sample of the highs and lows; the happy, the sad ("The minor key, Dad," Claude had explained); the excitement and crying and passion and exaltations that would show themselves in melodies of intricate variation. There was always something new to hear and something familiar to anticipate in works he had listened to before. A passage might be so sad, so wrenching, you wanted to turn it off, but at the end, you could accept that this was a part to be wept over. Regretted, possibly. Disliked, even, but it had its place.

He glanced in his rearview mirror. A large 4x4 had been following him for several miles as he tooled along. While other vehicles passed him or turned off along the way, this one—probably an older model Dodge Ram—kept a steady pace about thirty feet behind the Lariat.

Its lights reflected in his rearview mirror. Annoying as hell.

Harry let up on the gas and cruised at twenty-five so the truck would pass. But the testosterone pickup behind him, its chassis jacked up high above the wheels, slowed too. Curious, Harry pushed his foot to the floor and the Lariat shot forward. Forty-five, fifty, sixty, seventy. The truck behind him matched his pace. Harry slowed again, and when he reached the turn-off, he did so abruptly, with no warning, yet the driver behind him made no move to hide his intentions, seeming to know Harry's route home, and turned off as well.

Harry thought about stopping and calling his bluff, but when he reached his own street, the Ram went straight ahead. Frowning, Harry got out and went in the house.

He looked over the frozen dinners, ate a piece of cheese, and had just fed Zeke when the phone rang.

It was a voice Harry did not know. A man's voice, hoarse and flat. "You Harry Gill?"

"Speaking."

"Jack's father?"

"Yes."

"Got his phone number?"

"Yes." Harry looked at the sheet of paper taped above the phone and gave the number.

"It's disconnected," came the voice. Harry did not like the voice. Deep, and somewhat menacing. He regretted giving the man Jack's number.

"Are you the one who was following me?" he asked suddenly.

There was a pause. "Say, what?"

"Following me just now in a pickup. Somebody followed me home."

"I got better things to do," said the voice.

"Well, I don't see how Jack's phone could be disconnected," Harry said. "Did you try his laundry?"

"He's not there."

"Could I give him a message, then? I should be talking to him this week."

"Yeah, you do that. Tell him Arlo's looking for him. He may not want to talk to Arlo, but Arlo wants to talk to him. You got that?"

"A-R-L-O?" Harry repeated. "Last name?"

"Just Arlo," said the voice, and the phone clicked.

Harry stood with his hand on the telephone. He remained perfectly quiet as he felt worry crawl up his back. What to do? He thought of Beth's file box, but made no move to see if there was a SON, TROUBLE, HOW TO HELP card. Instead, he dialed Jack's apartment. There was not the usual ring but, as Arlo had said, a whistled tone and then the recorded message: *I'm sorry. The number you have dialed has been disconnected.*

IT WAS A one-story frame house converted to a grocery, then a shoe repair shop. Now it sported a blue canopy and a neon sign with blue and green bubbles that moved continuously around the border, like a nightclub marquee:

SUDS and SPUDS
More than a laundry
Welcome back, Coretta!

The last line changed every four days, Jack had told him—always something to do with a customer. It was good business to know who was on a trip, what couple was engaged and which of the once-married were back in circulation.

The laundry was on a side street in Silver Spring. It stood peculiarly alone, between a small parking lot and an alley. The recent addition, of which Jack was so proud, extended out into the parking area, and Harry could hear music as soon as he got out of the Cadillac.

He took the new entrance, the one with the bubble marquee, and went inside. The place looked more like a lounge. There were two modern sofas, a color TV, a large coffee table littered with magazines. All the furniture was black and chrome, sitting on a carpet of cobalt blue.

At the far end of the room was the snack bar, with a blackboard listing the various coffees, pizzas, and potato toppings. Beyond the large doorway at one side, the gleaming washers and dryers hummed away, accompanied by the gentle sloshing of water and the laughter of a few women at the sorting table, folding sheets. Maybe Jack had a head for business after all. While this was not the white-collar upwardly mobile clientele Jack had dreamed of—most appeared to be laborers, solid ethnic working class people—they all had need of a laundry. Harry counted fourteen customers. A few were reading, others methodically going about their business, but most were talking, laughing, pushing their laundry carts from washer to dryer. And this was nine-thirty at night.

A shapely woman in jeans and knit shirt came over. "Hello," she said. "How many machines will you need?"

Sort of a hostess, Harry decided—How many in your party?—or perhaps the change woman in a casino. He never knew if the women who came and went as employees of Suds and Spuds were women Jack had slept with, then hired for his business, or whether he hired them first, and then they ended up in his bed.

"I don't need a machine," Harry said. "I'm looking for Jack."

Her smiled slackened. "You Arlo?" she asked.

"No, I'm Harry, Jack's father."

"Oh! Nice to meet you. I'm Jennifer. I help out."

Harry tried to look pleasant. "I see he's got the new sign up."

"The new *name!*" Jennifer said. "I think it's really going to catch on."

"Is Jack in?"

"No. Well, that's what he said."

"Tell him his dad's here."

Jennifer went around behind the snack bar and opened an

unmarked door. There was a brief consultation, and then she came back out, followed by Jack.

"Hey, Dad!" he said. "Come on in. What are you doing over here this late?" He waited till Harry was inside the small office—a supply closet, really, with a desk crammed at one end—then closed the door and motioned him to the single chair. "How do you like the sign? Neat, huh? The bubbles were Jennifer's idea." Jack sat down on one corner of the desk. His shirt was wrinkled, his hair in need of a trim.

"Looks good," said Harry. "How much did it put you back?"

"I'll manage. It'll pay off in the long run. So what do you think—the addition and all?"

"*Seems* like a good idea. Guess you'll have to wait and see how business picks up."

"It's already up from two weeks ago. I changed the music, too. Rhythms are big here. Got a big Latino crowd. Man, I tell you, marketing is everything." He studied his father. "Were you just out driving around, or what?"

"No, I came to get your new phone number. I called your apartment and the operator said the phone had been disconnected."

"Oh, Jeez, I didn't tell you?" Jack slapped one palm against his forehead, then tore a paper from his notepad. "I just went unlisted, that's all. Less hassle." He wrote down the number and handed it to Harry, who stuck it in his shirt pocket.

"So who's hassling you?"

"Oh, the usual—salesmen, creditors. . . ."

"Who's Arlo?"

Jack startled for a moment, then adopted the sheepish look he'd had when he was twelve, smuggling *Playboys* up to his room. "He's been calling you?"

"He said he's trying to reach you, that I should tell you he wants to talk to you."

"Well, I don't want to talk to him."

"He said as much."

Jack was looking down at his knuckles, studying first one hand, then the other. "Did he say what it was about?"

"No. I thought maybe you'd tell me."

"Oh, it comes with the territory, Dad. You go into business, everyone wants a piece of you. *You* know how it is. Everyone wants his money yesterday."

"So who is he? Contractor? Electrician?"

"No. Just a guy I owe."

"How much, Jack?"

"I can *swing* it, Dad! I just need a week or two."

"How are you going to get the money in a week?"

"I've got some deals."

"Jack . . . " When his son didn't raise his eyes, Harry knew the answer, but he asked anyway: "What are you betting on this time? Horses? Games?"

Jack gave an impatient smile.

"You can lose your shirt."

"I'll *handle* it, okay? I'm not asking you for money, am I? If Arlo calls again, just hang up on him."

"All right." Harry got to his feet. He went over to the door and opened it, looking out at the blue carpet. "I like your color scheme," he said. "Good choice."

Jack smiled then. "Yeah. Big improvement. Here. Let me show you around." And after a quick tour of the new addition, Jack saw him to the door.

"Thanks for coming by. Sorry about the phone."

As he drove away, Harry mulled over the fact that he had two worries to occupy him now, Elaine's and Jack's. Three, if you counted the tomato sauce. Any distraction was welcome these days. Of the two, however, Elaine's seemed more serious. When sons erred, their mistakes were written broadly on their faces, but women could veer in a direction he never would have guessed, and not even Beth, he felt certain, could have known that Elaine would eventually drive her husband away.

Harry and Beth had had their problems, but somehow their children's seemed different. *Avoidable*, that was it. Their children didn't understand that life had structure, like a symphony, and you didn't leave after the first movement. You didn't go about building a marriage or a business and then put it in jeopardy.

Even at this hour, the beltway traffic moved slowly, long lines of cars snaking around a curve. Harry could see the day beltways would form concentric circles around the largest cities. The more people, the more anonymity, the harder one had to work to be noticed, much less recognized.

He realized suddenly that he had been wool-gathering and missed the Rockville exit. He'd have to get off at River Road, and after he made the turn, slowing as he went around the ramp, he merged into the stately quiet of space and affluence.

Here the houses had "great rooms," not "family rooms." Some had ballrooms and indoor pools. This was a neighborhood of gated communities, sporting little brick guardhouses with nobody in them. These were homes with designer kitchens, vast master bedroom suites with fireplace and sauna. A neighborhood where, if you no longer coveted your neighbor's zip code, you—player or not—envied his spot next to a golf course.

Harry turned off River Road at Seven Locks and headed home to where he belonged. Customers came to the garden center, he knew, not for its location, upscale as it was beginning to be, but because it was familiar. Because their parents had come. Because the same old rusty glider, wicker chairs and picnic table stood year after year in the grape arbor, and you could bring your anemic-looking plants to Wanda, who would sit on that glider with you and tell you what was wrong. Because there was coffee and a box of powdered doughnuts waiting just inside the door. Because as sure as New Yorkers wore black and community theaters opened or closed their seasons with *Our Town* or *The Cherry Orchard*, Barbie the goose would be standing outside Gill's Garden Center in a ridiculous new costume on the first of every month. You could count on it.

Was there any possibility that his truck was being mistaken for Jack's? Jack didn't even have a truck, of course, but the Progresso incident had happened soon after Jack left the house, and the phone call from Arlo had followed Harry's being tailed on his way home. Harry let out his breath. Well, if there was a connection, he didn't see it.

He had been home only ten minutes when the phone rang.

"I *hoped* you'd still be up! You won't *believe* what Don did now." Elaine's voice, full of exasperation.

Harry knew better than to guess. He wanted her back, the Elaine she had been. The young, dark-haired girl with the quirky smile who would address him in her twelve year-old smart-aleck tone and, laughing, leap on his back in a bear hug. Where did they go, these children—their softness, sweetness?

"You know that aerobics class I take on Monday evenings? And Jodie goes with me?"

Harry had a mental image of Don Wheeler showing up in Spandex shorts and a T-shirt.

"He came to the house while we were gone and went through his drawers."

"And . . . ?"

"He came right in like a burglar! I'm surprised the neighbors didn't call the police!"

"Elaine, that's his house! He has a key!"

"I'm going to change the locks."

Deranged. That's what she was. "I thought you *wanted* him to come home!" he said.

"Not creeping in while I'm gone, Dad! Not stealing from me!"

"What did he steal?"

"Socks, underwear. . . .some of his sweatshirts, maybe. I'm not sure what all."

"Honey, it's *his* underwear!"

"He's either got to come back or clear out," said Elaine. "To hell with now-you-see-him-now-you-don't."

"Elaine," asked Harry, "what's he got to come back to?"

The phone seemed to have gone dead. Then it exploded with fury: "What's *that* supposed to mean?" And without waiting for an answer, she hung up.

Harry went into the living room and sat in the dark, head resting against the back of the sofa. Zeke jumped up beside him, pawed his thigh a few times, and, after turning himself around, lay down against his leg. Harry absently stroked his head.

Why, he wondered, did fate wait for Beth's passing to unload on him? He did not *know* these two older children of his, and he tried to extinguish the thought that it would have been easier had it been Elaine rather than Beth who was gone. Easier for all concerned except Jodie, of course.

Was it easier or harder to lose a child rather than a spouse? he wondered, and tried to remember how he felt when his father died. When a parent dies, you lose your past. When a child dies, you lose your future. But when your spouse dies, you lose it all, including your now. That's what Liz had told him, anyway.

Max Bowen had kept his sense of humor right up till the end. A three pack-a-day lung cancer, that's what killed him, yet he smoked till the day before he died. "Won't make a bit of difference, so I might as well enjoy myself on the way out," he'd said.

Once, when he and Harry were following their wives home from a movie, walking along the sidewalk on a warm night, Max had confided that he still hadn't told Liz it was cancer and that the doctor had given him six months to live.

"And you know what, Harry? I'm thinking I won't ever have to go to the dentist again. Never have to go through another prostate exam. Probably won't even be here at Christmas to put up the damn tree. There's a certain satisfaction, you know, in all the things I'll never have to do."

He had pulled a cigarette from his pocket and lit up.

HARRY WAS NOT sleeping well. Kept drifting in and out of dreams of catastrophes large and small. The fact was, he couldn't get the hang of sleeping alone, even after all the months Beth had been in a hospital bed. Around ten of three, he got up and went to the kitchen for crackers and milk. Zeke, roused from slumber, came to the door of the kitchen and sat sleepily, yawning from time to time, the inner lids of his eyes half closed.

The phone rang.

Harry turned and stared at it there on the wall. At three o'clock in the morning? Should he answer? Then he thought of Elaine and Jodie all by themselves. He reached around and lifted the handset.

"Harry," came Marge Decker's voice. "I can see the light from your kitchen on your side lawn. You can't sleep, I can't sleep, and I'm just going to come right out and say it: Come over, Harry. You need some arms around you."

He was too stunned to reply. Every conceivable answer seemed out of the question.

"I was just. . . ." he began. "The cat was . . . I was pouring some milk. . . ."

"I'm asking, Harry."

"Really, Marge, I. . . ."

"Never mind," she said. And for the second time that evening, a woman hung up on him.

WHEN HARRY ARRIVED at the garden center on Saturday, no one was in sight.

Up to that point, it had been an uneventful week. He and Marge Decker had managed to avoid each other, and Harry felt confident there would be no more casseroles from that quarter.

On the drive in, he'd passed by the house of the gypsies but, as usual, neither the Spider Lady nor any of her relatives were in the yard. Waiting at the light, Harry's eyes roamed over the property and he could have sworn that not only was the ground in transition, but the house as well, for the shutters on the lower windows had been removed and rested on cinder blocks along the chain link fence, serving as shelves for several dozen flower pots of assorted shapes. Someone behind Harry beeped, and the Lariat shot forward again, Harry still shaking his head.

At the garden center, Wanda's car was in the lot. So were Tracy's, Bill's and Steve's, and five more parked at the back. The store was open and a customer was already looking at geraniums, but there wasn't a clerk to be found.

Harry went out the back door, checked the grape arbor where employees ate their lunch in good weather, and then, hearing voices from the greenhouse, followed the covered walkway to the door. A small crowd had gathered inside. Wanda was standing with her arms folded, head tilted to one side. Members of the group appeared quizzical, but Tracy stared with open mouth, her fingers pressed against the cross around her neck.

"Mr. Gill, look!" Rose Kribbs exclaimed when he came in, and pointed.

Expecting to see no less than a body, Harry looked. He saw nothing remarkable. The Apostle Paul still needed his final casting. The Chinese lady stood with her seams unsanded.

"Don't you see it?" Tracy cried. "The Madonna's crying! Church of the Annunciation called this morning to ask if you'd started on Gabriel, and when I came out here to check, I saw this tear!"

They parted to make way for Harry. He stooped and studied the old statue, which was missing a hand. The hand, actually, resided in a plastic bag tied to the lady's feet. The statue had been in the back yard grotto of a woman over in Kensington, and a new casting was wanted. Sure enough, there was moisture forming in the corner of the left eye, and a damp streak on the stone where it had trickled down her face.

"What do you think, Harry?" Wanda asked uncertainly.

"I'd say we have a lady with a moisture problem."

"She's crying!" Tracy repeated.

"You'd be crying too if you had a hand missing," put in Bill, giving Tony a nudge.

Tracy appealed to Harry. "Don't you think it means something?" she asked.

"There's a customer back in the shop, Tracy," he said in answer. "Would you mind? And tell Church of the Annunciation it'll be a while yet."

She left silently with Rose as Bill and the other workers headed on up to the back lot. But when Wanda showed no sign of leaving, Harry said, "You left the cash register untended, Wanda."

"It was locked, Mr. G. I know we shouldn't have all come back here, but Tracy was beside herself." She observed him for a moment. "You don't think there's anything unusual here?"

"What are you suggesting?"

"Nothing, really. Okay, Mr. G. I'll get to work," she said.

Harry got out the Portland cement, surprised he'd let Saint Paul drag on like this. He wiped the cement dust off the old cassette player on one shelf, blew on a cassette he retrieved from a cabinet, and put on a Haydn symphony. Music flooded the greenhouse.

After mixing the charge, Harry poured it carefully into the mold he had made of the apostle. Perhaps he'd been too gruff with Tracy, too dismissive of Rose. His own opinion was that the God of the Universe had a sense of humor and tested it now and then on Gill's Garden Center. He inserted a "donkey dick" on the end of his drill and whirred it around in the concrete to rid it of air bubbles.

Rose appeared in the doorway. In fact, Harry didn't know if she had just come or had been standing there for some time.

"Yes?" he said, turning off the drill.

"I . . . just wanted to apologize for leaving the shop," she said softly, her words fluttering out before her like feathers.

"Well, you can divide the blame among you, but I'm sure you'll know better next time," Harry said. He poised the drill again, waiting.

"It's just that. . . ." Rose hesitated. "Well, the Virgin chose *you*, Mr. Gill. This place, I mean. I think it's wonderful, and I wanted you to know that she couldn't have picked a better person, and you deserve a little joy in your life."

She accented the last word with a short nod of her head and, without waiting for an answer, turned and scurried back to the store again.

"I'll be damned," said Harry, staring after her. He started the drill again and, as he worked, glanced at the Madonna from time to time. A moist spot, that's all it was. He didn't know the exact composition of the stone—some substances were wetter or drier than others, some retained moisture, and sometimes a chemical could leak or weep—it wasn't all that unusual. But after twenty minutes or so, he thought he saw something glisten. When he looked more closely, he saw a small pearl of water forming in the corner of the Virgin's left eye.

Harry did not believe in miracles, but he would have liked to. "Mary," he said at last. He waited to see if she moved her head. "You're too important a lady for parlor tricks. If you wanted to send a sign, you could have told us what the terrorists were up to, or warned us about Beth's cancer before it spread." He removed the agitator. "No? Well, what about just telling me where the heck my son-in-law is? I'd even settle for that."

The Madonna gave no answer, but continued to weep. Harry would have liked to share this with Beth. "You'll never guess what happened this morning in the greenhouse . . . " All the little vignettes of the day, the small successes and shortcomings he related to Jack now when they went out to dinner, or to Claude when he called on the phone, or to Elaine when she came by with Jodie. And though they always listened, their own concerns took precedence.

He cleaned off his tools and prepared to wrap the mold tightly with straps cut from inner tubes. It was the minutiae of life, he discovered, that showed how a couple fit together, and minutiae that proved a steady reminder of all he had lost. Reaching for Beth's jar of favorite preserves at the store, for example, and then, remembering, withdrawing his hand. Missing her reminders—"Take a jacket,

Harry,"—that showed someone cared. Now, if he didn't come home at all some night, who would know?

ELAINE AND JODIE came by that evening, Jodie in a cotton dress with tiny green frogs on it. She wore three different necklaces that looked as though they had all come from a Crackerjack box. Elaine had picked up some fried chicken from Popeyes, and said she owed Harry a meal.

"How so?"

"For hanging up on you the other day."

"Apology accepted," he said, conscious that none had been offered.

It was evident they were not going to argue at the table. Elaine began removing containers from a paper bag and Jodie distributed the plastic spoons and forks.

Harry playfully examined the backs of Jodie's hands. "No more sad faces?"

She grinned and held out one fist. The inky remains of a happy face were still evident, the cheery smile caught at one corner by a Bandaid.

"She's had three happy faces this week," Elaine said.

"What do you have to do to get a happy face?" Harry asked.

"Make Miss Anna happy," Jodie answered.

"By being a good listener, a good helper, and a good friend," Elaine put in.

"I'm happy to hear it," said Harry.

Jodie opened one of the containers and made a face. "Eeeuuu! What's this?"

"Red beans and rice," said her mother.

"Yuk! Why did they have to put beans in it?"

"Because that's the way it comes. Just eat." Elaine put a spoonful on Jodie's plate.

For the next three minutes Harry watched his granddaughter

carefully separate the rice from the beans—rice to the right side, beans to the left. Every forkful of rice was ushered to its place by a whispered, "Okay," and every bean was accompanied by a "Yuk!"

He was growing exceedingly fond of this little girl, Harry decided, and wondered if he could afford it—all the worry that went with love. He remembered something his wife had said the day Elaine became engaged: At last there was someone else to worry about her the way a mother worries.

"I've started seeing a therapist," Elaine said.

Harry looked up.

"What's a ther-a-pist?" asked Jodie, still assigning her beans to purgatory.

"Someone who helps you with your problems," Elaine said. And then, to Harry, "One of my friends goes to her, and she charges on a sliding scale, so I can afford it."

"I see."

"I mean, whether Don comes back or not, I'm going to need it, I'm still so mad at him."

Harry raised his eyebrows and motioned toward Jodie, but Elaine said, "I'm not keeping anything from her. Kids feel more secure if they know exactly what's going on. If I get that full-time teaching job in the fall, I think I can make it financially, but if I don't and keep teaching part-time, I'm going to tutor on my off days—see if I can get by on that."

"You're going to make it, honey. However it turns out, you'll cope."

"What's 'cope'?" Jodie was looking from one to the other, trying to worm her way into the conversation.

"Get along," said Harry. "Do okay."

"*I'm* doing okay!" Jodie announced confidently, attacking a piece of chicken with an enormous chomp, then chewing with her mouth open. "Rosalind says if you're good, you go to heaven. If you're bad, the worms eat you."

"I'm going to have a talk with Rosalind's mother," said Elaine. "I don't know where she picks up this stuff." She studied her daughter's face. "Jodie, if Rosalind ever says anything to upset you, I want you to tell me. Okay?"

Jodie wiped one hand across her mouth. "More milk," she said, and held out her glass.

When Jodie finished, she went upstairs to Elaine's old room to look through her long-discarded costume jewelry. Elaine reached over and put one hand on Harry's arm. "How's it going for you, Dad? I get so wrapped up in my own worries I forget how you must feel."

"I suppose I feel like other men who have lost their wives. How can I say I feel worse? It only seems that way. You've lost your mother. . . ."

"You know what we learned in anthropology? I still remember. When one of the Bara people in Madagascar dies, the tribe designates two huts for grieving. One is the 'male house,' where the men organize rituals and plan for the burial, and the other is the 'house of tears,' where women cry and receive visitors. Isn't that interesting? Men deal with grief by staying busy, and women express their feelings. I cry every time I think of Mom. I wonder which is best."

"There is no best," said Harry. "And what works one day doesn't the next. That's one thing you learn about grief."

After they had gone, Harry picked up the phone. Arlo was looking for Jack, Don had left Elaine—he felt a sudden need to check in on Claude.

"He's out," Sue told him. "I'm not sure when he'll be back."

"Oh," said Harry. "Art show or something?"

"I think he's with friends. Any message?"

"Just wanted to touch base, tell him I love him."

There was a moment's silence. "I'll give him the message."

A FEW DAYS later, a reporter from one of the weeklies showed up at the garden center. Harry was stacking ceramic planters when a portly man with a camera bag over one shoulder approached him.

"Mr. Gill?"

"Yes?"

"Ken O'Hara from the *Montgomery Weekly*." The man put out his hand and shook Harry's. "We heard about your weeping Madonna, and I wondered if I could ask a few questions." He slipped a notepad from his shirt pocket.

"Mr. O'Hara," said Harry. "She's not *my* Madonna, and I make no claims for her."

The reporter's pen paused above his notepad, but he dutifully wrote it down. "Well, when we hear about something like this , we have to follow through on it, you know."

Harry went on stacking the planters.

"Could I just see the Madonna? Take a few pictures?"

Harry straightened up. "No," he said. "I'm sorry. I don't allow photographs of my customers' property, and there isn't any more to the story."

"Why don't you let me be the judge of that?" the reporter said.

"I am still quite capable of making some decisions myself, and the answer is no," Harry said.

It was a mistake. The following Thursday there was a picture of his greenhouse on the front page of the *Weekly:*

> *. . . Though the owner of the garden center, Harry Gill, refused to allow photographs of the Madonna, sources tell us that the statue is being kept out of the public eye in this structure behind the main building on Old Forest Road. Residents near the garden center report nothing out of the ordinary, though Gill is said to spend much time alone in this old greenhouse, restoring statues and other religious relics.*

Claude called. "Hi, Dad. Or is it Father Gill now?"

"Don't start," said Harry. Claude laughed.

"What's this about religious relics and statues crying?"

"Claude, it could be a number of things causing that stain."

"You're going to have a lot of people kneeling in your parking lot."

"God forbid."

Jack, of course, called next, then Elaine, followed by Harry's brother Wade, and finally, Liz.

"Harry, I know how you feel about Bloomingdale's, but whether you believe I saw Max or not, I think Beth may be trying to reach you."

"What?" Harry said.

"I mean, what better way than through a Madonna's tears? Maybe there's something she wants to say."

"If Beth had something to tell me, she could have told me in the last two weeks before she died. I was with her almost constantly," Harry said gently.

"All I'm saying is just be receptive, so if she *is* trying to contact you, you'll get the message."

"I'll keep an open mind," he said. If there was something Beth had been keeping secret all those years, did he really want to know?

The next day Harry unmolded Saint Paul and had put on his oldest work shirt to start the polishing when there was a tap on the greenhouse door. Tracy appeared with a group of seven.

"Mr. Gill, we have some visitors who would like to see the Madonna," she said in hushed tones. "Do you mind if we take a peek?"

Harry, liberally dusted with cement powder, looked something like an apparition himself, but he managed a cheerful decliner. "Sorry, folks, I'm just about to use my grinder, and this area's off limits. Tracy, point them in the direction of the grape arbor, will you? And then could I see you for a moment?"

Tracy blanched, then led the group away. Through the open door, however, he could see that they went only a few yards before turning to snap pictures of the greenhouse. Tracy came back in hesitantly, the pale freckles on her face looking somewhat darker.

"Now get this," Harry said. "The next time you bring anyone out here to see the Madonna, you can pick up your last paycheck. That's not what I'm paying you to do, and I want you to stop. Wanda tells me it was you who called the *Weekly* in the first place, and I want no more calls, no tours, no nothing. Is that understood?"

Her eyes filled with tears. "Oh, Mr. Gill, I didn't think—"

"No, I realize that. You didn't think. This is my private work area, and from now on I want you to refer all calls about the Madonna to Wanda or me."

Her face shriveled into silent crying, her mouth open, braces gleaming, and Harry immediately felt chastised. "Go take a break now. Wash your face and then go back to work," he said.

There were times he saw in Tracy a sixteen year-old Jodie, and he didn't want his granddaughter to be as gullible as that. *Grow up,* he wanted to say. *Open your eyes.* No weeping virgins will save you. No Gabriel.

He carried the apostle outdoors, plugged in the cord of the grinder, and soon the air was filled with cement dust and the whine of machinery. The question Liz had brought up, however, made him smile. Beth hadn't been the kind to keep secrets—well, her checkbook, maybe—but Harry had never known her to hold her feelings in.

"Harry," she had said four or five years ago, just after she'd placed a bowl of macaroni on the table. "When I was carrying this to the sink, just before I dumped it in the colander, I was thinking how easily I could pour the boiling water over you."

Harry, who had brought the sports page to the table and was awaiting his dinner, had slowly lowered the paper.

"It's because of the way you just get up and leave after a meal," she'd told him. "I don't ask you to cook, don't ask you to shop. All I ask is that you walk the damned dishes over to the sink and rinse them off. When I was carrying that boiling water, I was thinking, 'If he won't rinse them, I will.'" Beth sat down across from Harry and picked up her fork. "Not that I *would,* of course. I just wanted you to know how mad I was." And she began to eat.

She would tell a perfect stranger things about her life that Harry would not even have told his brother. Once, on a trip to Atlanta, they had not been on the plane more than twenty minutes when Harry heard Beth confide to the woman next to her that she used a diaphragm.

How, he wondered, had she got from "Hello" to birth control in twenty minutes? If she told this to a perfect stranger, what did she tell her hairdresser? What was the most intimate thing Harry had ever confided to his barber? That he had problems with ear wax, possibly? After twenty years, he still could not tell Jim Swann that his armpits stank.

The thought of Jim Swann made him want to visit the barbershop and share the Madonna with him. When the apostle was done, so was Harry. He wiped his hands, shook out his shirt, and locked the greenhouse.

"I'm off," he said to Wanda, poking his head in the store. "Tell a couple of the men to take care of that Bannockburn order. They can load the truck tonight. Anything else need doing before I go?"

"Nothing we can't handle, Mr. G. See you tomorrow," Wanda said. Tracy, looking subdued, kept her head down, and Rose, taking a count of hummingbird feeders, gave Harry a beatific smile.

LEROY SCHNEIDER WAS in the barber chair and for a minute Harry thought he was a customer. But as soon as Jim saw Harry he said, "Come on in, Harry. Leroy and me are just hanging out. Step on up here."

The short heavy man in the wide trousers clambered down and shook Harry's hand. There was a twinkle in his eye. "I see you've been making the news," he said.

Harry smiled wryly. "A funny business," he said.

"So what you got there, Harry? A miracle? First thing you know you'll have a bishop pay you a visit, then a cardinal, then the Pope," said Jim.

"Some flaw in the stone, some kind of moisture," Harry said as Jim tucked the cloth under his chin and pressed the Velcro tabs together in back. "Just a trim this time, Jim."

"But was it true, the tears? You saw them with your own eyes?" asked Leroy.

"They were there, all right. Corner of the left eye," said Harry.

Leroy sat shaking his head, sitting on the folding chair by the window, tapping his fingers on the card table. "Well, that proves it's a fake," he said. "Because a person doesn't cry out of just one eye."

Jim lifted the scissors and comb and began snipping away on one side of Harry's head. "She's no ordinary person, Leroy, she's the Madonna, the Holy Virgin, Mother of God, and I expect she can cry any goddam way she pleases." Jim was Catholic but had not been in a church for the past thirty years. Then he added, "But you, being of the Jewish persuasion, I doubt you'd understand."

Leroy held out his hands beseechingly and shrugged his shoulders. "What's to understand? Did I disrespect her? All I'm saying is it might be a bit more convincing if she cried out of both eyes. Know what I mean?"

Harry smiled, enjoying the debate.

"I had a dog once that only peed to the right," said Jim, poker-faced. "No matter what side the bushes were on, he'd turn himself around so his right side was facing the shrubbery and then he'd lift his leg and let go. Got hit by a car—broke his leg and had it in a cast—and I'll be damned if he just couldn't get the knack of raising his left leg and letting it fly. Imbecile of a dog would just stand there and dribble all the way down the cast."

Harry laughed out loud.

Leroy was leaning forward now. "Which goes to show. . . .?"

"That even a creature as lowly as a dog can be one-sided," Jim told him.

"But we're not talking dogs, Jim, we're talking. . . .how did you put it? The Holy Mother herself?" asked Leroy. "So maybe she has a message for half the population? The left half of the United States, maybe? Everything west of the Mississippi?" His knee bobbed up and down with enthusiasm. He was grinning again.

Jim nodded. "I'm not saying one way or the other, I'm saying you got something like this, it's a mystery. Let the church decide."

"Fair enough," said Leroy, winking at Harry. "Before you know it, Harry will have himself a shrine back there. You'll have to put in a grotto, Harry. Gill's Grotto, or Grotto at the Garden Center, or Our Lady of Chrysanthemums or something. The possibilities are staggering."

Harry closed his eyes and enjoyed the afternoon.

THAT MADE IT all the more difficult going home to silence. It was as though Beth had gone and taken the marriage with her, because all the memories they had shared, just the two of them, he couldn't relive with anyone else. He'd never thought of that before. The pillow talk, the struggle to get Harry's business off the ground, the births, the quarrels and the making up, early morning sex. . . .

He remembered one Sunday in particular. Beth had brought Jack into their bed to nurse him, and Harry, half awake, felt horny. While Jack pressed his face into Beth's breast, one small foot digging into her soft thigh which she had drawn up in the fetal position, Harry had caressed those thighs, running his hands up under her gown. Slowly they had maneuvered their bodies so that they managed to have intercourse with four-month old Jack between them, still nursing. As Harry's thrusts had grown stronger and the bed began to jiggle, Jack stopped nursing and laughed aloud. It was one of those rare, relaxed, never-to-come again moments that claimed a place in memory.

Harry turned off Old Forest Road and, a few blocks farther on, veered onto his own street. He turned his pickup into the driveway and came to a sudden stop.

A tall, thin young woman in jeans sat on his front porch, legs apart, a garment bag resting on her knees. Her long arms encircled a few bags and boxes at either side, and a suitcase overhung the top step.

FIVE

The Letter

HE COULD PUT the truck in reverse and back right out of the driveway. Any one of his kids would take him in for three or four days, and the Spider Lady would give up and leave.

Harry simply could not believe this was happening—that he had actually invited a woman he didn't know into his home. He couldn't even remember her name.

He took his foot off the brake.

She waved.

SPADAR, he thought. He was definitely into panic now. He turned off the engine and got out, conscious of the curtains moving in Paula Harrington's house. The Martians had landed, and the populace had taken cover.

"Hi. I took you up on it," said the female on the steps. "I hope your offer's still good."

This was his chance. He could say things had changed. That his daughter—one of his sons, maybe—was moving back.

"Well, Ida, I . . . uh. . . ."

"Iris," she corrected. "My sister's pregnant again, so she came back home. Guess where they put her? With me. I'm in this little bedroom with Kirsten—she's my seventeen year-old niece—and now Shirley. . . . That makes fourteen of us in all, with one bathroom, not counting the john in the basement, and I said, 'Look, I've got this offer. . . .' My brother drove me over. It's so *nice* of you, Harry!"

Did people really live like this? Just pick up their belongings and appear at a stranger's door?

"Your parents don't object?"

"Mom's dead."

"Your father?"

She shrugged. "A room's a room."

Harry's voice had taken on a bleating tone. "What about your grandmother?"

"If it's between me and a new baby, she'll take the baby." Iris began collecting her things together in the process of standing up.

She looked a little like Cher and was as flaky as old paint, but she was still one more distraction to keep sadness at bay. He was becoming a collector of distractions.

"Come on in," he said, and opened the door.

She stood in the front hall, surrounded by belongings, the tag on her shirt—the entire facing, in fact—hanging out the back like the puckered opening of a milk carton. He wondered if she ever looked in a mirror before she left the house, if there wasn't an aunt who could tuck her in, snip off the threads, *inspect* her, before sending her out into the world.

"You sure this is okay?" she asked.

Hell, no. Beth would—What *would* Beth say?

"For now, anyway," Harry said, as businesslike as he could

manage. "There's a possibility that my daughter might be coming back home with her little girl, but. . . ."

"Her marriage didn't work out, huh?" said Iris. "Well, I don't have to take her room. I can take another."

"The point is. . . ." Harry stopped. What *was* the point? The point was that he had offered this woman a room, she had accepted, and here she was.

"All this space!" Iris said, as she reached the second floor and looked around. "You could run a rooming house, Harry!"

"Hardly."

He led her to Claude's room. Elaine could be coming home for good, Jack could be coming to hide, but Claude was as settled a son as he could imagine.

"Nice," Iris said, and put her things on the bed. Then she went to the window and leaned down, palms resting on the sill, and Harry could see the bony ridges of her shoulder blades poking through her gauze shirt. Her hair was neater than he'd remembered it. Same heavy-lidded eyes, full lips, narrow face, a nose that did not just turn up at the end, it *bent* upward. And God, those legs!

"All this room for only one person!" she said again, surveying the yard. She turned. "As soon as I get a job, I can start paying rent."

"I don't need it, but if you can manage that, fine." Wearing his landlord demeanor, Harry checked to see that there were fresh sheets on the bed and hangers in the closet. He pointed out the linen cupboard and told her about the washer and dryer in the basement. Then he found himself apologizing for the dust that had accumulated on the dresser and bookcase.

"My wife never wanted a cleaning woman, so I'm afraid I've let the house go. A cleaning service is on my list; I just never got around to it."

"Oh, dust never hurt anyone," Iris said. "You show me where the vacuum is, I'll take care of my own room."

"Good," said Harry.

"And don't worry about meals. I'll eat out or bring stuff up here."

"I'd rather you didn't have food in your room, Iris. I'll clear off a shelf in the refrigerator. Buy what you like and feel free to use the kitchen. Make yourself at home."

"You're really nice, you know?"

Harry was surprised to feel warmth creeping up his neck and into his face. He wished his smile were more natural. He wasn't even sure how you smiled at a thirty-something woman residing in your home less than six weeks after your wife died, when you meant no impropriety whatsoever.

Iris must have eaten in her room anyway because she did not come down at dinner. Harry heated some leftovers in the microwave, and then did what he knew he must: he called all three of his children before any of the neighbors could tell them about Iris Shaw. Jack would be easiest, he decided, but he got a busy signal, so he dialed Claude next.

" . . . so here she is, Claude, and I wanted you to know before the gossips got wind of it. She's just staying until she gets her life in order."

There was a pause at the other end of the line. Then, "I know friends of forty-six who don't have their lives in order yet."

"As far as I'm concerned, it's a temporary arrangement. She's sort of up against a wall, and maybe it would be good for me to have someone in the house for the next few months."

"Whatever it takes, Dad," Claude told him genially.

That was easier than he'd imagined. Harry did not relish calling Elaine, but he took a deep breath and dialed. Jodie, of course, answered.

"Hi, Grandpa!"

"How are you, honey?"

"Fiiiine!" She strung out the word, her voice rising higher and higher, the way students used to say, "Good morrr-ning, tea-cher!"

"You and Mommy have dinner yet?"

"Uh huh."

"Anything good?"

"Yeeesss."

Elaine was raising the girl to be an automaton, Harry decided.

"Could I speak to mommy?"

"Yeeesss." Jodie remained on the line.

"It's important, Jodie. Go get your mom."

"Okay." This time she seemed to have dropped the phone, for there was a loud clunk, voices, then Elaine.

"Sorry about that," she said.

"Listen, I just wanted you to hear it from me so you don't get any crazy ideas. I'm letting a woman customer use Claude's room for a while. She's down on her luck, and is going to pay rent as soon as she finds a job."

"Really? Well, it's probably a good deal for both of you as long as she doesn't expect meals and maid service."

"Of course not."

"How old is she?"

"I didn't ask. Late thirties, maybe."

"Well, tongues will wag, but let them."

Harry couldn't believe how much his children had matured. Encouraged, he dialed Suds and Spuds again, and this time Jack came on the line. Harry repeated the news.

There was a long silence, and for a moment Harry thought they had been disconnected.

"Jack?"

"I'm here, Dad." More silence. Then: "You going to let her use the Cadillac?"

Harry blinked. "It didn't even occur to me."

"Well, you really ought to get some things down in writing, you know. What she can use, what she can't, when she's going to start paying rent, that sort of thing."

"I hadn't given much thought to a contract, Jack."

"You're letting a woman into your home and you haven't given it much thought? Just doesn't sound like you, Dad. I'm not saying you shouldn't do it, just be cautious, okay?"

"Okay. Glad to have your advice," said Harry.

For fifteen minutes, Harry Gill sat in the kitchen, arms on the table, trying to make sense of what he had done. Would he feel better or worse having this woman in the house? He didn't know. At each sound from above—footsteps going from one side of Claude's room to the other, the flush of the toilet, the squeak of a closet door, he told himself that anything was better than the quiet of the last month or so. These were sounds of *living.*

Out in the hallway, Zeke moved cautiously along the wall, tail straight up, ears alert, head turned toward the floor above. He sat expectantly on the carpet at the bottom of the stairs and then, with seeming delight, moved swiftly up to the second floor.

She's only a boarder, Harry told himself. You have no obligation whatsoever except to keep the plumbing working.

A key. Yes, he'd have to find her a key. Harry stood and went to the small chest of drawers by the umbrella stand in the hall. From the room above, he could hear a radio playing, the DJ introducing the next song. And then the singer's plaintive voice, with Iris joining in now and then:

"I don't want to steal your love,
I don't want to sneak and hide.
All I want is you to let me
Waaa-lk by your side.
I'm no burglar come to rob,
I'm no thief who strikes at night,
You can talk and I'll just listen,
Hold you in my arms so tight. . . ."

THAT SAME WEEK, the Pontiac Grand Am became hers. It had belonged to her sister, but it seemed there had been a family conference. It was decided that if Iris was turning her room over to Shirley, Shirley owed her something in return. So Iris got the car, just like that.

The Pontiac was of indeterminate age, with 87,000 miles on it. Everything about it seemed to squeal—the doors, the brakes, the gears. But—as Iris said—it ran. You could hear it when it was within a half block of the house. After a few days, in fact, Harry had come to listen for it.

For the first week or so, he didn't see much of Iris. She wasn't up when he left in the morning and either came in later or went right to her room. Then a carton of raspberry yogurt appeared in the refrigerator, along with a package of cheese Danish. Harry liked seeing them there.

The last week in May, Iris stopped in the living room on her way upstairs.

"I'm going to register for a couple of courses this fall, Harry, and I've got a job at Hecht's, starting next week," she said. "Cosmetics. You ever want any samples, we've got tons. Exfoliating cream, moisturizers, sun screen—"

"Thank you," Harry said.

"So I can start paying you a little every month."

Harry was impressed by her initiative. "Tell you what," he said. "You're going to need every penny you earn for school. Why don't you keep the upstairs clean, bathroom too, I'll do the down, and we'll call it even. And of course clean up after yourself in the kitchen."

"You sure?"

"If I see it's not working, I'll tell you."

She smiled at him, and leaned against the doorway. She did have a nice smile. "What'd your wife die of, Harry?"

There was a sort of good-guys-shouldn't-lose quality to her voice, but Harry answered anyway. "Cancer."

"Stomach? I had an uncle with stomach cancer."

"Ovarian. Then it spread."

"Jeez!" Iris gave a sigh and thrust her hands in the pockets of her jeans, which pulled the material even tighter across her pubic area.

She was wearing a red T-shirt and her small breasts made little points that Harry did not find especially attractive. He'd seen men with larger breasts than that. "You ever wonder what's going on inside your cells, that you don't know anything about?" She paused and reflected. "I'll bet you really loved her."

"Very much."

"Hmmm." Iris shook her head sadly. "I read once that hair dye can cause brain cancer, especially the dark colors. You can peroxide but you shouldn't dye."

"I don't know anything about that."

She studied him. "I'm not bothering you, am I?"

"No, course not. You want to sit down for a while?"

"Thanks, but I promised I'd call Shirley, and then I'm going to sack up. Goodnight, Harry."

"Goodnight."

THE PALE ORANGE of early morning shown on the angel Gabriel, so that his wings cast a shadow over Harry's work table like a large bird hovering overhead. Harry examined the chips and cracks, the missing toe, and got out the clay. He took these statues, with all their imperfections, and enabled them to carry on. Gabriel watched with lidless eyes, trumpet to his lips.

If the angel were to tap Harry on the shoulder and say that he could be recast, Harry would choose to have been one of the stone carvers at the National Cathedral.

They were all Italian, of course, those carvers—grandfathers teaching fathers, fathers teaching sons. Harry would have worked along with them and watched as each block and scroll and cornice and column was lifted high in the air and set into place.

He would have been inch-deep in stone chips and powder, laboring over the finials, reliefs and tympanums that laced the cathedral. He would have spent years on a scaffold carving keystones, bondstones, and grotesques. He too would have created a gargoyle in his own image to squat up there on the roof along with the parodies of the masters—a golfer in golf cap, cigar in his mouth; a businessman, dragon, griffin, even Darth Vader. They were all there, these heavy-jawed creatures with their jaded eyes, hunched open-mouthed high on the roof as the choirs below offered up their angelic voices. For centuries to come, perhaps, Harry—his image, chisel in hand—would remain as a testament to his craft.

But he had not been tapped. There were no heavenly visitors, and the Cathedral was done, finished at last. And so he contented himself with the wing of an angel and tended to its repair. Artificial resuscitation. A love affair with stone.

Had his wife been content? he wondered. She was the kind who thrived on the highs in her life—births of children, weddings, holidays—no matter how much work they entailed. It was the dullness, the grays, that got her down, but she had solutions for even the dreariest of problems; she was a collector of solutions.

Ha . . . rry . . .

Bent over Gabriel, Harry had just picked up the awl. He paused, slowly straightened his back and glanced about.

"Beth?"

He turned in a complete circle, then walked to the door and looked out. Looked up. In a far tree, a mockingbird began a new number, repeated it once, and went on. A car drove by on Old Forest Road, but the parking lot was empty.

Harry went back to the place he had been standing before. "Beth?" he called again.

He looked at the angel. Did the lips move just then—the slightest tremor, perhaps? He waited, listening to the throbbing of blood in his temples, he was that quiet. Then he bent over the statue once again because it was his work, and it was all he knew to do.

HE WENT HOME at noon to change clothes and get some lunch. When he walked into his house, Iris was standing barefoot in a light cotton robe in the hallway, her head wrapped in a towel. Zeke, all eleven pounds of him, was draped over one shoulder like a fur piece, purring loudly.

"Zeke and I were just going to have some breakfast," she told Harry. "You want a grilled cheese or something?"

"I could use one, I guess. I'll be going back to the garden center later."

Harry washed up and changed, and when he came back to the kitchen, there was a sandwich waiting for him on a saucer, a pickle alongside. Iris sat spooning yogurt into her mouth, Zeke in her lap, the comics spread out before her.

For a while they each sat reading their separate sections, Harry engrossed in an article on proposed zoning changes for Old Forest Road.

"Here's something I could never figure out," Iris said suddenly, pointing to the Spiderman comic strip. Harry looked up.

"See his costume? Fits like a glove, right? Can you imagine what a nylon body suit feels like in summer? I mean, can you imagine how he smells?"

Harry smiled faintly and turned a page or two of the Metro section.

"And every so often Spiderman *irons* it. Stretch nylon! You can sure tell a man writes that strip." Iris lowered her near-empty yogurt container so that Zeke could lick the inside. "The fact is, cartoonists aren't too careful. You know *Apartment 3-G*?" And when Harry looked blank, she added, "The comic strip? My aunt says she can remember when Louanne got married and moved to Georgia. She wrote her roommates that she'd had a baby. Well, later her husband's missing in action or something, and she comes back to the apartment to live. So where's the kid? The cartoonist never mentioned the baby again. To walk off and leave a little baby like that!"

Harry stared.

"And Mary Worth? My aunt says *she* used to have this son with a double chin who showed up from time to time, and then *he* disappeared. Nobody's heard from him in years. How do cartoonists get away with that? Do they think we don't remember?"

"I don't know," said Harry.

Iris studied him from across the breakfast table. "I talk too much," she said. "I drive my brother nuts. Women talk more than men, you ever notice that?"

Harry took another bite of the sandwich. "Have you ever been married, Iris?"

"Once. Lasted four months."

"I'm sorry."

"I'm not. He was a jerk. We got in a fight once and he broke my nose." She lowered her head and pointed to a raised place halfway down, hardly visible. "See that? I filed for divorce. Didn't stick around to let him do it again.One thing I won't do is let a man hit me."

"Nor should you," said Harry. He chewed for a minute, then said, "What if he was a pretty decent guy—didn't get drunk or run around or hit you—but he was. . . .predictable? Would you divorce him because you knew everything he was going to do before he did it?"

"That's a problem?" She turned her spoon over and licked the back. "I don't know. I never had the chance to find out." She put Zeke down, stood up and stretched. For a second Harry thought he caught a glimpse of pubic hair as her robe parted slightly, and then she padded lazily toward the stairs. A few minutes later Harry heard the high whine of her hair dryer.

He reached for the phone book where Beth had written down frequently-dialed numbers, and called Liz Bowen.

"Liz," he told her. "Beth's only been gone six weeks, Don's walked out on Elaine, I've got a Madonna weeping at the garden center, and I've let a young woman I hardly know have Claude's room."

"Good for you," said Liz.

She must not have understood. "There's been another woman here in Beth's kitchen, and I don't even know how old she is!" Harry said emphatically.

"So what do you want me to tell you, Harry? That you're all

right? I won't, because we may be normal, but we're not all right."

"I don't know. I don't even know why I called you," Harry said plaintively.

"All I can tell you is this," said Liz. "For the first few months after Max died, I was in shock. I thought I was handling things okay. But you know what, Harry? Things get worse. You can count on it."

HE STOPPED TO pick up some garlic shrimp with snow peas on his way home, then added lo mein to the order in case Iris was around. Afraid it still might not be enough for two, Harry asked for egg rolls to take along. But when he got home, Iris was evidently out for the evening. He ate half of everything and put the rest away.

He was just closing up the carton of rice when the phone rang. He lifted the handset to his ear. "Hello?"

What he got was an earful of tinny-sounding music. It was as though someone were holding the phone next to a cassette player.

"Hello?" Harry said again, more loudly. It was a familiar tune, but he couldn't place it.

The music continued, the volume increasing until the sound became deafening. Harry hung up.

At nine-fifteen, the phone rang again. Harry answered, and at first there was no sound at all. Then the music blasted in his ear, so loud it made him jump. This time he recognized the song: *O Sole Mio.* Goddam.

He hung up a second time and dialed *-6-9 to see what number had called him last. It was a number he did not recognize. The operator could not give him the name or address. Harry dialed the number. It rang and rang—twenty, thirty, forty times. No one answered.

When the phone rang again at two in the morning, long after Iris had come home, Harry picked up the phone and listened without speaking. The music again. The same song. One more time he hung up and dialed *-6-9 but this time the automated voice gave a different number. He dialed that too, but—just as before—no one answered. He left the phone off the hook for the rest of the night, and after he replaced it the next morning, the caller did not phone again.

THERE WERE SEVERAL things that had come to Harry's attention since Iris moved in: There were no more food donations left outside his door; Paula Harrington stopped picking up his newspaper along with hers and delivering it to his steps; Jack called every other night, obviously to see if "the girl," as he called her, had made off with the family silver yet; and his brother Wade paid an unexpected call at the garden center. Harry had just wet his finger with saliva and was using it to blend the shepherdess's new shoulder in with the rest of her body, when he looked out to see his brother lumbering through the walkway.

"Hi." Wade stood awkwardly just inside the door, large hands dangling like wrecking balls at his sides. Of the two brothers, Wade looked most like old man Gill—a horseshoe shaped mouth turning down sharply at the corners, even when he smiled. Deep furrows on either side of his mouth. His eyes were half hidden in a perpetual squint, and more often than not, he was covered with rock dust. On this Sunday morning, however, he wore freshly laundered jeans and a cotton shirt, handkerchief-thin from use. Outside the quarry, he could have afforded silk shirts and Gucci shoes, but he wore his clothes into the ground. Same with cars. An ancient Oldsmobile sat parked askew out in the lot.

"How you doing?" Harry asked him, motioning toward the stool. "Sit down. Take a load off your feet."

Wade just gave him a sour smile and went on standing. "Too hot to sit. Clothes'll stick to my butt," he growled. "How are things with you?"

"The same," Harry said. "Surviving. Business okay?"

"If the people in those townhouses don't complain. The old residents, they're used to us. But the new ones?"

"Yeah? What's the gripe now? You wash your trucks down before they leave the quarry?"

"Of course, and we keep to the blasting limit, but some group's after us for the level of chrysotile. I'll be long gone before we get all seven million tons of stone out of there, you can bet." He shifted his weight and leaned one hand against the door frame.

"Ever think about selling?"

"In five or six years, maybe, if they don't close us down before then. You tell me this: We were there before there were any houses to speak of on Old Forest Road. There before any of these developments. And all of a sudden *we're* a threat to *their* environment? Is that fair?"

Harry gave him a bemused smile.

Wade grunted and thrust two fingers in his shirt pocket for a cigarette, lit it, and turned his head so that the smoke rose outside the greenhouse. "Jack called," he said, flicking the ashes beyond the door. "Says you got a roomer."

"Boarder," Harry corrected. He ran a soft brush over a cake of soap and applied that to the shepherdess's shoulder.

Wade smoked a while longer. "When did you decide on that?"

"It's nothing I planned. She just showed up here one day, we got to talking, she needed a room, so I gave her Claude's."

"Hell, Harry! What do you know about the girl?"

"Not much."

Rooting about in his ear with one finger, Wade continued to study the floor. "This last year's been really hard on you. Guess I shouldn't be surprised at anything."

"I suppose not."

"Look. Your affairs are your business, mine are mine. But I hope you won't sign anything."

"Like what? You think I'm about to give her the house? I'm not senile, Wade."

"Hey!" Wade reached out and clamped one hand on his shoulder. "I promised Jack I'd look in on you, see what's what. I came, I saw, and I left. End of discussion."

Harry grunted.

"And anything I can do. . . . I keep saying that. But I wish there *was* something."

"I know. It's mostly stuff I have to sort through myself. I'm starting slow, tackling the easiest things first. It's her closet—her clothes—that will be hardest."

"Get Elaine to help you with that."

"I will."

"Well, then. Take care."

Harry watched his brother go back to the car, mission accomplished. He wiped his hands on his pants and thought about Wade and his loner life. Maybe he was happy! Who could say what happiness was for anyone else? Wade had said he kept his affairs to himself, but if Wade dated women, Harry sang at the Met. Harry put the shepherdess aside and turned to his next project.

BARBIE, THE GOOSE, stood by the door of the garden center in her polka dot bikini, sun shades, and hat.

"Wanda, really!" Harry said, when he walked in one June morning.

"Don't knock it, Mr. G.!" she laughed. "I've sold four of those bikinis already and have orders for seven more. Here," she added, handing him a folded newspaper as he started toward the greenhouse. A small story was circled in red. "Your jollies for the day," she called after him.

Harry read the news story:

MINISTER CONVICTED IN SEX CASE

DAYTON, OHIO –

A minister charged with sexually abusing three girls and a boy while pretending to be the Angel Gabriel was convicted of statutory rape and other charges. . . .

"Good Lord!" said Harry.

"Just thought you ought to know what Gabriel's been up to while your back was turned," Wanda joked.

Steve chuckled as he passed with his clipboard.

Rose Kribbs' eyes darted from one to the other, her mouth working in silent exclamations. Harry had begun to think of her as a security camera, the lens following employees from one side of the store to the other. Tracy, who was opening a roll of quarters at the cash register, said, "I don't think we ought to joke about things like this. It wouldn't surprise me if the Virgin showed up right here on Old Forest Road. We've already seen the signs."

Harry was reminded of a bumper sticker he'd seen on a car: *Eat, drink, and see Mary.* "In that case, he said, "we'd better start cleaning out the back lot."

He went into the small rest room beyond the urns and planters and, as he stood over the bowl, noticed a paperback book on the lid of the toilet tank. The title, *Fire of Longing,* was spelled out in raised red letters. Pictured on the cover was a young woman with flaming red hair, seated on a rock and bending backwards so that her breasts pointed skyward beneath her transparent blouse. A bare-chested man leaned over her, gripping her hair with one hand, her exposed thigh with the other. Harry wasn't quite sure whether a rape or a kiss was in progress.

He smiled to himself as he flushed and came back out. It certainly wasn't Wanda's. Cross out Tracy. Rose? He looked across the room to where the slim woman was fashioning a wreath out of dried summer flowers, threading the stems through the wire form, lips pursed as she held it out in front of her after each addition, studying the effect. If she got a new color job, a different pair of glasses, and an injection of self confidence, she wouldn't be half bad. She looked up momentarily and, finding Harry's eyes on her, looked so bewildered and embarrassed that he was sorry he'd stared.

"Looks good, Rose," he said quickly, and strode out of the room before she could crumble. Where *did* Wanda find their employees?

It was a day of unfinished business. Hostas had been delivered to the wrong address, a landscaper called to dispute his bill, and the sink in the restroom wouldn't drain.

"Mrs. Carmichael phoned about the Madonna," Wanda said, poking her head in his office. "She just got back from Europe and somebody gave her the write-up in the paper. I asked if she wanted to take the statue back, and she said not with it weeping, she didn't."

"I'll get to it next week," said Harry.

Still, he was beginning to find he had a handle on things. He'd made a point of going through at least a few of Beth's belongings each evening—a box of letters, perhaps; a fistful of bank statements; a drawer of old stationary—anything at all to assure himself he was coping, acknowledging, accepting, grieving, adjusting . . . whatever a normal man was supposed to do in the decidedly abnormal aftermath of losing the one he loved.

There was good news too, however. Elaine called.

"Two teachers turned in their resignations, Dad, so I'm assigned one of their positions. It'll be fifth grade, not fourth, but I can do it. What a relief!"

"Honey, I'm delighted. That's terrific!"

"And listen. A favor. I'm trying to set up a regular schedule with my therapist. Could you possibly sit Jodie on Tuesday evenings? I'll bring her over to your place; you won't have to come here."

"No problem at all."

"One more thing. Don called the other night."

"He did? Where is he?"

"I don't know. I didn't talk to him. Old predictable Don. You know when he called? When I was getting dinner. I could have told you he'd do that. It's the one time of day I let Jodie answer the phone for me."

"So. . . .what happened?"

"Oh, he fed her a line. Said he loved her and was still her daddy, and he'll see her by and by . . . not to worry, because this was between him and mommy, blah, blah, blah."

"At least he cares, Elaine."

Her voice took on the familiar sharpness. "Whose side are you on, anyway?"

"Look," said Harry. "I'm not involved in your war, but you shouldn't begrudge this to Jodie. And I don't think it does her any good to air your problems in front of her. He said he loves her and he'll see her eventually, and you ought to leave it at that. For her, anyway."

"You're right. I just get so mad, I can't see straight. Anyway, I'll see you Tuesday."

HARRY WORKED UNTIL seven that evening, and when he went to check the calendar, realized it was his wedding anniversary. He stood motionless, staring at that empty square as though expecting a magical notation to appear, telling him what he should do.

He did not turn on the radio during the drive home, because some commemoration seemed called for. Usually it was Beth who arranged these things—a celebration, a dinner out. Harry drove slowly, two fingers guiding the wheel. With the birth of each of his children and the death of his wife, he had witnessed the entrance of a presence that had not been there before and the exit of one he would never see again. Yet where had that presence, that consciousness, been all that time before, and where did it go after? How definite or impenetrable was that dividing line?

He did not believe, of course, and that was the trouble. If he could *will* her to speak to him again, *love* her back to life, she would be sitting beside him now. It was not that there was some huge thing left undone that he and Beth had wanted to do. He just wanted to do the same ordinary things over and over.

And once again the sadness got him and sank its teeth in his spirit. Harry suddenly felt so abandoned that nothing on his body seemed to move except his fingers on the wheel. Somehow he made it into the house and onto a chair in the dining room. And it was there Iris found him when she stopped in the hallway to pet Zeke.

She should not be here. Harry knew that as surely as the nose on his face, and he would take the first opportunity to tell her.

"Harry?" Iris looked around the corner. "Hey! What are you doing here all by yourself?"

Harry stared straight ahead as she came on in. She watched him for a moment, then placed her hands on the back of the chair opposite him. "You sick?"

His voice came out in monotone. "Just sad, Iris."

"Oh. I guess you've got a right to be. You've got a right to feel any way you want."

"Thank you very much," he said, not bothering to disguise the sarcasm.

She moved slowly around the dining room, running one finger over the decorative back of each chair in turn, stopping at the china cupboard to admire Beth's dishes, then turning toward the bay window and tracing the top of the ceramic jar with the black and purple flowers painted on it.

"Don't touch that," said Harry.

She glanced over at him. "It's beautiful. It looks like a Grecian urn."

"It *is* an urn," Harry told her.

Iris stared at it a moment. "I mean, like. . . ." And then her eyes grew larger. "You mean, *she's* . . . ?"

"Yes," said Harry.

Iris backed away and continued staring. "What are you going to *do* with her, Harry?"

He sat as stiff as a gun barrel, as though not even his neck had any give in it. "Maybe you ought to go on upstairs, Iris," he said. "This is our anniversary, and I'm tired."

For two or three minutes he sat in silence, eyes closed. Everything seemed disconnected somehow, hands from arms, thoughts from feelings. Gradually, he could feel his breathing slow, and when he opened his eyes at last, Iris was sitting directly across from him.

"You shouldn't be alone on your anniversary, Harry." If she had been looking at him with soulful eyes, it would have been one thing. Iris, however, was unwrapping a stick of gum. "Want some?" She offered him the pack.

He shook his head. Maybe now was as good a time as any. He could lie and say he was selling the place, she'd have to leave.

"How did you meet her?" Iris rolled the gum wrapper between her palms until it was a tight little ball, and dropped it in the pocket of her shirt.

Was there no stopping this girl? He didn't answer.

"Like, was it love at first sight?"

Harry gave a small stiff smile. "No, nothing like that."

"What, then?" At least she had the decency to chew with her mouth closed.

"You can't be interested."

"I *am,* Harry!"

"I don't remember exactly." His voice was flat, and Harry sighed as though to dismiss her.

"Oh, c'mon! It's your anniversary! Where were you when you met?"

It did seem disloyal not to even talk about her. "Beth always said she saw me first when a bunch of us went out to eat at O'Donnell's, but I don't remember seeing her there."

"Okay, when *did* you notice her for the first time?"

"She was sitting on the hood of a car."

Iris's eyes were laughing. "Bet it was *some*thing about her, though. Her nose or her legs, maybe."

"No, I liked her whole face. She was friendly." Why was he telling Iris all this? Talking made him feel better, however. Talking about Beth meant he hadn't forgotten her—their anniversary. Talking about her to a woman who was living up in Claude's room meant that everything was up front.

"You felt comfortable with her," said Iris.

"Yes, and the more I was around her, the more I wanted her to be a part of my life."

"Sure sounds like love to me," said Iris. "What did she like about you?"

"I don't know exactly."

"Oh, c'mon, Harry."

He smiled down at the table. It was embarrassing, but God, it felt so good to smile. "My stomach."

Iris gave an explosive laugh and her eyes widened. "Your *stomach?*"

"The fact that I didn't have a beer belly. Some of the men in our crowd, you never saw their belt buckles."

Iris nodded. "It all must have gone to your shoulders."

"Well, anyway, between her face and my stomach—her *smile* and my stomach—I figured we'd make a good match. Got engaged in January and married in June."

"Big wedding?"

"Her relatives, my relatives. A few friends. A hundred, maybe. She had a maid of honor and I had a best man. Reception there at the church. We didn't go for the big to-dos they have now, everything in black and white."

"Where did you go on your honeymoon?"

"Chesapeake Bay. A friend loaned us his cottage and boat. We had a good time." Harry sat quietly, smiling to himself. "Yes, we had a very good time."

And then, by God, a tear hit the back of his hand. He stared down as though it were some foreign substance, as mysterious as the tears of the Madonna.

Perhaps it frightened Iris, because she got up and left the room, but Harry scarcely had time to wipe his eyes when she was back again, holding a small bud vase with three yellow roses in it.

"I stopped by your garden center today, Harry, and picked these up. I want you to have them for your anniversary. For the good time you had at the Bay, all right?"

She took the flowers over and set them beside the ceramic jar in the window.

"Goodnight, Harry," she said as she passed and, bending down, kissed him lightly on top of his head.

THE FOLLOWING DAY began like any other. The slow awakening from a tenuous dream that kept slipping over the edge of memory. The sudden realization that he was alone except for Zeke and a woman upstairs. And then his rescue by the silent recitation of all the jobs that needed doing, and this propelled him out of bed, into the shower, and eventually on the road to the garden center.

The summer sun was already hot, and out behind the parking area where the herd loaded the truck or dug a trench or built a trellis, the air rang with the shouts of young men anticipating their weekend, ribbing the ones who would have to work.

No longer in school, Tracy came to work in khaki shorts and T-shirts. Wanda appeared in loose clothes that flattered her fullness, while Rose seemed entombed in the denim apron she always wore, with scissors, ribbon, tape and string stuffed in the pockets, a peasant blouse with ruffled sleeves above her elbows.

Harry went home that night to a frozen dinner of beef and macaroni, and while it was in the microwave, he sat down at his desk in a corner of the living room to finish sorting through a box of ancient business mail, twenty years old or more, when Beth was still doing the bookkeeping for the garden center. This he could do.

There were bank statements, bills, letters of complaint, each bundle held together with three or four rubber bands, most of them disintegrating, curled like dried-up worms among the papers. Each had the year written in magic marker on the first envelop in the stack. Beth was an incorrigible saver. "In case we're ever audited," she used to say.

"Out . . . out," Harry said aloud, thumbing quickly through one bundle, then another, and dropping them in the waste basket.

The microwave dinged as he picked up a fourth bundle, and he was about to discard that too when he noticed Beth had circled that year in pencil, as though to alert herself to something worth noting. The rubber bands had adhered themselves to the paper, and Harry pulled them off one by one, then made a quick examination of each envelop. Perhaps there was a bill a customer had never paid. A bank statement that never balanced. Nothing here worth saving, he thought, and then he came to a small white envelope with his name and home address typed out in black letters.

At first it appeared that the letter had never been opened, but on closer inspection the flap was unglued. The edges of the envelope were beginning to yellow with age.

Harry lifted the flap and slid out the sheet of paper inside, folded into sixths. When he opened it, he read a single line: *Maybe you should know that one of your children isn't yours. A friend.*

SIX

The Affair

A JOKE. OBVIOUSLY, a joke. You don't live with a woman for thirty-four years and not know something like that. Not even suspect that such a thing is possible. Harry's first impulse was to drop the letter in the trash with the rest, but his hand paused over the waste basket. He picked up his magnifying glass instead and inspected the postmark, so faint it was almost illegible. It had been mailed in Rockville eleven years ago, not twenty.

Harry hardly knew which question to entertain first. Why was the letter in this bundle then? Why would Beth have opened it in the first place, addressed to Harry here at home, and why in God's name, once read, would she have saved it? If it were untrue, she would have shown it to him immediately, indignantly, and together they would have speculated as to what it was all about. If it was true—what nonsense—who would the father be and of which child?

Claude was already twelve when this letter was posted. Why had that "friend" decided to send it then? Was Jack not his? Maybe that guy Beth had been dating when they met had come back briefly into the picture. Joe Wyman, from Glen Burnie. Harry didn't even know where Glen Burnie was. Was Elaine not his? Hadn't Windy had a thing for Beth in those early years? His mind rebelled at the thought.

Harry himself was one of the fifty percent of men who had not had an extramarital affair, though he'd idly carried on a dozen or more in his head. He'd really loved his wife, and the necessary secrecy, the hiding, lying, had simply put him off.

Okay, go with the ludicrous for a moment: If this was true, if Beth had been playing around, why wouldn't he have gotten some hint from their friends? Or maybe this was that hint—sitting for eleven years in Beth's keeping, tucked in among business letters so ancient she could be fairly certain Harry would toss them out unread should he survive her.

Loose ends were suddenly collecting on Harry like lint: the truck, the tomato sauce incident, the telephone music, the weeping Madonna. Now this. It had all begun after his son-in-law had disappeared. What was the connection? None whatsoever.

The letter he was holding was the most worrisome of all. When would Beth have found the time, three kids to raise? Where would it have happened? Ginnie Swann he could see fooling around maybe, but. . . . No, it was too ridiculous to think about, and he wasn't going to torture himself any longer. Beth was gone, this was an eleven year-old joke that hadn't got off the ground, and it didn't deserve another second of worry. He put the letter under his desk blotter and picked up the next bank statement in the pile.

Instead of the numbers on the page, however, he saw himself sitting at a table in a Red Roof Inn over in Virginia, Stephanie Morrison across from him. It was only five in the afternoon, and they were waiting for the restaurant to start serving dinner so they could . . . what?

After

It was her birthday, and Harry had told Beth the night before that he would be taking Stephanie out sometime the next day. He wasn't sure just when; they'd pick a slow time at the garden center. And he had known even when he'd said it, that it was to answer (even before it was asked) the question of why Beth might not be invited too.

Harry had dressed with care that morning. He had showered, clipped his nails, gotten a haircut two days before. Clean underwear, gray slacks, a silk-blend sport shirt.

Beth had studied him across the table at breakfast, silent, withdrawn, and no matter how he tried, he could not seem to come across as an ordinary man having an ordinary breakfast on an ordinary day. He knew that positively. Why couldn't she be reasonable? The facts were that he was the owner of Gill's Garden Center, and was taking his store manager out to eat on her birthday. What was the harm in that? He and Stephanie had gone out to lunch many times before. They'd even had dinner together once or twice, though he may have failed to tell his wife.

This time, though, he had picked a restaurant with a motel attached, in a neighboring state where no one would recognize them. And now it was awkward sitting in a less than luxurious restaurant, in a booth with vinyl seats, waiting for the evening chef to arrive to make the daily specials on the laminated menus. A workman was mowing the grass right outside the window, and each time he passed, their conversation was drowned out and they paused till they could be heard again.

Harry smiled at Stephanie and she smiled back. He had reached across the table and given her hand a squeeze. He said how much he appreciated her work at the garden center, and hoped he had been good at demonstrating that. They had both laughed a little then, and he gave her hand an extra squeeze before the waitress sauntered over to say that the dinner chef had arrived and it would be a few more minutes yet.

"Wonder if I should call work and see how they're doing without us," Harry mused at one point, looking at his watch.

"A Monday night, I should think there wouldn't be much traffic." Stephanie was wearing a scoop-necked dress, tight fitting around the bust, and a chunky gold necklace that Harry didn't find especially attractive. It seemed too heavy for the dress. He had not made a room reservation because he was not sure how the dinner would go. And he had not taken her to a more exclusive place because his intentions might have been too obvious. He would simply allow things to take their course, however they might turn out.

He glanced at his watch a second time, knowing that both Stephanie's husband and Beth would have questions if they got home much after nine. But the afternoon sun coming in had made it seem like noon, almost. Cars whizzed by on the highway, trucks making a labored sound. The kitchen help called back and forth to each other as they sauntered in, preparing for the evening shift. And when the waitress came at last to take their orders, they had already waited forty-five minutes.

Why did it seem so different now? Harry wondered. So unlike the playful pats he gave her occasionally at work when he passed if no one was looking. Or when she touched his arm in the greenhouse. Where was that surge of adrenaline now?

"Well," he said, smiling again. "I didn't think we'd have to wait this long."

She smiled back. "For what?"

"For . . . dinner, of course." He smiled with his eyes this time.

So did she. "Of course."

"Unless. . . ."

"What?"

He looked toward the registration desk, then at her again, smiled innocently and turned his palms upwards.

"It's not the most romantic place in the world, is it?" she said, possibly mistaking his gesture.

"I guess not." What was *that* supposed to mean? he'd wondered. Did she want to go somewhere else? And then, in case she had *not* intended anything more than dinner out, he said, "I don't think the meal will mind. It should taste just as good without violins and candles."

It didn't seem the thing to say, and Harry began to sense that each was feeling the other out, each waiting for the other to make a definitive remark that would determine the course of the evening. The canned music was awful, far too raucous. Harry considered asking the waitress to turn it off, then thought better of it. It would focus far too much attention on them.

When the food still hadn't come twenty minutes later, Stephanie said, "Kurt gets up early tomorrow morning, so I can't be too late."

Harry glanced toward the kitchen. "I really thought we'd be served by now." God, he had blown this, that's for sure. He forced another smile. "I could ask for the birthday cake to be delivered, and we could have dessert first. . . ."

"I don't eat dessert," Stephanie said. "I hope you didn't order something special."

"No, but I would have liked to," he told her. "Anyway, I did get you a little present." To redeem what he could of the occasion, he pulled a small box from his coat pocket and handed it to her. He had tied it with yellow ribbon from the shop, and she laughed at the way he had arranged the bow, which leaned far to the left as though blown by a strong wind.

"My thumb was in the way," he explained, grinning, and they laughed.

She opened the box and found a watch on a thin gold band.

"Oh!" she said, and pressed her lips together.

He studied her face. "I hope you like it."

"It's beautiful, but I already have a watch."

"I know. I just thought this was particularly suited to you—the narrow band."

She turned it around and around in her fingers. "It's very nice, really," she said.

"I can easily exchange it for something else."

She handed it back and shook her head. "Oh, I can't. Kurt would ask. . . ."

"Just tell him I appreciate my employees, and it was your birthday. There's no reason he should be upset."

"Is that the truth?" she asked.

"That I appreciate my employees?"

"That there's no reason he should be upset."

"Well." He waited. "I guess that's up to you."

"Why me?" Her eyes fell to the table. She turned her water glass around and around. "I don't think we're very sure of anything, are we?"

Harry took her hand. "I'm sure that I appreciate you very much."

She looked at him questioningly and they both fell silent as the food arrived.

"Thank you," said Harry.

"Will there be anything else?" asked the waitress. "I go off duty soon."

"Not at the moment," said Harry, and she had taken off her apron and left.

Harry tried to start over, turning the conversation back to the garden center to see if they could segue into the flirtation mode from a different angle. But everything sounded artificial. The momentum had slowed. He found himself asking questions she had already answered on the drive over. Even their laughter sounded forced after a while.

I don't think we're very sure of anything, are we? She had asked. He hadn't answered. Would he have taken her to bed if she'd answered differently? Probably. He would have reacted first and examined later. Justified it, perhaps.

Stephanie had pulled back. He tried to tell himself he was in it for the flirtation only. Curiosity. Variety, even. He didn't love his wife any less. He ordered a dessert wine after they'd finished eating, then coffee, attempting to give themselves more time, in case.

"I've got to get home," Stephanie said finally.

"Really? We could still—"

"Yes," she said decisively, reaching for her purse. She was not smiling.

Harry recognized defeat. "All right," he said.

But there had been an accident on the American Legion Bridge and traffic was tied up for two miles. They were stuck near the bridge for an hour and forty minutes. When they got back to her car at the garden center, she was frantic.

HARRY HAD COME home in a reserved and cautious mood. He had a perfectly acceptable alibi for being late, but it would involve telling about the tie-up on the American Legion Bridge, and that would raise questions about why he had taken her to a restaurant in Virginia.

Elaine was at the dining room table wearing a headset and doing homework; Claude, sitting on the floor by the couch, tracing the latest Cadillacs from a brochure and adding his own details. Beth, curled up on the couch with a magazine, lifted her eyes when Harry came in and went on reading.

"Well!" Harry had said pleasantly, looking around. "Everybody in for the night? Should I lock up?"

"Jack's still out," Claude told him.

"Oh," said Harry, and added—unwisely, he discovered—"Where'd he go?"

"We might ask the same of you," Beth replied without taking her eyes off the page.

"Well, we had a long wait for dinner, but I think Stephanie appreciated the thought." Harry went over to the closet to hang up his sport coat. "The big problem was an accident on the beltway. I'll bet we sat there for two hours and couldn't move."

No one responded.

The flare-up didn't come until after both Elaine and Claude were upstairs. Harry went to the bedroom to undress. When Beth came in, she kicked off her shoes, then picked them up and threw them, as hard as she could, into the closet.

"Something eating you?" Harry asked.

"You need to *ask?* "

"Well, I'm asking, aren't I?"

"And should I ask if you and Stephanie enjoyed yourselves?"

"It was a so-so evening," he replied.

"And the other employees—they'll get a night out with the boss on their birthdays?" she snapped.

"It's not the same, and you know it. She virtually runs the store single-handed. It's the least I can do. I didn't expect to be home so late, but it's not my fault there was an accident. You'll probably read about it in the *Post* tomorrow."

"I'm not a fool, Harry. I'm not one of those wives who's the last to know."

"Know *what*?" He felt his own temper rising. Hell! The evening was a non-event, a wash-out, and he was still being raked over the coals.

"To know that something's going on between you and Stephanie," she said, her jaw so tense it trembled.

"I've *told* you," Harry said tersely. "Stephanie's a valued employee, and I enjoy her company."

"Oh, come on, Harry! *Say* it! She's your mistress and you're having an affair."

"She is not my mistress and it's not an affair! She's a special friend. I think I'm allowed to have friends."

"And what am I?"

"You're my wife, Beth! That's the difference."

"Really? Well, maybe I'd like to trade places. *I* want to be the one you get a haircut for and put on a clean shirt for. *I* want to be the one you take to lunch and dinner in your brand new underwear. Let *Stephanie* cook your meals and iron your shirts. Let me be the one who smells your after-shave, the one you take to some hotel while Stephanie stays home helping your kids with their homework."

"Beth, for Christ's sake, keep your voice down! I swear to you, nothing happened."

"I'm not your mother or your housekeeper, just keeping things humming so you'll have a nice secure place to come back to when the fling's over. I would rather hear nothing at all than be lied to, Harry."

"Look. I'm leveling with you. Stephanie's an attractive woman, but she's not you."

"Now that's profound."

"I like being with her, and I did give her a birthday kiss, but if you're thinking we made love, you're wrong. It's just a nice change, Beth. A break in the day." He didn't know if that would pass a lie detector test, but it was the best he could do.

"Change?" she had cried. "You never even want to change the furniture around, Harry. Like we might make some irreversible mistake. But you're willing to put our marriage at risk for a little 'change'?" And when he didn't answer, had no answer to give, she said, "Harry, if you were ever truthful to me, let it be now."

"I swear it! Ask Stephanie if you like."

"You know I wouldn't." Her face began to crumble. "Maybe it's true this time, but what about the next? What about all the other times you've taken her to lunch or dinner?"

"She only has one birthday a year, Beth."

There were tears in her eyes. Harry came over and put his arms around her. He pulled her to him and felt her tears moisten his shirt. He swallowed, stroking her hair. They heard Jack come in and go upstairs. Still they clung to each other. Finally Beth let go and went in the bathroom to bathe. But just before they went to sleep that night—a restless sleep for both of them—she had said, "The thing about life, Harry, is that sometimes when you take one path, you can't go back and take another. You have to choose."

It had been a week after Stephanie's birthday dinner before Beth would make love to Harry again. Yet even before she reached for him, even before Stephanie left the garden center for a job in a bank, Harry had known that it would have been a one-night stand with Stephanie—nothing more than a wet spot on a motel bed. He would not have given Beth up for that. It would have been more to his credit, of course, if he had told Stephanie that his marriage came first and their relationship would have to be strictly business. But Stephanie had gone, tension eased, and Harry had discovered how much he valued peace.

It was only when Iris came in around eight with a dinner from Boston Market that Harry realized he was still at his desk with an old bank statement in his hand. She wore a black tank top above her jeans and bracelets up one arm. Zeke immediately roused himself from the couch and went over to brush against her legs.

"You want some chicken?" she asked from the doorway.

"No, thanks," he said, and dropped the statement in the trash.

She set to work in the kitchen—the clink of a fork, the clunk of a plate. There was a pause, and Harry heard her say, "Did you know there's a Hungry Man dinner in the microwave? Don't you think it's about done?"

CLAUDE CALLED THE following evening.

"I think I saw Don," he said.

"You think?"

"I was in my car on MacArthur Boulevard, and I saw this man cross the road up ahead. He was carrying a sack. Groceries, maybe."

"And?"

"He disappeared into the trees."

"What makes you think it was Don?"

"Everything about him—big, burly, sort of stoop-shouldered. I couldn't see his face well or I'd know for sure. I just thought I'd mention it."

"Is there a house along there somewhere?"

"I don't know. I took a good look as I passed. Just woods. The canal. Maybe he's camping out, though I doubt it. Not on park property."

"If he's camping, he should be tired of it mighty quick," said Harry. "Wait till fall sets in."

"Fall's a long way off, Dad. I think Elaine wants to do something before then."

"Like what?"

"I don't know. Claim desertion or something. She calls pretty often. A lot of anger there."

"I know."

"Sue and I thought we might hike along the canal some evening, see what's there. I won't mention it to Elaine, though. Might not have been him after all."

"And even if it was. . . ." Harry offered.

"Exactly. What are we going to say? Listen, I've got some paintings in a show this weekend if you're interested."

"Oh? Where?"

"Here at the Yellow Barn in Glen Echo Park. Ten to four, Saturday and Sunday. Come by if you want."

THE AIR WAS heavy and warm on Sunday. Harry decided to drive to the exhibit as soon as it opened before the temperature rose any higher.

"Going to work in the greenhouse?" Iris asked him from the chaise lounge on the patio. Zeke was in her lap as usual, tom-cat that he was, and even though he'd been neutered, it always seemed to Harry that he was snuggled down as close to her crotch as he could get. He glared at the cat.

"No, Claude has some paintings in an art show at Glen Echo. I'm going to drive over and take a look."

"Didn't that used to be an amusement park?"

"You've never been?"

"No."

"Come if you want."

"Shorts okay?"

"Whatever you like."

As he waited for Iris, Harry realized how odd it seemed, going some place with her. He had hoped that the neighbors, seeing Harry's Lariat and Iris's Pontiac coming and going at different times, leading their separate lives, would conclude finally and rightly that neither had designs on the other.

Five minutes later Iris came down. She had taken to curling her long hair in a more attractive fashion, but she still—at thirty-seven or eight or nine—had not learned to put her clothes on properly. The cuff of one leg of her shorts was turned up, the cuff of the other hung down. The left strap of her tank top was caught under the strap of her bra. Silently Harry vowed to remove the full-length mirror from Elaine's room and put it in Claude's.

As they went out to the driveway, Harry saw Marge Decker sweeping her sidewalk. "Hi, Marge," he called.

She looked up, studied the tall, skinny-legged woman in the tank top and shorts, and went on vigorously sweeping without a word.

"Friend of yours?" Iris asked as Harry led her around to the Cadillac.

"Probably not," he said, and opened the car door.

Iris seemed glad for the chance to get out of the house and do something different. Harry automatically turned on the radio, but kept the volume down.

"How's your sister?" he asked. "The one who's pregnant?"

"Pukes every day. Did the same with her first kid. I'm sure glad I'm not there. She and her little girl and Kirsten are all in the same room now. 'The Grand Hotel,' Kirsten calls it."

"I've been wondering for some time," Harry said, realizing that he was going to have to word this carefully, "about the soil in your yard."

Iris turned. "The soil?"

"That pile of dirt."

"Oh, that. We got it free. A friend of my brother's got this fill for a customer and she changed her mind, so he just brought it home."

"Just dropped it there in your yard?"

"Where else would he put it?"

"That's a point." Harry tried to contain a smile. "I guess I was wondering why you keep it around. That day you saw me sitting outside your house, I was just curious. Being in the garden business, you know."

Iris opened a box of Tic Tacs, shook out a few and popped them in her mouth. She offered the box to Harry, but he declined.

"Why should you be curious?" she asked.

"Well, the dirt. I mean, it keeps moving!"

Iris shrugged. "We just haven't decided where to put it yet."

"But the work!"

"Oh, we all help. One of these days we'll get it right. Some people move furniture, Harry, and some people move dirt."

He smiled a little broader and turned the radio up a notch. The announcer said the next selection would be a fugue by Scarlatti. Harry didn't know fugue from fungus, but he decided that Scarlatti sounded something like Bach.

"You like this kind of music, huh?" Iris asked.

"Yes, I learned to like it some years back."

"I like country," Iris told him. "You ever hear Jeanette Fay sing *Take Your Love and Leave Me?* "

"Probably not," said Harry.

"Oh, it's the best song. She puts her whole heart in it, you know?"

Harry turned off the radio. "How does it go?" he asked.

"Well, I can't do it like Jeannette does, but here's the first verse." Iris began singing in a low, plaintive voice with a slight tremolo. Not half bad, Harry thought:

"When we met, you said you loved me,
When we kissed, you said you're true.
Tell me why, if love is lovely,
Do I sit and cry for you?"

She tipped back her head, and when Harry glanced over, he saw that her eyes were closed:

"I don't want another evening,
Waiting by the telephone.
Take your love, go on and leave me,
I can cry for you alone."

"Isn't that just the saddest song, Harry?"

"Hmmm," he said.

"She writes them herself. Some of these country singers, you know, have other people write their songs, but Jeanette's had three unhappy marriages, so she writes from the heart."

"You have a nice voice," he said.

"Thank you."

It was about then that Harry discovered he did not know what to talk about with someone her age. He did not always know what to talk about with his own children either, but if nothing else, he could ask if they still went to the same dentist.

"How's the car?" he said at last, out of desperation. "What kind of gas mileage are you getting?"

Iris stared at him, incredulous. "What kind of a question is *that?*"

He tried again. "How are you liking the Pontiac? Is it giving you any trouble?"

"It runs," said Iris. "The radio's shot, though." She stared straight ahead. "It's hard to talk to me, huh?"

"Oh, no! You do fine, Iris. I just . . . sometimes I don't know what to say to my kids, either."

"Really?"

"I think it's a male thing. We're different, you know, the way men and women look at things." Harry had no idea where this conversation was headed, but it was filling up space in the car, so he just kept going. "I remember when Jack was small, we took him to the circus, Beth and I. And when we got home, I was talking about the lion tamer and the flying trapeze. Beth talked about Jack, and how much he'd enjoyed it. How he'd sat on the edge of his seat, swinging his feet, and hadn't taken his eyes off the performers once. And it suddenly occurred to me that I had been watching the circus, but Beth had been watching Jack."

They were both quiet a moment.

"It's the same with my sister," said Iris. "She gets pregnant, and the guy takes off."

"I didn't 'take off,'" Harry said curtly. "I was *there* for them. I may have been watching the circus, but I was there."

"Oh, I didn't mean you. I just mean that men and women don't care in the same way. The baby's growing in *her* body, after all. If it was growing in yours, it would be different."

That was reassuring, somehow, coming from a woman. But the conversation had got off center and was accompanied by a feeling of unease on Harry's part. And then he knew what it was—the letter. Beth . . . babies . . . Would there always be this question mark about his wife, absurd as he felt it to be?

As they neared the Yellow Barn at Glen Echo, Harry directed his thoughts toward the exhibit, and hoped to see lots of cars in the parking area. There were only four, including his. If Beth were alive, she would have spent the last week calling friends, inviting them to the show. Harry gave himself points for simply showing up.

Iris got out and stretched. "I think my folks used to come here on Saturday nights to dance," she said. "I heard them talk about it."

"So did we," said Harry.

The Yellow Barn was a dilapidated building of painted wood and gray stone in the slow process of restoration. An artists' studio during the week, it was available for exhibits on Saturdays and

Sundays. It stood near the front of the park, just off MacArthur Boulevard. Inside, the large white room had been divided by movable partitions into smaller areas. Paintings hung so as to lure the visitor from one space to the next—still lifes next to abstracts next to Jackson Pollock imitations. The five or six viewers moved slowly along, listless in the humidity which even the ceiling fans could not dispel.

Claude came over. He looked particularly good, Harry noticed—white pants, white shirt with white stripes woven into the cloth.

"Hi!" he said to Harry. "You came!"

"Of course." Harry turned toward Iris. "Iris, this is Claude."

"Oh, hey!" she said. "I'm in your room." She held out her hand and Claude shook it cordially.

"Hope Dad cleaned out the drawers. Mom was a saver," he said. "I think she saved every paper I brought home from school, every picture I ever drew."

"I've got enough space," Iris said. She thrust her hands in the pockets of her shorts and hunched her shoulders slightly as she looked around. "These are all your paintings, huh?"

Claude laughed. "Hardly. Just a few. But take your time and look around."

Iris walked up to the first painting and stood two feet away, staring at a huge blob of orange and yellow paint that looked for all the world, Harry thought, like a squashed tomato. The paint was so thick in places that it protruded a quarter inch from the canvas.

"Sometimes it helps to stand back and let your eye take it in," Claude suggested.

"Oh." Iris moved back and studied it again. "What's it supposed to be?"

"Well, a friend of mine did this one. He calls it 'Reflection in Orange.' It can be whatever you like."

"But what's the point?"

Claude smiled. So did Harry. "That's the beauty of it, there is no point except that you see whatever you want to see in it."

Harry studied him as Claude moved off again. Who did he resemble the most? The broad forehead? Beth's. The deepset eyes? Harry's. The mouth? The chin? Not his, certainly. *Stop it!* he chided himself.

They walked around the perimeter of the little cubicle, and Harry decided, with a pang, that about two thirds of the artists showed more talent than his son. It pained him. Not that he was disappointed in Claude or even embarrassed for him. It was more a grieving that his son might spend a lifetime, perhaps, doing something he did only competently, but with no particular gift. When they reached the third room, with its paintings of sailboats listing left and sailboats listing right, Harry could not help but notice how the few wandering viewers scanned the work and walked on through.

He found himself standing in the doorway trying to *will* a couple to stop, to study and comment. When he saw that Claude was observing the scene from the opposite entrance, he wished with all his heart that Beth were there. She'd know what to do.

Do. That was the key word. She was so good at doing that she found it easier to do something tedious than to refrain from something pleasurable. Harry was exactly the opposite. For Harry, what could be easier than taking the path of least resistance—the *not* eating a favorite dish, for example, as opposed to writing a letter to a customer? To Harry, these were differences as distinct and profound as physical dissimilarities.

Iris had lingered at a picture in the previous room that seemed to have been painted sideways. In fact, she was leaning to one side, her head almost parallel to the floor, and finally straightened up again. She saw Harry waiting for her and went past him into the third room.

"Oh!" she said, and stood still. "Oh! Well!" She looked slowly about her, then went directly over to a sailboat against the most brilliant of sunsets, the brightest of yellows, the most vivid of crimsons. "This," she breathed, "is beautiful."

Harry watched as Iris moved along the wall of paint-box colors. Claude, observing still, seemed clearly pleased.

Was this a natural homing instinct? Harry wondered. How did

she *know*? Claude's signatures were the only interesting parts of his paintings, not decipherable in the least. She turned to Harry.

"How do you go about buying one of these? How much does this one cost?"

Claude came over. "There's a number by the title there on the wall. You ask at the desk over by the door, and they'll look it up for you."

"I really want this painting," Iris said to Harry. "That's *real* art! Did you ever see such a sunset?"

"Can't say that I have," he told her. "The composition's nice too." Harry put himself in full throttle. "The balance. See how the edge of the pine tree sort of balances the mast of the sailboat?"

"Yeah." Iris studied it some more. "Well, it's the sunset I like. It's like that Jeanette Fay song. It's got *feeling*, you know? Maybe you haven't ever seen a sunset that beautiful, but you'd like to, and so the artist imagined it for you." She leaned forward to read the sticker. "Number seventeen," she said, and went to find the sales desk.

An electromagnetic field, Harry decided. Women had radar that could detect emotional stress at a range of seventy feet and didn't even know they had it. Might not even have known the distress was there till they heard the beep. He remembered the way Beth used to look at one of the children on a family outing and say simply, "You need to go to the bathroom." There was not the slightest sign of discomfort that Harry could see, and yet—when he finally located a restroom for Jack or Claude—the kid barely made it before he let fly.

Harry followed Iris back to the desk. Sue was handling purchases. She wore a print vest over her beige T-shirt and pants, a Peruvian pattern of magenta and jade, and looked more attractive than Harry remembered. There was a wide gold band on her ring finger, a pendant around her neck. Behind her rose-colored lenses, her eyes lit up when Iris asked about number seventeen.

"Sunset Study II, by Claude Gill," she said, checking the list. "It's ninety-five dollars."

"That's Claude's?" Iris exclaimed. And then, in dismay, "Ninety-five dollars?"

"Well, it's framed. You get the whole thing," Sue told her.

Iris turned to Harry. "His are the best in the whole show."

"I know he's pleased that you like them so much," Harry said.

"Could I pay half now and half later?" Iris asked Sue.

"I'm sure we could arrange that," Harry said hastily, and Sue put a *sold* sticker on it.

Iris went back to admire the painting. "I just bought it!" she told a woman standing nearby.

The woman smiled.

On the ride home, Iris sat humming to herself, Sunset Study II on her lap. "I never owned an original painting before," she said. "I'm going to hang it above the dresser."

Harry said nothing, because along with his astonishment and gratitude was the realization that he could hardly evict her now. She had just purchased, on the installment plan, a piece of Harry's life. Something that belonged there in Claude's room. It was hers, but it belonged in his house.

IN LATE AFTERNOON when Iris had gone out for the evening, Harry walked to the dining room and stood for a moment before the green ceramic jar in the bay window. Emboldened at last, he lifted the lid and looked inside.

He had expected to see it filled almost to the top with ash. Instead, he found himself looking down upon a plastic bag about the size of a loaf of rye. Taking a breath, he put his hand in the jar and retrieved the package, then sat down in a dining room chair and placed it on his knees.

Strange to be sitting here like this, his wife on his lap. He had to know; had to touch her. Harry didn't understand why. It seemed necessary. He took the clip off the top, unrolled the bag, and gently,

gently, as though he were caressing a lock of Beth's hair, he fingered a handful of ash.

It was more coarse than fireplace ash, grainy, with small bits of bone in it. Holding some in the palm of his hand, he ran a finger over it. An eerie kind of closeness settled over him—a feeling that he had gone as far as he could with Beth, that he had shared in some small way her experience of death. He had been in the room with his wife when she died, had gently stroked her forehead. But this was a step beyond.

Slowly he let the ashes go. When he closed the bag and started to put it back, he noticed a folded piece of paper at the bottom of the jar.

He knew why his heart was pounding so as he reached in and got it. Was it possible that she had dictated a note to one of the nurses in those last few weeks—some little message to console Harry after she was gone? Had she, before she died, placed a confession in this jar, knowing that eventually Harry would find it?

He stopped, forcing himself to breathe more slowly for a few moments. Then he fumbled with the paper and leaned forward to read in the light from the window:

Dear Fletcher Patron:

In accordance with your wishes, we return to you the cremated remains of your loved one. It should be noted that due to the cremation process itself and the nature of the facilities, we cannot absolutely guarantee that all of the remains are included herein or that these are entirely those of your loved one. But we assure you that the procedure was carried out with dignity and respect for the person who shared your life.

THE BIGGEST PROBLEM Harry had so far with Iris was that she often tied up the phone. It wasn't so much a problem for him, it was that others complained. She couldn't afford a cell phone, she'd told him.

"Harry, what the heck?" came Wade's voice on the answering machine. "Either you're never there or the damn line's busy, and I forgot your cell phone number. You need anything from the store, you call me." They talked in code, these brothers. They talked groceries instead of loneliness; offered errands in place of love.

"Wade never paid me a compliment in his entire life," Beth had complained once to Harry. "In fact, I could put all the words he ever said to me on the back of an envelope."

"Well, he's never paid me a compliment either," Harry had told her, but it was no secret that Beth had never liked his brother, and didn't make conversing easy for him.

One phone call from the Mitchells slipped through, however.

"Now listen, Harry. It's not everybody who gets a second chance. The lady from New York's going to be in town again next weekend. I know it may feel a little soon for you, but why don't I set up something for the two of you? Rita says she's not going to cook again unless you promise to show up."

"No, don't do that, Windy. Every blind date I ever had was a bust."

"This woman's a looker. I'm not kidding!"

"I'm not interested in—"

"Bull. Don't give me that."

"I'm no fun anymore, Windy."

"You've got to get *out*, fella! You can't just shut yourself up in a house full of memories! They'll eat you alive! Listen, she doesn't get down here that often. May not be back this way for six months. Hell, she could be married by then."

"Why don't you give me her phone number and I'll call her. I'll set up something myself." He was beginning to hate Windy. *Could* it have been Beth and Windy?

"*Now* you're talking! Set something up for the two of you, and Rita and I will play dumb. Got a pencil?"

Harry wrote the number down, but when he looked at it again later, he couldn't tell if the last digit was a zero or an eight. Saved.

ELAINE BROUGHT JODIE by on Tuesday.

"I'll be back in about an hour and a half, Dad," she said. "Each session's fifty minutes."

"Take your time," he said.

The minute the door closed behind her, Jodie trained her eyes on Harry.

"Well?" she asked. "What are we going to do?"

There it was again. *Do*. Beth must have left a list somewhere.

"Maybe you could suggest something," Harry said.

"That's *your* job."

My God, was this going to be another Elaine? What was the harm in letting kids figure out some things for themselves?

"Well, what do you *like* to do? Maybe we don't like the same things."

"Grandma always liked what *I* did."

"Well, I'm not your grandma, Jodie. I'm going to finish the newspaper, but there are puzzles over there you could try." He amazed himself.

Jodie went across the room to the game shelf beside the fireplace and returned with a five-hundred piece jigsaw puzzle of a covered bridge. Kneeling beside the coffee table, she dumped the contents out and sat looking at him, chin in her hands, fists pushing back the skin at the sides of her eyes.

"It might be easier if you turned all the pieces right side up first," Harry told her.

Dutifully she set to work, and Harry figured he had a good five minutes before the task was completed. He settled down with the editorial page. When he looked up again, however, Jodie was leaning back against the couch, eyes accusing. All the pieces were turned right-side up.

"See here." Harry leaned forward. "What you have to look for are pieces with straight sides, like this." He propped up the lid of the box at one end of the table as their model.

"Here's one, Grandpa!"

"Hey, that's a corner piece! Very good. Check it out." He watched as she studied the piece in her hand. "Sometimes you have to turn it a little."

They set to work looking for straight-sided pieces, and when Elaine came in later that evening the border was finished.

"We'll do some more next week," Harry said to his granddaughter.

"But guess what!" she said brightly, with mock exasperation, hands on her hips. "You didn't give me anything to eat, Grandpa!"

Harry laughed.

"Why don't you give Jodie some ice cream to eat in the kitchen, Dad, and we can talk a little in here," Elaine suggested.

"What are you going to talk about?" asked Jodie.

"Just grown-up things."

She's found out something about Don, Harry guessed. He took Jodie to the kitchen, gave her a dish of fudge mocha, closed the mahogany door and came back to the sofa. Elaine was holding a sheet of paper and a pen.

"This therapist thinks that my problems with Don go a lot deeper than what happened after the funeral service. She's right, of course. But she feels that everything that happens to you in later life can be traced to a specific event in your first four years."

"Right," said Harry. "Beth was born, therefore she died." He did not mean it to sound as sarcastic as it did.

Elaine was patient. "She's doing this study, Dad, to see if she can predict what kind of problems a new client's having based on what happened in early childhood."

"You find her through the Yellow Pages?"

"This friend at school says it's really uncanny the way she can analyze things. Linda, the therapist, gives a discount to clients who agree to be in her study, so I said sure. I think she's going to publish. We'll all be anonymous, of course."

"Okay, shoot. What do you need to know?"

Elaine scanned the list. "How old was I when I was toilet trained?"

"Certainly by the time you started kindergarten."

"You don't *know?* "

"You want the day and the hour?"

"Don't kid around, please. Things like this are important."

"Well, maybe your mother made notes in your baby book or something."

Elaine moved her pen down to the next question. "How was I disciplined? Was I ever spanked?"

"You bet your booties."

Elaine cast him a look. "I don't think that will get you any points, Dad. Did I ever have separation anxiety? Fears? Phobias?"

Goddam you, Don Wheeler! Harry was thinking. Why the hell did he pull something like this on Elaine right after Beth passed away? If he was going to leave her, why couldn't he have done it while Beth was around to answer these fucking questions?

He grasped at straws. "I think you were afraid of snakes, maybe."

"Snakes? When did I see any snakes?"

"I suppose you might have, at some time or other."

The door to the kitchen swung open. "I'm done!" Jodie said. There was chocolate down the front of her T-shirt.

"Just a few minutes more, honey," Elaine said. "Go back in the kitchen."

"I'm *done!* "

"Then go wash the chocolate off your shirt," Elaine said.

"How?" she whined.

"Go outside and use the hose," Harry growled.

"Dad!" said Elaine. "Pull a chair over to the sink and use the dishcloth."

Jodie banged back into the kitchen.

"One more," said Elaine. "Did I ever witness parental nudity or the primal scene?"

"The primal scene?" Harry exploded. "The primal *scene?* You think we sold tickets and herded you kids into the bedroom? This therapist have a problem or something?" *If one of the kids wasn't his, please let it be Elaine!*

"I'm just trying to get it right."

"Well, I'm sorry, but you're asking the wrong person. Your mom might have had the answers. I don't. Yes, you may have seen me step out of the shower a time or two, and no, you did not, to the best of my knowledge, witness the primal scene unless you were hiding in the closet."

Elaine jotted down his answers on the sheet of paper just as the sound of splashing water came from the kitchen. Harry found Jodie trying to pour a glass of water down her shirt front.

"Okay, kid, time to hit the road," he said, mopping up. "See you next week."

"Thanks, Dad," Elaine told him, taking out her car keys. "I'll treat you to dinner sometime soon."

"Elaine," Harry said as Jodie skipped on outside and was jumping about on the steps. "Let me ask you: Is there any possibility Don would take all the money from your bank account and wipe you out?"

"Jack asked me the same thing. He thinks I should close it and open another in my name only. But last week Don made a six-hundred dollar deposit in our checking account."

"That's encouraging."

"Is it?"

"It means he's working somewhere, I would think, and wants to provide for you and Jodie."

"Sure. He just doesn't want to live with us. How is that supposed to make me feel?" The shrillness was in her voice again. There were times Beth had sounded like that, and Harry had to admit Elaine got it from her mother.

"It's supposed to show he cares, maybe, and for now, you'll have to settle for that."

"I guess."

He watched them drive off and wondered what he really knew

about any of his children? This therapist of Elaine's was going to go down a checklist and tell his daughter's fortune, while Harry, who had known Elaine all her life, couldn't even begin to guess.

As he turned away from the window, he remembered the cat.

"Zeke?" he called, and tried to imitate Beth. "Zeke? Zeke?"

Nothing.

Harry went from room to room, turning on lights and looking around the furniture. He found the cat at last, upstairs on Iris's bed. Even though she was out for the evening, there was the scent of her shampoo. Zeke opened his eyes, yawned, stretched, and then—with claws extending and retracting in pleasure—settled down once more against her pillow.

Harry went back down and phoned.

"Windy," he said. "I haven't called her yet."

"I know, you son-of-a-bitch. I already checked. You're missing a good thing, Harry. If it weren't for Rita, I'd snap that woman up. Get her between the sheets, at least."

Yeah, you go, boy, damn you! Harry thought. "I couldn't read her phone number. That last digit."

"Shit, Harry! Why didn't you *call* me? It's an eight! It's a goddam eight! *Call* her!"

"Oh, I just don't—"

"She knows all about you—all you've been through. She knows about Beth. I told her how happy you two were together, and she said it's like she'd known you both for years. *Call* her!"

"I'll think about it," Harry said, and hung up.

He knew that if he took his hand off the phone, his resolve would disappear. This would be either one of the best things he had ever done—a step, at least, in the right direction—or an enormous mistake. The fact was, when he thought about women at all, the married ones seemed more attractive. Single women were more desperate, some of them. But hell, he was desperate too. Who was he kidding? He thought of Zeke sleeping upstairs, secure and loved on Iris's bed, while he slept alone downstairs, and he lifted the phone once again.

It rang four and a half times, and it wasn't until a woman's voice said hello that Harry realized he didn't even remember her name. He had her phone number but not her name.

"Hello?" the voice came again, slightly louder.

He couldn't hang up. She'd be expecting his call. She probably had caller ID. He'd have to wing it.

"Uh, hello. I wonder if I'm calling at a bad time. This is Harry Gill, and I think we have some mutual friends in the Mitchells."

"Hello, Harry." Her voice was low, smooth. It was the most comforting, terrifying, reassuring, disorienting sound Harry had heard in some time. "Windy's told me all about you."

"Oh?"

"Any friend of Windy's and Rita's is a friend of mine," the voice said.This was too fast. Too easy. She was leading, and Harry had never learned to dance that way.

"I'm so sorry about your wife. Rita showed me some pictures of the two of you together. It must be hard. . . ."

"Yes, it is. I miss her a lot."

"I'm sure you do."

"Unless you lose a spouse, I guess, you just don't know."

"I think not. I've never had the misfortune."

"Anyway," he said quickly, "Windy said you were coming down next weekend, and I thought . . . well, perhaps we. . . ."

"I'd love to meet you, Harry."

He swallowed.

"What did you have in mind?" she asked.

Words ricocheted around in Harry's head. *Companionship, conversation, dinner and sex? A meaningful relationship and ultimately marriage?* His wife had only been gone for three months, her ashes not even disposed of yet, and already he was inviting another woman into his life, name unknown.

"Have you . . . ever been to the Chesapeake Bay?" he asked in desperation, his head trying to keep pace with his mouth.

"Not for a very long time," the woman said. "But I love the

water. What were you planning to do?"

"Well, I thought . . . perhaps we could drive over to the Bay and . . . scatter Beth's ashes. . . ."

There was a silence so long, so deadly, that it almost had a ring to it—an echo inside Harry's head.

"Why on earth would you ask me to do that?" said the woman at last. "I didn't even *know* her."

Harry reeled. "I'm sorry. I just . . . I thought . . . Look, this was all a very bad idea. I'm sorry to have bothered you." And he hung up.

He sat staring at the clock. Nine forty-three. They should lock up men who had lost their wives, he decided. Such men should not be allowed to go out in polite society. They should all be placed in a ceremonial house until a year or two of mourning had been completed.

The enormity of the debacle made his body flash first hot, then cold. He opened the phone book to Liz's name and called. "Liz? Harry. I've done something incredibly stupid."

"Tell me."

He did.

"God Almighty, Harry!"

"I think I'm cracking up."

"No, Harry, you know what it means? It means you're alive. Some days the only way you know you're alive is you do something so stupid that you have to surface. You come up for air."

He was hyperventilating. He could hear his own breathing coming back to him.

"Listen, Harry. You know what I do when I can't take it any longer?"

"What?"

"I drive to the drugstore and call my own number."

"What?"

"I listen to Max's voice on the answering machine and I sit there in the booth and talk back to him. Then I cry."

His second mistake of the evening—calling Liz. "Oh, I'm sorry, someone's at the door. Can I call you back?" he asked.

"Sure," she said.

He didn't call back.

The evening wasn't over yet, however. At twenty past ten, Windy called.

"Harry, you okay?"

"No. I'm a raving lunatic."

"That's what Connie told me."

"That's her name?"

"Harry, have you been drinking?"

"Not a drop."

"She phoned me after you called. She thinks you're a nut case. She says you asked her out to scatter Beth's ashes."

"That's exactly what I did."

"She hasn't even met Beth!"

"I thought you told her all about us."

"I did, but Harry, Harry, listen to me! You invite a woman to the Chesapeake Bay, she's thinking 'boat.' She's thinking 'sailing.' 'Drinks on the water.' That kind of thing."

"I told you it was a bad idea. No more set-ups, okay?"

There was one more phone call that evening. Harry had just taken off his shirt and was untying his shoes when the ring cut through the silence of the bedroom.

"Dad," came Jack's voice. "I'm in kind of a jam, and can't reach Jennifer. I'm here at the laundry, and need a ride home. I just went out to the parking lot, and all my tires are slashed."

SEVEN

The Pizza

HARRY STOOD OUT in the July midnight, hands in his pockets, and looked at the Lexus squatting there on the asphalt. Someone was out to get them? Both him and Jack?

"So how do you explain this?" he asked. "This guy Arlo, he have anything to do with it?"

Jack shrugged, saying nothing.

"What's happening, Jack?"

This time there was an edge to his son's voice. "Look, Dad. I don't *know* who did this. Okay?"

"Are you in debt? Seriously, I mean?"

"I'm always in debt. What else is new? You don't start a business without going in debt."

"How much?"

"I'm not asking for a loan."

"I'm not offering any. Just asking how much."

"I can handle it."

They got in the DeVille and drove to Jack's apartment near East-West Highway. Like Jack himself, the high rise was extravagant, its curving balconies, terraced walkways and pool more like a country club than an apartment complex.

"This Jennifer, is she your current girl friend?"

"Something like that," Jack answered. "Listen, Dad, I really appreciate the ride. Don't worry about me, okay? I've just got some business problems, that's all, and what happened tonight I needed like a hole in the head." He opened the car door and put out one foot.

"Okay," said Harry. "But Jack . . . leave off the horses or whatever you're betting on. You need that like a hole in the head too. It's not helping."

Jack reached over and squeezed his arm. "G'night. I'll get Claude to drive over with some tires tomorrow. Sorry to add this to your own life right now."

Harry sat in his car and watched Jack go up the steps to the sidewalk, shoulders drooping slightly, then up more steps to the front door with its brass panels gleaming beneath the globes overhead.

"Jack, Jack, Jack," Harry breathed, watching him go inside. Through the glass doors he could see into the lobby, the contemporary paper on its walls, the huge black lamp, the black and white silk flowers.

He felt his own shoulders give and sat for some time on the circular drive, hands resting loosely on the wheel. What more could he have done? How do you sit by and watch a son, your first-born, self-destruct? All his stored-up fatherly love wouldn't save him. How long had Jack's gambling been going on? At what point had it all begun? You might as well ask when Elaine was toilet trained. He simply didn't know.

He chose a back way home this time, over deserted streets, the windows of the Cadillac down, radio off, only the hum of the motor audible along with night sounds of crickets and katydids. He liked the quiet, liked seeing a different mood settle over streets and neighborhoods. The loneliness of night did not seem so intense when he was in a moving car, the dark air heavy with the scent of honeysuckle.

A light shown from Iris's window as Harry pulled in the drive. It was good to see it, as though someone were waiting up for him. When he got inside, he heard voices coming from above. He stopped in the hallway, listening.

It was another female voice, and a moment later Iris called down, "Hi, Harry. My niece is here, okay?"

"Fine," said Harry, and went to bed.

When he got up Wednesday morning, a teenage girl—sixteen or seventeen—was sitting groggily in the kitchen eating corn flakes. She hastily wiped one hand over her mouth when she saw him, and swallowed.

"Good morning," said Harry, as though strange young women appeared at his breakfast table with regularity.

"Hi," she said. "I'm Kirsten."

"Iris's niece."

"Yeah. Except we're more like cousins? I mean, I don't call her 'aunt' or anything?"

When did young people start speaking in question marks, Harry wondered, but answered with a question of his own. "Iris up?"

"She's in the shower. She's driving me to summer school? I flunked a course last semester."

"Oh. What grade will you be in?"

"Senior." She grinned. "This will be my last year."

Harry started the coffee and set the cream on the table, glancing now and then at his visitor. Kirsten had a rather chunky build, with long brown hair and a pretty, childlike face. Both she and her aunt had the same heavy-lidded eyes. Kirsten could be Iris's daughter for all he knew, but he didn't believe that somehow.

He put bread in the toaster, then broke two eggs into a skillet.

"What are you going to do after high school?" he asked.

"Job somewhere? Iris said maybe she could get me in at Hecht's? I'll probably get married in a couple of years."

"Oh. A boyfriend, then."

"Of course." She took another spoonful of cereal. "He works at the AutoWash on Rockville Pike? You ever need a Simonize, I could get you a discount."

"That's good to know," said Harry.

Kirsten looked at her watch. "Well, gotta run." She started to leave the room, then stopped and carefully picked up her dishes, depositing them in the sink.

A few minutes later Harry heard both Iris and Kirsten come downstairs and drive away in Iris's car. He rinsed off Kirsten's dishes and put them in the dishwasher, wondering if he should have some kind of house rules.

It was noon when Claude called him at work. Harry was in his office tallying Tuesday's receipts.

"It's Claude, Harry," came Wanda's voice over the intercom. "Will you take the call in there?"

"Yes."

Then Claude: "Dad, I just took the morning off to pick up some tires for Jack. What's with him?"

"I was hoping you could tell me."

"He says it was probably some neighborhood kids."

"And his were the only tires slashed? All four of them?"

"Yeah, I told him I didn't quite buy that either."

"Claude, did you ever hear Jack mention someone named Arlo?"

"No, why?"

"I wondered if there's a connection. Someone named Arlo's been looking for him." Harry paused. "Is that Italian—Arlo?"

"I haven't the faintest idea. Anyway, I just wanted you to know that Jack's got a car again. He said you drove him home last night, I thought you might be worrying." A pause. "How are *you* doing?"

"Holding up. How about you?"

"I miss Mom a lot. More than I imagined, really. Anyway, I'll talk to you later."

Harry liked to be asked how he was doing. Nobody asked that much anymore. The difference between the first month after his wife's death and the second had not been so profound, but there was a noticeable change now that it was July. As though people supposed the hurt had healed somewhat, and that asking how Harry was doing, not to mention *talking* about Beth, would be like picking at a scab. It was the aloneness of grief that struck him—a singular sadness.

Wanda always gave him a warm "Good morning;" Tracy, with her serious demeanor, never changed from day to day. The men assigned to the trees and shrubs worked in green polo shirts with *Gills* on the pockets, but in the heat of the July afternoons, they frequently stripped bare to the waist, and their brown limbs glistened golden-tan as they lifted saplings or unloaded a truck. No one said the words "Beth" or "wife" or even "Mrs. Gill."

Of Bill and Steve, who supervised the outdoor work, Bill was the larger, with black hair that covered his chest before dwindling down to a fine line dividing his rib cage, then disappearing behind the buckle of his belt. His cut-offs were frayed and thinned almost to the point of indecency. Steve, a biker, rode in every morning in his Spandex shorts.

Harry couldn't help envying their youth, their health, their strong white teeth, their animal fragrance. How could his own flabby body compete with theirs? Not that he had let his go to pot, but he'd noticed the fold of skin beneath his chin, the wrinkles developing on his abdomen, receding gums. . . . The list was endless.

Live! he silently urged them. *Risk, you golden-backed boys of summer! You'll lose it all in the end.*

It was the apparent normalcy of the days that bothered Harry, as though anyone could assume that he was the same man he had been before. He was not the same. The whole world was divided between those who had lost a spouse and those who had not, and the bone-crushing, soul-dampening magnitude of what had happened to him made him feel old.

The one person especially calibrated to Harry's moods was, strangely, Rose. It unnerved him sometimes, the way she read his face each morning, like a cartographer studying a map, and then her own face took on whatever degree of sadness or resignation, courage or cheerfulness he might be feeling. He was almost tempted on occasion to pull out a pocket handkerchief and weep profusely to see if Rose would cry along, and wondered idly if she might have had anything to do with the Madonna's tears.

One of the things Harry did when he needed a lift, however, was get a haircut. He liked to drive to Jim Swann's over the lunch hour when Leroy and Fred were likely to show up.

Jim was standing in the doorway in his nylon shirt, one hand against the frame. He grinned when he saw Harry.

"Well, well, well! Decided to chop off that mane, huh?"

Harry followed him inside and climbed into the chair. "Where's Leroy today?"

"Oh, he'll be by, I imagine. Been having some trouble with gout. How you doing?"

"I'm still here. That's about the sum of it. Took in a boarder."

Jim shook out the cape and put it around Harry's neck. "So I've heard."

"Customer at the garden center sort of down on her luck. I figured she could use one of the kids' rooms for a while. Sure don't need it myself."

Jim took the comb and scissors from his pocket and began to snip. "The way I see it, Harry, nobody else is in the same situation exactly, and you've got to call the shots. Nobody's business but yours."

Harry studied him in the mirror. "What's that supposed to mean?"

"Oh, you know. People don't have anything to gossip about, they'll invent something."

"What's there to say?"

"What do they ever say? Your wife's not been in the ground three months and already you're sharing your bed with a girl no older than your daughter. That sort of thing."

"Well, they're wrong on two counts," said Harry. "She's older than Elaine and she's not in my bed." Three counts, actually. Beth was not in the ground, either.

"That's how I figured it, but you know, Virginia was saying just the other day, 'What Harry needs is a love interest.'"

"Furthest thing from my mind right now. Every morning I get up, I've got to face the fact all over again that Beth's gone. You'd think it would have sunk in by now, but every morning it's new."

Fred Fletcher and Leroy Schneider came in together while Harry was talking, Leroy with a sandwich rolled up in butcher paper stuck beneath his arm, and Fred with a sack from the hardware store. Fred smiled with sympathetic eyes, but Leroy's had a decided twinkle as he sat down at the card table by the window.

"The Casanova himself," said Leroy, studying Harry, prepared for a good time. Jim Swann, working on Harry's sideburns, smiled even broader, but Fred Fletcher looked nonplused.

"Seems our Harry took in a boarder," Leroy said by way of explanation, "and one of Harry's neighbors has been burning up the phone lines."

Harry was exasperated. "Sounds to me like Marge Decker doesn't have enough to do," he said. "I'm letting a woman customer use Claude's room, while she saves up some money for college. As simple as that. She's gone most evenings and I don't even see her."

Fletcher leaned back in his folding chair, head resting against the wall, fingertips touching in his lap. "I can imagine," he said, "that a young woman might find an older man attractive who works with flowers and living things. Young women are always attracted to garden centers."

Leroy gave a chuckle. "And living right there with Harry, she can get her petunia watered whenever she wants."

A rumble came from Jim's throat as well: "Her petals plucked," he said.

"Her soil fertilized," coughed Leroy, amid the chuckles.

Fred looked from Jim to Leroy and back to Harry again, but Harry dismissed it with a wave of the hand. "Have your fun, boys."

"Hey, listen, Harry," Fred said. "I was telling Leroy. I've got this friend with a cottage over on the Eastern shore. He's going out of state next weekend. Jim's going to close up shop that Saturday and we'll all drive over for a couple of days. Do a little fishing, a little golf, get some barbecued ribs in Easton. You come with us."

"Can't. We've got this huge sale at the garden center."

"You'd like it, Harry," urged Jim.

"You don't like to fish, you can stretch out on the porch," said Fred. "We'll take some beer, send out for chicken—not a thing to do but relax."

Harry would have loved to go. He imagined himself sitting out on a dock with a rod and reel, talking with old friends. "Just can't do it," he said. "I told the rest of them nobody gets off next weekend. We've got all our spring flowers to unload before summer burns 'em up. Weekend after, maybe."

"It's the one weekend he offered," Fred said. "And it's his cottage."

"Well, I'm sorry. I'd sure like to go," Harry told them. "You boys go catch a ten-pound bass for me."

"We're sorry too," said Fred.

Leroy was unable to stop himself. "Don't feel *too* sorry for Harry, now. He has his compensations. What's her name? Iris, was that it? He'll be cultivating his Iris, maybe."

"Checking her buds," Jim chuckled.

"Plowing her bottom land," yelped Leroy, slapping one hand on the table, and the shop exploded in laughter, Harry's included.

HARD AS HE tried, Harry could not forget the letter sitting beneath the blotter on his desk. Somehow, when he tried to picture his wife making love to another man, he sensed it would be more out of revenge than love. And the one time she had been angry enough to cheat, he decided, was over the non-affair with Stephanie Morrison.

After Stephanie had given her two weeks' notice and things had settled down, Harry had felt himself forgiven. But what if it had festered all those years in Beth? What if her feelings for him had never been the same after that—the dreaded proof that we are not loved unconditionally? Loss of her love, then as now, was also loss of self. Of mooring.

The irony was that the years after that, up until Beth's illness, had been some of the most satisfying of their marriage. He and Beth became more aware of each other, and Harry found solace in the fact that he had really tried to make her happy. More than that, he had *wanted* her to be happy.

But it made no difference as far as the letter. Their last child was in seventh grade when Harry took Stephanie to dinner. Whatever sin Beth may have committed would have happened a long time before that. Could he, in turn, forgive her? Could he forgive the intrusion of another man's child he had supported all these years, father unknown? Was it someone he saw every day? Passed on the street?

So what was he going to do? he asked himself. Tell his kids about the letter and suggest they submit to DNA testing? Destroy their faith in their mother?

He imagined calling Jack and making the request.

Are you nuts? Jack would say.

He imagined calling Elaine.

How can you do this to Mom?

He thought of calling Claude. And for reasons he didn't know, he abruptly reached for the remote, turned on the TV, and put his mind on the evening news.

HE WAS GLAD for the extra work at the garden center. Harry organized the sale tables, dividing the plants between sun, sun/shade, shade, and posting the signs Wanda was painting, marking down the shrubs which cried to be planted before the August sun parched them irreparably.

He also tried not to think of Jim and Fred and Leroy lolling on the Eastern shore, and wished he could have gone. How many chances did you get to be with old friends in a rent-free cottage? If it weren't a two-day sale, he would drive over that evening, but one of the drawbacks to owning your own business was that you often had to say no.

Saturday night he made himself a late supper of fried potatoes and ham. Iris had gone home for a few days and Harry was just putting some forks in the dishwasher when the doorbell rang.

He shook the water off his hands, rubbing one sleeve of his T-shirt over his forehead, and went down the hall, lifting Zeke out of the way with his foot and depositing his body in the bedroom. Cats had a way of doing that: determining where you were about to put your feet and staying one step ahead of you.

He opened the door to find Virginia in the July twilight, smiling at him tentatively, her hair long and loose about the shoulders.

"Hi, Harry. Could I come in?"

"Virginia!" Harry stood dumbfounded.

She stepped inside and closed the door.

"Where's Jim?" Harry asked quizzically.

"Fishing, remember? The guys? They'll be back tomorrow."

Jesus, Joseph. . . .!

"I can't help myself, Harry. I saw the way you were looking at me at our place. The crab feast?"

Harry stared at her. "Virginia!" he said again.

"Shhhh." She reached up and put one finger on his lips. "I know how this looks, Harry, but we're all adults, right? We're grown up. It won't change a thing.'"

"But Jim?"

"What about him? He's a wonderful guy." She stepped closer and put her arms around Harry's waist, smiling up at him with her gray-green eyes, all the little lines of her face pleading.

"Listen, Ginny," he said, "he's been my friend for a real long time."

"I know. But sometimes we need a change. A little appetizer. Nothing heavy-duty. No strings, no obligations. And tomorrow, I promise, we'll never mention it again. We'll forget it ever happened."

She withdrew her hands and slowly parted the front of her rayon blouse which, Harry realized, had been left unbuttoned. She was nude from the waist up. Her breasts, sagging slightly, tilted in his direction. She took his hands and put them on her breasts. The nipples seemed to give off an electric charge against his palms, and Harry drew back.

"Virginia, let's don't do this." Harry gently clasped her wrists. "Please."

She studied him intently, head cocked to one side, eyes playful. "Are you rejecting me?"

"How could anyone reject you? I'm just saying I don't want to do this to Jim. I wouldn't want someone doing it to me."

"How can it hurt, Harry? How would he know?"

"We'd know."

"I can't believe you!" She shook her wrists free and gave him a mocking look.

"Neither can I." Harry smiled. "Come on. You want some coffee?"

"Before or after?"

He ignored it. "Go ahead. Sit down and I'll get you a cup," he said. "I was just doing the dishes."

"The answer's no, then?" She followed him halfway down the hall toward the kitchen.

"It's no," he said gently, and went over to the stove. But he had scarcely got the mugs from the shelf when he heard the front door click and then, a minute later, the sound of Virginia's car pulling away.

"THANK YOU," HE said to Wanda the next day as bargain hunters milled about the sale tables.

The statuesque woman in the jade green dress turned toward him, pausing over the philodendron she was re-potting for a customer. "What for, Harry?"

"For not making a play for me since Beth died," he told her.

Hilarity danced in her eyes beneath the arched brows. "Why, Mr. G! I've been flirting with you for the past twelve years, and you just never noticed."

He looked at her with such consternation that she burst into laughter. "Listen," she said. "I've got one man to please, and that's enough. But if I was single, I'd chase you from here to Baltimore."

Harry found himself whistling later as he tagged a tree.

That evening as he finished up the potatoes he hadn't used the night before and heated the leftover ham, the doorbell rang again. What was he, caught in some kind of time warp? Virginia didn't take no for an answer? He glanced at the clock. It couldn't be Virginia. Jim would be home by now. Harry considered not answering, but knew he couldn't stand the suspense. The drapes had been drawn for the night, so he couldn't see the porch. He walked to the door in his bare feet and opened it.

In the split second it happened, Harry's first impression was that of the full moon coming toward him at lightning speed and suddenly his face collided hard with something flat and warm and fragrant and sticky. He almost toppled backward from the force, his nose stinging from the frontal attack. As he fought to disentangle his face from the cheese, a man's voice said, "Here's Italian!" before footsteps receded on the porch, a door slammed, and there was the sound of a motor racing as a vehicle roared off down the otherwise quiet street.

HARRY GOT ON the phone to Jack.

"What's up, Dad?"

"I just got attacked by a pizza," Harry said.

A pause, then a laugh. "You *what?*"

"It's the darndest thing. A few months ago it was tomato sauce on the hood of my truck, and a note saying *You like Italian? Here's Italian.* Tonight it's a pizza in the face. You sure this Arlo guy isn't Italian? Part of the Mafia or something?"

"Dad, believe me, Arlo isn't interested in you."

"Well, the first time it happened, you'd been here in the house. We'd had dinner that night, the night after the funeral service."

"And tonight? I wasn't anywhere near your place tonight."

"Right," said Harry, considering. "I don't know what to make of it. I'm taking care of Jodie on Tuesday nights while Elaine sees a therapist, and I'd hate to have some nut hanging around while she's here."

"The pizza stalker," Jack said, laughter in his voice.

"It's not that funny to me."

"Sorry, Pop. My guess is that it's some disgruntled supplier. You importing something from Italy now that you used to get here in the states? Planters? Urns? Garden ornaments—that kind of thing?"

"Well, that's a thought. But I haven't. Using the same suppliers I always did."

"Maybe it's time to report it, Dad."

"Call 911, you mean? Tell them I just got hit with a pizza?" They both began to laugh. "Anyway, how goes it with you?" Harry said. "How are things?"

"Not bad. Business is good. Got a few bills paid last week."

"Jack," Harry began, and wasn't sure just what he was going to say next. "Was there . . . was there ever anything your mother told you that she didn't tell me?"

Silence. "Like what?"

"Oh, anything at all. Anything I should know?"

"What got you started on this, Dad? You think the pizza stalker is connected to Mom somehow?"

"No, no, of course not. It's just natural, I guess, after you lose somebody, to want to know all about her after she's not here to ask."

"Nobody knew her better or longer than you did, Dad."

"That's true."

"If Mom had any secrets, she probably would have told Elaine, not me."

"I suppose. Look, forget I ever brought it up. You lose someone, you go a little crazy for a while."

"It's understandable," Jack said.

"I even began to wonder if Don had anything to do with all this."

"I can't imagine him pulling something like that. He thought you were cool, Dad. Even Elaine would tell you that. Listen. Get some sleep. You sound tired."

"I am, I guess."

"Take care."

MONDAY AFTER WORK, as Harry was leafing through his mail at the kitchen table, he came across an envelope addressed to Harry M. Dill, the same last name that had appeared on six other envelopes since he had entered the world of the bereaved: a brochure for cemetery plots, an advertisement for a life-care community, and a medical supply catalog selling blood-pressure kits, hernia trusses, knee braces, and a men's brief called Sir Dignity Plus for incontinent males. He was about to toss it all when the word *confidential* caught his eye on still another envelope, and he opened it to find a letter from a dating service, with a questionnaire he was invited to fill out. There were fifty statements, and the same five possible answers for each one: *a) definitely agree, b) agree, c) undecided, d) disagree, e) definitely disagree.*

The first statement: *I would never fly in a plane with a female pilot.* Harry smiled to himself and sat down.

Number two: It would be no problem for me to spend a week by myself. Three: I am in favor of any sexual activity that brings people pleasure; Four: Science can explain the world without the need for a Supreme Being.

So this was how young singles hooked up these days! How had couples of his generation ever made it to their first anniversary, he wondered, when all they asked of each other was Republican or Democrat, chocolate or vanilla, your place or mine? He was still reading when Iris came in.

"Homework?" she asked as she dropped her shoulder bag on the counter and reached for the jug of ice water in the refrigerator. "Looks like a multiple-choice test."

Harry chuckled. "It's a dating service. Suddenly everyone knows what's good for me."

Iris took a sip of water. "Well, Harry, you never know. Don't try to find someone through a personal ad, though. Boy, you sure get some weirdos."

Harry tossed the questionnaire in the trash and opened his gas bill. "You've tried, I take it?"

"Once. A friend of mine talked me into it. My ad ran for a month and I got seventeen replies. I agreed to meet four of them, and I sure learned a lot."

"Yeah?"

"Any guy who only wants to see you at lunch time or after work—especially at some place dark—never on evenings or weekends, is married. That's number one. Any guy who says 'looks unimportant' is probably pretty unspectacular himself. ACDC, of course, means bi-sexual, so you could end up going out with a couple; 'youthful looking' means he's probably ancient; and if a guy wants to correspond for a while before you meet him, he's fat."

Harry had to laugh. "I imagine you could find yourself in some dangerous situations, going out with someone you don't know."

"Yeah, but I never got that far. There was only one guy I liked. He never called back. Two hours we sit in this coffee shop and I'm telling him the story of my life, y'know? And guess what he says when he pays the check? He says, 'Thanks, it was fun. I enjoyed talking to you. Take care.' I'm standing there on the sidewalk, tears in my eyes, and he's saying, 'It was fun, take care,' and heads for the Metro."

Harry felt an ache in his chest for Iris just then. "Well," he said, and smiled. "His loss."

AUGUST: A SLOW month at the garden center. What was to bloom had blossomed, and the air was too hot for fall plantings. Harry's employees and customers alike took off on vacation, and the humidity of a Washington summer clung to clothes and skin. The Madonna surveyed it all and wept profusely.

It was as though Harry's friends and relatives had taken vacations from him as well. He saw Elaine only when she dropped Jodie off on Tuesday evenings. Claude and Sue had gone to be with friends at the beach, and Jack seemed to be avoiding him, so Harry let him be. Even Iris was gone more than she was there. Harry saw her in the kitchen some mornings, or he would hear her come in late at night, but for the most part they communicated by way of Post-It notes on the refrigerator:

I used the last banana, Harry. I'll pick some up on my way home.

Iris, be sure to double-lock the door when you come in.

Think Zeke has another hair ball. Any more of that medicine, Harry?

It would be good if you could please rinse off your supper dishes, Iris, before you put them in the dishwasher.

ABOUT THE TIME Harry thought that Marge Decker and Paula Harrington could not possibly go any longer without making a comment of some kind, he proved himself right.

He was quietly eating a supper of scrambled eggs and baked beans one evening when he heard Iris come in and go upstairs. Zeke, who had been drinking from his water dish, turned toward her sound and padded softly from the room with not even a glance in Harry's direction.

Harry went on reading *Newsweek*. He heard Iris's shoes hit the floor, the music from her CD player, and after that her footsteps on the floorboards in the hallway and the running of bath water. Harry had never known a person to bathe so often—a shower each morning and a bath at night.

"It relaxes me," she'd told him once.

"No problem," Harry had said.

After the water started to run, Harry thought he heard a knock at the door. He cocked his head, unsure of the sound, but got up when it came again. He walked into the hall, wary of doorbells ringing in the evening.

Paula Harrington stood on the steps, straight as a yardstick, face as set as a clock.

"I would like to speak to the other occupant of this house," she said.

"Iris?" Harry studied her for a moment, then realized he had no right to question. "I'm afraid she's indisposed," he said.

Paula's eyes took in Harry's shoeless feet, and focused on his face again. "I'll wait." She folded her arms, leaned against the side of the porch, and stared out over the lawn.

"Would you like to come in?" Harry said, as cordially as he could.

"No, thank you."

Harry walked upstairs. He could hear the water running, and Iris singing along with it:

"Tell me why, if love is lovely, / Do I sit and cry for you?"

Harry knocked, but both the singing and the running water continued full force.

"Iris?" he called, and knocked louder.

The singing stopped first and finally, when he rapped again, the water.

"Harry?"

"Sorry to bother you, but one of the neighbors is at the door and wants to speak with you," he called. "I told her you were indisposed, but she says she'll wait."

"What the heck does she want?"

"I couldn't guess."

"Well, shit." A pause, and then, "I'll come down."

Harry went back downstairs. "She's coming," he said.

Paula looked pointedly at Harry and turned to stare at the yard again. He walked on into the living room, but stayed within earshot of the door.

He heard the creak of the stairs a few minutes later, and glanced around the corner just long enough to see Iris take the last step, her thin robe glued to her body, nipples pointing through the cloth.

"I'm Iris," Harry heard her say.

Then Paula: "I want to know why you insist on parking bumper to bumper behind my car."

Silence.

"You do it all the time!" Paula went on. "Every evening you pull right up behind me till the bumpers are touching. I could get boxed in like that some day."

Harry heard the front door open, and Iris's voice out on the porch. "What are you talking about? You could pull a bus out of that space!"

"*Some* people in this neighborhood have standards," replied Paula in precise tones. "And one of those standards is that we allow each other room to get in and out of our parking spaces."

"Lady, if it will make you happy, I'll give you a whole city block," Iris said. "But right now I'm in the bathtub."

The door slammed again, Iris went back upstairs, and Harry chuckled as Paula marched militantly across the lawn toward her own property.

"Another country heard from," he murmured, but Marge Decker was soon to follow.

When Harry put out his trash cans the following morning, Marge was putting hers at curbside as well.

"Good morning," Harry called.

This time she straightened and looked him right in the eye. "You surprise me, Harry. You really do."

"Excuse me?"

"I thought you had more respect for your wife than that."

"Than what?"

"Taking in a woman half your age."

"My boarder, you mean?"

"You *know* what I mean, Harry."

"I'm afraid not."

"The entire neighborhood is talking."

"Good. Everyone pulling together for a change," said Harry, and got in the pickup.

As he passed Iris's house on Old Forest Road, where a new eight-pound baby had been born, Iris had told him, he noticed that the huge heap of dirt was disappearing into smaller piles scattered throughout the yard. The damn thing was spawning! Some of the soil was packed down around the post of an American flag by the fence in front. Some had been scattered between a few rose bushes along the sides, and some formed a flower bed, a repository for dead geraniums, their roots entombed in the thick clay soil.

It irritated him that people suspected him and Iris of carrying on an affair, as though anyone who invited a young woman into his home had the consolation of warm limbs and a moist mouth, not to mention the haven between her legs.

Still, what upset him more was that he had dreamed of Iris. He had been sitting in his living room, and Iris had simply walked in and opened her robe. Yet it wasn't her nakedness he remembered as much as her face. She had not said a word—just looked into Harry's eyes—and then she had lain down on the rug. She'd wanted it all along, he had thought in his dream as he ran his tongue over her nipples, stiff and hard as pencil erasers. He was surprised—amazed—that the whole thing was so easy, so guiltless, so devoid of awkwardness. Then he had wakened, stunned, gotten up an hour early and driven to work.

JODIE WAS IN a strange mood. When Elaine brought her by on Tuesday, she seemed on the verge of tears. Her mouth tugged down at the corners, and she sat on the couch, head thrust hard against its back in a valiant effort not to cry.

Harry stood in the doorway, a beer in hand. "Bad day, hon?" he asked.

She pressed her lips tightly together, the mouth sagging even more.

Harry came over and sat down on the chair next to the sofa. "What's wrong?"

A small pitiful voice responded. "I'm sad."

"I can tell."

Her chin quivered. "I miss my daddy."

A stab in the heart.

"I want him . . . to come back," Jodie said, and suddenly turned her head to one side, cheek against the damask. Her face wrinkled and she sobbed quietly, wrists turned up helplessly in her lap.

Harry moved over beside her and enveloped her with one arm. She buried her head in his armpit and let the tears come.

He could think of nothing to say. He looked stoically across the room, his large hand patting Jodie's shoulder, and felt a tug at the corners of his own mouth.

"I wish I could find your daddy and make him come back and make everyone be happy together, but I can't."

"I know," she said miserably, in a voice as high and resigned as a kitten's mew. And when she had cried herself out at last, she clung to him like seaweed, a wet bedraggled waif tossed onto a strange shore.

IRIS DID NOT seem to have a boyfriend. At least no man came to the house that Harry knew of, and if she was not out with girlfriends from work, Sunday often found her at loose ends, discontented, by all counts, with herself and the world. She seemed to Harry a woman who had been disappointed by life early on, and who found it safer to stick close to home than to venture out. And so, because there was a lull in the heat over the weekend, Harry called up the stairs where she had gone only moments before.

"I'm not going to the greenhouse this morning, Iris. I'm taking a walk along the C&O Canal. You interested in getting out?"

"Where is it?" she called back.

"Runs along the Potomac, the other side of MacArthur Boulevard. Nice scenery. Come on. You might enjoy it. I've told the garden center I won't be in this afternoon."

The silence made him hope she would consider it.

"How long?"

"Oh, a couple of hours, maybe. But we can quit any time."

"Okay. Wait'll I put on my sneakers."

She slid beside him in the DeVille. "Mom used to tell me that when a man asks you to go somewhere you should say yes, because if you don't he may never ask you again," she said, guilelessly.

Harry smiled. "Hmmm," he said.

"She meant people you know, of course. Whenever Dad invited her some place, she always went, whether she wanted to or not."

"So has it worked for you?"

"Not really. I was going with this one guy, and you know where he took me? Stock car races. You want to know the stupidest thing in the world? Men driving cars around a track like crazy, bumping into each other."

Harry laughed. "Oh, I don't know. You could say the same about football, except it's bodies, not cars." Then he asked, "How are things back at your house?"

"Well, Dad's got emphysema. Hasn't worked for seven years. But everyone else is okay."

"That's a lot of people for one house."

"Everybody helps out. Dad owns it, so my uncles pay the expenses."

"Who does Kirsten belong to?"

"Sam, my oldest brother. I've got two, Sam and George. Only Sam and his wife are divorced, and she's seeing somebody else, so after Kirsten lived with her awhile, she wanted to come back. We all sort of look after her."

"She gone this weekend? I haven't seen her lately."

"Kirsten's got this boyfriend," Iris told him. "None of us see much of her anymore."

They drove for a few minutes in silence, except for the music Harry kept at low volume.

"What about you, Iris? No man in the picture?"

"Not at the moment," she said, and Harry realized how rude his question had been.

He tried to redeem himself. "Well, you're certainly attractive enough."

"You think so?" She asked the question honestly, and looked over at him, waiting.

"Of course. I'm sure I'm not the first person who's told you that."

"This one guy I went with, he said my eyes were too close together. And I know for a fact that my nose is ugly."

"I think your eyes are lovely, and your nose seems perfectly fine to me."

"You're a nice man, Harry, you know that?" Iris said. And then, as Harry pulled into the next lane, "Oh!"

He glanced over. "What?"

"I could never do that! Pull in front of a car like that."

"I signaled," Harry said.

"That's the thing, Harry. When men signal, they're, like, making a statement, you know? When women signal, they're asking a question."

Harry laughed. "I think you're right. I used to tell Beth that if she were driving to Chicago, she'd start signaling about the time she reached Cleveland."

Iris laughed too.

After they'd parked and Harry pointed out the trail, they walked side by side for some distance, but gradually, as the trail narrowed, Iris moved ahead of him, her long legs taking even longer strides than Harry's. She had never been on the towpath, she said, and seemed to delight in each new vista as they rounded a bend or climbed over a rise, the canal on one side, river on the other.

Harry, too, enjoyed the view. Iris's long, long legs, her lean thighs, the slimness of her body, so that the narrow belt holding up her shorts seemed to encompass no more than a twenty-three inch waist. It was the tightness of her cut-offs, however, that fascinated him—would captivate any man, he was sure. The seam hugged the cleft of her buttocks so tightly that he was conscious of getting hard. Just watching the shift of her behind as she walked made him imagine doing all kinds of things with her, and his genitals felt warm, his stirrings urgent. He forced his eyes on the brush instead, and what he could see of the river through the spaces in the trees.

Of course he knew why he had come. He had not promised Jodie anything, but he had promised himself. If it *was* Don whom Claude had seen crossing the road, and he *was* hiding out over here by the river, Harry intended to find him. All he wanted to do was tell Don Wheeler what his absence was doing to Jodie.

He had parked a half mile south of where Claude thought he'd seen Don, and they hiked about a mile past it. Several times, when they reached a clearing that led to the river, Harry detoured to the water's edge and looked up and down the bank as far as he could. But there was nothing that suggested a camp. An old sock one place, a soda can another. That was all.

On the way back, they took a different fork in the trail that eventually connected again to the main path, and found that it dipped into a gully, still wet with mud from a recent rain. There was a tangle of branches that someone had laid over the middle to form a bridge. As Iris stepped gingerly on it, arms straight out at her sides for balance, Harry put one hand on her waist to steady her, and Iris placed her fingers over his hand. Harry felt his penis lunge to attention again, and he kept his hand on her a few seconds longer than necessary after Iris let go.

They did not say much going home. Harry's thoughts turned alternately from his disappointment at seeing nothing of Don Wheeler to the feelings Iris had aroused in him. He asked if she'd be going out later after dinner, and she said she'd promised her dad she'd eat there. She went upstairs to change. That night Harry ate alone, but he went to bed early to relieve his cravings. In his mind he slid one finger along the seam of Iris's shorts as it ran tightly through her crotch, and later his orgasm was so cataclysmic that Harry lay panting when it was over.

He could certainly allow himself this, he decided—fantasies of Iris. He had no doubt that from time to time Beth had fantasized other men. In fact, she had told him sometimes of these fantasies, and one of them, about a window washer, had brought such pleasure to them both that Zeke had jumped up on the bed to see what was going on.

In the moist stillness of the bedroom, Harry lay listening, wondering what he would do if he were to hear, at that moment, Beth calling his name. But he did not hear the word "Harry," did not feel Zeke walking paw over paw along the edge of the mattress. Only the soft scrape of drapery rings broke the silence as the breeze blew the curtains back and forth in the dark summer air.

EIGHT

The Bedroom

WHAT HARRY WAS discovering was that the six stages of grief did not necessarily follow in the proper order. There were days he got up and felt shock, panic, anger, despair and apathy all in the space of an hour. Recovery, he guessed, was a long way off. In the weeks following Beth's funeral service, he had even begun to miss the things about her that annoyed him.

"Harry, can you believe this?" she used to say over the newspaper. And then he had to pull himself away from his own story to listen to a paragraph he would read later anyway.

She also told friends she was a year younger than Harry and left piles of clothes on a chair in their bedroom. But only the night before, Harry found his own shorts on the chair, and was struck by how bereft they appeared.

What he was feeling now, on and off, was anger—hard for him to recognize, more difficult still to admit. If she *had* been unfaithful, how many others knew and pitied him? The person who wrote the letter, surely. While he had been a straight arrow, relatively speaking, had she been fooling around? Still, he was lonely, and he missed her. He chastised himself for distrusting her on the basis of one yellowed letter.

"I don't want to grow old alone," he said aloud.

He did not like to think of himself cooking his solitary suppers of scrambled eggs with an ancient, probably incontinent cat looking on. Did not like the idea of no arms to hold him, no scent of a woman's hair on his pillow. For all their faults and differences, he and Beth brought out the best in each other. Symbiosis: two dissimilar organisms in a mutually beneficial relationship.

ELAINE CALLED ONE night about ten.

"You heard about Jack, didn't you?" she asked.

"Do I want to know this?"

"Probably not. He lost two-hundred dollars in a card game, hoping to bail himself out of another debt. He told Claude."

"I could have done without that, Elaine."

"I'm sorry."

"How is Claude?"

"Okay, I guess. He sounded a little depressed. He sold only one painting at the art show, he said."

And it hung back here in his bedroom, Harry knew.

"Dad, do you have time to talk for a few minutes?" Elaine went on.

"Of course," Harry said, but did not anticipate that this would make him feel any better.

"I just wondered how you would describe our relationship when I was little. Were we close? I mean, did people ever refer to me as a 'Daddy's girl' or anything?"

Harry could not remember who had taken Elaine to the prom

when she was seventeen or whether or not she played the piano at twelve. How in hell could he remember their relationship when she was small?

"I'd like to say we were close, Elaine, but it seems as though that would be for you to decide."

"Well, that's the point. My therapist says it's really hard to remember events before the age of four—it's all buried in the subconscious. If someone jogs your memory, though, it'll come to you, she says. She wants to know what kind of relationship I had with you and Mom."

Harry really did want to help out. He certainly had loved his daughter, he knew. "Well, I don't remember feeding or bathing you, but I do remember how I'd lift you from the car sometimes when you fell asleep on a trip—the way your head rested against my neck as I carried you inside. That was a good memory. I remember taking you to the park, teaching you to skate, taking you around to the neighbors' on Halloween."

"Anything else?"

"Seems as though my mother may have called you a 'Daddy's girl' once or twice," he offered vaguely. "I *know* you were close to Beth. It was always her you went to when you scraped your knee or something."

"Okay. Thanks, Dad."

"How's Jodie?"

"Fine. Why?"

"Just wondered. She's seemed a little . . . serious . . . the last few times she's been over."

"Yeah, she has a lot to be serious about."

KIRSTEN AND HER boyfriend began dropping by the middle of August. Hahn, the boyfriend, was as huge as a linebacker, with a neck that seemed to start at the ends of his shoulders and grew straight up, like the trunk of a tree. He wore a black tank top stretched as tightly across his chest as a sail in the breeze, and his feet were size thirteens, at least. Hahn the Hun.

Iris, Kirsten, and Hahn usually congregated on the patio. Hahn and Kirsten appropriated the metal glider, while Iris sprawled loose-jointed on the chaise lounge.

Harry listened and watched as he puttered around the yard—pulling a weed, removing dead blossoms. Among Hahn and Kirsten's friends, who sometimes came by, there was a conversational gambit Harry thought of as "beating the system." How to speed without getting a ticket, drink without getting caught, smoke a joint without getting busted, and who knows what else they mentioned when Harry wasn't there.

When Iris left Kirsten and Hahn alone for any length of time, the young couple would start a kiss that began at a quarter to seven and end at ten of. Harry felt as though he were witnessing oral copulation. Sometimes Kirsten would lie at the opposite end of the glider, her legs over the lap of the Hun. He would stroke them intently, concentrating on every curve, caressing the tender skin behind her knees and watching her face to see if he was turning her on. Other times he would lie with his head in Kirsten's lap, and with great studiousness she'd trace and retrace his profile with one finger. How was it possible, Harry wondered, to look into the eyes of another person for ten minutes—twenty, even—and never tire of the scenery?

But Harry found the patio more interesting when Iris was there alone. On a hot August day she would lie on the chaise lounge, her shirt stuck to her body in the heat, the buttons undone as far as her bra. Her shorts would be wrinkled and, beneath her raised leg, he could follow the line of her thigh until it met the fleshy cheek that disappeared into her underwear.

Her hair hung in sweaty curls tucked behind her ears, and she lay languidly, uncaring, her thighs slightly parted. The back of her shirt showed damp when she leaned forward to swat a fly off her foot.

Heat did not seem to bother Iris. It had bothered Beth. In the heat of summer, if Beth had to be outside at all, she would sit with arms spread, fingertips resting lightly on the bench beside her so that no part of her body would be touching any other. When she spoke, even her words seemed widely spaced.

Iris, by contrast, lay in a lump, her scent sweet in the wet warmth of afternoon. When *she* spoke, her speech was slurred, sluttish, her words stuck together in the heat. There was something about Iris lying moist and glistening, her eyes half closed, lips slightly open, that mesmerized Harry. He ached with forbidden want of her, angered that the neighbors assumed he had been enjoying her all along. Here he was imagining himself with another woman, and Beth had still not been laid to rest.

He thought he might feel better if the ashes were disposed of. It was a hurdle he had to face, so he called each of his children and made a date for the following Sunday. Elaine was having brunch with a few of the teachers from her school that day, Jack had something planned for evening, so they agreed to meet at Claude's in the early afternoon, drive to a restaurant on Kent Narrows, scatter Beth's ashes from the far end of the dock, have an early dinner, and drive home again, all in the space of an afternoon.

Anything that was preordained, however, was already programmed to go wrong, Harry discovered. First, Jack decided he needed to see a man in Annapolis on the way back, so he drove his own car. Harry, therefore, sat in the front seat beside Claude, who was driving, while Elaine sat in back with Jodie. Sue had decided that this should be an intimate family thing between Harry and his children, so she did not come. The plastic bag holding Beth's remains rested in a grocery sack between Harry's feet.

He had thought they might spend the drive over talking about Beth, sharing something of their memories that the others may have forgotten. Jodie, however, had been promised that she could listen to Raffi's *Singable Songs for the Very Young,* and as soon as the car began to move, the tape began. It lasted almost until they reached the Bay Bridge, and after that, silence seemed such a welcome relief that Harry did not feel like starting a reminiscence.

"How much farther?" Jodie whined. "Are we almost there?"

"Almost," Elaine told her. "You watch. We'll be going over a long bridge in a minute."

"When do we throw in the ashes?" Jodie wanted to know.

"We'll see when we get there," Elaine whispered.

Jack was waiting for them on the dock outside the restaurant. He was looking at his watch and pacing. When Harry got out of the car, Jack came over and embraced him, then patted him on the shoulder as they pulled apart. Harry had reached that stage in life, he discovered, when his children looked out for him. He was grateful, of course, but not that fond of the turnaround.

"They don't open for dinner for another twenty minutes, Dad," Jack said. "You want to have the ceremony first, then eat?" And when Harry hesitated, he said, "I may be leaving a little early, so. . . ."

"Then of course we'll do the ashes first," Harry said.

Jodie stood very still now, her eyes on the sack in Harry's hands, the sea breeze blowing wisps of hair about her face. Elaine stood behind her on the dock, hands on Jodie's shoulders, a tissue wadded up tightly in one fist. Claude walked over to the water and looked down.

"Well, we're all here—the immediate family, I mean," Harry said. "As we were driving over, I thought it might be appropriate to share some of our memories with each other. I was thinking about our honeymoon on the Bay. And since none of you was present"—Here his three children chuckled politely—"I thought I'd share this little episode with you. A friend had loaned us his cottage in St. Michael's, but we didn't get away nearly as soon as we'd thought. Everybody was having a good time at the reception. By the time we finally got changed and into my car, it was after nine in the evening. We didn't reach St. Michael's until almost midnight.

"Well, we hadn't thought about the fact that restaurants would be closed. There wasn't a single one open after we crossed the bridge. Not so much as a diner. We'd hardly eaten a bite at the wedding, you know, but didn't want to drive all the way back to Bay Bridge either. So Beth got out the slice of wedding cake they'd wrapped up for us for good luck. We also had a bottle of champagne, and we located a snack machine outside a motel. Our wedding supper consisted of a bag of Fritos, a bag of peanuts, a package of cheese crackers, the champagne, and the wedding cake."

More laughter.

"I remember she made cheese crackers for me once," said Jodie helpfully. "She put peanut butter on my crackers and then she cut up little pieces of cheese and put them on the peanut butter and made faces." She smiled hopefully around the circle.

"That was a nice memory, Jodie," Elaine told her.

The others appeared to be thinking. Finally, from Claude: "Mom bought me my first box of paints. It wasn't just a box of eight colors. There were thirty-six shades and two brushes. I don't remember how old I was, but I can thank Mom for whatever I accomplish, which is more, I hope, than I've done to date."

Harry was not entirely sure whether this was a requiem for Beth or for Claude's talent, but it moved him.

Elaine cleared her throat, but her voice still sounded choked: "You could count on Mother to come up with a solution to any problem. Dad, do you remember that old Buick I used to have at college? I was coming back from a job interview once, and realized there was something wrong with the latch on the passenger-side door. It kept swinging open. I veered off the highway, found a phone booth, and called Mom. 'Elaine,' she said, 'are you wearing panty hose?' 'Yes,' I told her. 'Take them off and use them to tie the door shut,' she said. It worked!"

Everyone laughed aloud. Harry had not heard that one.

"She had it in her file box under 'fanbelt,'" Elaine explained, "because she'd read somewhere that you could use panty hose in a pinch. That's what I remember about Mom."

Then it was Jack's turn: "One of the things I remember is that she always insisted on knowing where I was. Where I was going, I mean, when I went out. I used to hate it, but now I realize how much she cared." His voice broke, and Harry was surprised. Children were a constant surprise after they'd left the nest.

They were all looking at Harry now. Not exactly at him. Their faces were turned in his direction—Elaine's eyes, behind her sunglasses; Jack's squinting thoughtfully; Claude's overshadowed by his thick blond brows—but they seemed to be focused on the wooden boards of the dock, as though embarrassed for him, at his sadness.

Other than the honeymoon story, Harry did not have any one thing he wanted to say. He had volumes, so trapped in his memory, imprinted on his heart, that to choose any one of them over the others would seem to devalue the rest. And so he said simply, in a raspy voice, "Goodbye, Beth. A piece of my heart goes with you."

Then he stooped over and lifted the plastic bag out of the grocery sack at his feet. He walked to the edge of the dock, put his hand in the bag, scooped up a handful of Beth and then, holding the ashes gently in his large callused palm, cast them over the water. He held out the bag toward the family next, thinking each child might like to hold this little bit of their mother one last time. Jodie frankly stared.

"Dad," Jack said quickly, "just scatter them."

Harry did, and they sank, but fine dusty particles floated out over the water of the Chesapeake Bay. The family stood there unspeaking, watching the grayish film change patterns, like a cloud moving across the sky. And then, Harry saw a crab swim to the surface and nibble at the ashes. A fish, two fish.

Jodie screamed. "They're eating her!" she cried.

"Oh, my God," whispered Elaine.

Some of the restaurant personnel had come to the window to watch.

"It's okay, Jodie. That's just what Beth would have wanted. Feeding the fish. She's part of nature now," Harry said.

Claude put one hand on his father's arm. "Come on, Dad. Let's go inside."

AT WORK, THOSE of "the herd" who were not at the beach spent their lunch hour sitting in the open back of the large delivery truck. With a red bandanna tied around his forehead, a tanned arm resting on his bent knee, Bill regaled the others with such risk-taking adventures as bungee-jumping off the bridge over the New River Gorge.

The other men, enjoying the shade of the truck's high roof, let their legs dangle over the back end, chowing down their Kentucky Fried Chicken or the packaged sandwiches they'd purchased from the vending machine at the Texaco.

The women preferred their lunch in the grape arbor, a favorite place too for a Coke in the August heat. When school was in session, Tracy sometimes took her homework out to the picnic table on her break, while Rose curled up in a wicker chair with her romance-of-the-month novel, whose cover brought snickers from the hired men.

One lunch hour, when Rose and Tracy were out at the picnic table, Wanda followed Harry into his office and closed the door only enough so that she could still see the sales counter.

"Got a minute, boss?" she asked. She was wearing a loose-fitting dress of moss green that flowed unhindered over her full figure, embellished only by a white necklace resembling flower petals. Harry marveled that she could look so cool.

"Sure. What's on your mind?" He motioned her to the extra chair, taking the one at the desk himself.

She continued to stand, and lowered her voice as she nodded toward his window. "I'll just take a minute. Rose and Tracy have been having lunch together since Tracy started full-time over the summer, and I'm a little concerned at the things Rose has been telling her. I've only heard bits and pieces, but enough to make me wonder."

Harry was mildly amused. "Rose? I can't imagine what. She's confessed to killing her grandmother?"

"She told Tracy she once had a date with Johnny Mathis."

Harry could only laugh.

"And Tracy believed her," said Wanda.

"Heck, maybe she did."

"And she says she knew John Lennon, though she never went out with him."

"Rose gets around, doesn't she." Harry grinned.

"You're not taking this seriously, are you?"

"How can I take it seriously unless she's raiding the cash register or something? She hasn't, has she?"

"No, but I just thought you ought to know. If she was sixteen and telling tall tales, that would be one thing, but not a woman her age. I'm the one who hired her, so I feel responsible."

"How's her work?"

"No complaints there. She does a good job with wreaths. I have to restrain her from putting on too many bows and berries, but customers like her, and give her special orders sometimes."

"Arrives on time, does she?"

"Like a railroad time table."

Harry shrugged. "So she does her work, entertains Tracy, and gets her jollies on the job. Heck, Wanda, she can say she's slept with Prince Charles if she keeps the customers happy."

"Okay. Just wanted to be sure you were in the loop," Wanda said smiling, and went out to the counter.

How could he deny an employee her fantasies when he had his own? Harry mused. Was imagining herself with Johnny Mathis any more improbable than Harry in the arms of Iris Shaw?

JACK ANNOUNCED THAT he had purchased a new coffee machine for Suds and Spuds.

"You should see this thing, Dad," he said over the phone. "All I do is open the top each morning and pour dry mix in six different compartments. The machine does the rest. Customers put their cup under the drink they want, pull a lever, and they get coffee plain, expresso, latte, mocha, hot chocolate, or chocolate orange. They love it."

"You charge for this?"

"A dollar a cup, that's all. But the increase in customers offsets the price of the machine. It'll pay for itself in eighteen months, I figure."

"Sounds good, but I thought you already had some pretty stiff debts, Jack."

Jack's voice showed his irritation. "I'm working on that, Dad. You don't have to remind me." Then, "Stop by sometime and get yourself a coffee mocha. You'll love it."

"I'll do that," Harry said.

After he hung up he turned to Iris, who was leaning against the refrigerator eating a bagel. "You want to drive to a laundry sometime and have a coffee mocha?"

"Why would I want to do that?" she asked.

"You probably wouldn't," Harry laughed, and poured some corn flakes for himself. "Jack's put in a new machine."

"If I don't have anything better to do, maybe," Iris said. She spread a lump of cream cheese across the top of her bagel with one finger, the nail painted cinnamon. Taking a bite, she studied Harry while she chewed.

"I think you're feeling a little lonely, Harry," she offered.

Was it so obvious, then? "Sort of obligated, actually," he said, to explain. "It's not that I don't have anything else to do, it's that whatever your kids are up to—art shows, coffee machines—you're supposed to be supportive."

"I'll bet you were a good father."

"No. Average, maybe."

But she wouldn't let it drop. "You know what Shirley and I used to do to entertain ourselves?"

"Your sister? I can think of a lot of things, but they're probably all wrong. What?"

"We'd go someplace—any place—a coffee shop or the mall or a gas station or something—and we'd decide who we were going to be."

"I don't get it."

"Like, maybe we were going to be cousins having a quarrel. Or we'd walk in a coffee shop like we were about to cry, and we'd have this conversation about how Shirley had just lost a baby or something. Shirley, she was real good at this. She can think of something sad and start crying. The tears just come, you know? The waitress, she'd ask if something was wrong, and we'd tell about this tiny baby, and one place, we looked so sad because our brother had died that the manager said our pie was on the house. Wasn't that nice of him, Harry? I said we ought to pay for it anyway, because George at that very minute was in Las Vegas at the slot machines, but Shirley said no, an actress never gets out of character as long as she's onstage, so we ate the pie and thanked the manager and left the waitress a really good tip."

She put the last bite of bagel in her mouth and smiled. "That's what *we* do when we're feeling lonely."

He smiled. "I'm sure you're a lot better at that than I'd be, Iris."

ON THURSDAY AFTER dinner, Harry drove to the Super Value to stock up on essentials—paper towels, napkins, detergent. He kept them stacked in the basement, which saved trips to the store. He was feeling negligent at everything these days, including landlordship. Twice Iris had to ask him for toilet paper, so after he got home he filled his arms with paper products and went upstairs to the hall closet.

He did not like closets or cupboards, anything with doors, behind which some reminder of Beth might be lurking. Shelves weren't so bad, because every memory on them was visible upon entering a room, and you could steel yourself before you got too close. Harry wasn't sure he had opened this closet more than once since Beth died. Since long before she died. She had been the stocker of cupboards and closets.

There were sheets and towels, soap and shampoo. And hanging

on a hook to one side was a satin sachet with the scent of peach and almond.

He drank in the scent and stood looking out the hall window beyond, where the leaves of the box elder brushed the screen. He felt his chest grow tight with the emptiness. Beth often left that scent on her pillow, or the pillow case, possibly, scented her hair. This was their house, their screen, their box elder, and she should be here, but she wasn't. His eyes grew moist.

He was aware suddenly of Iris standing in the doorway of her room, studying him. In a green jersey tank top and shorts, barefoot, a Sprite in hand, she watched as he came out of his reverie and deposited his bundle on the closet shelf. He did not know how long she had been there, but when he shut the door again, avoiding her glance, she put out her hand.

"Harry?" she said simply and, grasping his arm, led him just inside her room.

His first thought was that something in Claude's room was not working. The curtain rod had come apart or a lamp was malfunctioning. But then Iris placed her Sprite on the dresser and put her arms around his waist, a gesture of consolation, Harry imagined. God knows how many women had hugged him since Beth died, so he put his arms around her also.

And then he knew. Perhaps by the way she laid her face against his neck. Or because she didn't let go. Harry didn't either. Iris was humming. She was humming one of the country songs she liked so well, and was moving almost imperceptibly from side to side as though they were dancing.

The smell of her hair, the feel of her body. Her pelvis pressed against him ever so lightly and Harry felt an instant response in his groin.

"Harry," Iris whispered, her lips moving against the skin just below his ear.He kissed her then—as gently as a whisper. Their lips touched and parted, touched again. A mere brushing of lips. Harry's hands dropped lower until he was pressing her buttocks toward him He felt her body crumple slightly in an attitude of surrender.

And then, still without words, he helped her remove the green tank top, her small breasts bare beneath it. She took off her shorts while Harry removed his own clothes, but she came to the bed in her panties. They lay down together and Harry drew her to him. It was as though he'd forgotten how smooth was a woman's skin, how curved her bottom, how soft those breasts.

He slipped one hand in her underwear, stroking the bare cheeks of her buttocks, then moved his fingers around to the front, combing the hair of her pubis until he felt the welcoming wetness.

The underwear came off, her long, long legs crossed behind his back, hugging him tightly, pulling him down, and soon, but not too soon, he erupted inside her and laid his head upon her pillow.

THE MORE HE pondered what had just happened in Claude's room, the more uncertain Harry was as to whether his mind was going. If it was, it was sweet madness. He didn't care. He drifted in and out of sleep.

Iris stirred and Harry gently helped her disentangle her body from his. She rolled over, then turned back again, her lips against his shoulder.

"What time is it?" she asked.

"I'm not sure. We both dozed off, I think." He kissed her forehead.

Iris sighed, then jerkily rose up on one elbow. "I'm gonna take a bath," she said.

As she moved to get up, Harry put out one hand and stopped her. "Iris, we . . . took no precautions," he said, sounding revoltingly formal.

"Don't worry," she said. "I just had my period, and you're the only man I'd sleep with without a glove. I figured, well, y'know, with your wife and all . . . you're safe."

"I'm safe," he assured her, smiling, and watched her long torso move out the door of the bedroom.

He closed his eyes again and drifted off. Once he woke convinced that intercourse could not possibly have happened. Then he put his fingers to his face and smelled her scent. He sniffed his shoulder and got a faint whiff of her hair.

"My God!" he said aloud, and opened his eyes.

Harry was thoroughly awake now, and his mind was in an uproar. Had she had sex with him because she found him attractive or because she felt safe? She'd invited him, hadn't she? If he was the only man she would sleep with without a glove, how many had she slept with properly attired? Heck, couldn't he just enjoy it?

But no. The questions came at him like bullets. What if Elaine had come by with Jodie? What if Claude and Sue had dropped in? How did this change the arrangement he had with Iris?

Harry could not help but wonder if Beth, on some astral plane, had seen. What if her consciousness had never left this house, and she knew somehow that within days of feeding her bones to the fish, Harry was locked belly to belly with a woman he did not even know the age of, up in their younger son's bedroom?

He tried to return to that delicious semi-conscious state once again, and for a while succeeded. But when Iris didn't return, he got up finally and pulled on his trousers. He wondered if she had wanted him to stay all night. He'd hoped that they could talk a little, perhaps. Should he leave a note on her pillow? *Thank* her, even? Good God, no! What then?

He tapped uncertainly on the bathroom door.

"Yeah?" Iris called.

"I'm . . . I'm going downstairs now," he said. "I know you need your sleep."

"Okay," she answered.

Harry waited. "Goodnight, Iris," he said at last.

"Goodnight, Harry."

The water was turned lower in the bathroom until it was running at only a trickle. He imagined Iris's long leg extended out of the water, toes curled around the faucet. And then she began to sing softly to herself:

"You want mah loo-ve . . . baby!
You want mah hearr-t . . . so true.
I'll tell you onnn-e thing, baby!
I'll give it allll . . . to you."

FOR THE NEXT week, Harry did not know how to behave. There were times he felt like a seventh-grade boy in the girls' locker room. When he heard her coming in the door, his first impulse was to run and hide.

As she passed the living room, he said hello. Warmly. If she stopped, they talked. If she went directly upstairs, they did not. The thing was, for Harry it felt that what had happened between them had changed their relationship completely. But it seemed that for Iris, it changed nothing.

She made no reference to it at all. She could stand in the doorway talking about the shipment of cosmetics that had arrived a week too late for the big sale, or the red-haired bastard who had cut her off as she was trying to turn onto Westlake, seemingly oblivious of the fact that she was speaking to a man whose most intimate organ had, only days before, penetrated her private space. Amazing.

Didn't she know that the longer she stood there talking, the further Harry undressed her with his eyes? A guileless woman could control him with her body as surely as Elaine had controlled Don with her tongue. Didn't Iris realize that he was fingering the pages of the newspaper and remembering the feel of her nipples? How do you look into the face of a man who has had intercourse with you and go on yammering about the intersection of Democracy Boulevard and Westlake? Maybe what had happened upstairs had taken her by surprise as well, and she had her regrets. No, he didn't believe that.

Modesty, he guessed. A cover for shyness. Embarrassment for being so forward.

Two weeks later, however, on a Wednesday night, Harry was mopping up some apricot juice he had spilled beside the refrigerator when Iris came downstairs to make a cup of tea.

They exchanged a few pleasantries. Harry stepped again on the linoleum where the juice had been, and once again the soles of his shoes made a smacking sound as he raised each foot. He sighed and attacked the floor with a rag.

"Harry?"

He looked up.

"You want to come up to my room?"

Harry slowly got to his feet, managed a smile. "I'd like that very much," he said. "Be there in a minute." Iris seemed to have second thoughts about the tea, and left both cup and tea bag on the counter.

Harry stared after her. What had turned her on? The sight of him down on his knees? The smacking sound of his shoes on the floor? The smell of canned apricots in heavy syrup? The older he got, the less he understood, but did it matter?

He went into the bathroom, washed his armpits and groin, then put on his robe and went upstairs. This time he brought a condom that he had purchased the day before, more out of hope than expectation. Maybe she had been thinking about him too.

"I don't want to take the chance of getting you pregnant, Iris," he told her. "I think we'll both enjoy it more if we don't have to worry about that."

"It won't bother me," she said.

He could not understand her unconcern. It was both refreshing and unsettling to have been living with a woman for thirty-four years whose entire life was a marvel of organization and to be around someone now who whirled through each day like a leaf in the wind. Yet after a few continuous hours with Iris, it was comforting to fall back on his memories of Beth, the certainty of her.

"If the phone rings," he said to Iris, smiling, "we'll let it ring."

She was lying on her back, completely naked this time. And once again she crossed her legs behind him and pulled him down until he could feel her hip bones dig into his abdomen. He had a brief vision of a praying mantis being eaten by his mate, but then they began moving rhythmically together, and finally they were side by side, one of Iris's thighs tucked under his waist, the heels of her feet touching his back, the musky scent of their love-making drifting up between their warm bodies.

How good it was to be in a woman again! If every woman knew how sweet, how inviting, how perfectly delicious was that opening between her legs. It was the same and yet it was different, being in bed with Iris. Harry was used to the soft fullness of Beth's thighs, like pillows beneath him, supporting his weight. Iris's thighs were not full and they were not soft. They were just different.

"You're so very nice, Iris," he said, into her hair. "I like making love to you."

She made no response. Thinking she might be asleep, he ran one finger up and down her arm, then her back. What did a contemporary man say to a contemporary woman after having sex?

"Do you like being in bed with me?" he asked finally.

"Uh huh. It was me who asked you up here, remember?" She moved away from him a little. "Come on and take a bath with me."

Harry blinked. "Now?"

"Sure. C'mon."

What the hell, he was fifty-six going on sixteen. Why not?

He drank some water while Iris leaned over to fill the tub. What surprised him was that she got in first and settled herself at the back, instead of scooting forward so he could climb in behind her, as he used to do with Beth. It was Iris now who invited him to sit down and lean back against her, head between her breasts. Fifty-six going on seven.

At first he felt embarrassingly awkward, knees drawn up, but then he extended his legs, bracing his feet on the tile at either side of the faucets: two hairy legs, like flying buttresses, holding up the wall of the bathroom.

He allowed Iris to soap his chest, running her fingers through the dark matted hair, sliding her soapy fingers under his armpits and caressing the sides of his body, bending forward as she did so, her hair brushing the sides of his face. Her fingers reached his penis and she gently soaped him there. The penis strove valiantly to stand at attention, and after a few reeling tries, succeeded, more or less. They both laughed at its antics.

It felt good being in a tub with a young woman. He could come to like this ritual. She was caressing his shoulders, his eyes half closed. He could so easily drift off again, asleep in the arms of Iris.

"Harry!" she said suddenly. "Look at that!"

He opened his eyes.

"Your navel!" she said. "It's off center."

Harry lifted his head and studied the abdomen protruding from the water. He closed one eye and surveyed it carefully, then raised his head even higher.

"Son of a gun," he said. His navel appeared to be three quarters of an inch to the left.

"You know what that means, don't you?" Iris continued.

"That the doc did a sloppy job with the umbilical cord, I imagine."

"No! Harry, you *came* that way, with an off-center navel."

Harry's penis too rose up to take a look, then flopped down again.

"So?" Harry said. "I should get a refund?"

"It means you have special powers. I read it somewhere. You can sense things other people can't."

"Sure."

She squeezed both his shoulders hard, then gave him a little shake. "It *does!* There was this article in one of Kirsten's New Age magazines. Everybody's got something asymmetrical. I mean, one person might have a shoulder lower than the other, or a foot that's bigger than the other. But the navel is the focal point of your own particular universe, Harry, and if the navel's off center, it means your body is slightly out of balance, and you compensate for that by developing really acute, almost mystical abilities in your senses."

Harry's eyes closed again. He rested his arms on Iris's knees, fingers trailing up and down her shins.

"I feel things, all right," he said.

"Seriously!"

"Well, if I have special powers, they've escaped me, but I'll keep an eye out for them," he told her.

It was later, down in his own room, that he heard his name again.

"Harry," it said. Just like that.

He stopped, holding one sock in the air, and stood like a statue. Then he realized the phone must have been ringing when he flushed the john because the voice said, "Harry!" again, and it was coming from the answering machine in the front hall. "It's Liz, Harry. Call me sometime. I'm commissioning you to make a bust of Max, something to remember him by."

IT WASN'T UNTIL Liz left a second message on his answering machine ten days later that Harry returned her call.

"You've got the wrong man," he told her.

"Harry, you can do it! You're the only one I'd trust to get it right. Just his head and shoulders, that's all."

"But what would you do with it? Put it out in the garden, the birds'll desecrate it."

"The mantel."

Good grief.

"You don't have to worry about his eyes. Look at any statue, almost, and you'll see that most of the eyes look like grapes without any pupils at all," she continued. "I've got lots of side views of Max, so we'll work on the nose and chin together. I'll help."

"Liz, I can't even remember the shape of his head. Only that he was bald. That makes it all the more difficult. The head has to be right."

"I've already thought of that." Her voice tapered off, and Harry wondered if she was on the verge of crying. She *was* crying. "H . . . Harry, do you remember when he was in a coma there at the end? And we brought him home?"

"Yes, I remember. That was a rough time for you."

"It was awful! But I felt I had to have something of him to remember, and I couldn't cut off a lock of his hair because he didn't have any, so. . . ."

A feeling of horror crept up Harry's spine and lodged between his shoulder blades.

"One evening when I was there with him alone, I just took a pair of scissors and cut a roll of paper towels into little strips. Then I dipped each piece in flour and water, and after I greased Max's head, I applied the strips. Just over his forehead and scalp, of course. I didn't cover his eyes and nose."

"Liz, I don't *believe* this!"

"What was the harm, Harry? I was really, really careful. I just put layers of paper and paste on as much of his head as I could reach, let it dry, and then I lifted it off. And I said to myself, 'Someday I'll give this to Harry and ask him to make a bust of Max.'" Here she began crying again. "Well, it's that some day, Harry. I want you to use the mask I made and fill in the rest." Her voice trailed off. "Don't let me down, Harry."

Lock her up, Harry thought. That was the only thing to do with widows who wouldn't stop weeping.

ELAINE CAME BY on Tuesday a half hour early, but Jodie wasn't with her.

"Rosalind was having a birthday party, so Jodie's there this evening," she explained. "Anyway, I wanted a chance to talk with you alone."

"Sure. Glad to have you, honey," Harry said. "Want some coffee?"

"No." Elaine moved on into the living room rather stiffly, Harry thought. He followed her in and sat down on the couch. His daughter, in her beige cotton skirt and top, took the chair across from him. She let her shoulder bag slide off her arm and drop with a determined clunk onto the floor. "All I want is for you to be honest with me."

Iris, thought Harry. Was it possible she had come by the other night when they were upstairs together, and surmised?

"About what?" he asked cautiously.

"I know this is going to be embarrassing for you, Dad. You can imagine how it makes me feel, but I have to know."

"So ask," he said, bracing himself.

Elaine stiffened even more, her arms straight out in front of her, hands on her knees. She hunched her shoulders to an impossible height, then let them drop to signal the awkwardness of the question to come.

"Did you . . . ever do anything sexual to me?"

Harry could feel his lower jaw drop. "*What?*"

"I want the truth, Dad. Did you ever molest me when I was little, even if you didn't hurt me or anything?"

"Elaine, are you out of your mind?"

"I thought you might say that." She seemed surprised, however, at his surprise. Yet she continued on with resolve. "What's done is done, and I'm not going to press charges or anything. I just want to know for my own peace of mind."

"Well, the answer is no. Not unless Martians took over my body and I was temporarily brain-dead. I'm your *dad*, Elaine!"

"That's what makes it all the worse."

"Makes *what* worse? For God's sake, what are you getting at?"

Elaine swallowed. "Well, just things I wonder about. Dreams I've been having."

"Elaine, anything at all can happen in dreams. You can devour your own children in dreams. What got you started on this?"

"Things I've been talking about with my therapist. I really don't want to get into that now. Mainly I just wanted your impressions about the kind of relationship we had."

"Well, you can cross molestation off your list. If I'd wanted an affair, I sure wouldn't have picked a little skinny-legged girl in training pants."

Elaine gave a nervous laugh. "I just wanted to ask."

"It offends me that you would even *think* this, Elaine! This therapist, is she certified? I mean, did she graduate from an accredited university? What do you know about her?"

"My friend Claire says she's worked wonders for her."

"I'd do some checking around if I were you."

"I *like* her, Dad."

"Well, *I* don't. And you can tell her for me that I'm damn mad. But other than this, if she's helping you I suppose that's the main thing."

Elaine stood and picked up her shoulder bag again. Harry walked to the door with her, and she gave him a quick hug. "Next week I'll bring Jodie again. She's already on her Halloween kick—has a mask to show you."

"Okay, see you then."

After Harry closed the door, he stood staring at it blankly. If this wasn't the limit! Where did thirty-somethings come up with things like this? He tried to force his memory back three decades to anything at all that might have seemed seductive to a three or four year-old. All he could conjure up was the memory of changing her diaper when she was under a year old—mopping her with a cotton ball—and once, out of curiosity, examining the bud of her clitoris. Was that any worse than examining her infant ear, which he had also done? Her navel too, come to think of it.

He felt the need of arms around him, and when Iris came in later—she must have gone out to eat because it was nine when she got home—Harry opened the door for her and put one hand on her waist as she passed. She offered her cheek and he kissed her. "I'd like to come up later, if you'll let me," he said.

"Better not," she told him. "I've got my period."

He wasn't sure if he was more disappointed or relieved. No

paternity suit this month, anyway. "Oh, okay then," he said. He hadn't minded having sex with Beth when she was menstruating, but you had to know a woman well to do that. What he knew about Iris Shaw he could write on a half sheet of paper.

Harry was glad, however, when she came back down to sit with him later. She made a cup of tea and sat in Beth's favorite armchair with her feet drawn up under her.

"So how are things going at Hecht's?" he asked.

"I'm switching to handbags," she answered, and blew at the steam before taking a sip.

"Oh?"

"I didn't like the way they were always trying to change me in cosmetics, you know?"

"What's to change?" Harry asked genially. "You've got great-looking skin."

"They put this Swedish woman in charge of us. Elsa says I'm one of the winters."

"Winters?"

"Yeah. That used to be real big, and now it's coming back again—dividing women into seasons. You're only supposed to wear colors that go with your group. Colorations, we call them now."

"You can only wear white?" Harry asked, curiously.

"No. I'm lucky. Winters look good in most anything. Springs get stuck with pastels. But they wanted me to put on this makeup each morning before I came to work. Astringent, turnaround cream, moisturizer, the works! I would have had to get up an hour early just to do my face! And once you get there, Elsa wanted us to do a face check every hour. I was a freaking doll! I'd look in the mirror and wonder if it was me!"

She uncurled her body and stretched her long legs out in front of her. Harry had never seen such legs in his life. They started at her armpits and didn't stop till they were under the coffee table.

"Last week Elsa tells the boss I'm not happy in cosmetics. 'You want handbags?' he says. 'Yeah,' I tell him. Not so much pressure.

The customers are looking at the inside of purses, they're not looking at you. I'm more at home in handbags."

"That's good," said Harry.

"The story of my life, everybody wanting me to *change* somehow. I had this boyfriend once—this was maybe four years ago—he wanted me to learn golf. A friend of my brother's. Even bought me a set of clubs. 'I'm not the golfing type,' I tell him, and he says, 'Sure, you are.' I must have gone to the golf course with him five or six times, and I didn't like it any better than when I started. Once I hit the ball, I didn't much care where it went, you know? Drove him nuts. He said if I didn't learn golf, we wouldn't have anything to talk about in bed. Can you imagine?"

Harry smiled.

"That's what I like about you, Harry. You don't try to change me. I'm just Iris to you."

"I'm glad."

He watched her go up the stairs later and felt the stirrings. The small waist encircled by her narrow belt, the little bounce of her bottom in her long pants, her tangled hair. He couldn't help himself. He felt passion for this disheveled woman, and a certain tenderness as well.

Harry got up and went out on the steps to enjoy the still warm air. The aura of fall hung over the lawns up and down the street—a dry, golden heat that made him think of . . . what?

He tried to trace this feeling as he stood there. He and Beth had married in the summer, so it could not be memories of that. She had died in the spring, so that was out. Liz came inexplicably to mind. The nutty phone call, the even crazier request. A bust of Max, no less. Something to remember him by.

And then it came to him. Once, possibly five or six years ago, Beth had mentioned that she would like a fall garden, a small plot on the east side of the house, with flowers and shrubs that reached their full glory in autumn—mums and Japanese maples; a burning bush, and the small purple flowers of the lariope.

Somehow Harry had never got around to it. Beth hadn't been that persistent, maybe, or he'd been unusually busy, or he had forgotten, he didn't know what.

But now he was filled with an odd mixture of remorse, regret and resolve. He would plant this garden in her memory on the east side of the house.

The following afternoon, Harry took the shovel and was hard at work spading up the dry earth, when Kirsten and The Hun arrived in Hahn's rattle-trap of a Toyota. They waved at him and went inside to see Iris.

For two hours Harry worked, right through the dinner hour. He transplanted three azaleas to the south side of the house to make room, then mixed a bag of peat moss with the well-dug earth, turning it over and over with enormous satisfaction. At last there was something he could *do.*

Iris, Kirsten and Hahn came out on the patio as dusk set in and watched him idly, leaves floating down around them. Iris sat with her legs up on a lawn chair, Zeke fat and smug in her lap, his paws dangling contentedly over one of her thighs. Kirsten and Hahn had the glider, and as the sky went from gold to orange to gray to purple, they became silhouettes, exploring each other's faces. Whenever Harry paused to wipe his brow or rest for a minute on the handle of the hoe, they reminded him of chimpanzees, endlessly grooming.

At work the next day, Harry walked through the back lot and chose the best of the Japanese maples, the most brilliant of mums, some red-tipped photinia. Somehow Beth would know, and would be at peace. He walked back and forth from nursery to truck, loading things, and when he finally went to the greenhouse about noon, he found a sealed box sitting on his work table.

Harry pressed the intercom button. "Wanda, what's this package here in the greenhouse?"

"I don't know, Mr. G. A woman delivered it just before you came in this morning."

Harry took a knife and slit the tape that held the flaps together.

Inside was the papier-mâché mold of Max's head, along with photos front, side, and back, and a note from Liz: *You have to, Harry.*

GOING HOME THAT night at dusk, Harry was annoyed by the headlights of a vehicle behind him, shining in his rearview mirror. He slowed. "Okay, buddy, go around. It's clear," he said aloud. But the truck, a pickup, made no move to do so. In fact, came closer still until it was tailing him, almost on his bumper.

"Not again!" said Harry. Yes, definitely. It was the same old high-riser Ram as before, deliberately menacing. How long had it been following him? About the time he left the garden center, he figured.

Somebody, obviously, had been waiting for him. He remembered now. He had seen the truck parked on the shoulder of Old Forest Road, perhaps fifty feet down the highway, when he had got out and pulled the chain across the drive.

This time Harry made a turn several miles short of his usual route. The Ram behind him did the same. At the next corner Harry turned right. So did the Ram. Left . . . right . . . right . . . left. . . . No matter how he drove, fast or slow, the old 4x4 was almost touching his bumper. No horn, no flashing lights. It was just there.

He'd had it. He slowed, then slowed some more until he was going as slow as he could and still be moving. Suddenly he slammed on his brakes and leaped out, fury welling up inside him, and started around to the back. The Dodge motor suddenly revved, the Ram went into reverse a few feet, then raced on around Harry, missing him by inches, and went roaring down the street and into the dark of the next intersection.

He tried to get the license number, but couldn't. Blood throbbed in his temples. *Just hang around long enough for me to get a good look at you, you bastard,* he thought. He took the long way home so he could think, but was no closer to solving the mystery than he had been before.

IT OCCURRED TO Harry that with fall settling in, it would be nice to have his three children over for a barbecue. He would invite Iris, of course, and Kirsten and Hahn the Hun, so it would be just a casual gathering of friends and family. Iris and Claude had already met, and this way Elaine and Jack could meet her without any special introduction. He'd invite Wade as well.

He worked hard to finish the fall garden. The leaves of the burning bush were as brilliant as a sunset, and the heavy pine scent of shredded mulch perfumed the air. Harry stood back with mud-stained hands and observed his work with satisfaction. He wished he had saved Beth's ashes and buried them here.

"Harry."

He turned to see Paula Harrington standing a few feet away, and braced himself for the onslaught. But her voice was soft and her face chagrined.

"Harry, I want to apologize."

"For what?"

She appeared truly anguished. "Oh, I . . . I had this needless suspicion about you and that girl. It just didn't look so good, but that was no reason to think what I did. I want you to know I believe you, she's just a roomer. I see her coming and going to work, and her friends coming over, and you out here making a garden in Beth's memory, and I said to myself, 'Paula, you go over there right now and apologize.' I hope you can forget everything I said."

"As I remember, Paula, you didn't say a thing. Not to me, anyway."

"Maybe not, but I thought plenty, and I couldn't have been more wrong."

"Well . . . things aren't always what they seem, you know."

"That's it exactly. Anyway." She took a few steps closer, admiring the small flowering stalks of the spikey liatrobe. "Beth always wanted this garden. I can't believe she isn't around somewhere watching."

It was what Harry both hoped and feared.

HE CALLED EACH of his children and invited them to a cook-out the following Sunday. Jack, answering first, said Sunday was out, it was their busiest night at Suds and Spuds, but he could come Saturday if he could leave by seven. Iris had to work till six, so Harry set the date for Saturday and told people they were free to come and go as they pleased. Jodie squealed with pleasure upon hearing that her Uncle Claude would be there.

Claude had a way with children. They could cling to his leg like a ball and chain, yet he would uncomplainingly drag them around from room to room. Jodie would lunge at him, using her head as a battering ram, showing her aggression and fondness in equal measure, and Claude would wrestle with her until she was tired.

"Anything I can bring?" Iris asked Harry a few days later. "I could pick up some wine."

"Sure, that would be good," Harry told her. They were eating dinner together, Iris mastering the use of chopsticks which had accompanied their take-out meal, and she held out a water chestnut for him to eat. Her eyes watched his, and Harry recognized the invitation.

It was the novelty of her that enticed him. At fifty-six, his penis did not stand out at a right angle to his body any longer. When he was in his twenties and thirties, Beth used to playfully hang her bra on it when undressing. This time, as Harry took off his trousers and laid them over Claude's chair, he realized that "fun" was not exactly the object here. When he'd followed her up the stairs, he had resisted the urge to hurry her along with a pinch on the bottom as he would have done with Beth. In fact, much of the foreplay he had enjoyed with his wife seemed inappropriate with Iris, he wasn't sure why. He was at a loss sometimes to discover just what it was on Iris's part. Simple physical need, perhaps. Compassion, maybe.

"Two lonely people," Iris murmured as Harry lay down beside her, one long leg entwined over his.

"Not any more," he whispered, kissing her, but she only clung to him. Harry felt as though he had a third arm when he was in bed with Iris. He knew where to put his arms when his wife lay snuggled against him, the way they fit together, but with Iris he seemed to have one arm too many. Where *had* he put it before?

Novel as it was, their sex seemed restrained. Perhaps it had been this way at the beginning with Beth and he couldn't remember, Harry thought. There was still a certain inhibition to overcome, after all. Finally, still erect inside her, Harry rolled over, pulling her with him and instantly an inhuman cry filled the room.

He jolted and lurched, afraid he had hurt her, and Iris fell away from him as Zeke crawled out from beneath the covers, hissing at him before dropping to the floor.

Harry lay on his back, heart pounding, and wondered if his obituary would state that he had died from fright or simply expired at home. Some day forensic science would be able to develop the last image seen on the human retina before death, and in the case of Harry, the killer would be a cat.

"Zeke's got to go," he said, panting.

"Don't you dare," Iris chided. "He's my number one man, sleeps with me every night."

"Lucky Zeke," said Harry.

As he stroked her side, Iris said, "I signed up for a course, Harry."

"Terrific! What are you taking?" His voice was groggy with impending sleep, but he welcomed the invitation to talk.

"CPR."

Did Harry only imagine it, or did he stop breathing for a moment? Was this what young women did when they found themselves in bed with men old enough to be their fathers? Harry took condoms up to her bedroom and Iris took CPR?

"Why?" he asked.

"I just wanted to start with something I knew I could handle. I've been out of school a long time, y'know."

"You're taking this course for me, aren't you?"

"For *you?* " She lifted her head and looked at him.

"You're worried that some night when we're having sex, I might kick the bucket."

"I never thought about that," said Iris. "I guess if anything happened to you up here I'd call your daughter."

"Oh, Lord, no!"

"What if I was in a restaurant, Harry, and someone started choking? Or we were walking along the canal and some hiker had a heart attack? I could do something really special."

"Well, you kiss very well," Harry told her, touching her lips with his.

"Do I? Really?"

"An exceedingly good kisser."

She kissed him again.

"The trouble is, we're supposed to have partners for CPR," she said. "If I don't come as a pair, they'll sign me up with just anyone, so I wondered if you'd go with me."

Harry's eyes opened and focused on the ceiling. "Now, Iris. . . ."

"I didn't put your name down or anything. I just wrote 'Iris Shaw and partner.' If you can't come I could probably find someone else."

Harry did not like the thought of her finding someone else. Did not like the thought of this girl with legs up to her armpits leaning over a man on the floor and putting her mouth to his. "When does the class meet?"

"Thursday evenings at Montgomery College for three sessions, seven to nine."

"I suppose I could manage that," Harry said, pulling her toward him again, wondering if he had the strength for another round.

Downstairs, a door clicked. Harry opened his eyes, one hand on Iris's belly. He knew he should leap to his feet and pull on his trousers, but he was still recovering.

Footsteps. Then Jack's voice. "Dad?"

Iris startled. "Harry!" she whispered.

"Shhhh."

The footsteps were going from hallway to kitchen, then back again, and finally came halfway up the stairs.

"Dad?" Jack called again. Harry swallowed.

There was a long pause, and finally the footsteps went back down. After a time, Harry heard the front door open, then close again. He let out his breath. If it was important, Jack would call. He'd assume Harry was out for the evening, that's all. Then he realized that both the Ford and the Cadillac were in the driveway, Iris's car at the curb. Jack would know. He'd be on the phone that very evening with Claude and Elaine.

When Harry went downstairs later, there was a note on the table:

Dad—
Sorry I missed you. Guess you were busy.
I wanted to talk with you, but suppose it can wait. Take care.
Jack

Harry called him back, but Jack was out.

NINE

The Boat

AS SATURDAY APPROACHED, the number of guests had grown to include Jim and Virginia Swann, the Mitchells, Leroy Schneider, Fred Fletcher, Marge Decker, Paula Harrington, and Wade. It seemed a perfect way to repay obligations and, at the same time, get people used to seeing Iris about the place. He had asked Wanda Sims and her husband too, but they had theater tickets.

Harry was especially glad when Marge accepted—animosity in the neighborhood made life so awkward. "You know, Harry," she said, "I've been meaning to tell you—when I propositioned you back in May I was half asleep, and when I woke the next morning, I couldn't imagine why I'd picked *you,* of all people."

Harry laughed, glad for the out. "Don't we do strange things in the middle of the night, though? Our minds play tricks on us, Marge, I swear it."

The day of the cook-out, however, he woke to rain. Not a brief shower, but a steady sound, as though in his subconscious he had been hearing it all night and it would continue forever. His first thought was that Beth would know what to do. Then he remembered, and felt lost.

Rain did not figure in his plans. People would come inside! Iris may have been keeping her part of the house clean, he did hear the vacuum now and then, but except for wiping off the kitchen counter, he had not touched the rest of the house for he did not know how many weeks. Even if the sky were to clear, someone might come in to use the bathroom. Damn. He got out of bed before it was light and began an inspection of his quarters. Harry even put on his glasses, and was appalled.

There were finger marks on the doors of the kitchen cabinets. In fact, the wood all around each handle had turned gray. Grime on the stove, crumbs in the drawers, the glass shelf inside the refrigerator was caked over with a crust of spilled milk.

At eight he called the garden center. "I won't be in today, Wanda," he said.

A pause. "On a *Saturday*, Mr. G?"

"Too much to do around here."

"Pardon my saying so, Harry, but there's one heck of a lot to do here. That truckload of dogwoods is coming in. You wanted to look each one over when they arrived."

"Have Steve inspect them. He knows what to look for."

"You have an appointment with a landscaper at eleven."

"Call and change it to Monday."

"Harry, is everything all right, or is that cookout proving a little too much?"

"I'll manage. See you Monday."

Harry hung up, reached under the sink for the Ajax, and began.

HE WAS EXHAUSTED by three, but he had the ribs and hot dogs yet to buy. At least the rain had stopped. He returned at four, sank down in a chair, the groceries still waiting on the table, tipped back his head, and was awakened ten minutes later by the sound of the doorbell.

"I just thought I'd stick this Jello mold in your refrigerator, Harry, till we're ready for it," said Paula. She looked past him to the freshly scrubbed floor in the kitchen. "My goodness, you *are* keeping this house up, aren't you? I know I'm early, but if there's anything I can do."

"There is," said Harry. He led her to the kitchen. "Take this charcoal out to the grill and light it, and after that you could start the coffee and set up some card tables while I finish scrubbing the tub." She stared.

To her credit, Paula simply pulled out a dish towel from the second drawer, tucked it in the belt of her slacks like an apron, and took over. Harry liked that in women, the way they just *did* things, didn't bother to discuss all the ifs and buts. Paula Harrington even looked better than he remembered. At one point when they passed hurriedly in the hallway and he saw how inviting the patio had become with the tables and chairs set up, he put out his hand to give her a pat on the fanny, then checked himself.

The sky had cleared, and the sun came out warmer than before. Claude and Sue arrived shortly, then Wade. Harry washed up and changed his clothes while Wade took over the grill. Elaine and Jodie showed up with dessert, then the rest of the guests. The party picked up a momentum of its own, and the air was fragrant with the scent of barbecued ribs.

Jim Swann, however, came alone. "Ginny couldn't make it," he said. "Just not feeling quite herself today. She'll take a rain check."

"Sure," said Harry.

Elaine and Jack seemed to be talking earnestly on the glider, while Jodie threw herself onto Claude's neck and he piggy-backed her around the yard.

Kirsten and Hahn got there even before Iris arrived at a quarter past six with some rolls from the Giant and a bottle of spumante. She and Harry were in the kitchen, putting the rolls in a basket, when Elaine brought Jodie into the house. Harry introduced them.

"Elaine, this is Iris Shaw. Iris . . . Elaine. And this is Jodie, all of four years old."

"Four and a half!" Jodie corrected.

"Hi," said Elaine. "We were wondering if there might be some popsicles in the fridge."

"Sure." Iris opened the freezer. "Green or pink?" she asked Jodie, who was studying her carefully.

"Pink." Jodie turned to her mother. "Is that Grandpa's girlfriend?"

Jesus! thought Harry.

"Just a friend," Elaine told her. "It's a nice cookout, Dad."

"It turned out to be a good day after all," Harry said.

Jodie was still looking at Iris. "You're almost as tall as my Grandpa."

Iris laughed. "Yeah. I was always a tall skinny kid."

"My grandma died."

"I know," said Iris. "I'm sorry."

That out of the way, Jodie decided she needed to use the bathroom.

"It takes her a while to sort things out," Elaine said to Iris, and hustled Jodie down the hall.

Somehow Harry had expected more from Elaine. Had hoped she would spend time talking with Iris. She had seemed so accepting when Harry first told her about the arrangement. Well, it took adults time to sort things out too, he concluded.

He moved around among his guests and actually heard Paula ask Fred if it was true that an undertaker had been arrested in New Jersey for sexually abusing a corpse. Fletcher choked on his glass of beer, holding it out away from him, wiping off his chin, and Harry laughed aloud. By God, this was a first rate party. He began to wish he had invited every person who had sent a card to Beth during her illness, everyone who had extended sympathy to him after she was gone.

"Did you want to talk with me, Jack?" Harry asked his son at one point, but Jack merely waved him off. "Hey, that was business, and this is a party, right? Never mix business with pleasure."

As Iris came outside with more ice, Jack said, "Dad tells me you work at Hecht's. Good job?"

"It's okay if you like handbags," she replied. "Not a whole lot happens, though. What about you?"

"You'd be surprised at the customers we get," said Jack. "And the amount of clothes they leave! You want an orange jersey top? A denim jacket? Size eight jeans? They've been sitting in lost-and-found a couple months now. Nobody seems to miss them."

Harry filled a plate for himself and sat down between Wade and Leroy, admiring the ribs that were seared to perfection.

" . . . just normal people?" Iris was saying.

Jack nodded. "Well, we've got this woman who walks around the laundry with a huge keyboard strapped to her chest. Never plays it, but never takes it off."

Iris smiled. "That's weird, all right."

"Then there's this guy who comes in and gets on his knees in front of the machine and does a little ritual before washing his clothes."

"Really?" asked Rita Mitchell. "Have you ever asked him why?"

"No, we just stay away from him," Jack said, and the others laughed. "And then, of course, there's a man who washes his money. Really! Change and bills both. Puts them in this little mesh bag."

"I've heard of laundering money, but that's ridiculous," Wade said. More laughter.

Harry had just taken a bite of baked beans when he heard Elaine give an exuberant declaration: "Sue, that's wonderful!' And then, turning to the others who had glanced her way, she grabbed a spoon and noisily tapped a table leg. "News flash!" she called gaily. "News flash, everyone! Sue and Claude are going to be parents!"

"Well, hey!" cried Jack, slapping his brother on the arm.

Harry grinned broadly and watched as Claude gave an embarrassed shrug, then playfully snapped at Jodie's nose as she stood waiting for her hot dog. Sue simply smiled from the chaise lounge she had preempted for herself.

"Well, Claude, are you going to make an honest woman of her and set a date?" Jim teased.

Claude continued snapping at Jodie and she giggled, fighting back. "Well, we haven't got that far yet," he said.

"I'd say you got pretty damn far!" said Leroy, to more laughter.

"When is it due?" asked Marge.

"Next May," Sue replied.

"Take it from me, that's a great time to have a baby. You'll skip all those hot summer months," Rita told her.

As Claude gave Jodie her hot dog, Harry said, "Pretty exciting news, isn't it, Jodie? He'll make a great father, won't he?"

She lifted the bun to her mouth, then paused. "He's going to be *my* father?"

"No, sweetheart. He and Sue are going to have a baby."

"But I'll still be your Uncle Claude," Claude told her and, winking, scraped a layer of marshmallows off Paula Harrington's Jello salad and put them all on Jodie's plate.

Harry couldn't seem to stop smiling. Was this a happy occasion or what? Jack had to leave early, of course, but the others all seemed to be enjoying themselves. The October wind was warm, the sky turning from pink to violet, the barbecued meat giving off a heavenly fragrance that wafted over the lawn, and even Marge and Iris had become friends, deep in a discussion of handbags.

He liked the way people fit together—the generations mingling here in his backyard. He walked about the lawn refilling Styrofoam cups. The lives of his children were not exactly going the way he might have wished, but a year after his wife's death, there would be a new grandchild, Elaine would be teaching full time, the leaves would be coming back on the trees, fresh and small and new, slowly unfolding, like a baby's ear. Life would be. . . different. That's all he was prepared to say.

Harry could hear the phone ringing back in the house, and climbed over Jodie on the back steps to go inside. He was afraid he had missed the call because he could hear a slight clunk at the other end at the same time he said, "Hello?" He repeated it more loudly when he realized they were still connected. "Hello?"

A pause. And then a voice as low as thunder: "Leave her alone, or else." Followed by a dial tone.

HARRY TOLD NO one about the call, not even Iris, who had gone back home to spend the night. What was this, some jealous boyfriend? She'd said she had no boyfriends. Who had she been talking to?

Buoyed by the success of his party, Harry slept with a peculiar soundness, and woke ready for a quiet Sunday morning at the greenhouse. He managed to finish several projects, and felt a rare sense of elation that he was getting on with things.

He put down the sandpaper he was using to smooth the fin left on a lion. The beast had his mouth open in a perpetual roar that made Harry's jaws ache. He focused on the Virgin standing at the other end of his work table. From where he stood, Harry could see a thin dark streak extending from the Madonna's left eye down her cheek, a blotch on her bosom where a drop had landed.

He walked over and bent down, observing her closely. She did not feel wet at the bottom, so what was it with these tears? Cement of indeterminate mixture, he guessed, with just enough bentonite to soak up any available moisture and release it through some minute crack or hole in the surface which, in this case, just happened to be in the left eye.

By noon, when the others came in, he surveyed the property to see what else needed doing. Most of the herd had taken steady jobs for the fall and winter. Tony Berto had been the first to leave, then Kenny Haines and Mike Zapata. Soon the staff would have dwindled down to the regulars. But meanwhile the plastic garden ponds, the submersible pumps and filters, the wind chimes and fruit tree netting must all go into storage, making room for more bird feeders, firewood, and a load of pumpkins. Harry could have asked Bill and Steve to do all that, but today he felt physical, and his legs welcomed the trips back and forth to the storage shed.

There were two calls that day.

"Hi, Dad," said Claude. "Just wanted to say that Sue and I had a good time yesterday. Everyone did."

And his brother Wade: "Hi, Harry. Say, I wrapped up the rest of those ribs and stuck them on the bottom shelf of your refrigerator, in case you're wondering. Good news about Sue and Claude, huh?"

Nothing, however, from either Jack or Elaine.

ELAINE SEEMED TIGHT-LIPPED and tense when she brought Jodie by on Tuesday. In fact, she seemed to be talking mostly to Jodie and ignored Harry altogether.

It's Iris, he decided, remembering Jodie's remark at the cookout.

"Don't forget what I told you," Elaine said to her daughter before she left.

The door closed and Jodie stood in the middle of the living room with her jacket still on, holding her little tote bag of amusements.

Harry surveyed her fondly as he flipped channels on the TV, then decided there was nothing worthy of his granddaughter's attention, and turned it off.

"Are you going to take off your coat and stay awhile, or are you just passing through?" he asked genially.

Jodie put down her bag, pulled one arm out of her jacket, then the other, and dropped her wrap on a chair. She sat down on the rug by the coffee table and took out a circus sticker book.

Harry went to the kitchen for more coffee, then sat on the couch when he returned, watching the work in progress. Opened, the sticker book presented the inside of a circus tent with some of the props but none of the performers. On a separate page were vinyl figures of people and animals that could be removed and pressed onto the scene wherever a child happened to want them.

"Hey, that's something!" said Harry. "Make your own picture, huh?"

Jodie nodded, intent on what she was doing. It pained Harry to see how precise she had to make things—seals lined up exactly in the right order, from tallest to smallest; elephants marching in precision, each with its trunk hooked around the tail of the animal in front; the acrobats swinging their perfect legs in perfect unison.

"No!" Jodie would whisper occasionally to herself, removing a figure she had just placed on the page and then pressing it down a mere centimeter to the right or left of where it had been before.

Where was the originality, the creativity, he hoped to see in his progeny? Claude seemed not to have it. Jodie didn't exhibit it either. How could Harry pass on something he didn't have? No stone carvers here, but he loved them profoundly, nonetheless.

The precision even tired Jodie, for at last she fell back on the rug dramatically, her arms straight out at her sides and announced, "I'm tired."

"Could I play with your book awhile?" Harry asked.

She studied him suspiciously for a moment, then began to smile. "Okay." She sat up and slid the book down the table toward him.

Harry removed all the figures from the page and Jodie crawled over beside him, curious. She watched as he took two lions, their limbs taut, and had them springing off the trapeze on either side of the ring.

"Not *there,* Grandpa!" she cried in disbelief.

"Why not?" said Harry.

She looked at him dumbfounded as he chose an elephant next and turned it upside down, legs in the air, in the safety net below.

"Not *there!* " Jodie shrieked indignantly. "The elephants are supposed to be in the parade!"

"Not *my* elephants," said Harry.

By the time his picture was done, he had the lion balancing on a ball on his nose, and an acrobat flying through the flaming hoop.

"There!" said Harry, and handed her the book.

Jodie stared at the picture a long time, and finally began to smile. "You old silly!" she said. Harry laughed and pulled her over on his lap.

Instantly Jodie jerked away.

"What's the matter?"

"This is *my* body, and you can't touch it without my permission," she declared.

It was Harry's turn to be dumbfounded. Jodie scooted to the other side of the couch.

"Did I do something wrong?" Harry asked.

"You hugged me," said Jodie.

"Oh," he said. "That's about as bad as seals on horseback, huh? Twice as bad as tigers on the tightrope?"

She appeared to be holding back a smile, but did so successfully.

"It's *my* body," she said again.

"You always liked hugs before," he countered.

She sighed. "Mom says to be careful!"

Sadness crept over Harry, compounded by grief that had nothing to do with Beth. "I'll be very unhappy, Jodie, if we can't hug anymore," he said.

She sat with her legs out stiffly in front of her, tapping the edge of the sticker book against her knees. "So will I, Grandpa," she said in a small voice.

Harry swallowed and turned away.

Cardiac-Pulmonary Resuscitation, Room 24B, read a sign on the door of a classroom.

"I'm glad you came with me," Iris said as they walked down the hall, looking for the right room. "You sure don't want to be paired up with a stranger. Somebody could be blowing AIDS right into your mouth, you know? You come in to get certified and you leave HIV positive."

"Can't be too careful," said Harry, bemused.

At the door, everyone was to write his name on a tag with a big red *Hello* at the top. Most of the participants wrote their names so small and faint that Harry could not read them anyway, and he decided he was getting to the age where he would simply have to go around calling everyone "Hello."

HARRY, he wrote in big letters.

The class sat on plastic chairs, each with a blue folder containing colored diagrams of the head and chest—thorax, esophagus, sternum, lungs and heart. The sixteen or so members of the class were mostly women in their forties, though there were three healthy-looking men, and two women who appeared younger.

The instructor, a woman Iris's age, stood in the front of the room with the no-nonsense enthusiasm of a starchy headmistress. "Just so there's no misunderstanding, this is room 24B, ladies and gentlemen, not 24A, and this is a class on CPR, or Cardiac Pulmonary Resuscitation."

She paused as some of the class members took out their pens or began inspecting the material in their folders.

"Again," the woman repeated, "I am Carol Graves, and this is 24B, *not* 24A."

She smiled condescendingly. "Each class, we seem to get people who are supposed to be somewhere else. If you are here for Edible Plants, Conquering Phobias, or the Creative Christmas Workshop, you are in the wrong room." Her eyes slowly scanned the group like those of a customs official looking for contraband.

One of the women stood up pink-faced and reached for her sweater. "Phobias?" she asked in a whisper.

"Twenty-four A," said the instructor patiently. "The other side of the folding doors."

The woman and her sweater made a hurried exit. A minute later Harry, who was sitting in the back row next to the partition, heard a male voice say, "Come on in, don't be shy," and then the scraping of a chair on the floor.

Two courses for the price of one, thought Harry, keeping an ear out for both.

"Now," said Carol Graves, gravely. "Why are we here? After all. . . ." She laughed. "You could have been learning to make your own Christmas candles. What was it that made you decide to enroll in three weeks of CPR?"

Harry listened while each gave a reason. One of the men was a high-school football coach, and the two younger women were healthcare workers needing certification. But most were wives of men who had heart disease. What was it like, Harry wondered, to be fairly sure of how you were going to die? Was there a certain relief in meeting your adversary face to face? *So this is who you are, you son of a bitch.*

He snapped to attention when he realized that Carol Graves was waiting for him. What was the question?

Iris answered: "We're together. Harry's my partner, and I just wanted to get back into courses and things."

"Still," said the instructor, "there must have been something about CPR . . . "

"There's nothing worse than feeling helpless when someone's life is on the line," Harry offered.

"Thank you, Harry," said the instructor.

"Flying," came a woman's faint voice from the other side of the partition. "I'm absolutely terrified of planes. It's not the taking off, it's the landing."

Harry tipped back in his chair. Carol Graves was writing A-B-C on the board. *A=Airway,* she wrote. B stood for breathing. *C=cardiac: check to see if the heart is beating.*

There were murmurings beyond the wall. A man who seemed to be sitting just behind Harry was saying, "I've got this worry that when I use the bathroom in someone's house, the toilet won't flush."

Harry wished he was in 24A. He wanted to be with people whose biggest problem was how to get on a plane and fly to Florida. Or being invited out to dinner and worrying about the toilet. He would have taken on all of them in exchange for a wife who would leave you for the silent stalker who carried her name in his pocket.

AS HE AND Iris drove home, Harry stroking her knee, he said, "You've sure got a big family, Iris. I think you're smart to be taking CPR—you just never know in a group like that."

"That's how I figure," she said.

"Anyone in your family Italian?" he asked. "They don't have many heart attacks, do they?"

"Italian?" She appeared to be thinking it over. "I don't think so. A cousin married a Gonzales, but I don't think that's Italian."

"No, it's not." Harry waited a moment. "Something else I was wondering about," he continued. "Can you think of anyone who might be upset that we're sleeping together?"

She looked at him blankly. "Who would it be?"

"That's what I'm asking you. Your father? One of your brothers? An old boyfriend?"

"My family's glad I've got a place to stay, and they don't know what we're doing. There's no boyfriend, either."

"Well, I got this call," Harry said, and told her what the voice had said.

"Must be about some other woman you're seeing, Harry, not me."

The casualness of her tone upset him. "You think I'm sleeping with someone else?"

"I don't know. It's not any of my business."

"Well, I'm not."

"I'm okay with that," she said.

What was she to him, or he to her? Harry wondered. He wasn't even sure, if asked, how he would describe their relationship. An affair? A service arrangement? No, he was underrating it, he told himself. It was the beginning of a friendship, and who knew where it would lead?

"You coming up?" Iris asked when they reached home.

"If you'll let me," he answered.

"I gotta brush my teeth," she told him.

Unaccountably, Harry changed his socks. You did weird things when you went to bed with a stranger. Her body parts were different from Beth's—her breasts, for instance—more like Christmas decorations than mammary glands. But he liked her youth, the firmness of her thighs. The thing he did not like about Iris was her feet. They were narrow, but they were long. He had loved Beth's tiny feet, size five and a half, but when Iris rubbed one of hers up and down his shin, it looked as though it belonged to a plowman.

He went upstairs to her room. She wore only a long T-shirt. When she bent over to pull back the spread, he had a sudden desire to spank her, and wondered if she'd let him.

As she came around the bed, he caught her, kissing her hard on the lips. "I'm going to spank you," he whispered.

She pulled away a little. "Why?"

"I'd just like to do that. I won't hurt you."

"You mad about something?"

"Of course not. It just . . . turns me on."

Iris crawled onto the bed and rested on one elbow, looking at him. Harry tried to turn her on her stomach, but she resisted. "It seems sort of weird, Harry."

"Okay," he said agreeably. "It was just an idea." He lay down beside her.

But Iris was curious. "Did you ever spank your wife?"

"Of course. She enjoyed it."

"What did you hit her with?"

"God, Iris, I didn't hit her! Just spanked her bottom lightly." He tugged at her playfully, and Iris put her head back down.

"You ever read that book by Stephen King?" she asked.

"What book is that?"

"*Gerald's Game*. This husband's into kinky sex and they're out in this cabin. He's got her handcuffed to the bed and then he dies of a heart attack. So here she is, you know? And this stray dog comes in and starts eating the corpse. . . ."

It took some doing to keep his erection after that, but somehow Harry managed. The thing was, the really weird part was that when Harry had made love to Beth in the last ten years of his life, he sometimes fantasized a younger, more physically attractive woman. But the last few times in bed with Iris, he had found himself, at the peak moment, fantasizing Beth.

As he lay there stroking Iris's hair, he pondered this phenomenon. What was it he missed, besides their past and future? The familiarity, he decided. The same thing that had driven him to imagine a younger body was now the thing he missed—the gentle, slow casualness of the way sex had become for them. The easiness of it, the acceptance of each other's quirks. He missed the scent of her brand of shampoo on his pillow or her vagina on his fingers, as familiar to him as the shape of his own chin. He simply missed Beth's body, a road map to home. Was this a sign of aging or of love? All that mattered was that it was real. He felt his eyes grow moist so he closed them. Sighed, and flirted with sleep.

The phone rang as Iris was getting up to do her ablutions. Before she could reach the phone in the hallway, the answering machine at the foot of the stairs kicked in with, "Leave your message after the beep." Harry could just make out Jack's voice: "Dad? Hey, Dad, it's Jack. Are you there?" Pause. "Dad? Can you come to the phone?"

"You want me to pick it up?" Iris asked. She was holding her T-shirt over her breasts.

"No," Harry said drowsily. "Let him leave a message and I'll call back."

"Dad?" came Jack's voice again. "Well, I guess you're not there. Or else you're doing something pretty interesting," and he laughed. Harry's eyes opened wide. "Listen, Dad, I'm sort of in a jam. I need a loan of about three hundred dollars, and I've got to have it tomorrow. It's only for four days. I can pay you back on Tuesday. Could you possibly get the money out tomorrow, and I'll come by the garden center and pick it up? I really appreciate it. Just a small cash flow problem, nothing serious. Thanks a—" The machine cut off.

HARRY HAD A theory about the Madonna. He was tired of looking at her, for one thing. She was an old statue, made in France, and in addition to her hand, one of her elbows and a piece of her forehead were missing. She was still weeping from her left eye. Harry would mop her up in the morning and a few hours later he would see a tear forming once again. It was spooky as hell.

The owner wouldn't take her back till the Blessed Mary stopped crying. Harry suggested that perhaps she was crying because she wanted to go home, but the woman wouldn't hear of it. "I don't want busloads of people kneeling in my front yard," she said. Harry could understand that.

So when he got to work the next morning, after stopping at an ATM machine for Jack, he examined the statue under a strong light with a magnifying glass and detected what he should have suspected all along: There was an almost invisible fissure on top of the Virgin's head. She had been sitting out in a garden year after year, and had undoubtedly been soaking up rain water. If there was a crack or hole lower down on the figure, the water would leak out at the first opportunity. An eye—the corner of an eye, especially—was usually one of the deepest points on a statue. All it took was a microscopic hole, and the Madonna would cry.

It was even possible that she was hollow at the core, and if this were the case and she was actually harboring a well, he could insert the smallest diamond bit on his drill and have her leaking any place he chose. He smiled at the possibilities.

There was a tap on the door and Rose Kribbs stepped timidly inside.

"Say, look here," said Harry, motioning her over to his work bench. "I want to show you something."

Surprised, Rose came over to where Harry was holding a magnifying glass above the Madonna's head. "Look through there and tell me what you see," he said, and slowly raised, then lowered the glass.

"Oh! There!" said Rose, steadying the glass herself to hold it in place. "It looks like a crack."

"That's exactly what it is," said Harry. "This lady has been out in the garden soaking up rain all these years, and she's probably got a well inside her. The water will come out wherever it finds an opening which happens, in this case, to be the corner of one eye."

"So—she wasn't really crying?" asked Rose.

"Not exactly," said Harry. "Some 'miracles' are actually made by human hands, but I think this is an old fissure that's been there for a long time."

"Well," said Rose, handing him the little tinfoil-wrapped package she carried under one arm. "This was made by human hands too. I just thought you might be tired of your own cooking, Harry. I mean, Mr. Gill. So I made you some banana bread last night."

Harry looked down at the little package. "That was very kind of you," he said. "I appreciate it, Rose."

She smiled back, and when it appeared she might linger, he said, "Would you mind explaining the Madonna's tears to Tracy when she comes in today? I think she should know that there's a scientific explanation."

A SECOND VISITOR came to the greenhouse that afternoon.

"Get my message?" Jack asked.

"Yes."

"Hope you can help me out, Dad. I'll have the money back to you on Tuesday, no problem there at all."

"Aren't you running things pretty short? You don't have any savings?"

Jack put up the palm of one hand. "No lecture, please."

Harry took the envelope from his pocket. "Okay, Tuesday it is."

"How are things, Dad? How's Iris working out?"

"All right, I guess. We both stay busy. She comes and goes."

"Yeah. Well, good. Thanks a lot. See you Tuesday."

When Jack had gone, Harry told himself that it was a different world than it was when he and Beth were starting out. Who would have thought that one of his children would be paying over fifteen hundred dollars a month for an apartment! Almost twenty grand a year, and no equity to show for it.

He remembered a wedding they'd gone to five or six years ago—some friend of Elaine's—and the kids were going to live on a houseboat. If it got too expensive one place, just untie the ropes and float somewhere else. Maybe that was the way to go.

Harry finished restoring the swan he'd been working on and set it aside. Then, with frost warnings imminent, he went out to help Steve and Bill bring all the remaining plants inside. Max's cranium still sat in its box. Liz had not called lately, and Harry began to hope she'd forgotten. Maybe all she really wanted was to get it out of the house—felt that once the mask was someone else's project, miraculous things would happen and she would recover. Miraculous things did not happen all by themselves. You had to work at miracles.

JODIE WAS ON his mind. Every time he thought of her unhuggable little body sitting woefully on the couch, he was sad, alarmed, and angry in turn. Angry at Don Wheeler for deserting her and her mother; angry at Elaine for driving him away; furious at Elaine's therapist for even entertaining the thought that Harry could have molested his daughter. He also was angry at Beth for leaving him when he needed her most, and possibly for other transgressions as well which he could not think about for more than a minute at a time.

So maybe he had passed through shock and panic and was up to anger now. But when he thought of Jodie and Elaine, it seemed they were all adrift on an ice floe, and that he could hear sounds of its cracking. Some day soon, perhaps, there would be a split in the ice, and he could only watch helplessly while his daughter and granddaughter drifted away from him.

When he rose Sunday morning and made his coffee, he decided to go through Elaine's room and see what he might find of hers that would interest Jodie. A game they could play together, perhaps. A favorite doll. Elaine, like her mother, had been a saver.

He didn't want to wake Iris by clunking around upstairs, so he waited until he heard a toilet flush. Then he went up and opened Elaine's door. A young woman was asleep in his daughter's bed. Her hair was a tangle, and she had one arm up over her face. He wasn't sure, but he suspected she was sleeping in the nude because he caught a glimpse of a bare breast. She didn't stir.

One moment Harry was standing inside the door of his daughter's old room, and the next he was standing out in the hall, the door closed behind him, staring at the wall. Who the hell was that?

He heard the shower turn on next—Iris, he assumed, though now he wasn't sure of anything. He went downstairs and poured some cereal. He was halfway through breakfast when Iris appeared, her vest mis-buttoned, the cuff of one shirt sleeve flapping around her wrist. She tried to roll it up while she reached for the bread.

"Better check that top button," Harry said.

"Hmmm," she murmured sleepily, fumbling with it, then stopped and re-buttoned the vest.

"Iris, I started to go in Elaine's room this morning to find something for Jodie, and someone's in there," he said.

"Just Kirsten," said Iris, slowly shaking some cereal into a bowl for herself, then reaching into the refrigerator for the milk. Her eyes were half closed.

"Oh," said Harry thoughtfully. Of course. She'd spent the night here before and he hadn't objected. Did he expect both girls to sleep together in the same bed? But then another troubling thought came to mind: in addition to the bare breast, which had almost blotted out everything else, Harry had noticed some boxes and at least one suitcase parked there on the floor. Yes, now that he thought of it, he was sure.

"How long is she staying?" he asked.

"Well, Harry, we were wondering if you'd care if she moved in for a while. My sister's baby cries half the night, and the room always smells of diapers. I mean, Elaine's room's just sitting there, and we'll do all the cleaning. Your whole house, I mean, if you want."

Harry stopped chewing.

"Kirsten doesn't eat a lot of breakfast, and she'll eat lunch and dinner out, so except for her showers and a little electricity and Rice Krispies, she really wouldn't cost you much. And all you have to do is say so, and we'll both start paying rent, as much as we can afford, I mean. I'll get her a key."

"She's just a high school girl, Iris. I can't take on a responsibility like that."

"Oh, she's *my* responsibility," Iris declared. "If she gets in any trouble at all, it'll be up to me. We already talked to Sam—that's her father—about it, and he said it was okay. You were out yesterday, so I told Kirsten she could bring her stuff over, but she couldn't unpack until you said it was all right."

The one thing Harry had learned in his fifty-six years was to never, if confused or confounded, give an immediate answer to anything.

"I'll have to think about this," he said. "I'll let you know tonight." And then he added gently, "It's not that I object to Kirsten. Maybe I was thinking about our privacy more than anything."

Iris smiled at him sweetly. "She's out almost every night with Hahn. We'll manage."

Harry sat turning his coffee mug around and around on the table. "And if Hahn decides to sleep over?"

"I already told her you wouldn't like that," said Iris. "Besides, she's signed a chastity card."

"Come again?"

"It's the thing now. The school counselor got about a hundred kids to sign cards promising not to have sex until they're married. AIDS, you know."

"And they stick to it?"

"Most of the time. They do everything but," she added. "Things I wouldn't even *think* of doing."

"Well, as I said, I'll let you know."

Iris lifted her eyes and studied him as she chewed. "She's practically my best friend, Harry. I mean, you'd think with her so young and all, we wouldn't have much in common, but we really get along."

"I know," said Harry.

He left the house as soon as possible and was surprised to see Paula Harrington getting in a car with Fred Fletcher, both dressed as though they were going to church.

I'll be damned, thought Harry.

He did not especially enjoy his work at the greenhouse that day, but he did not know why. Life was moving too fast. Later, as he drove toward home listening to Mendolsohn's *New Hebrides Overture*, there was a part he particularly enjoyed, a haunting theme that came back in first one place, then another, and finally Harry asked himself, Why *not* let Kirsten have Elaine's room? It might insure that Iris stayed, for one thing. Also, better to have music and laughter and strange containers of food in the refrigerator than to have old ghosts wandering from room to room. With both Beth and Don Wheeler gone, Harry was gaining a boarder for every member of the family he had lost. Zeke would be delirious.

He stopped at the Tastee Diner in Bethesda for their blue plate special, which happened to be pork chops and mashed potatoes, and then drove home as dusk settled in.

Kirsten and Iris were sitting together on the couch looking

through a hairstylist's magazine. They looked up tentatively when Harry hung up his jacket.

He faced them in the doorway. "I've been thinking about your staying here for a while, Kirsten," he said. "I realize that things are difficult for you at home, with so many people under one roof, and I don't see how I can charge you rent, since you're still in school. You need a room, and I need someone to clean the house, so if you girls. . . ." Here he corrected himself. " . . . If you women will agree to keep the house clean, upstairs and down—all except my room and bath, which I'll do myself—I'll consider the rent paid. As for rules, I guess we'll make those as we go along, and if things don't work out, I'll let you know."

Both Iris and Kirsten smiled broadly.

"Thanks, Harry," Iris said.

"I really, really appreciate it," Kirsten told him.

"Well, that's settled then." Harry went into his own room to change clothes. Did he know what he was doing, to have a seventeen-year-old girl in the house, only slightly older than Tracy? Was he prepared for her music? Her friends? No. He knew the answer to that already.

HE WENT AGAIN with Iris to her CPR class because he needed to stay busy. There were no shortcuts to grieving, he knew. He had to go the whole nine yards. But there were times he felt more disturbed than sad.

"The thing about the first year," Jim Swann had told him once, "is you feel fine for a while, and six months later you think you're going to have a nervous breakdown." What would Jim do, Harry wondered, if he knew that his own wife had opened her blouse to Harry? And then, because he couldn't help himself, he wondered if Beth had ever opened her blouse for Jim?

Iris climbed in the Cadillac beside him as she always did, with an air of naïve expectancy, as though this class, this expedition, *this* time was going to fill an empty space in her life. Where Beth seemed to have an answer for everything tucked away in a file box, Iris had no solutions at all. She appeared to be perpetually searching.

The DeVille rolled down 355 toward Montgomery College. There was an implicit understanding between them that if Iris listened to Harry's choice of music going—a Bartok *Romanian Rhasody* this time—she could tune the radio to whatever station she desired coming home.

"I kind of like this one," she said, and Harry smiled.

Most of the people in the CPR class assumed that Harry and Iris were father and daughter. She approached each session with a gung-ho attitude that Harry found delightful and amusing, and when she was handed the small doll model to practice infant resuscitation, and was praised by the instructor, she looked around the group and said proudly, "I don't know what I'm doing, but I'm doing it!"

Harry liked sitting back by the partition, however, listening to the angst of the inhabitants of 24A. This time they were relating their successes and failures of the previous week:

"I actually drove to the airport and watched a take-off."

"My son found a spider and I didn't panic."

But Harry was especially taken with a woman who had a phobia about food deliveries. After agonizing all week, she had finally entered a Mexican restaurant to ask for a take-out menu, and ended up by the cash register with her head between her knees.

The instructor was asking for Harry's attention. Today she was introducing the class to a life-size model named Suzy, dressed in blue sweatpants and a loose-fitting top. She was an approved CPR model with a flexible diaphragm and slightly visible rib cage, so that when the instructor demonstrated the chest compression part of CPR and lifted the top to expose the chest, Harry was somewhat shocked to see life-like female breasts. His penis registered a slight ping as though, even asleep in his trousers, it could detect an amatory object within fifty paces.

"Okay, Harry, what about you?" the instructor said. She yanked down the model's top again.

Harry stood up uncertainly.

"Let's say you're in a tour group and suddenly a woman ahead of you falls to the ground. Everyone else seems to panic. Take over." She stepped back and left the stage to Harry.

Reciting the basic steps to himself, Harry ran over to the mannequin, bent down, and gently shook its shoulder. "Are you all right? Are you all right?" he asked, and, getting no answer of course, pointed to the instructor and said loudly, in a voice of command, "You! Call 911."

"Good!" she said.

Harry looked down again at Suzy. She wasn't put together quite right. One pupil was dilated and one was not. He did the customary breathing check, then, tipping her head back to open the airway, he pinched her nostrils shut, covered her mouth completely with his, and gave five hard quick breaths. He felt like a desperate man who had received an inflatable doll by UPS and was trying out the first orifice.

Okay. Five breaths. Now the chest compression. Quickly he flipped up the woman's top, and those breasts stared up at him, like two sundaes topped with nutmeats. They befuddled him momentarily.

Her sternum! Where the heck was her sternum? Harry placed the palm of one hand over the knuckles of the other and laid them on her chest. Then, rising up on his knees for leverage, he pressed down in what he thought was the right location, and fell backwards as a mechanical scream issued from the rubbery throat.

"Holy Jesus!" Harry said, and the instructor could not help smiling.

"Surprise," she said. "I forgot to mention that this one's a super model. If you do it wrong, she lets you know."

Iris and Harry were still laughing when they got in the pickup later, and Harry thought perhaps they could just talk on the ride home. He and Iris never really unburdened themselves to each other. But Iris turned on the radio instead, and fiddled with the dial.

". . . if you leave me,
I will cry, if we part,
But if you say you never loved me,
Little gal, you'll break my heart."

Iris sighed and leaned back against the seat, singing along.

She wanted to make love when they came home from CPR. Beth had wanted to make love when they had seen a movie together, or after a back rub, or when she was simply in a good mood and feeling relaxed. Iris wanted to go to bed with Harry after they had been kneeling on the floor at the community college blowing air into a mannequin's plastic mouth. She also wanted to eat first, as though her thin frame could not support him without nourishment. So after Iris and Harry stopped for coffee and doughnuts, they went home and sat on the edge of her bed. Iris locked the door in case Kirsten came back. Then she took off her clothes and lay down beside Harry. He caressed her until she was on the edge of either excitement or sleep, he was never sure which, and then their bodies came together and the evening was over.

It bothered him that Iris insisted on a bath after sex. Harry remembered how his wife had stayed glued to him, enjoying the afterglow. That had pleased him. This did not.

WHEN HARRY CAME home from work on Tuesday, there was an envelope on his bed.

Thanks, Dad, it said on the front. Inside were fifteen twenty-dollar bills.

"I'll be darned," said Harry.

Jodie arrived that evening wearing a witch mask with warts on the nose, her fingernails painted black.

"Ye gods!" exclaimed Harry when he opened the door.

"Mom wanted me to be a butterfly, but I wanted to be a *witch,*" said Jodie gleefully, making clawing motions at him.

"She insisted on those nails," Elaine said, coming inside and helping Jodie off with her jacket. As Harry hung the coat in the closet, he heard Elaine tell her daughter, "Now remember. If anything happens, the number is right there in your pocket."

"What's this?" asked Harry amicably.

Elaine kept her eyes on Jodie. "It's a good idea for Jodie to know where she can reach me."

"In case I have a heart attack or something?" asked Harry.

"In *any* kind of emergency," Elaine said. And then, to her daughter, "'Bye, Sweetie. See you later."

When Elaine was gone, Jodie put on her mask again and went to look in the hall mirror. Harry checked her jacket pocket and found the slip of paper: *Linda Bainbridge, family therapist*, it read, with a phone number.

"I think maybe I've got a little headache," Harry said to his granddaughter. "Maybe you ought to call that number in your pocket and tell Mommy."

Jodie took off the mask again and studied him. "Why?"

"Isn't that what she said? Call her if anything happens?"

"Not *that,*" said Jodie, giving him a look.

"What, then?"

"*You* know." The look again. "If you touch me."

Anger whipped through him. "Oh, absolutely!" he said. "No touching."

He had found a game in Elaine's closet. Each player was supposed to eliminate the other's marbles by sending them through a grid into the pit below. Jodie took to the game with much screeching and cheering. Once, when she successfully caused four of Harry's marbles to disappear at one time, she leaned against him, whooping in delight.

Harry immediately backed off. "Oops! No touching!"

She glanced at him, then looked away.

They made milkshakes afterwards, and when she clutched his arm to beg for two straws instead of one, he gently shook her off.

"No touching, Jodie." He felt like a heel.

She grew quiet after that, sucking through her straw. Then she silently got down out of her chair, carried her milkshake to the other side of the table, and stood next to him. "Hug me, Grandpa," she said in a small voice.

His heart ached. "I'm afraid we can't, Jodie. It seems to upset your mother."

"Hugging's okay," she said. "You're just not supposed to touch me *there.* " She pointed between her legs.

"Jodie," Harry said, "Have I ever touched you there?"

She shook her head.

"Have I ever touched you anywhere I shouldn't, or done anything at all to you like that?"

"No," she said.

"Then I think you ought to tell your mother that. If there's not going to be any more hugging, it's going to be a very sad world."

Jodie put her milkshake on the table, turned to Harry, her arms outstretched, and they hugged. *Cherish the moment*, he thought, as the balsam scent of her shampoo reached his nostrils and the small arms hugged him about as tightly as they could. She took a deep breath and retrieved her shake.

"*Now* I'm happy!" she said. "You know why?"

"Because we can hug again?"

She nodded. "And because you know why else? Because Daddy's going to come back for Christmas and surprise me."

Harry was nonplused. "How do you know that, honey?"

"Because he always puts on his Santa Claus suit at Christmas. I think he's just waiting till Christmas, and then he's coming back as Santa Claus. And *then* he's going to get a big, big, *big* hug!" She held out her arms as wide as they would go.

Goddam you, Don Wheeler! Harry thought. *Goddam you to hell!*

IT WAS SOMETIME in the night when Harry woke and remembered a wedding. For a few minutes he could not recall whose wedding it was, but it was outdoors, it was somewhere near the C&O Canal, and there was a pulley-type raft that conveyed guests across an inlet of the Potomac to Chestnut Island.

A girlfriend of Elaine's, that's whose wedding it had been. The parents had decorated the raft with flowers, and the ceremony was held in the woods. The reception took place in the lodge there on the island, owned and maintained by a canoeing club. Yes! This was the couple who had lived for a time on a houseboat. After the reception, Harry remembered, the newlyweds had simply got on their boat and drifted away. The island's caretaker, too, lived on a houseboat, an old thing tied to the dock, and Harry had a distinct memory of Don going down to the water's edge to look the boats over, talking awhile with the man. Was it possible?

He dropped off to sleep again for an hour or more, but woke early and got up to make breakfast. He called the garden center and left a message that he would be in late. As soon as daylight broke, he got in the pickup and headed for MacArthur Boulevard.

It took a while for Harry to find the right turn-off, much less the right path. He probably hiked a half mile in the wrong direction before he realized he had to cut back and go the other way. Finally the path grew more familiar, landmarks more certain, and then, yes, there it was, the mud-caked landing, the water's edge, and sitting high on its stilts, serene and sure on Chestnut Island, the lodge.

Harry stood on the bank, hands in his jacket pockets and surveyed his options. There was a thick cable stretched across the gray-blue water of the inlet, attached to a bell on the island, and Harry remembered that were he to yank on the cable, the bell would ring and the caretaker would respond. The young man would unleash the raft on the island and, holding onto the cable, hand over hand, pull himself and the raft with him to the other side to inquire about Harry's business and ferry him across.

Harry did not want to waken the caretaker at this hour. Besides, he was studying not one houseboat but three, two of them not more than floating shanties. But what caught his attention was a black and white plaid jacket that was flung over an old chair on the deck of one. It looked very much like the jacket he and Beth had given Don for Christmas a few years back. Bingo.

He began walking south along the bank, beneath sycamores and mulberry trees, maples and elms, looking for Fletcher's Boat House and was about to turn around and go back when he caught a glint of something silver up ahead. Tramping on through the weeds, he found a small encampment—two pup tents and a canoe.

Harry thrust his hands in his pockets and tried to think what to do. There was motion, however, in one of the tents, and a minute later a hairy-backed male, bare to the waist, with pants slung low over his buttocks, backed out of one of the tents dragging a sleeping bag, and shook it out.

"'Morning," said Harry.

The man looked around quickly, eyes still puffy with sleep, and ran one hand through his hair. He gave Harry a nod, then reached into his tent again to retrieve his boots and sweatshirt. He was obviously trying to break camp before discovery by park police.

"I was wondering if I might use your canoe for a short while," said Harry.

The man shook his head. "We're clearing out. You've got to rent one from Fletcher's."

"Well, that's the problem. I've got to see a man over on Chestnut Island, and he may not be there by the time I get back from Fletcher's. I'll show you where I want to go." Harry took a step toward the water and pointed to the island. "I'll be glad to rent the canoe for an hour and I won't even be out of sight. Twenty bucks?"

The man wiped one arm across his forehead and didn't answer. A second man crawled out of the other tent, turned his back and urinated into the bushes.

"What's he want?" he asked over his shoulder.

"Wants to rent the canoe for an hour. Twenty bucks."

"Shit. For twenty bucks, we can pack up and hang around for an hour. Why not?"

The deal was made, the money delivered, and Harry pulled the canoe to the water's edge and picked up a paddle. It had been years since he'd paddled, and he knew he had climbed in awkwardly. But after a few strokes, he found himself moving through the water cleanly, evenly, the rich dank-earth smell heavy upon the air. The trees on both sides of the inlet were brilliant in the early morning light—red, then red-orange, then as intense a yellow as he had ever seen. If he had known, when Elaine and Don married, that eight years later he'd be out here trying to retrieve a straying husband. . . .

And then he remembered that retrieving was not his business. Beth would have made it hers. Beth would probably have delivered an ultimatum in a motherly manner that left no mistake about it. But Harry was neither pointer nor retriever; a simple messenger. He could not make Don love Elaine any more than he could make Iris love him.

Within a few minutes he glided past the larger houseboat, the caretaker's boat, and approached the smaller, more run-down of the other two. His idea was to tie up, cross the plank, and knock at Don's door, taking him unawares.

It did not work that way.

"Hello, Harry."

Harry had just swung the canoe around, ready to head for the bank, when he looked up to see Don leaning on the railing of the boat, a coffee mug in his hands. Don studied him some more, then said, "I'll be damned."

"Good morning," Harry said, and waited for Don to invite him in, but the large man on deck gave no indication that he was accepting visitors. That was bad. Still, Don obviously had seen him coming, and he could have simply not answered the door.

"Care if I come up?" Harry asked.

Don gave a slight toss of his head toward the cabin behind him. "Place is a mess. Rather you didn't."

Harry had not planned to give his little speech hunkered down in a canoe, his head tipped back, but he had no choice. "I know it's early," he said, "but I had a hunch you might be here."

Don let out a long, uneasy sigh, and turned his head in the opposite direction, staring sideways out over the water. He was dressed in the navy blue jumpsuit of an auto mechanic, and there was an insignia on the pocket that Harry couldn't read. Finally, when the silence had gone on for some time, Don asked, "Elaine send you?"

"She doesn't even know I'm here."

"How'd you find me?"

"Claude thought he saw you crossing MacArthur Boulevard. Just a hunch."

Don tapped his fingers on the railing, and finally straightened up. "I've got to leave for work in twenty minutes, but you can come in if you like."

"Thanks." Harry rowed to the bank and tied up the canoe. "Go ahead with your breakfast," he said to Don, stepping inside. "I don't have too much to say, actually."

"That makes two of us."

"Where's your car?"

"I let a guy at the garage keep it during the week. He's doing some work on it, and picks me up each morning, drops me off at night. Not much use for a car here on the river."

"You're working at a dealership?"

"Yeah. Same work, different company."

The boat smelled like a bachelor's abode—dirty socks, musty blankets, mildew, and coffee. There was a bunk at the back of the houseboat, unmade, a sink full of dirty dishes, an array of canned food stacked on top of the single cupboard, its green paint peeling.

Harry slid onto the vinyl bench of a stained dinette table; the Formica felt sticky to the touch. Don was grilling a slice of Spam in a skillet, and added a couple of eggs. The smell of the Spam was sickening. Harry didn't know they still sold the stuff.

"Had breakfast?" Don asked.

"Yes. I'll take a little coffee, though, if you have enough."

Don nodded toward the pot on the dinette. "Help yourself."

Harry poured himself a half cup, using one of the mugs on the table. Don worked on in silence, then dumped the mess from the skillet onto a plate and turned off the propane stove.

"So how goes it with Elaine?" Don sat down heavily at the table. He looked a little plumper about the face, the pasty color of a man who wasn't eating right or getting enough exercise. Belly more prominent.

"What do you want to know?" Harry took a sip of coffee. Damned if it didn't taste like Spam too. Single men were a pathetic lot, he was thinking. Could kill off an entire population.

"What's she telling everyone?"

"That you up and left, what else? She's teaching full time this fall."

"I figured she would. I wanted to be sure she and Jodie could keep the house. I only take out enough from my paycheck to get by, and put the rest in our account. She can have it. I don't care."

"And Jodie?"

"Don't, Harry," Don said.

"Just a message, that's all. Actually, not even that, because Jodie doesn't know I'm telling you. But she's got this idea that you're going to show up on Christmas. That's when you're coming back, she says. Not only that, but you're coming back as Santa Claus to surprise her."

"Harry. . . ."

"I think it's her way of trying to explain things to herself. I've been taking care of her on Tuesday evenings while Elaine goes to therapy sessions. Jodie was real down for a while, but last week she was cheerful. That's when she said you'd be coming back at Christmas."

This time Don stopped eating and rested his forehead in his hands.

"I'm not advising you one way or another, but Jodie's got to know where she stands in all this."

Don let out his breath and tipped his head back, eyes closed. For a while neither of them spoke. Then: "Leaving Elaine . . . was the hardest . . . and the easiest thing I ever did in my life."

Harry waited.

"I can take a lot, Harry. I *did* take a lot from her. But that day—the day of the funeral service—it was like something inside me said, 'This is it. Curtain time.' Walking out of that house and into my car, it was like a magnet pulling at me from both directions. I went to a Holiday Inn that first night. Then I remembered the caretaker's houseboat, a couple other old boats he said he kept around for friends who dropped by. I wanted a place to think things over, so I came here."

Don looked out the small grimy window. "At first I saw it as a short separation—probably just a couple of nights. Week at the most. But the longer I stayed away, the easier it got. When I thought about going back, I asked myself, 'For what?' Even Jodie was beginning to sound like Elaine."

"She's *four*, Don!"

"Oh, I didn't mean that. It's Jodie who's tearing me up inside. I called her, you know. . . ."

Harry nodded, withholding judgment.

"It's not as though I don't care about them. A neighbor—Elaine doesn't know this—will let me know if there's an emergency, anything I should come home for, and I would. But, I don't know, Harry. I never thought I'd stay away this long. Here I am, with half my clothes still hanging back home in a closet. I've got mice for bed mates and this junk heap of a boat I'm renting, yet there's something about my life I like. The quiet, maybe. Not having to second-guess Elaine, and always guessing wrong."

They sat for some time in silence as Don finished his breakfast. Finally Harry said, "This is a strange question to ask, I know, and completely off the subject, but did Elaine . . . did she ever mention that I sexually molested her as a child?"

Don bolted back in his chair. "*God*, Harry!"

"I didn't, of course, but she seems to think I did. I'm just wondering how long she's been under this delusion."

"All she ever said to me was that she never felt you really loved her. Never hugged her, kissed her. Do you suppose any kid ever thinks she's loved enough?"

Harry wished Don hadn't told him that. It wasn't true. He did love her, and had loved her, and there had been plenty of hugs and kisses, but, as his son-in-law said, probably not enough to satisfy. And what was truth, if a child's conception of it was different? Do you ever convince her otherwise? He wasn't sure whether he felt better or worse for finding out he had loved Elaine too little instead of supposedly loving her too much in the wrong way.

Don got up and put his dishes in the sink, stuffing the last bite of Spam in his mouth. Chewed thoughtfully for a moment, then reached over and put one hand on Harry's shoulder. "Listen, I'm sorry this all dumped on you right after Beth's funeral. I'm really sorry about Beth."

"I know."

"And I'm sorry about Jodie. I don't know what I'm going to do."

"Do you still love Elaine, Don? At all?"

"I don't know that either. I truly don't."

They went outside together where the caretaker, a slim man in his twenties, was waiting for Don. The man untied the raft as Don got on, then ferried him to the other side of the inlet. Harry waved, got in the canoe, and paddled back to the campsite.

He began to feel like a man who had gone to the store for his wife and forgotten the grocery list. If Beth had been waiting at home to find out how the conversation had gone, Harry felt quite sure he would not have been able to answer a single question he was asked.

Why had Don left? Beth would have wanted to know. Was he out of his mind? Was he seeing someone else? Why hadn't he filed for divorce?

Harry had asked none of those questions. Women always complicated things. This whole problem boiled down to whether Don loved Elaine enough to come back and live with her again. If he did, he would. If he didn't, he wouldn't, and all the other questions were irrelevant. But Beth would want to *know.*

A gull soared over the island. It looped back around, flew over Harry's head again and then, spreading its wings wide, sailed out toward the Potomac beyond.

WHEN HE REACHED home thinking of Don, of Elaine, of Jodie, of Beth, he sat down at his desk and unearthed the cryptic letter in its yellowed envelope from beneath his blotter, as though reading it for the seventh, the eighth, the ninth time would reveal something he had not seen before.

It did. For the first time he noticed that, in addition to the top of the capital "T" in the address being missing, each letter "g" was almost too faint to be read. There was something familiar about the "g" and the "T," and suddenly Harry's heart began to pound. He pushed back his chair and went to the storage closet in the hall, searching the shelves for Beth's old typewriter that she had brought with her to the marriage. When Harry first started the garden center, she had used it to type the addresses on customer's bills.

He carried it to the dining room table and inserted a piece of paper. The platen was so old and dry it had fine cracks on its surface, and the mechanism gave a rusty squeak as Harry turned it. There was scarcely enough ink in the ribbon to leave any imprint at all, but with his index finger hovering over the keys, Harry pushed down each letter of the alphabet in turn. He removed the paper and compared it with the yellowed sheet in his other hand. On both pieces of paper, the "g" was especially faint and the top of the capital "T" was missing.

TEN

The Therapist

HARRY FELT HE had been married to a woman he didn't know. With the knowledge that Beth had sent the letter, he had been transformed from a man bereaved into a man deceived. Yet she had typed it, sealed it, mailed it, and then—when it arrived at the house—opened it. And decided, after all that, not to show it to him. Still she had kept it. It didn't make sense, and Harry's shaky peace with himself had been shattered, no closure in sight.

Had his wife made up the story to hurt him as he had once hurt her? Or was she confessing a truth she had intended to keep secret, but—because of Stephanie Morrison—no longer cared if it came out? In that case, take your pick. Who was the bastard child—Jack, Elaine or Claude? And who was the father?

Once again, he considered each friend. Jim Swann? Fred

Fletcher? Surely not Leroy. Max, his best friend? Was it possible? Or the likeliest candidate of all, Windy Mitchell. *Surely* not Wade!

He was through with this business of mourning, he told himself angrily, and was glad he'd taken Iris to bed. Life was for the living. And yet . . ?

The hurt was unmistakable. His chest felt inflamed. It was the worst a wife could do, to keep such a letter, leaving him with the question unanswered for the rest of his life, should he find it.

Perhaps, after eleven years, she had truly forgotten it. Forgotten where she had hidden it, maybe. The one irrefutable fact was that she had not mentioned the letter to him. Whether she had held back because she lost her nerve, resolved her anger, or found her peace, Harry didn't know. Could he possibly consider that she had held back out of love? Could he live with that?

He rested his head in his hands. "Oh, Beth," he murmured. "Beth."

JACK LOOKED THINNER. It was November before Harry saw him again. He came over to help put on the storm windows, an annual rite Jack had continued long after he left home. He'd just show up some Sunday and say, "I've got a couple hours, Dad. Let's do the windows," and they'd get the job done. Paying his filial dues.

"You working out at a health club or something? Look a little thin," Harry said.

"Heck no. Haven't got time for a health club." Jack lifted the frame Harry hoisted up the ladder toward him. Then he laughed. "I don't have to work the weight off. I worry it off."

"Any problem in particular?"

"Running a business is problem enough," Jack said.

"Anything I can do?"

"Not unless you can fix a dryer that keeps overheating and a washer that skips the spin cycle. It's okay. I've got a repairman coming tomorrow."

Harry washed the next window while Jack fastened the first in place. They seemed to be reversing roles these days. When Jack was in college, Harry drove over occasionally to see how things were going and put up a shelf in his room, maybe. Now it was Jack calling to see how the old man was making it.

"When are you going to get yourself some thermal pane windows, Dad?"

"I get those, I'd *never* see you."

"Oh, I'd be around," Jack said.

IT WASN'T WORKING—anger as an antidote to grief. When he thought of Beth lovingly, Harry was sad. When he thought of the letter, he was miserable. And because he did not care to be either, he kept busy.

He had been invited to Claude and Sue's for dinner that evening. He'd planned to eat crackers and cheese before he left, so he wouldn't discover that what he assumed to be the appetizer was, instead, the whole shebang. He forgot, but this time was pleasantly surprised. Claude had made paella, and Sue baked bread. The seafood concoction was served in a huge ceramic bowl, and there was plenty of it, so Harry ate heartily.

Sue was dressed in a loose-fitting shirt and baggy pants, and if Harry had not known she was pregnant, he might not have noticed. But when she stood in the doorway, her folded arms resting on her abdomen, he could see a slight roundness to her body beneath her shirt. He liked the thought of another Gill coming into the world, liked the thought that at least two of his children had reproduced. And then the random thought: *Was* this a Gill, after all? Which of his three children would *least* likely be his? He would not allow himself to answer, even if he knew. He wasn't certain he wanted to know.

"Who's Jack dating now?" he asked. "I can't remember."

"Still Jennifer, I believe," Sue told him.

"He looks thinner to me. What do you think?"

"I think all parents figure their kids look thin," said Claude. "You ever notice how every time I'd come over for dinner, Mom would try to send food home with me?"

Harry smiled. "She didn't have to twist your arm."

"How about some pumpkin pie, Harry? I know it's rushing the season, but would you like a piece?" Sue asked.

"Love it."

"Whipped cream or plain?"

"The works."

Eat like there was no tomorrow. Keep the mouth going, hence the mind. Pretend it never happened: there had never been a letter. When Sue left the room to get dessert, Harry said to Claude, "Well, you and Sue *are* going to marry, aren't you?"

Claude just smiled and shrugged, and worked at stacking the plates. "Don't jump to any conclusions," he said.

"Meaning?"

"I'm just saying that 'baby' doesn't necessarily mean 'marriage.' It's not a natural antecedent. Sue just really wanted a baby."

Harry wished he had never asked the question. They had a house, they had been living together two or three years. How could they have a child together and not commit? For that matter, how could Don Wheeler abandon a child he had created? And then the question, how could Beth. . . ?

Each day he understood less than he had the day before.

WHEN HE WENT to bed next with Iris, Harry tried to increase his understanding. He told her about Claude and Sue having a baby because Sue wanted it, and how Elaine had wanted a child almost as soon as she and Don were married.

"What's to understand?" Iris wanted to know.

"I can understand how women want a baby, but how can they be so eager to go through childbirth?"

"What about men going to war? Who would ever join the army knowing he might get his head blown off?"

"It's not quite the same, Iris, and not all men want to go to war."

"Not all women want to have children."

"What about you?"

He felt the little sigh against him as he held her. "There was this guy once. He said he wanted to marry me. Only he wanted me to promise that if I ever got pregnant, I'd have the baby by C-section so my body wouldn't stretch. Down *there*, he meant. That really ticked me off. It was the last time I went to bed with him."

Harry would like to have known how many lovers she'd had. He thought about his own history. There was that girl in high school when they were seniors, and the two in college. And a woman he'd thought seriously of marrying until she confessed she didn't love him enough, no matter how many times they'd slept together. After that, it was Beth. He was sure that if he asked, Iris's liaisons would outnumber his own.

He lay still for so long that Iris asked, "Wha'cha thinking? You think I should have had a C-section just for him?"

"Course not. Just wondering—say, on a scale of one to ten—how much you would like to have a baby."

"A five or six, maybe."

Harry stroked her thigh and smiled. "How about a husband? Scale of one to ten?"

"About the same, I guess."

Maybe this was the key to intimate conversations with Iris, Harry was thinking: the questionnaire.

"Question number three," he joked. "How important is sex in your life?"

"You mean like water, food and air?"

"Well . . . yes."

"A four, maybe."

His hand stopped in mid-caress. "A *four*?"

"You *have* to have water, food and air, Harry, but did you ever hear of a person dying because he didn't get enough sex?"

He chuckled. "No. Time or two I felt I might." Harry turned his head and studied her. "You don't—regularly—get a craving for it?"

Iris looked thoughtful. "In high school I did. And I used to feel that way sometimes with a house painter I was going out with. I don't know what it was. I just liked the smell of turpentine on his hands."

Harry waited, but what he hoped to hear never came. Iris seemed to sense his disappointment because she said. "Sometimes it's a seven or eight. Like right before I eat? Sometimes it's hard to tell if you're hungry for food or for someone to hold you, know what I mean?"

"Not exactly."

"Well, see, if I go out with a guy to eat and afterwards I'm still hungry, I think, 'Maybe it wasn't a hamburger I wanted after all.' It's different for men, though. You're always a ten, aren't you?"

"Uh, let's make that an eight or a nine."

"Only *they* want to eat *after*," she said. "There was this one guy—his life was like a bus schedule. Always trying to save time: make love, eat a sandwich, watch the eleven o'clock news. Every night the same. Finally I told him he had to choose between me and the eleven o'clock news. He chose the news. Said he could eat a sandwich and watch the news at the same time, but he couldn't do anything else when he was having sex."

Harry laughed aloud.

She turned and drew up her knees, facing him again. "What I like about sex is—it's like CPR, you know? Somebody's—well—in pain, sort of. And I'm there to fix it. For a man, I guess, I'm water, food and air."

That said, she went off for her ritual bath.

IT WAS TIME to call the police, Harry decided. He had not been tailed again, but when he and Iris left the house one Sunday morning to have brunch, he found that someone had glued an Italian flag, a foot square, over the driver's side of the Cadillac's windshield. He swore.

"Is it some sort of holiday, maybe?" Iris asked, studying the red, white and green flag.

"Yeah, Idiot's Day for folks like me. I should have reported this stuff a long time ago."

"What stuff?" asked Iris.

"Some vandalism that's been happening off and on."

"If it was *our* flag," Iris continued, "I could understand, maybe, but this?" She tried to pry up one corner of the cheap, stiff cloth with one fingernail. "Do you think they're Italian terrorists? I mean, if at eleven o'clock, all on the same morning, all over America, people couldn't drive because their windshields were covered."

"Just keep working at it, Iris," Harry muttered. "Maybe it will pull off." But try as they would, they could barely lift a corner. The flag had been firmly cemented to the glass with epoxy. He'd probably have to have it towed to a dealer and replace the whole windshield. He swore again.

"I'm sorry," he said to Iris. "We'll have to take the Lariat."

"Oh, I don't mind," she said. "But what do you suppose they'll do next? Let out the bulls or something?"

"What?"

"You know. Once a year they let the bulls out and they chase people down the street."

"That's Spain."

"Oh."

They got in the pickup, and Harry knew he would have to work to remain pleasant. Inwardly he seethed, mostly at himself.

"Well," said Iris, "at least they didn't put a horse's head in your bed."

"*What?*"

"*The Godfather!* Now I *know* that's Italian."

Harry smiled in spite of himself. "Yes," he laughed. "I'm glad they didn't decide to do that."

"I like to make you laugh, Harry. You don't look so old when you laugh," Iris said.

"I'll try to remember that," he said, and turned the truck toward Old Forest Road.

ON MONDAY HE stopped by to see the Cadillac dealer and they suggested a solvent he might try. "Your insurance will probably cover this," they said. But Harry knew what would happen to his premiums if he told them the whole story, and their first question would be, "Did you call the police?" So he applied the solvent and then, inch by inch, with a plastic ice scraper, removed the flag in sections and called the county police.

The officer was a tall man, six foot five, with skin almost as black as his shoes, who carried a clipboard under one arm.

"Officer Mark Collins," he said, extending his hand. "Heard you've had some vandalism."

"Come in," said Harry, holding the door open for him. Iris was visiting her relatives and they had the house to themselves. Zeke jumped up on the couch beside the officer and sniffed at one sleeve. Mark Collins smiled at the cat and scratched him behind the ears.

"Something happened to your car, they said."

"Yes. It's pretty adolescent stuff, but it's beginning to get ominous. Somebody epoxied a flag onto my windshield."

Officer Collins began writing something on his clipboard and didn't even look up, as though flags were glued to windshields weekly.

"American flag?" he asked, pencil pausing.

"Italian. I had a devil of a time getting it off."

The officer gave a grunt of sympathy and went on writing, the noon sun from the south window reflecting off the wristband of his watch. "Did you keep the flag?"

"In that bag there on the coffee table."

Mark Collins opened the bag and looked in. "Not very big, was it? Looks like dime store stuff." He wrote some more, than looked at his watch to get the date and wrote that down too. "When did this happen?"

"I didn't discover it till about eleven yesterday morning, so I suppose someone put it on Saturday night."

"You the only person living here?"

"No. I rent out two rooms upstairs."

"Names?"

"Iris and Kirsten Shaw."

"How long have they lived here?"

"Iris has been here since May. Kirsten moved in about a month ago, I think."

"And when did the vandalism begin?"

"April. Near the end of April. Neither of the women was here then."

"What was the first incident?"

Harry shook his head and smiled a little. "Somebody poured a can of tomato sauce on the hood of my pickup and left a note that said, 'You like Italian? Here's Italian.'"

Now the policeman stopped writing and studied Harry carefully, laughter in his eyes. "An Italian flag on your windshield and tomato sauce on the hood? Do you have another car, a Ferrari, maybe?"

"No. It's a Ford Lariat."

"Anything else happen?"

Harry decided not to divulge the phone calls—the one from Arlo and the one telling Harry to let her alone. "Yes, when I answered my door one evening, a man shoved a pizza in my face."

Officer Collins hid his face in the crook of his arm. "Sorry," he murmured, but now the laughter came in spite of himself. "Just when I think I've heard it all."

Harry smiled ruefully.

"How did you know it was a man? You see anyone?"

"No. There was cheese on my eyelids. But it was a man's voice. 'Here's Italian,' he said. But I heard what sounded like a truck driving off, and I've been tailgated twice by a souped-up Dodge Ram. Each time it followed me almost all the way home. Once I stopped and jumped out."

"Not wise," the officer interrupted.

"I know, but I was pissed. The driver tore around me—almost grazed my arm—and sped off."

"Get a license number?"

"It was too dark. Maryland tags, though, I'm sure of it."

The officer wrote some more, then rested his pencil. "Can you think of anyone who might be doing this, Mr. Gill? Any quarrels with people at work, any fights with neighbors?"

Harry shook his head, and told how he'd run through his list of employees, suppliers, neighbors, acquaintances.

"If you think of anything, you get back to me," the policeman said, standing up. "We've got an officer who lives about a mile away. We'll ask him to make this street part of his route going to and from work for a while. Wouldn't hurt to have a visible presence in the neighborhood. But I'll take in the flag if you don't mind, check it out. Can't be too many places selling these."

Harry shook his hand and walked with him to the porch. He couldn't help noticing, however, that the officer was chuckling to himself when he slid into his cruiser.

HARRY SELDOM HEARD from Elaine anymore. They saw each other Tuesday evenings when she brought Jodie over, but she did not phone during the week to see how he was doing.

"Are we incommunicado, Elaine?" he asked one Tuesday as she prepared to leave.

"Dad, I have mixed feelings about you these days," she told him, hands in her pockets. "I'm just going to have to sort some things through till I figure out where we stand."

"Where we stand?" Harry said. "I'm your father, you're my daughter. Has that changed?"

"I didn't *think* it had, but I don't really have time to talk about it right now."

"Then sometime," Harry said emphatically.

At least he was back to hugs with Jodie, and there was satisfaction in that. It was the first thing she wanted, in fact, when she came through the door, and Elaine watched without comment. Each time Harry felt those small arms around his neck, he realized that if Elaine was not his daughter, then some other grandfather was missing out on this child.

"Know what?" Jodie said that Tuesday. "I can't wait till Christmas."

Harry was teaching her to play pickup sticks on the coffee table. "Yeah?" he said, wishing she hadn't brought it up.

She nodded in such an exaggerated sweep of the head that her chin touched her chest. "I'm going to get up, put on my tiger slippers, and come downstairs, and my Daddy will be sitting on the floor." Here she punctuated each word by slapping both of her knees hard. "Right . . . by . . . the . . . tree!"

She made a face at Harry, as though daring him to contradict her.

"That would be nice, Jodie, but sometimes we don't always get what we want. I can remember a lot of times I didn't."

"He'll *be* there!" Jodie said and, turning, pushed against his chest hard with both hands.

When she was getting her things together later, Harry said to Elaine, "You know she expects Don to be here for Christmas, don't you? She's mentioned it several times."

"That's Don's problem, not mine," Elaine said bitterly.

LIZ SHOWED UP at the greenhouse again. This time she was wearing a pair of Max's gray sweat pants and his PENN STATE shirt. Harry recognized the outfit Max wore when they used to play handball.

He had suspected all these years that Liz dyed her hair because it stayed so dark—a deep chestnut. But now he saw more silver in it than before, and realized it was naturally brown. She wasn't unattractive, but God—those sweatpants, baggy at the knees! A crazy woman in her deceased husband's scruffies.

He was repairing Venus, who had several chips that the owner had overlooked, and Harry worked carefully, pleased that his eyesight was still so acute. But there was Liz, blocking the doorway, scanning the bench.

"You haven't even started!" she said accusingly. "I thought we were friends!"

"Now, Liz."

"When was the last time I asked something really big of you, Harry? The night you drove Max to the hospital, right? Did I ever wake you at two in the morning and tell you my car broke down? Did I ever ask you to balance my checkbook or clean the gutters? All I'm asking is something to remember my husband by."

"Liz, listen. You've got his photos, his watch, his clothes. . . ."

"I want his head," Liz told him. "If it doesn't fit on my mantel, I want it on that white marble table inside the front door."

"I'm no sculptor."

"You can *do* it, Harry! Is it asking too much for you to try?"

Dear Lord, would the woman never quit?

"There may not be enough here to work with," he explained patiently as he walked to the end of the work table and lifted out the papier-mâché mask that resembled a misshapen hornets' nest. It bent slightly in his hands, and gave the surreal appearance of a man whose skull still throbbed with a sort of half life.

Yes, Harry could see the shape of Max's head in that hornets' nest, but the back of the skull had been somewhat knobby, as he remembered it. Liz hadn't been able to duplicate that, of course, because Max's head had been on a pillow, but Harry could almost feel it beneath his fingers, as though his hands could resurrect what he could not see with his eyes.

"If you don't," Liz threatened. "I'm going to start deconstructing our house until I get it down to the part that was there when Max and I married; at least I'll have that to remember."

Harry gasped in astonishment. "Liz, you wouldn't! That's an $800,000 house!"

"I would!" she replied, and Harry knew she was crazed enough to do it. Just off Falls Road in Potomac proper, it wasn't one of those ostentatious castles, but the white brick house had gone through three different transformations, elegant in its wooded setting, and here was Liz and her ultimatum!

"When I finish Venus here, I'll give it a try," Harry said. For old times' sake. For the fact that, if Max knew that Liz had gone off the deep end, he would have expected Harry to control her. And if he couldn't control her, at least contain her.

THANKSGIVING LOOMED BEFORE him like a root canal. The names of the holidays on his Sierra Club calendar were printed in color, but if there wasn't that to remind him, there was Barbie the goose at the garden center, incongruously dressed in a pilgrim's white starched collar and wide-brimmed hat.

This was the first big holiday since Beth had died. Iris and Kirsten, of course, were going back home for the whole weekend, and Claude had said something about how he and Sue would have everyone there for Thanksgiving this time. Last year, despite her illness, Beth had somehow gotten together a traditional turkey dinner. They had all helped, of course, but underneath the forced gaiety, the mood was definitely Last Supper.

Harry did not want to be reminded of it. He did not want to sit at the table musing over which of the children were his, or whether he could forgive his wife. The best way to spend Thanksgiving, he decided, was to do something entirely different.

And so, when the official phone call came from Sue, giving the exact time and the assurance that Harry need not bring a thing, he said, "Actually, Sue, I've got other plans for Thanksgiving this year. I should have told you. I hope you don't mind."

A pause. "You do? Why, Harry, that's wonderful! I see we're getting out and around more, aren't we?"

The news soon spread.

"I hear you've got an invitation for Thanksgiving," Jack said in a phone call. "That's great, Dad."

"Yeah. I decided on something a little different."

"You're not coming to Uncle Claude's for Thanksgiving?" Jodie asked him the following Tuesday as she put together a Hallmark turkey.

"Not this year, sweetheart. But you'll have a nice time, I know."

HE AWOKE THANKSGIVING morning to the sound of silence. Now and then there was a ghostly creaking of the floor, however, and Harry listened without opening his eyes. Then he felt the mattress give a little, as though the shadow of a woman had sat slowly down beside him.

He put out one hand and felt fur. Zeke, bereft of feminine companionship, had settled for third choice, and gave an impatient *meow*.

Harry got out of bed and went in the kitchen. Standing there in his shorts and T-shirt, he took down the box of Kitty Chow and reached for a china plate. Sprinkling a few pieces on it, he said aloud, "Turkey." A few pieces more, "Dressing." More. "Sweet potatoes." He set the plate on the floor. "Enjoy," he told the cat. Zeke gave him a token brush against one leg and hunkered down for his meal.

Harry read the paper until eleven fifteen. He straightened his room and ran the sweeper over the rug. He ate a piece of cheese and a cracker, and at three that afternoon, decided he was hungry enough to go out.

He changed his shirt and drove to Normandy Farm, sure that there would be tables available in the afternoon lull. Inside, a group of people in holiday finery milled about, awaiting seating, and in the great hall, flames snapped smartly in the fireplace. A man in a dark suit checked his roster.

"Time of your reservation, sir?" he asked.

"I'm afraid I neglected to make one," Harry told him. "Gill. Harry Gill. Party of one."

The man shook his head. "I'm sorry," he said. "We have no tables available until nine this evening."

"Forget it," said Harry.

He went back to the Cadillac and drove to the Tastee Diner, but he didn't even get out. There was a line waiting outside and they were all men. All men with nowhere else to go on Thanksgiving. Depressing as hell.

Harry ended up at the Jade Palace, and was one of only eight customers. The owner's wife came over to greet him, and the waiters treated him like a long-lost relative. Tea was brought at once, and ten minutes later Harry feasted on hot and sour soup, Peking Duck, vegetable lo mein, and a fortune cookie: *He who wants no more than he has will live the happy life*. Well-spoken. This was exactly what he wanted, and he enjoyed every bite.

IT WAS THE Sunday following Thanksgiving that Elaine called, and asked to come over.

"Jodie's playing at a neighbor's," she said.

"Come ahead," Harry told her. Iris and Kirsten were still gone. He didn't know how their household managed when the girls went home. Perhaps people slept in shifts over the holidays.

Elaine came in wearing boots and leggings, a long sweater over the top. She did not hang up her coat, but threw it over the back of a chair, then sat down, obviously upset. She'd been crying, and there was a tissue in her hand, another stuffed under the cuff of one sleeve.

"What's the matter?" Harry asked.

"Dad," she swallowed. "I know this is hard for you, but it's been hard for me too—Mom's dying, Don's leaving, and now this."

"Now what?"

"At first I couldn't believe it myself, but then I started having these dreams, and finally I began to remember."

"*What* dreams? Remember *what?* "

Elaine stiffened and thrust her body against the back of the chair. "If you're going to shout, it's just going to be that much more difficult."

"I wasn't aware I was shouting, but I think that a man about to be hung has a right to a little emotion."

"Okay. To start at the beginning, you know I've been depressed since Don left. Not just depressed—anxious. Panic attacks. I mean, there have been times I've wakened in the night with my heart pounding. Everything hit me at once. Would I get a full-time job? Could I keep the house? How do I raise Jodie without a father?"

"Those are questions that would make anyone wake up in a cold sweat," said Harry, in as gentle a voice as he could manage.

"Well, Linda—"

"Linda?"

"My therapist. She says that sometimes we *think* we're anxious about things that are happening currently, things that are worth being anxious about, but when we're abnormally upset it's usually mixed up with something else—possibly something that happened to us long ago—that's making us overreact to things now."

"I see," said Harry, beginning to see very clearly indeed, like a movie scenario before his eyes.

"Then I started having these dreams. I'm a child again in my dreams, and in this one dream I'm at the bottom of a well or an elevator shaft or something, and this big weight is coming closer. I don't see any way out, and this thing starts pressing down on me. I think I'm going to be crushed, and I'm terrified, only the weird part is that I can't feel my bones breaking or anything, but I can't breathe."

"And this is supposed to mean?"

"Then there's this other dream. I've had this one a lot, even before Don left—where I have to go somewhere—catch a bus or plane or something, and I can't find my ticket. I'm running to catch a train, maybe, and the strap breaks on my purse and all the stuff spills out. I have to stop and pick it up, but the conductor's yelling for me to get on, and the train is moving, and at that point I always wake up."

"Seems a fairly common dream. I've had a variation of that a time or two."

"Well, Linda's specialty is dream interpretation. She says that when you dream about wells and shafts and things, it represents the vagina. And my fear, in a sexually-charged situation that something is pressing down on me, is a long-repressed memory of an adult forcing himself on me, especially since my bones don't break."

"Elaine." Harry leaned forward, arms resting on his knees. "*Did* someone ever assault you sexually?"

"I can't remember, but it's got to be somebody."

"So naturally, then, the elevator must be me. Right?"

"Who else would it have been?"

"Jesus Christ!"

"Don't try to be funny, Dad."

Harry was almost shouting. "Funny? You think this is funny? Elaine, if anyone assaulted you when you were young, or when you were grown, for that matter, he deserves to be strung up by his thumbs. I've no mercy there. But *I* don't remember assaulting you, *you* don't remember, and you're going to go the rest of your life distrusting me because of a dream about an elevator?"

"But Linda thinks the other dream confirms it. She says that purses represent vaginas too, and something happening to the purse usually means pregnancy, particularly when it's connected to missing something that comes on schedule, like a train. And she thinks that the dreams about being crushed and the dreams about a missing period could mean that not only were you abusing me before the age of four, but maybe you continued up to the point of puberty and I've just blocked it out."

Harry rose from his chair, catapulted by his own anger. "And where was your mother while all this was going on?"

"I don't know." Elaine's voice was soft, like a small child's. "Linda says that sometimes the mother knows about it and doesn't do anything, and sometimes she just doesn't know."

"That you would *ever* think Beth would allow such a thing!" Harry exploded. "Why the hell would I want to have sex with an underage daughter when I had Beth? We enjoyed each other, and I don't mind telling you that."

Elaine was staring down at her legs. "I know." Her voice was shaking now. "Dad, I'm just so confused."

He came back and sat on the sofa across from her. "Elaine, listen to me. You can't believe what this therapist is putting in your head, because you are one of the most caring, responsible mothers I know. And if you for one moment believed that I had abused you, you would never, ever allow me to take care of Jodie alone on Tuesday nights. Never."

Elaine looked at him steadily and, as Harry watched, her eyes began to fill with tears and her mouth tugged down at the corners. God, she looked so much like Jodie!

Harry let his shoulders drop. "Come here," he said, holding out his arms. And suddenly Elaine rushed over, sank beside him on the couch and crumpled against him, face against his chest. She sobbed big, deep, gasping sobs.

Harry gave a sigh and stroked her hair.

"Sweetheart," he said at last, "I think my crime was not showing you enough love, even though I felt it, and for that I'm really sorry. You had the bad luck to be born when I was working the hardest to get my business going, and I'm afraid you missed out on a lot of hugs."

She sobbed all the harder.

"If I can make up for any of that, I will. But meanwhile, we've got some problems to face, and the story that I fooled around with you when you were small isn't one of them, because it didn't happen and I think you know it."

"But Linda seems so sure," she wept, her nose clogged, her face wet against his shoulder.

"I don't know Linda. I don't know what her problem is, but I can't help wondering if she gets her jollies by imagining sexual encounters her clients might be having. Would it help if I had a talk with her?"

"She'd never allow that. I already suggested it. She said she never sees two members of the same family, that you'd have to get your own therapist."

Like hell, thought Harry.

What surprised him was that Elaine didn't pull away, just kept clinging, and he stroked her back until she began to breathe more deeply and he almost thought she'd fallen asleep. But finally, slowly, she disengaged herself. "I just feel like an enormous weight has been lifted off my shoulders," she said.

Harry grinned. "The elevator, what else?"

IT MAY HAVE relieved Elaine, but Harry was sleepless half the night, and found he wanted to defend Beth as much as he wanted to defend himself. When his pillow didn't suit, he pounded it into oblivion, and the first time his blanket twisted around his foot, it landed on the floor. At eight the next morning he picked up the phone and dialed the number he had found in Jodie's jacket pocket.

After a number of rings, a voice like that of an answering service said, "Linda Bainbridge's office."

"I'd like to make an appointment with Miss Bainbridge, please."

"She prefers to set up the appointments herself, but she won't be in until nine. May I have her call you?"

"Well, it's rather urgent. I'm. . . ." Harry's mind whirred on ahead of him. "I think I'm suicidal."

"Then I suggest you come in at eleven o'clock today," the woman said. "She could see you for perhaps a half hour. Your name?"

Harry paused. "Harried," he said. "Mr. Harried."

"H-a-r-r-i-e-d?"

"Yes."

"Phone?"

"No point in giving a number. I'm calling from a phone here by the bridge."

"Mr. Harried, I'm sure Miss Bainbridge can help you. If you need to talk with someone before then, please call the Suicide Hot-Line," and she gave him the number. "We would like very much for you to keep this appointment."

"I'll . . . try," Harry said.

He had never felt more energized. He drove to work where he unloaded half a truck of Christmas trees himself, and he and Steve set them up in the north end of the parking lot, stringing lights from pole to pole.

Ten-thirty. Harry got in the pickup and drove to a Wheaton office building, a little two-story in a strip shopping center that had been zoned for demolition at some unspecified date.

Ten fifty-three: Out of the truck, up the stairs, and through the door that read, *Linda Bainbridge, family counselor.*

There was a waiting room about the size of a small bathroom with two vinyl chairs, a magazine table between them, and a hanging plant against which Harry bumped his head as he sat down.

Instead of leaning back, he tilted forward and cupped the fist of one hand into the palm of the other, and was engaged in cracking his knuckles when the inner door opened six minutes later and a woman in her mid-forties surveyed him with professional compassion.

"Mr. Harried?" she asked. "Am I pronouncing that correctly?"

He nodded, rose, cracking his knuckles still. She looked at his large hands.

"Please come in," she said gently, and held the door so that he preceded her. None of that nut-case walking behind you sort of thing.

"Sit down," she said. "I do have a form here for you to fill out, but my answering service said you seemed rather upset, so perhaps you'd like to talk first."

Harry nodded. He looked from left to right, right to left, as though looking for an escape route. A window ledge, even! God, he'd missed his calling. Best supporting actor. . . .

"Something is bothering you, and I'm concerned," said Linda Bainbridge, PhD. She folded her hands in her lap, eyes intent on his face.

"It's . . . it's this feeling that I'm out of control," said Harry. "I mean, it's so unlike me. I've never hurt anyone in my life, and suddenly I feel like the world would be a better place if I . . . I just wasn't part of it."

He expected some response on her part, but she continued listening, head cocked expectantly.

"I mean, how can you go all your life thinking it's been worthwhile, and then suddenly. . . ." He slumped back in his chair. Oh, *God,* he was enjoying this.

"Can you tell me about these thoughts you've been having that make you think about taking your life?"

"It's . . . it's this *rage!* " He doubled his fists again and pressed them against each other. Her eyes, he knew, were on those fists. Harry clenched his teeth for effect. "This almost uncontrollable impulse to *maim* someone."

Did Harry only imagine it or did her concerned look seem to stiffen just a little?

"To torture and kill, with these very hands." He held them out in front of him as though he had never seen them before, foreign flippers attached to the stubs of his arms.

"Tell me what's going on in your life right now, Mr. Harried. At home, at work."

"Work is going fine. My wife is dead, so—"

"I'm sorry."

"Wasn't your fault." Harry took a deep breath. "But it's my daughter."

"Yes?"

"We've always had this good relationship. I mean, not perfect, but we certainly respected each other, and suddenly she's met this Svengali."

"How old is your daughter?"

"Old enough to know better."

"Is she having a sexual relationship with this person?"

"I have no idea what goes on between them, but she's changed."

"In what way?"

"It's made her suspicious. Almost paranoid. And I keep having these fantasies of taking this Svengali by the throat and just pressing my fingers on the windpipe, finding the precise place, the exact spot, and then. . . ." Harry put both hands on the arms of his chair and tensed his fingers.

"Mr. Harried, do you live alone?"

"No. I have three boarders, two females, one male." Zeke may have lost his balls, but he was still male.

"Then your daughter doesn't live with you."

He shook his head.

"When did she meet this man?"

"A few months ago. Only it's not a man, it's a woman."

"Oh. And this is what's upsetting you?"

"No. It's the effect this woman has on her. She has the weird idea that I must have molested her as a child. This Svengali—this so-called therapist, who undoubtedly has sexual problems of her own—keeps interpreting these dreams, and—"

A chair creaked as Linda Bainbridge stood up.

"This session is over," she said, and Harry could see her mentally measuring the number of steps she needed to reach the phone on her desk.

Harry stood up too, essentially blocking her path.

"You are Elaine's father, and you used this ruse to get in here."

"A ruse? I am what I am, lady. Harry the Harried, and the session is not over until I've said what I have to say."

"Are you threatening me?"

"I am telling you to sit down."

She seemed to be considering it, and finally she sat. Harry, however, remained standing.

"Very well," she said. "I'll agree to listen, but I can't discuss Elaine's therapy with anyone but her."

"What you have to say about my daughter, I don't want to hear. What *I* have to say about her, you had better listen. If at any time in her twenty-nine years I molested her in any way, I deserve to have the book thrown at me. But I know and Elaine knows that I never did any such thing. And if you continue to suggest that it happened, I intend to take you to court. I will charge you with implanting false memories and alienating my daughter from me." Harry picked up his jacket. "I have the money, I have the time, and I'm determined to see it through. This will, I assure you, be great publicity for your practice."

He went to the door, closed it after him, and stepped out into the waiting room, then the hall. When he got halfway to the stairs, he heard the outer door to Miss Bainbridge's office click as though a dead bolt lock had just been fastened in place. It was, he decided, one of the best days of his life.

INSTEAD OF GOING back to the garden center where people ordered subs for lunch, Harry drove straight to Swann's Barber Shop to have lunch with the boys, and was delighted to find Jim, Leroy and Fred all sitting at the card table by the window, eating together.

"Harry! You want half this tuna salad?" Jim said. "Business is slow. Everyone got their hair trimmed before Thanksgiving."

"Sure you don't want that?" Harry took off his jacket and threw it over a chair.

"We already got an egg salad on rye going begging."

Leroy reached around and turned the *Open* sign on the door to *Closed*. He grinned.

"So how's it going?" asked Fred, as Harry pulled over a chair.

"Not bad," Harry replied, smiling broadly. He took a bite of tuna salad and, with scarcely time to chew, a bite of the egg salad sandwich as well. Fred, Jim, and Leroy studied him with amusement, and passed knowing looks among themselves.

"Things working out okay with your boarder, huh?" said Leroy, his grin widening, his knee bouncing up and down with anticipation.

"Yeah, what you been up to, you rascal?" asked Jim.

"Well, this morning I went to see a therapist," said Harry, scarfing down another bite.

"You know, I'm glad to hear that, Harry," said Fred. "Takes a big man to admit he needs help, but I tell you, grieving is no easy matter. Looks to me like he did you some good."

"She," said Harry.

Jim and Leroy smiled at each other, then at Harry.

"She must have been reeeeal good," said Leroy.

"I feel one heck of a lot better," said Harry. "She's Elaine's therapist. I told her off."

The three friends sitting at the table stopped chewing.

"Because," Harry continued, "she got Elaine to believe I sexually molested her as a child."

Leroy's mouth dropped open and a small piece of liverwurst hit his hand. He sat unmoving.

"You don't mean that!" said Jim. "Elaine told you this?"

"And so," Harry continued, "I took the bull by the horns and went to see her. You're looking at Mr. Harried, calling from a pay phone by a bridge where I might or might not jump."

"Hot dog!" said Jim admiringly.

Harry drew the story out—the way he got her to see him, his role as a distraught man, and when he got to the "I have the money, I have the time. . . ." Leroy let out a whoop and the others joined in.

"Way to go, Harry!" Leroy said, when the racket died down.

"I thought that kind of thing went out in the eighties, all that repressed memory stuff," said Jim.

"Not with all these priests lowering their blessed britches," Leroy smirked.

"You got to be so careful nowadays," said Jim. "You better keep your eyes on a female's face, 'cause you study any other part of her body, you're looking at a lawsuit."

"But can your kid come at you thirty years later 'cause you paddled a bare behind?" Fred asked disbelieving.

"Don't you even *say* 'bare behind,'" Jim warned him. "You know these dads who bring their little girls in for a trim while they go to the drugstore for cigarettes? I say, 'You got to stay right with her, buddy.' I'm not going to court because some kindergarten kid says I put my hand under the cloth. No sir."

Nobody was eating now.

"What do you think ever got Elaine started on that molestation business?" mused Fred.

"Her dreams," said Harry. "She's down in an elevator shaft and this heavy thing is coming at her. It can only be me, right? That's what the therapist said."

Leroy looked genuinely startled. "My daughter used to dream about her car. You don't suppose. . . .?"

Harry tried not to smile. "Oh, that's the worst."

"What? Don't kid me, now."

"A big machine like that? And who was in the driver's seat, do you remember?"

Leroy looked anxiously around the group. "Me, she said."

"Oh, man, you've had it," said Harry. "She's in the car with you and you're in the driver's seat, and you're going eighty miles an hour, I'll bet."

"Something like that."

"Why, Leroy, it's plain as the nose on your face! All those pistons going up and down."

Fred and Jim got in on the act.

"Giving her gas," said Jim.

"Checking her oil," said Fred.

"Lubricating her parts," said Harry.

Leroy looked around. "You're joking, right?"

The other three broke into laughter, and Leroy joined in.

"Well," said Harry. "It could be we're just four old farts, but I tell you, I had one heck of a time today. Beth would have been proud."

"Indeed she would," said Fred.

ELEVEN

The Son

SUE WAS UPSET. That Harry had gone to the Jade Palace on Thanksgiving was bad enough, but that he deliberately misled them into thinking he'd had another invitation was inexcusable. Somehow, Harry discovered, he'd let it slip. Then, of course, he got it from the kids.

"Is there some problem, Dad? Coming to our house, I mean?" asked Claude.

"You can eat Chinese every night of the week. What do you have against Thanksgiving?" Jack asked him.

And from Elaine: "We all sat there trying to guess who you were out with, hoping you were having a great time. Why did you do it?"

Harry was curious. "Who did you *figure* I was with?"

"I guessed the Mitchells, Jack guessed Iris Shaw, and Claude guessed one of your cronies from the barbershop. You're avoiding the question, Dad."

"It was just hard to face Thanksgiving without Beth," Harry said at last. "So I decided to do away with it this year—Thanksgiving, I mean."

And with those fatal words he paved the way for Christmas. Jack, Elaine and Claude put their heads together and decided to make Christmas as memorable for him as they could. Whatever their mom had done for Christmases past, they would do again, right down to the rum sauce.

"We're all coming to your place on Christmas Day, Dad. We've got it all planned," Elaine told him.

All right, let them come, Harry thought. He could not hide out at the Jade Palace for the duration. He would do his best to respond, if only to be there for Jodie. The problem was that Harry's contribution to Christmas in years past had been selecting presents for his wife and buying the tree. Now he had to cope with the whole works in the space of four weeks.

He went to the mall on Sunday intent on doing his shopping in one day. But after staring at bread makers and waffle irons, at electronic versions of things he'd always done manually before, and at the many possibilities of the Hold Everything store, Harry went home empty-handed, convinced that women's clothes were taking over the world and that the human hand would soon be obsolete.

"Shut up," he growled at Zeke, who was sleeping peacefully on a chair. The cat opened one eye and moved not a muscle.

"How's the shopping coming?" Wanda Sims asked him the next day as she and Rose stood in the back room spraying pine cones with artificial snow.

"Checks," he told her. "I'm giving checks."

"Oh, Harry," said Wanda, and Rose looked appalled.

It was the way she said it that hung over him all week, and the more he tried to visualize a half dozen white envelopes dangling from the tree, the more convinced he was that it would not do. He had to buy at least one gift for each person that could be boxed, wrapped, and properly tagged. No getting around it.

The Lands End catalog, taking up the whole of the mailbox that evening, told him how. Looking around the house, he realized that catalogs were accumulating on end tables, chairs and the space beneath windows. Living trees had been sacrificed to produce the slick, full-color pages that would be his salvation. That *must* be how Beth had done it. How else could she have presents wrapped and ready for every event that came along?

Harry got as far as opening a beer, sitting down in the middle of the sofa, and lifting the first catalog to his lap. Iris and Kirsten came in, laden with bright red shopping bags decorated with a frosted Santa.

"Well, there's Mr. Christmas himself," Iris exclaimed, amused.

"I'm pretty new at this," Harry told them. "Are some of these better than others?"

"I'd take anything from Victoria's Secret," Kirsten said, and the two young women went giggling up the stairs.

Harry thumbed through the pile and, by God, there it was—women in various stages of undress with that languid look in the eyes that invited you to linger, not be in too big a hurry to turn the page. He quietly slipped the catalog under the rest for safe-keeping, but found himself distracted and thinking of Iris.

He did not understand her. She initiated sex from time to time, yet he'd remained abstinent once as long as three and a half weeks to see if her own need would kick in. She didn't seem to miss it. If they made love, that was fine and she was ready, but if they didn't, no big deal.

"It doesn't matter, Harry," she said when he apologized because a cold kept him out of her bed for a week.

With Beth it had mattered. She understood, but it mattered. He *wanted* it to matter. Wanted, himself, to matter to her. With Iris there seemed to be no intense passion to do anything. Not that she didn't yearn, perhaps, to do or be or feel or give, Harry mused. She didn't appear to know what she was searching for, and if she did, she didn't know where to look.

It was important to want. Important to need. To try, even if you never made it. Because it was in the reaching that you knew you were alive. How could you go through life with no great stirrings, Harry wondered, sexual or otherwise? Iris slept, she woke, she came, she went. Harry longed to rouse her with music, with books, with kindness, with intimacy. Yet she seemed to prefer his body around her rather than in her. Preferred sleep to conversation. He began to feel as though she had invited him up to her room that first time or two as one would take in a stray dog, lost and disoriented on the street, not really intending to make the situation permanent.

Harry picked up the next catalog and idly turned the pages. Christmas placemats, Christmas potholders and tablecloths. Holiday bathrobes and shorts. Many of the catalogs had been sitting around since summer, and Harry was astonished to see that you could order Fourth of July wind socks by mail, platters specifically designed for fish or corn on the cob. Thanksgiving candles. You could, if you had enough closets, reserve one for each holiday of the year.

The phone rang.

"It's me, Dad," said Elaine. "I'll be getting another therapist. I just thought you'd like to know."

"Oh?"

"Linda told me what you did." Her tone was affectionately scolding. "I went back for one last session to tell her what I thought. She said she can't be effective in the hostile environment you've created."

"*I've* created?"

There was a smile in Elaine's voice. "She said you were an animal! That you practically attacked her!"

"No such luck," said Harry, and he wasn't sure, but he thought Elaine laughed a little.

"Actually, I'm calling about Don. He phoned."

"Really!" Harry sat down on the bench in the hallway. "Where is he? What did he have to say?"

"He's living on a boat somewhere. He wanted to talk about Jodie." Elaine gave a deep sigh. "Oh, God, we talked a long time, but I'm not sure we decided anything."

"Did he say why he left?"

"Me, of course. It was just as I said, Dad. I *told* you he was predictable. I—" She stopped. "I guess there are worse things in life than being predictable, aren't there? I asked if he was going to come back. He said he didn't know. He asked if I wanted him to. I said I didn't know that either. I guess that's where we left it."

"I see."

"But he's going to come back for Christmas Eve. He said we could talk some more then. I'm just not sure *how* I feel, Dad."

"I wish your mother were here. She'd know how to advise you."

"Then again, maybe not," Elaine said. "There was this guy I was crazy about in high school. We went out a few times, but I was never sure how he felt about me. I thought maybe I should come right out and ask him, but Mom said I should date other guys and then, if he really liked me, he'd be jealous and let me know."

"Beth suggested that? Making him jealous?"

"That's what she said. So I dated other guys and he dumped me. Told a girlfriend I'd probably never liked him much in the first place. He'd just been shy. Mom was dead wrong." A pause. "You seem surprised."

"I didn't think your mother was much for manipulating people."

"Ho! Mom had a scenario for every possible problem. Not just a solution, Dad. She could write a whole screenplay, if she had to."

Harry didn't answer.

"Listen, what will I say to Don when he comes over?"

"I don't know, Elaine. You've got a couple of weeks to think about it and decide what you really want from the marriage. Maybe Beth would've had a screenplay you could follow, but I think you should trust yourself. And maybe, when the time comes, you'll know what to say."

THE STORES AT the mall were opening at eight to accommodate shoppers, and Iris left each morning right after breakfast. On this particular morning, however, she went out the front door, then paused, then stepped back inside again, holding a homemade wreath.

"What's this?" she asked.

Still nursing his coffee, Harry came out of the kitchen and stared at the object in her hand. It was made from a wire coat hanger, bent in the shape of a circle. Someone had taken black crepe paper and wrapped it loosely, awkwardly, about the frame in a funereal arrangement. And taped to the bottom was a little card shaped like a tombstone with the name *Harry Gill* printed with Magic Marker.

"It was taped to the door," Iris said.

Harry took it from her and quickly deposited it in the waste basket. "Just someone's idea of a joke," he said.

She studied him uncertainly. "It's not a very good joke."

"Don't worry about it. Have a good day," he said.

She left, and Harry dialed Mark Collins at the police station. He wasn't in, but they expected him shortly.

When the phone rang twenty minutes later, Harry told the officer about the wreath. "Anyone could have made it," he said. "Plain wire clothes hanger, crepe paper, Magic Marker—nothing special."

"I checked around some about that flag, Mr. Gill, and found two variety stores that sell them. One told me they were pretty sure they hadn't sold any Italian flags in the past year and a half. The other said they'd sold six or eight—a grade school was doing an international festival, and they figure that's who bought the flags."

"I'm just uneasy having my granddaughter visit with a nut case on the loose," said Harry. "I'm going to install those motion-detector lights on the house this weekend."

"Not a bad idea," the policeman said. "We'll step up the patrol of your neighborhood, Mr. Gill. I'll talk to the sergeant about it this morning."

"Appreciate it," said Harry.

HARRY TOOK TIME out that week to install the lights, but a week later he was still ordering Christmas presents. There was a cut-off date, he discovered, beyond which a Christmas arrival could not be guaranteed; he was making a science of it now.

Call the toll-free number, wait for the taped instructions, then, *Press one.*

Harry pressed. Christmas music flooded his ears. *Let it snow, let it snow, let it snow.* Then, miraculously, a human voice.

"Desert Crafts. How may I help you?"

"I'd like to place an order."

"Certainly. Please look on the back cover, in the blue box above your name, and give me your customer number."

Harry recited it dutifully.

"To the right of the blue box is a yellow box with a source code. Could I have that number, please?"

Again Harry read it off.

"Beth Gill?"

"I'm her . . . was . . . her husband."

"Spell your first name please. . . . Will you verify your home address?"

Where would he like the items sent? What credit card? Expiration date? Express mail or UPS? Harry answered all.

"And the number of the item you wish to order?"

Finally! "Two X one-forty W," he said.

"The children's plaid cowboy shirt?"

"Yes."

"What size, please?"

"Five."

"I'm sorry, sir. That item is on back order and we don't expect delivery until the middle of January."

THERE WAS THE usual Christmas party at the garden center. At nine o'clock on a Wednesday evening, when the sign at the driveway read *Closed,* employees and spouses and significant others gathered for the customary buffet. Wanda had platters of food delivered from Sutton Place Gourmet, a CD of carols flooded the store, and people milled about in better-than-usual attire, with Santa Claus hats on their heads, helping themselves to finger sausages and mushroom ravioli, bite-size pieces of fried catfish and chicken wings. Those of The Herd who hoped to be hired again next summer showed up with their girlfriends, passing up the wine in plastic goblets and opting for beer instead.

Rose's husband had to work so she came alone, but Wanda's spouse was there—a large, jovial man who took charge of the drinks, as he did every year, and made sure everyone had something in hand. Tracy brought a boyfriend, a tall skinny youth with a complexion like raw meat, who stepped gingerly to the right or left when people passed him, as though he felt himself continually in the way. Harry longed to just hit him over the head and say, "Relax."

Steve or Bill, one or the other, had rakishly carried the weeping Madonna into the store from the greenhouse, and she stood crying in one corner with a small elf's cap perched over her stone shawl.

"Oh, Bill, you *would!* " Wanda scolded when she saw it, then burst into laughter.

Harry gave his usual speech about how everyone had pulled together to make this season a stand-out, and he wanted to thank each one for seeing him through what had been a difficult year. Then he made the rounds of his employees, thanking them personally for their service and slipping the anticipated envelope and check into a hand or pocket.

Well, that's over for another year, Harry thought with satisfaction as he drove home, pleased that the gathering had gone well.

Dear God, let Christmas go as easily, and make Don keep his word.

AND SO THEY gathered for Christmas.

Claude had come over earlier in the week to put up decorations the way he remembered them, then added his own embellishments—a long rope of evergreen to frame the doorway, a bouquet of live holly from a hanging planter beside the front door. Just as his mother had done, he set a small electric candle in each window, to welcome the weary traveler. Iris and Kirsten had gone home for the holidays, but the candles would still be there when they returned, weary or not.

Christmas morning began with a call from Wade who had gone to New Orleans for the duration, while Zeke hunkered down in Iris's room, prepared to be depressed without her.

Claude and Sue arrived first, bringing the ham and mince pies; then Elaine and Jodie, with vegetables and bread, leaving Jack and Jennifer—if he was still going with her—to bring the salad and wine. Each put his offering on the table before the Ghosts of Christmases Past. *I'm not the only one who's missing Beth,* Harry reminded himself, conscious of the wistful looks on the faces of his family when he caught them unawares.

But it was still an occasion for celebration.

"I saw my Daddy!" Jodie shrieked the moment she came in, and showed Harry the pair of roller blades Don had brought her—too big, of course and, as Elaine pointed out, not very practical in a neighborhood without sidewalks—but Jodie carried them around with her from room to room and wouldn't let them out of her sight.

"Aren't those beautiful skates!" Sue exclaimed, and no one asked the question until Jodie had gone upstairs to find Zeke and give him some fresh catnip.

"You and Don iron things out?" Claude asked his sister. The

adults stood grouped in the kitchen, waiting for Jack, while Harry sliced the ham.

"Not really. We just talked," Elaine said. "He says if he comes back, there have to be some changes." Then she added, sardonically, "I haven't received his Bill of Rights yet. I guess it all boils down to whether we still love each other."

"You both love Jodie," Harry said.

"That's not enough, Dad."

Jack arrived with a new bed-mate. Her name was Lisa, an artificial redhead who smiled a lot and said little. He looked even thinner than he had before. Could he possibly have AIDS? Harry wondered, a knot in his stomach. Not only was he thinner but he seemed nervous, and more than once during the meal, Harry caught him looking at his watch. But the food, the wine, and the general merriment infected them all, and even Jack seemed to relax as the various dishes made the rounds.

His cell phone rang halfway through the meal, and he was on his feet in an instant, backing into the kitchen. A look passed between Elaine and Claude as Jack closed the door behind him.

The talk turned to New Year's Eve and what everyone was planning to do. Jack did not come back until it was time to serve the pie.

"Listen, I don't want to cut the festivities short, but I'm going to have to leave in another hour," he said apologetically.

"On Christmas?" Elaine said, her voice scolding.

"Believe it or not, some people even wash their clothes on Christmas," Jack said feebly.

"Well, then! Let's take our pie into the living room and open the presents!" said Claude, as though hurrying for Harry's sake to salvage what spirit of Christmas was left.

"Yay!" shouted Jodie, tipping her chair over in haste.

There was a scramble to place more chairs around the tree, and Jodie eagerly volunteered to fetch gifts from beneath, deciphering those that had her name on the tags and guessing at the others. It was not until the first presents had been distributed that Harry realized some of his were not there. Some were not even wrapped! In fact, several had arrived a day or two before Christmas, and there was nothing to be done now except retrieve them from his closet, still in their Lands End wrappers, their L.L. Bean boxes, in thick yellow envelopes from Brookstone, and the large cardboard container from I.F. Schwartz.

No matter. It provided a laugh for the others, and whether he guessed right or not, everyone said the gifts were wonderful, the best, just what they always needed, wanted, longed for, craved. It was as though, now that their mother was gone, his kids were staging a *This Is Your Life.* There were bits and pieces of traditions he'd like to remember and others he'd just as soon forget. Only they didn't do it by direct reference, but by the idiosyncrasies they'd learned from him—his own generosities or foibles, disguised as their own. His usual "Bah, humbug," for example. Variations on a theme, hauntingly familiar.

Jack rose to go, saying goodbye, but his eyes implored Harry to follow. While the others were helping Jodie assemble the huge dinosaur Harry had given her, Harry stepped out on the porch with Jack. Lisa headed for the bathroom.

"Dad, I'm really embarrassed about this, but I'm in a bind. Is there any way you could write me a check for five grand? Just until the middle of January?"

"Five grand!" Harry felt his jaw go slack. "Jack, what in the world?"

"Listen, I got myself into this and I have no one else to blame. But I owe this guy."

"Gambling."

"Yes, and I swear to God, this is the end of it."

"I've heard that before, Jack."

"This is serious. I'm flat broke."

"How can that be? Are you sick? You look thinner."

Jack gave a bitter laugh. "I'm worried as hell."

"I can't give it to you."

Jack blanched.

"I let my checking account get below a thousand. I couldn't write you a check if I wanted. And I don't believe you and wish that I could. But I see no end in sight. This wouldn't solve a thing in the long run."

"I paid you back last time, didn't I?" There was desperation in Jack's voice.

"And I know you would again if you had the money. But you're broke! You'd try to pay me back by gambling some more, and would go right on putting your future on the line. I can't stand by and watch."

Jack turned away and went down the porch steps. "Okay," he said tersely. "Sorry I asked."

When Lisa came out, pulling on her leather gloves, she got in the front seat, but Claude had come out now, and walked over to where Jack was standing beside the car. Harry watched as Jack spoke earnestly, animatedly, gesturing with his hands. Then Claude answering, hands in his pockets. It ended with Claude shaking his head, and finally Jack got in the Lexus and drove away.

If one of those two was not his, which son would it be? Harry wondered. The impulsive Jack? The sweet-tempered Claude? The plodding artist? The passionate entrepreneur?

Claude came back to the porch and exchanged looks with Harry. "So what do you think, Dad?"

Harry blinked. "I don't know."

"It would have been a mistake to loan him anything. You know that."

"Of course. We did the right thing, but he'll have to sell his business, this keeps up."

"It wouldn't be the end of the world."

All Harry could think was how glad he was that Beth had not seen this. He went back into the living room where Christmas was unraveling and helped put the dining room table together again, taking out the extra leaves.

"*Damn*, Jack!" Harry heard Elaine say to Sue.

In spite of all this, he had enjoyed having the family there. When the last bow had been picked up, the last dish washed and put away, the last coat removed from the closet, the goodbyes were affectionate, and then they were gone.

WHETHER IT WAS Jack, or Iris's absence, the days between Christmas and New Year's were the worst for Harry. Even worse in some ways than the days following Beth's funeral service. He went about his work at the garden center mechanically, scarcely conscious of Wanda's scrutinizing eye or Rose's breathy attempts at conversation. He had no desire to drive to Swann's, and felt perhaps it was a good thing that Iris and Kirsten were not subject to his long, sad face.

"You okay, Mr. G?" Wanda asked. "You don't look okay."

"I'll get over it," he said, and let it go. Wisely, so did she.

At least he had put a label on it. It helped to know that his sensation of having been sucked into a black hole was a process, and that he might still hope to come out of the vortex and live. With the discovery of the eleven-year-old letter, he had thought that his sadness would be tempered with the realization that Beth was not quite the wife he had thought her to be, but found no consolation in that. He had nothing more than suspicion, and though never-to-know seemed worse than knowing, he could not bring himself to foist this surprise on the children. He loved her still. They deserved to love her too.

In the days before New Year's, Harry found himself walking through the rooms, around and around, through bedroom, hallway, kitchen, dining room, while Zeke watched warily from the stairs. He lingered over the perfume bottles on Beth's dressing table, musing over the fact that if she had worn a perfume every day for the rest of her life and lived to be ninety, she could not possibly have used up all those bottles.

And the dreams. . . . Harry rarely remembered his dreams. Mostly they were dreams of anxiety—a stranger walking off with Jodie, Elaine in a car crash, Claude losing the use of his hands. But then, with the waning of the old year, Harry came out of the bedroom one evening to see Beth sitting in her favorite chair, the gold one. She was in her robe, the rayon robe with the shafts of bamboo on it, and she was barefoot, her tiny feet drawn up on the chair beside her, her hair damp. She may have washed it, she was combing it out. Beth was combing her hair and smiling at him.

Harry had never felt such joy. A golden liquid seemed to flood his body.

"Beth," he said from the doorway, smiling back. "I knew you weren't dead."

"I just wanted to see what it was like," she replied.

"Why did you tell me one of our children wasn't mine?" he asked. "You were joking, weren't you?"

But she didn't answer, just went on smiling.

He came across the room and gently lifted up one of her feet. He was surprised how cold it felt, but he warmed it in his hands, then placed it between his thighs and held it fast. She continued to smile up at him as he leaned over her, and she extended her other leg, the robe falling away to reveal her nakedness. He put both of her feet between his thighs, and then he was on his knees and Beth slid down beside him. He was undressing her on the floor, and he was happy, so *happy*, and he knew this was really, really happening this time. She felt so soft—the sweet, sweet sameness of her—and he told himself he wouldn't feel this good if it weren't really happening, and he smelled her hair, and then. . . .

Harry found himself in bed alone, lying on his stomach, his arm around Beth's pillow, the urgency in his groin fading fast.

He was so filled with the immediacy of the dream that he would not allow disappointment to intrude. He struggled to relive that pleasure, recapture that happiness, like a phone call from the Great Beyond. The scent of her hair, the feel of her skin, the sound of her whisper against his neck. What *had* she whispered? He opened his eyes, trying to bring it back.

But the dream was growing fainter and fainter, like a landscape overtaken by fog, until his memory of it became only a brief recitation, and the pleasure, he knew, was gone. He waited until the sting had passed, then got up.

ON NEW YEAR'S Eve, Harry made himself a pitcher of martinis and sat with a stack of *Newsweeks*. Iris and Kirsten came by to pick up some clothes and dress for a night on the town. They trotted back downstairs in skin-tight jeans, heels, and sequined tops. Iris's brother George drove over to pick them up, and Harry recognized the resemblance.

"We're off," Iris said. "What are you going to do tonight, Harry?"

"Oh, catch some old movies, I suppose," he said, nodding toward the TV and trying to look genial. He held up his martini glass. "I'm all set. Have a good time."

They trooped out, debating which club they should head for first.

Harry knew that Jack would be out for the evening, as well as Claude and Sue, but he figured Elaine would be lonely.

Jodie answered the phone. "Happy New Year!" she chortled.

"Heeeey! What are *you* doing up so late?" Harry asked.

Instead of an answer he got a yawn. Then, "Mom said I could stay up and watch the big silver ball."

"Happy New Year yourself! Now what big silver ball would that be?"

"*You* know, Grandpa!"

"Like a dance? Cinderella goes to the ball?"

"No!"

"A beach ball?"

"No, silly! It drops down from a building."

"Good grief! Does anyone get hurt?"

Jodie gave a dramatic sigh. Then, "Mom! Grandpa's talking stupid again!"

Elaine came on the line. "Hi, Dad. Happy New Year. I told Jodie she could stay up, but I doubt she'll make it. How you doing?"

"Don't worry about me. I've got a martini to keep me company. How are *you* doing?"

"Okay. Don came by earlier. Read a book to Jodie, ate some pie. I *almost* asked him to stay all night, but it would only have got Jodie's hopes up. 'Never trust yourself on New Year's Eve,' Mom told me once."

Harry managed a laugh. "Might be interesting to know what made her say that. Anyway, I just wanted to wish you a happy new year, and hope it's better than this one."

"Same here."

Jodie grabbed the phone again. "Here's a joke, Grandpa! Rosalind told me. How do you keep a bull from charging?"

"I don't know."

"Take away his credit card!" she yelped, and laughed uproariously. Then, a second later she asked seriously, "What's a credit card?"

Harry bellowed with laughter and Elaine joined in.

"Happy New Year, sweetheart," he said. "Duck, now, when you see that ball!"

He sat in his chair a long time, nursing the rest of his drink, then another, thinking about Beth. About New Year's Eve, present and past. What she could have meant.

He stood up to use the bathroom, and as he did so, heard his name.

Ha . . . rry. . . .

Was it a voice? A squeak? A moan?

"Beth!" he called. "Are you here? What do you want?"

He stood in the center of the room so still that he could hear the steady click of the second hand on the kitchen clock. That was all.

"Beth!" he called again, turning slowly around, listening for the slightest whisper. The phone rang instead.

"Hello?" he said cautiously.

"It's Liz, Harry. Happy New Year. I'm really down, and I had to call somebody."

"You and me both, Liz. I'm losing it. I thought I heard Beth calling my name."

"Oh, I went through that," she said. "Wait till you see her sometime, Harry. That's worse."

"It's hell, Liz."

"Yeah, tell me about it."

"How are you spending New Year's Eve?"

"You don't want to know."

"I asked, didn't I?"

"I'm having a seance."

"What?"

"Max and I promised that after one of us died, we'd try to contact the other on New Year's Eve. It's when we met. Just in case—you know—there *is* part of him still around."

The good thing about talking to Liz was the realization that someone was even crazier than he was. The bad part was that someone who used to be beautiful (still was) and funny and generous and a good friend to Harry and Beth could now be losing her grip in a slow slide downhill. Scarier still was that he understood completely how she felt.

"We were half joking," Liz continued, "but then when he died, I got to thinking, what if Max remembers? Last year I tried. I had this horrible cold, so even if I got through, he'd probably never recognize me. I'm trying again for good measure."

"May it be a happier new year for you, Liz. Say hello to Max for me."

This time when Harry hung up, he was surprised to find he felt better. He decided he needed no more martinis, and went back in the living room to finish his magazines. Thirty minutes later the phone rang again. Hell, maybe Liz got him! Maybe Max had a message for Harry. Anything was possible.

"Hello?"

There was no answer. Harry's skin began to crawl. "Max?" he said tentatively.

"It's Arlo," came a deep voice. "I got a message for Jack."

"So why are you calling here, and who the hell are you?" Harry said angrily.

"It's nothing to you," the man said, "but just in case you see Jack, tell him this: he's got till midnight."

"For what? What do—"

The phone clicked.

Harry slammed the phone down, then picked it up again and dialed Jack's number. No answer. None at Suds and Spuds either.

He put on his coat, went out to the Lariat and drove the slower back roads to Silver Spring. If Jack wasn't at his apartment, he'd leave a message at the desk. No, damn it, he'd sit in the lobby and wait for the creep with the coal mine voice, show the punk a thing or two. Damn right, that's what he'd do. And when the boys at the barbershop asked how he'd spent New Year's Eve, he'd say, "Waiting for Arlo."

He welcomed this surge of adrenaline; anger was a good antidote for despair. How could it be, he wondered, that one child was so different from the others? There was not much resemblance between Elaine and Claude either, but at least they put in an honest day's work; didn't ask something for nothing. Jack worked too, but he expected the moon. He wanted everything yesterday.

Harry turned onto Georgia Avenue, and drove to Colesville Road and the huge apartment complex with its manicured grounds, its brass and glass lobby. A silver tree with ornaments commanded attention in the center of the Oriental rug, and off to one side, a fire burned in a large stone fireplace.

"Could you ring Jack Gill?" Harry asked at the desk.

"I'll try, but I saw him leave earlier and it appeared he was going out for the evening," the desk clerk told him. He rang Jack's apartment but there was, of course, no answer.

"I'll wait," Harry said.

The clerk looked surprised. "Could be a long one. He and the lady had on their party clothes."

"It's okay. I'll read," Harry said, and went to the stack of magazines on the table. He settled himself near the fire and picked up a copy of *Forbes.* What was Jack doing living here? What was he doing out on the town when he probably hadn't even paid for the socks on his feet? Where did he learn such irresponsible living—to lose five grand in some crap shoot? Beth would wonder where they had failed.

The problem with parenthood was that the job description kept changing. What it was, Harry decided, was a persistent, chronic attempt to get it right. *He* hadn't succeeded yet; how could he expect it of Jack?

Beth always felt responsible for the flaws she saw in their children. Harry never did. There had been a sort of understanding between them, unspoken and possibly unacknowledged, that neither had the time nor energy to take on all of life's worries, so they had simply divided them up. Beth took upon herself the health and safety concerns of the family, and Harry worried about investments, the roof-over-their-heads.

It worked. He'd kept his troubles to himself and Beth had kept hers in a file box. Harry never worried about cancer or heart attacks because Beth worried for him; she never worried about putting their kids through college, because that was Harry's department.

But now, with Beth gone, Elaine deserted, and Jack in trouble, the old formulas didn't work anymore; he had to deal with his grown children himself, and he didn't know where to begin.

HARRY WAS EMBARRASSED to discover that he had dozed off. He woke to a strange popping sound, that of his own lips giving way to breath, and the *Forbes* lay on the floor beside him.

He wiped one hand across his mouth and picked up the magazine, then massaged the back of his neck and looked around. The clock above the desk said four minutes past midnight. There was no one else in the lobby, and the music and laughter coming from the room behind the desk was evidence of a party in progress.

Harry got up and went to the men's room, then came back. The clerk looked out the door of the back room and grinned sheepishly. "Happy New Year," he said. "Like some champagne?"

"No, thanks," Harry said. "I wonder if my son came back yet. I'm afraid I dozed off."

"Jack Gill? Not unless I missed him. I'll ring."

Jack was not in.

"Did anyone else come by asking for him?"

"No, sir. You're the only one here tonight. You're welcome to stay, but it wouldn't surprise me if Jack didn't get in till three or four. Maybe later."

Harry was getting tired, he had to admit. "I'll stick around a bit longer," he said, "but if I miss him, tell him to call his dad, will you?"

"Sure thing, Mr. Gill." The clerk wrote it down, then went back to the party.

Harry walked through the glass door of the lobby and stared out into the night. Horns were still blowing and, off in the distance, the rapid *whap, whap, whap* of firecrackers. Now and then a siren. All over the metropolitan area, couples were dancing, kissing, toasting all their hopes for the year to come.

He and Beth used to go out with Liz and Max, hit a couple of night spots before they went home again. More recently, the couples had taken turns having a midnight buffet, along with the Mitchells and Swanns. In the last few years, it hadn't been unusual for one of the couples to fizzle out before midnight came, and no one felt compelled to stick around for the obligatory kiss. A sign of age, but with a plus: they didn't care.

Harry waited till twelve-fifteen, then decided to call it quits. If Arlo came, let *him* sit on his hemorrhoids till four in the morning. Maybe he and Jack had connected somehow. Maybe Harry was like a nervous nanny, waiting here in the lobby while Jack was out having a good time. He pulled the keys from his pocket and got in the pickup. There were still firecrackers, horns now and then, still the sound of sirens, and a yellowish cast to the night sky.

The air was mild for New Year's Eve, and Harry rolled down his window as he backed the Ford out of the lot, moving onto Colesville Road, then immediately pulled over as a fire engine raced past him. He waited as the lights of a second truck loomed in his rearview mirror.

He looked at the sky again, then leaned his head out the open window and inhaled. The acrid smell of smoke.

Suddenly his hands went cold, his throat grew tight, and Harry put his foot to the gas and followed the last truck. It turned off Colesville, raced to Wayne, turned again, and Harry braked, skidding to a stop.

Suds and Spuds was merely a black silhouette against the bright orange glow of the sky.

TWELVE

The Visitor

He slid from the seat, then leaned heavily against the pickup.

A policeman walked over. "Yours?" he asked.

"My son's. Was he—?"

"No one inside that we know of. Residents say the place was dark." He touched Harry's arm. "You okay?"

"How did it happen?"

"We don't know. The marshal's investigating. You'd better call your son."

Harry simply shook his head.

Beyond, in the orange glow, the small building began to divide into two sections. The smoke grew blacker, billowing faster now. Flames, like short locks of orange hair, greedily lapped up the water from the fire hoses, and the whole house grew transparent.

Finally Suds and Spuds was consumed by a huge ball of fire, swirling up into gray smoke. Every so often a piece of debris flew up and outward, rolling toward the sky.

As the building burned down, the chimney seemed to grow taller, till at last all that remained was the chimney and a grillwork of iron posts at the entrance.

A radio blared, the dispatcher's voice an accompaniment to the grind of the engines. Some of the hoses were being rewound, a few of the helmets removed.

A car turned into the parking lot and rolled to a stop. Harry looked over and saw Jack staring at the charred remains of his business, his face a mask of disbelief. And then he was leaping out of the car, banging the door as though he were throwing a grenade. He whirled around and rammed his fist against the side of the Lexus.

Harry went over, but Jack seemed not to know he was there. He stood with his legs apart, head thrown back, and howled at the sky.

"Jack."

Harry watched while Jack turned and laid his arm on the roof of the car, then his face on his arm.

"Jack, Jack . . . " Harry said, and placed one hand on his shoulder.

Jack did not try to shake it off. He seemed to shrink in Harry's eyes, like a tire slowly deflating. And finally he turned. Together they surveyed the scene before them.

The narrow walk, encroached on both sides by the stubble of winter grass, led to a concrete platform. And there, like the remains of supper on a plate, sat what was left of Jack's dream. One corner of the roof, with eaves attached, had come down nicely over the front right edge of the platform. Far less tidily, the twisted water pipes lay over the whole in huge loops and curves, swirls and arches, and the furnace, its heat ducts fallen away, looked out toward the street with one hole for an eye.

The fire marshal and two policemen were talking off to one side.

"Jack, do you have any idea how this could have happened?" Harry asked him.

Jack's jaws worked but they could not seem to open.

"I got a message from Arlo earlier this evening. I tried to call you, then drove over."

"That fucking *bastard!*" The words spat from Jack's throat, husky and wet.

"You need to tell the police."

"No!" Jack turned toward his father. "Don't you tell them *anything!* "

"But why?"

"Because it'll be me next. They'll do it, Dad! You don't know them!"

"Who's 'them'?"

"Listen Dad, it's over now. There's nothing left. Let it go."

"Maybe with your insurance you can—"

Jack let out his breath and stood with arms dangling loosely from his shoulders. "There *is* no insurance."

"Jack!"

"I was *this* close, Dad!" He held up a thumb and finger. "*This close* to sending the check. I thought I was still in the grace period." He voice broke. "It's gone. It's all gone."

Harry reached out and steadied himself against Jack's car. The fire marshal came over carrying a clipboard.

"You the owner?" he asked.

"Was," Jack replied.

"Got any idea how this happened?"

"We were closed," said Jack. "All the machines were off when I left."

"We may be looking at arson here."

"Goddam," was all Jack said.

Beth had been spared the calamities of their two older children. Harry wondered if he didn't believe in some higher power that could foresee the future, and removed her from it. If so, Harry had been allowed to remain. The why seemed even more mysterious than it had before.

~

BACK HOME, HARRY could not escape the feeling that he should be *doing* something. Elaine was coming around, maturing out of necessity, and if Claude was having problems committing to Sue, he would work them out. But Jack?

One thing he knew, Beth would be with Jack right now. She would not have let him go home alone. Would have insisted he come back to their house for the night. Harry had tried.

"Come on over and stay the night," he'd offered.

And when Jack refused, Harry had said, "Would you like me to follow you back to your place?"

"No, Dad. I'm going to bed," Jack had told him, and after talking with the marshal, got in his car and drove off.

Beth would have followed. If he didn't invite her up to his apartment, she would have insisted on it, and fixed his breakfast the next morning. Harry did neither. Instead, he went to bed himself about three. He heard his roomers come in, Iris's footsteps on the floor above, while Hahn lingered with Kirsten on the stairs.

"*Don't*, Hahn! He'll hear us."

"Let me come up then."

"No! He'll see you in the morning and kick us both out."

"Let's do it right here then."

"Hahn!" Giggling. A small shriek.

Surely Iris would come to the top of the stairs and call her niece to come up. Both Kirsten and Hahn had been drinking, Harry could tell, and wondered for the thousandth time about the wisdom of letting a high school senior board in his home.

"Hahn . . . " More softly now.

" . . . crazy for you. . . ."

"Let me get them off first. Stop it! You'll rip them!"

Where the hell was Iris? Harry rolled out of bed, his steps heavy on the floor, and turned on the light. He opened the bedroom door to find the young couple at the foot of the stairs, trying to pull up their jeans in a tangle of arms and legs.

"Oh, God!" cried Kirsten, and broke into a giggle.

"Go home, Hahn. It's late," said Harry.

The Hun was on his feet now, back to Harry as he zipped up his jeans.

Harry went inside the room again but left his door open. Kirsten had followed Hahn to the front entrance.

"You animal! I *told* you!"

"You wanted it."

More giggling. "You're still a beast."

"Come on out to the car and I'll give it to you."

"Shhhh. Jeez, Hahn!"

There were whispers at the front door. Kirsten must have been holding it open because Harry could feel the draft. When the laughter and protests began a second time, he went out in the hall.

"Good*night*," he said. "Close the door."

Kirsten gave Hahn a quick kiss on the cheek, then scurried on past Harry and up the stairs. Harry bolted the door and went to bed.

HE WOKE ABOUT eleven. Someone was using the shower upstairs, but other than that, the house was quiet. The neighborhood was quiet. The new year had arrived with the wail of sirens and the odor of charred wood and metal. In the sunshine of late morning, there was a new calendar to hang on the wall, three hundred and sixty-five unknowns.

Harry got up and dialed Jack's number. It rang seven times before it was answered.

"Jack, how are you this morning?"

"How do you think?" The voice was flat.

"Listen, I know you're depressed, but you are going to get through this."

"Don't make me laugh. I can't even look in the mirror."

"Hey, you aren't planning to do anything stupid, are you?"

"Couldn't do anything stupider than what I've done already."

Harry couldn't think of what to say next. "Would it help if I came over?"

"I'll be all right, and I'm not in the mood for company."

Harry, the man with no answers, put on his clothes without washing up, drank some coffee in the kitchen, and was about to leave for the greenhouse when Iris came downstairs. She was either hung over or extremely tired. She'd evidently gone to bed without removing her makeup, for there were smudges of mascara around her eyes and a dark line down one cheek. Her hair was a mess, but Harry doubted she looked any worse than he did. Besides, they needed to talk.

"Iris," he said, cutting right to the chase, "you went upstairs last night and left Kirsten down here alone with Hahn."

He didn't think she had heard at first. She reached blindly for the handle to the refrigerator, missed, and tried again. "Yeah?" she said.

"Well, I didn't want that to happen."

She ran one finger under her nose to suppress a sneeze and stood perfectly still as though to keep her balance. "Jeez, Harry, all you had to do was tell him to go home."

"I did tell him, but I thought we agreed that Kirsten is your responsibility."

"Well, they probably wouldn't do anything they haven't done before. Those chastity cards aren't worth diddly," she said.

"That's not the point! Kirsten's underage, and I don't want her unsupervised with Hahn in my house. I'm concerned that they've probably been here alone a lot together after school."

"He works days at the car wash, Harry."

"It doesn't mean they haven't been here alone."

Iris didn't answer. She pulled her robe about her, sat down on a kitchen chair, eyes closed, feet apart, head tipped slightly back.

"Okay, for what it's worth, here's the deal," Harry told her.

"Hahn isn't allowed in the house unless I'm here and awake. Understood?"

Iris's head tipped back a little farther, then jerked forward again. "Got it."

"Iris, are *you* awake?"

In answer, she held open the lids of her right eye with two fingers, and the pupil rolled in his direction.

He almost smiled. "Happy New Year," he said.

She put her arms on the table and her cheek on her arms. "Happy New Year, Harry."

THE ROADS WERE fairly empty, the houses quiet, yards undisturbed. The people of the greater Washington area greeted the New Year with half-closed eyes, he decided. Harry passed the gypsies' house where part of the chain link fence had been detached and rolled to one side, and a car had been driven through. It sat at the bottom of the sloping yard, two tires flat.

At the garden center, he drove past the store, with its *Sorry, We're Closed* sign on the window, and parked near the greenhouse. Inside he turned on the oil heater and for a long time stood staring at the box Liz had brought him. Finally, when his breath was no longer visible in front of his face, he stepped forward and lifted out the mask. Holding it out before him, he pressed it slightly with his fingers to extend the skull and forehead.

"Old friend," he murmured. Could he do it? Could he produce an original piece, and did he have the guts to find out?

Harry closed his eyes, holding the delicate replica of Max's cranium in his hands. He could feel his friend's head as he slowly ran one hand over the top, his imagination filling in the missing sections. The high rising forehead, the deepset eyes beneath, the bushy brows, the small ears, the knobby protuberances at the back of the skull.

What's the worst that can happen if I fail? he asked himself.

Liz Bowen would never ask for another thing.

"Not to worry," he said aloud. He put on Vivaldi's *The Four Seasons,* and began.

HE STOPPED ONCE that afternoon to call both Elaine and Claude to tell them about the fire and, in both instances, had to tell their answering machines. When he went home later, Claude phoned.

"What's Jack going to do now, Dad? He's not just lost everything, he still owes a bundle on the place."

"I don't know," said Harry. He was amazed how easily he could say those words. He was not a file box or an encyclopedia or a minister of God. He did not have all the answers. Those three words were remarkably refreshing in their honesty.

"Did you suggest anything?" Claude asked, sounding puzzled.

"If he's lost everything and he was uninsured and he has debts, then he'll have to file for bankruptcy, I suppose," Harry said at last. "He'll have to start over. He doesn't need me to tell him that."

Claude let out his breath. "Man, it's a good thing Mom's not here to see this."

"Yes, I guess Jack spared her that."

"What I mean is, she'd want to *do* something. And we can't."

"No," said Harry with finality. "We can't."

ELAINE CAME BY on Sunday to leave Jodie a few hours while she hit the January sales. Don was talking about the possibility of moving back, and she wanted to fix up the place a little.

"I had lunch with Jack yesterday," she said. "He sold the Lexus and bought a cheaper car."

"Good move."

"Has he talked to you about a loan?"

"No. Is he going to?"

"He was wondering what you'd say."

"Jack always has a place here if he wants to come home," Harry said. He found Elaine studying him as he hung up Jodie's jacket.

"You're so different from Mom. She'd be out selling the family jewels to get Jack back on his feet."

"And you think that would help?"

Elaine pursed her lips thoughtfully and shook her head. "Probably not."

After she had gone to the mall, Harry gave Jodie the task of taking all the wooden ornaments off the tree, the ones he and Beth had saved for the lower branches when the children were young. He had already removed the breakables and laid them out on the coffee table.

Then he went through the house taking down the wreaths and holly. He was too old for this. Christmas didn't have the same flavor and texture anymore. It had lost its anticipation. He had lived through fifty-six Christmases now. How many more times could he expect his heart to go thump when he plugged in the lights?

As he moved around the house, he remembered that you don't have to watch young children every minute when they're in your care; you only have to listen, for they emit constant noise that indicates activity. It's when they fall silent you take notice. And so, when he had removed the window candles from their holders and still heard no noise from the living room, he peeked in.

Jodie was sitting on the hassock holding the angel ornament on her knee. It wore a little pipe-cleaner halo, sprinkled with glitter, and its gossamer wings were gold and purple. Jodie was bouncing it around as though the angel were flitting about in her lap.

She looked up when she saw Harry. "I'm not going to break it," she assured him.

"It's very old, so be careful."

"Grandma's an angel now, isn't she?"

Harry considered, then opted for science. "No, Sweetheart. She's just dead."

"Rosalind says she's an angel."

"Rosalind's full of beans."

Jodie clasped her hands hard around the angel's puffy skirt and twisted the fabric.

"*Careful*, Jodie!"

"I can call her an angel if I want!" Jodie said defiantly as Harry gently took the ornament from her hands.

"Yes, I suppose you can."

"When *I* die," Jodie said with certainty, "I'm going straight up to be an angel and play with the baby Jesus."

"Good for you."

Jodie followed him back out to the dining room and crawled up on a chair to watch him put the candles away. "Daddy's coming back," she said. "I *told* you he would, didn't I?"

"Yes."

"See?"

"So?" said Harry.

"So Grandma's an angel," Jodie repeated, and scrunched up her face at him mockingly.

HARRY WAS SURPRISED to discover that he was enjoying January. He found that he liked the lack of obligations there at the house and the nothingness of the garden center after Christmas. The red poinsettias were replaced with the pink of Valentine's Day, and Wanda and Rose were busily gearing up for the lace and satin that would decorate the windows in a matter of weeks. But it did not concern Harry, and he ignored completely the goose who welcomed customers to the store in a muffler and stocking cap adorned with hearts.

As Harry came out of the office, Tracy pointed to a lavish valentine posted on the employees' bulletin board next to the office. Scribbled in bold black script along one edge were the words, *To Rose with affection, Luciano Pavarotti.*

"Look!" she said. "It's *him!*"

Harry stared. "The tenor?"

Tracy nodded. "She showed it to me and Wanda this morning, and I said why didn't she put it on the bulletin board. Isn't this exciting?"

"When did she get it?"

"Last year, but she thought we might like to see it."

"How does she know Pavarotti?"

"She wrote him a fan letter once."

Wanda passed by just then with one raised eyebrow and Harry made no comment. He went on into the storeroom to check his supply of plasticine and found Rose stacking rolls of ribbon on an upper shelf. As he squeezed by her in the narrow aisle, he touched her waist briefly as he said, "Good morning," and was startled by her instantly springing away from him, her face flushed.

"I didn't mean to startle you," Harry apologized. "I thought you heard me come in."

"Oh . . . I . . . No, I didn't know you were there, Mr. Gill!" she said, so flustered that she didn't notice the spool of ribbon that had slipped from her fingers and was unwinding on the floor.

Harry stooped to pick it up. "Beautiful valentine out there, Rose," he said. "I didn't know you knew Pavarotti."

"Oh, I don't really know him!" she said, her words coming out in a rush. "But when I read how he left his wife to be with his mistress and they were saying such awful things about him in the newspaper, I just thought how nobody understood what love can do. So I wrote and told him I understood. I didn't think he'd ever answer, but then one day I opened the mail, and there it was!"

"Really!" said Harry. "Imagine that!"

When he went back out into the store again, Wanda came over. "Do you think we ought to call her on it?" she said.

"Oh, why bother?" said Harry. "Maybe it really was from Pavarotti. Let's opt for joy."

In the greenhouse, where he had constructed an armature of screen wire in the shape of Max's head, Harry was applying plasticene to the framework. He smiled as he worked, thinking of the early years in his marriage when he and Beth made a ritual of having sex on Valentine's Day. It was understood that, no matter what, there was a scheduled romp that evening. And then one day when he was shaving, he'd looked in the mirror and decided he did not want to make love on schedule. Maybe he would prefer to have Beth the night before or the morning after.

He had gone back in the bedroom where Beth was still dozing, leaned over the bed and said softly, "Would it make any difference to you if we took a rain check on tonight?"

Beth had turned, reached up, put her arms around his neck, and pulled him down on top of her. Harry was an hour late for work that morning and Claude missed his bus, but it was worth it. Was that before or after the non-affair? he wondered. Before or after the fateful letter had been mailed? He wanted to go through the remembrance a second time, but the first visitor of the year was Liz Bowen. Harry saw her getting out of her car just when he discovered he had probably made Max's chin too pointed.

She came in the greenhouse wearing her late husband's trench coat, reaching almost to the ankles. This time, however, she wore her own clothes underneath, a lavender turtleneck and wool pants, her dark hair tossing about her face in the winter wind as she stepped inside and closed the door behind her. She went directly to the heater and held out her hands.

"I hate January," she said. "Max's birthday was in January, remember?"

Coming face to face with Liz was like traveling down a highway and finding a car stalled just ahead in your lane, Harry thought. Widows and widowers should be required to put warning signs on their bumpers—*Caution: Grieving*—so you could move to the left and go around.

"The chin's too narrow," said Liz, studying the sculpture.

"Yes, I realize that, Liz. I've barely started."

"I brought some more photos—side views, this time. I was going through my old pictures and found these. Of course they were taken when he still had some hair."

Harry studied them, propping one up on the work table.

Liz sighed and dusted off the seat of Harry's work stool, then hoisted herself on it and sat listlessly, swinging one foot in its slender black boot. "I never did reach Max on New Year's Eve," she said morosely.

"Hmmm," said Harry, and reworked the chin.

"He's either not there—wherever 'there' is—or he's not answering." And when Harry didn't reply, she said, "Why did this have to happen to us, Harry? We're not old, are we? Max and I could have had thirty more years together!"

"I know." Harry wiped his hands on the loose ends of his shirt. Maybe Wanda would ring him from the store. He did not want someone sitting here who could so easily tip the balance of his mood.

Her foot went on swinging and she clasped her hands around one knee. "You know what I read in the Harvard Health Letter? No, maybe it was Mayo's. Eighty percent of bereaved spouses are still grieving four to seven years later. *Seven years*, Harry! I've got five more to go!"

Get her out of here, Harry told himself. *Just pick her up bodily and set her on the ground outside.*

"Well," he said, grasping the spatula again and putting his hands on the clay. "Back to work." He paused, waiting for her to leave.

"Don't let me interrupt you. I'll just watch," she said.

What was bothering him more at that moment was not her presence as much as her perfume. Iris wore perfume that was too strong—astringent smelling, and chemically flowery. But this was the kind of perfume that made you want to seek out the scent, follow it right to the source, and in this case it would lead him to Liz. Harry wanted her as far away from him as she could get.

"The only good part," she went on, "is you lose track of time. You don't realize it's been a month since your husband died, then three, then six. . . . People don't have any idea till it happens to them. Right, Harry?"

"Yes, but some days are better than others."

"I don't have too many of those 'some days.' No matter what kind of a day it is, Max isn't here." Liz let out her breath, long and slow. "What I can't get used to is the finality of it, you know? I still find myself thinking, 'When this is over. . . .' and it *won't* be over. This 'death is just a part of life' stuff is crap. Dead is dead, dammit. My one survival skill is to wake up every morning expecting to feel the worst I have ever felt, and then, if I don't, it's a bonus."

"You're a fun person to have around," said Harry.

"There's before and there's after."

The phone rang and Harry lunged.

Wanda's voice: "Harry, I just wondered if that order for . . . "

"I'll be right there," he said.

"What?"

"Hold on, and I'll be there."

"I only wanted to ask if. . . ."

"I'm leaving this minute," said Harry, and plunked down the phone. "Sorry," he said to Liz. "Problems in the store."

"The only thing I *don't* miss is his smoking," Liz said, following him outside. "And you know what? It's what I try to focus on, because it's the one thing about him I don't miss. I wake up in the morning and before the sadness can grab me, I try to remember Max smoking. And then I wonder if I'm in some altered state."

"I feel that way too," Harry said as he walked her out to her car. "I feel that way a lot, in fact."

"We *are* a little nuts, I think."

"Take care, Liz," Harry said, and walked swiftly away.

If he had died before Beth, he was thinking, what would she *not* miss? His sweat-soaked T-shirts after jogging? His belches? The way he let his toenails grow too long? Why is it we let it all hang out with the person we supposedly love the most? But wasn't that the miracle of marriage, that we could?

AT JODIE'S REQUEST, she continued to come to Harry's on Tuesday evenings. Elaine used the time to catch up on lesson plans. Harry was a substitute father, he knew, but was glad to have found a niche.

"Jodie left her green sweater at your place," Elaine said one evening when she called. "Why don't you bring it over and stay for dinner?"

Harry retrieved the sweater from one of the living room chairs—Zeke had been sleeping on it—and drove to Elaine's around six. Hers was an attractive townhouse with holly growing on a large bush beside the door. Snowmen cutouts decorated the front window.

Jodie, in red tights and shirt, was demonstrating how she could maneuver herself down the hall stairs like a Slinky.

"Grandpa, look!" she crowed from the top where she had obviously been awaiting his arrival. His attention gained, she started her silver-ringed Slinky end over end at one side of the stairs while she, on the carpet in the middle, turned awkward somersaults down the incline, legs colliding noisily with the stair railing.

"Good Lord!" said Harry, catching her halfway down.

"Rosalind taught me to do it," Jodie said, not even breathless.

"Friends!" Elaine said, rolling her eyes.

It felt incredibly good to be eating at his daughter's table again, especially to know that Don might soon be sitting in the chair that Harry occupied. And then he thought of all the months Jodie had missed her father, and his eyes grew moist as he reached for the crackers. For every emotion there was an equal and opposite emotion.

"You already *have* crackers, Grandpa!' Jodie scolded, laughing.

"So I do," said Harry.

In the kitchen later, after Jodie had gone to bed, Harry asked, "Elaine, did your mother ever tell you anything you think I should know?"

She paused, a graham cracker between her fingers. "Like what?"

"I don't know. I guess there's just that desire to know everything about her . . . to hold onto whatever I can get."

"Secrets, you mean?" He didn't fool her. "You're asking if she confided any secrets in me?"

"Perhaps. That or anything else."

"Nothing she told me outright."

"What do you mean?"

"Oh, you know. That difficult time between you and Mom."

"I'm not sure that I do."

"I'm thinking about my senior year in high school. Mom never said anything, but I sensed there was something going on between you. You don't have to tell me what it was."

The non-affair, of course. "I suppose there are rough patches in any marriage," he said.

Elaine gave a little laugh. "And I'm the shining example of that. But you and Mom obviously worked yours out. Thirty-four years. Wow!"

JACK LOOKED AWFUL. He sat across the table before a huge Western omelet which Harry divided between them. He ate without relish, but finished his share. That must count for something.

Harry knew that Jack had not come over to be fed, though. And he had not come for advice. Jack hadn't asked Harry's opinion since he was thirteen years old.

"So what's happening?" Harry inquired after a while when Jack poured his second cup of coffee. This was a sweater morning—Harry in an old blue fisherman knit, Jack in a tan cashmere.

"Well, I'm going to file the papers. Chapter seven. You know what that means, of course."

"A new start, for one thing."

Jack sneered. "I'm zilch. Who would want to give me a chance after this? An idiot who lets his insurance lapse."

"Well, you won't starve. Either Wade or I could find a place for you at the quarry or the garden center. We'd work your tail off, of course, but it's a paycheck."

"If you want to help, I'd prefer another way."

"Yes, I imagine you would," said Harry.

They should not be holding this conversation, he was thinking as he reached for the butter and lopped off a triangular piece from the stick. He and Jack were treading along the edge of a cliff, and at any moment the earth might crumble beneath them.

"You won't consider it?" Jack sat tensely, swirling the coffee around and around in his mug, tilting it in his hands.

"A loan? Would you, in my place?"

"If I had the money, sure. Listen Dad, there's this guy I know has a sports bar franchise. Business is great, but it's more work than he bargained for, and he wants a partner. He said I could come in on the deal at a third of the cost, and buy my way up to full partner when I get the money. I've got some ideas; I could double his business."

"The answer's the same, Jack."

Jack slid his coffee away from him, shoulders slumped, arms extended out in front of him so that his fingertips barely touched his cup.

"You don't think I can do it, do you?"

"The work? Certainly. The financial commitment, you'll have to show me. But you'll have to show me with your own money, not mine."

"I don't *have* any goddamned money, I'm telling you! I'm wiped out!"

"Then you'll earn it."

"Fuck!" Jack's jaws clamped in anger. "I'll be an old man before I get on my feet again! Christ! Mom would be outraged if she knew."

Harry reacted. "At what? At you? At me? At the money you blew at the track and the casinos?" he demanded. "Who's to answer for what here, Jack?"

Jack pushed away from the table, got up, then slammed his chair forward.

"You're so judgmental," he said, reaching for his jacket. "Mom could see possibilities. She believed in giving someone another chance, and she did, too!" He flung one arm in a sleeve, then the other, overturning the pepper shaker as he did so.

It took a moment for Harry to understand. "How many times did she bail you out, Jack? Four? Five? A dozen? And each time you gambled her money away again?"

"Just tell me this: Did Mom leave anything to me in her will?"

It was all Harry could do to control himself: "No, Jack. In Maryland, everything goes to the spouse, unless stated otherwise. You can look at it yourself if you like."

"Fuck the will," said Jack, and left, his boots thudding down the hall, out the door. He didn't bother to close it after him. "Fuck *you!*" he yelled, the sound of the crunching snow growing fainter as he went across the yard to the street.

Harry stood unmoving at the door, watching him go. Was it remotely possible that Jack was the mongrel child, and that to help him succeed, Beth had gone out of her way to support, disguise, and enable his habits? Where were the instruction cards for dealing with a grown son who gambled away a good thing?

Zeke wandered into the kitchen, walking his sideways gait, rubbing his backside against a table leg.

"Be glad you have no children," Harry said to the cat, who studied him without interest, then sauntered off again to see if Iris was in.

HE HAD NOT seen much of Iris since New Year's. He had not seen much of Kirsten either, and nothing at all of Hahn, although he and Kirsten were on the phone every night. Iris always seemed to be on the run—would poke her head in the kitchen before she left in the morning and sometimes grab a carton of yogurt to take with her. Harry himself had been working in the greenhouse in the evenings after the garden center closed, and when he came home, Iris was either out with friends from Hecht's or upstairs with her door closed. Harry took a closed door as a *No* and didn't feel he should ask, much as he wanted her physically.

Both she and Kirsten were there the following Sunday, however, and lounged about the house in flannel pajamas and robes. It might be safer, Harry was thinking as he watched them work a crossword puzzle together, to invite Iris down to his room instead of going up to hers. He was not sure he was ready for this—another woman on Beth's sheets, in their bed—but it was too risky making love upstairs anymore with Kirsten about. So far they had been lucky, the girl was almost always gone. Harry decided that the next chance he got, he would say, Why don't you come down to my room, Iris? We'll enjoy the privacy.

He waited all morning and half the afternoon to talk to her alone, but Kirsten stuck to her like rubber cement. Harry left at last for the greenhouse, disgusted with himself for wasting so much of the day. When he came back, Kirsten was watching TV in the living room, but Iris was nowhere in sight. There were two Coke cans on the coffee table, however, and a rumpled pillow at the opposite end of the couch. Harry was all but certain Hahn had been there.

"Thought you were out with Iris," Harry said casually, picking up the pages of the newspaper, glancing around for more evidence of the boyfriend.

Kirsten's eyes never left the screen. "She might be staying at the house tonight, I'm not sure."

"Oh. Well, then." He made himself a sandwich.

Kirsten went upstairs about eleven, and at last even Zeke tired of waiting for Iris and cuddled up in a corner of the couch. Harry showered, just in case, but went on to bed.

He woke before the alarm went off and knew Iris had come in because the shower was running upstairs. Kirsten always showered around seven, and caught the bus at seven-forty. Iris would use the bathroom next, and right now the clock read ten of eight.

Harry stretched slowly, reluctant to leave the warmth of his bed, but he wanted to be up and dressed when she came down—to tell her he had missed her—that he wanted, soon, to make love. He washed and shaved, putting off his shower until evening so as not to rob her of hot water. Then he went to the kitchen and started the coffee. She liked the blend with almonds and chocolate in it, and soon the kitchen windows were fogging up with steam and the aroma filled the room.

There were footsteps overhead, and Harry wondered if she would like to share an omelet with him. He took out a carton of eggs and walked to the kitchen doorway.

A man in his early forties was coming down the stairs, dressed in loafers, a white shirt and jeans, and a suede aviator's jacket. He paused only a millisecond when he saw Harry, then turned up the collar of his jacket and thrust one hand in his pants pocket for his car keys.

"'Morning," he said, and went out.

HARRY STOOD BETWEEN stove and refrigerator, solid and unfeeling, like a third appliance. The fact was, there was absolutely nothing to say. He had no claims on Iris. He was her landlord, and, he'd hoped, her special friend upon whom she occasionally bestowed her favors.

He was still standing there, holding the eggs, when Iris came hurrying down, the front of her blouse unbuttoned. She realized her error as she opened the refrigerator—stopped with the door half open and rebuttoned herself—then took out a package of English muffins.

"Hi," she said and, breaking one open with her hands, dropped the two halves in the toaster.

"Good morning," said Harry. Why, he wondered, did he—a man of the earth who had worked in a quarry and spent his life handling loads of brick and mulch and stone and soil—forever end up sounding like a country squire where Iris was concerned? Somebody out of *Masterpiece Theater*.

"You want me to pick up some orange juice?" she asked, searching for the jelly.

"Not for me," he said. And then, "I saw your friend in the hall a moment ago."

"Yeah? Pete?"

My God, how many were there? "I didn't realize you'd had a visitor."

She straightened up then and looked at him. Her lipstick was somewhat pointed at the top so that two small peaks appeared above the lip line. Harry, standing not three feet away, could not help himself: he inhaled deeply, searching for a scent of sex. He got her perfume instead.

"You mad about something, Harry?"

"Not mad. I didn't know you were seeing someone, that's all."

"I can't have friends?"

"Of course you can have friends, Iris. I just didn't know you'd invite a man here without mentioning it to me."

"I'm supposed to ask?" Her tone had an incredulous note to it. "He's a friend, Harry!"

"He stayed all night."

"So?" She did not say this defiantly. There was something so guileless and sure in her expression that Harry felt even more the old fool. *It doesn't matter*, she would say if he persisted.

He shrugged and smiled. "Want some eggs?"

"No. I don't have time." She retrieved the butter and stood by the counter, waiting for the toaster to spring. "I don't know how you can eat eggs in the morning. Especially the yolks, you know?"

She was wearing a silky white blouse with a black band at the collar and cuffs, and a black skirt, tight enough to show the high roundness of her bottom. Harry felt himself go from middle-aged man to school boy. He moved up behind and pressed against her, kissing her on the neck.

"Harry," she chided, smiling and frowning at the same time. She moved away a little.

"Is your friend coming back tonight?" Harry asked.

"No. He works Mondays, I think."

"What does he do, this Pete?"

"Waiter. One of the hotels downtown. Is there a Sheraton? I think it's a Sheraton."

"Then you're mine tonight," he told her, and smiled.

"Sure, Harry. I'm having dinner with my dad, though." She gave his right hand a tap. "Leggo. I'll be late."

She disgusted him almost as much as he disgusted himself right then. He did not *want* to be this pathetic older man begging for sex anymore than he wanted to be a widower in the first place. Yet here he was, completely at her disposal. It made him sick.

She was watching him. "You going to work today?" She broke off a piece of muffin and popped it in her mouth.

"Yes." Then, "I guess I don't want any eggs either, come to think of it." Harry put them back in the refrigerator. "It's the yolks."

THINGS ALWAYS LOOKED better in the light of day, however, and by lunch time, the sun was so bright, the air so clean, that Harry felt renewed, strong, vigorous. So what if Iris enjoyed the attentions of a younger buck? He could compete with the best of them. The rules had changed since the days he and Beth were going out. So what if you hooked up with more than one? By today's standards, that didn't make you promiscuous. No one seemed to be keeping score.

Like a sophomore preening for a big date, Harry went to Jim Swann's over the lunch hour.

"Leave it a little longer at the sides," he said, settling into the chair. "Hi, Leroy. How you doing?"

The man by the window was picking his teeth over his empty sandwich wrapper, and the shop had the spicy smell of peppers and cheese.

"The usual," Leroy said. And then, "It's Fred you should be asking."

"Fred sick?"

Jim and Leroy exchanged smiles.

"Sick as a puppy in love," said Jim. "He's dating that neighbor of yours, Paula Harrington. Robbing the cradle, is what he's doing. There's got to be a twenty-year age difference there. Fifteen, anyway. Think he's planning on moving in with her."

The barber chair swiveled around, Harry in it, as Jim began trimming the top.

"What do you suppose they talk about in bed?" Harry said idly.

Jim gave a chuckle. "What everyone talks about, I suppose. 'Was it good for you, honey? Was it really, really good?'"

"No, after all that, I mean. Or over the dinner table. Do you suppose undertakers talk about their work?" Harry could see Jim's smile widening in the mirror.

"That would put the skids on the evening, all right," Jim said.

"Unless they're into necrophilia," Leroy laughed. "When you come right down to it, what does a garbage man talk about when he's in bed with a woman and she says, 'How was your day?'"

"Or a urologist," suggested Jim.

"A proctologist," said Harry.

Leroy crumpled up his sandwich wrapper. "You know, I can't remember saying much to my wife at all. I suppose we did . . . talk some . . . but mostly we just crawled between the sheets and went at it." He sighed. "Bet Paula is really something in the sack, though, the lucky devil."

"Was it Ben Franklin who said to marry an older woman because they're so grateful?" Harry ventured.

"I say marry one who never had children, 'cause they're so tight!" Leroy laughed, and stretched himself out full on the folding chair, his heavy ankles showing beneath the cuffs of his trousers.

"You can never tell about women nowadays," Jim observed dryly. "Used to be we'd sit at the beach and try to guess which girls were virgins. You ever do that, Harry?"

"I suppose."

"It was something about the eyes, we always said. A knowing look in the eyes."

"And the mouth. Playful at the corners," Harry added, smiling a little.

Leroy aimlessly massaged his thigh and looked out the window. "Now? Shoot! To find a virgin you got to go all the way down to ninth grade."

They smiled and grew silent as the clip, clip of the shears filled in for conversation.

"How *you* doing, Harry?" asked Leroy.

"Hanging in."

"That girl still room with you?"

"*Boards* with me, in my house," Harry corrected. "She and her niece."

"Well, you'll meet somebody one of these days," said Leroy. "I say start with someone new. You go out with someone you know, they've heard all your jokes already. They know you got a bad back. That you can't lie down after a meal. Hell, where's the mystery in that?"

HARRY INVITED IRIS to his room that evening. "One of these nights Kirsten's going to come home and find me in your bedroom," he explained as he kissed her and helped her off with her bra.

"Oh, she already knows," said Iris. "She wouldn't walk in if she knew you were with me."

Harry's fingers paused. "You've told her?"

"She came home once and heard us together. Said she'd guessed as much, anyway."

Good God! "You didn't mind?"

"Why should I?"'

Harry pulled her down beside him. "You're a mystery," he said. "I can never quite tell what you're thinking."

"I'm thinking I'm here with you," she replied which, Harry decided, was exactly the right answer, and he kissed her again.

As he stroked her arms, rubbed her back, repeated the turn-ons which had worked for Beth, he said, "Do you ever think of settling down with one man, Iris? I confess I'm probably behind the times, but when I was going out with girls before I married—when I was in a relationship, I mean—I just went with one woman at a time."

She appeared to be thinking it over. "I guess I'd have to go with a guy for a while to think of it as a relationship," she answered. "The last relationship I was in was the guy I married, and he broke my nose. So I don't get too excited about relationships."

They didn't even have that then, Harry thought as he leaned over her slim body, lips grazing her nipples. *I'm thinking I'm here with you*, she had said. All they had was the moment, and for that, at least, he was grateful. But later, when he came, he had an image of his sperm mixing with Pete's—of young energetic sperm with long tails charging forward to challenge his. He wondered if Iris ever talked about him to the waiter.

He asked, "Iris, do I please you?"

"Sure you do. You're good to me."

"In bed, I mean. I'd like to think I satisfy you."

"Well, I don't think we need to be talking like this," she said. "I mean, we're not married or anything. What's with all these questions, Harry?"

In the glow of the night light, Harry blinked at the stucco ceiling that had watched over him and Beth for thirty-four years. At the drapes she had made herself, the picture of them on their fifth anniversary with Jack in her arms, on the wall.

Go take your bath, he wanted to say, withdrawing his hand. *Take your long sinewy body out of my bed and leave me my memories.*

But it wasn't as black and white as that. He liked the firm, young feel of her. What he did not like was that there was only one connection—skin. The rest was missing, and their separate selves rubbed and chafed against each other.

As she headed to his bathroom later, he followed to show her where to find the fresh towels. The robe she hung on the back of the door looked familiar.

"Have I seen this before?" he asked, fingering the rose-colored sleeve with the satin trim.

"Probably so," said Iris, stepping over the rim of the tub. "Kirsten found it in Elaine's closet. Figured she wouldn't mind if we used it."

ON VALENTINE'S DAY, Harry brought home a dozen long-stemmed roses and left them on Iris's bed. When she had not returned by ten, he went up and put them in a vase, setting it on her dresser. She didn't come back till the following day. Then she said, "Long-stemmed roses! Thanks, Harry!" And, laughing, "Musta been left over, huh? They look a little wilted, but hey—that's all right."

THIRTEEN

The Brother

THE PHONE RANG just after dinner, and when Harry picked it up, he thought at first no one was there. Then he heard breathing, and finally, a feminine voice: "Mr. Gill? This is Rose, and I . . . I need to talk with you. Really! I was wondering if you could meet me somewhere."

What? he thought. "Tonight? We can't talk in the store tomorrow?"

"I don't think so. It's personal, and . . . well, sort of urgent. I was wondering, could you meet me at Gallagher's about nine?"

Gallagher's was a bar popular with the younger crowd, just down the road from the garden center next to a Holiday Inn. It was the favorite watering place of The Herd when they'd finished work.

"I suppose so, Rose, if you're sure it can't wait."

"It can't, Harry." She rarely called him Harry. "I really appreciate this. I'll be there at nine o'clock," she said, a strange note of excitement in her voice, and hung up.

Now what? It was only a twenty minute drive, but Harry resented having to go out again. He would have preferred going immediately and getting it over with. All he could guess was that she was going to confess to not knowing either Johnny Mathis or John Lennon or Pavarotti, and beg forgiveness. That she was too embarrassed to do this in front of Wanda and Tracy. Forgiveness, however, he could dispense over the phone. Maybe she was in financial trouble and needed a loan.

At eight thirty he brushed his teeth and put on his jacket. He took the Cadillac to Gallagher's parking lot. Only four or five cars were there, a slow mid-week night.

Harry went up the paved walk and into the bar. A hockey game was playing on a TV up near the ceiling, and two couples sat at tables in the middle of the floor. A waitress was joking with the bartender, and they looked up, smiling, as Harry entered.

He slid into a booth facing the door as the waitress came over. "Bourbon and water," he said. "But hold off. I'm meeting someone."

"Sure," she said. "Just signal when you're ready." And she went back to the bar and leaned her arms on the counter.

At exactly two minutes after nine, Rose Kribbs entered hesitantly, carrying a small satchel. She was wearing a dress of blue satin and a jacket of white fake fur, dangling earrings with matching choker. She looked as nervous as a cat.

"Hello, Mr. Gill," she said, putting her bag on the seat across from him and sliding in next to it. Her jacket caught on the back of the seat, and she had to stand up again to retrieve it. Harry had visions of her opening the satchel to reveal the contents of his cash register, with the announcement that she had wanted to return what she could before flying to Brazil.

The waitress came over and smiled at Rose. "What can I get you?"

"Wine," said Rose. "Any kind." And then, "Red."

The waitress smiled again and moved off.

"It looks as though you're going somewhere special," Harry remarked.

"Not really. I just . . . put this on because I was seeing you," she said, avoiding his eyes. She sat twisting her watch band around and around on her arm.

What the hell? "You said you wanted to talk about something personal, Rose, and I wondered if you were having problems at work."

"Oh, no!" she said.

The wine came along with Harry's bourbon. He felt like swallowing it all down at once and ordering another, but resisted.

"Are you in some kind of trouble?" he asked.

This time her eyes, still timid behind her dark frames, seemed to dance. "Not yet," she said, and giggled.

So Harry smiled too and took another drink. "What's so important that you had to see me tonight?"

"Well," she said hesitantly, and leaned over to peer out the window. "I just. . . . " She pressed her lips together, then turned again, lifting her eyes now and then to look at him as she spoke: "I've been working for you for a year and a half, Harry, and I just . . . couldn't get up the courage to tell you how I felt about you. And then, when your wife died, I said to myself, 'Rose, it's either now or never.'"

This can't be happening, Harry thought, and decided to treat it as lightly as possible. "You know, Rose, there must be something about a widower that brings out the nurturing instinct in women, because it seems like there are a lot of women around who want to take care of me all of a sudden."

She gave him a swift, shy glance. "Well, some men won't even *let* a woman care for them. Some men keep all their affection bottled up. Just corked up!" she said, lifting her glass and looking at it. She took another sip of wine but it went down the wrong way and she choked, reaching for a tissue. The clasp on her purse said, RGK.

Harry desperately played for time to get his mind in gear. "I see your middle initial is a G," he said. "You wouldn't be another Gill, would you? Maybe we're long lost cousins or something."

"Oh, no. It's Gardini. My maiden name."

He started to tell her about a girl he once knew named Gardenia, and suddenly his mind was in overdrive. "That's . . . Italian?"

"Yes," she said, and her eyes darkened. "It doesn't matter, does it?"

"Rose, tell me this," Harry said, putting both palms on the table. "Does your husband drive a Dodge Ram?"

She looked startled, then pressed her forehead to the window again, peering out into the dark. "Yes. Why?" she asked. Suddenly she reached across the table and awkwardly grabbed his hand, like a woman going down at sea.

At that moment Harry was conscious of a short slight man striding through the door and coming swiftly toward them. The waitress at the bar, leaning back with her elbows on the counter behind her, suddenly straightened as the little man charged on past to where Rose and Harry were sitting, Harry managing to retrieve his hand. The little man reached across the seat for the satchel, then held it upside down over the booth, spilling an aqua negligee, a hair brush, and various cosmetics among the drinks on the table.

"Roger!" Rose cried excitedly. Harry stared at the small man facing him, whose every crease on his face was deepening. He wondered if he might have only one arm, for the right sleeve of his jacket was tucked into a pocket.

"Just like that!" Rose's husband said to Harry in a voice too low, it seemed, for a man who wore a size fourteen shirt collar and probably lifts in his shoes as well. "Sitting right here by the window with another man's wife, fine as you please!"

"Now just a minute!" said Harry. "Roger, please sit down."

But Roger Kribbs made no move to sit. He tossed the now-empty satchel back on the seat beside Rose, glaring at Harry all the while.

"You'll not be sweet-talkin' me so you can diddle my wife," he said.

Diddle? Over by the bar, the bartender ducked his head, and the waitress began to smile. An Asian man behind the counter stared poker faced at the scene.

"Look! This is not what you think," Harry began, turning to Rose, but knew he would get no help from that quarter.

In fact, Rose looked up at her husband, and said, "We just couldn't help ourselves, Roger."

"Rose? What the hell is going on?" said Harry, looking from one to the other. But then he noticed that there was a bulge in Roger's right jacket pocket and suddenly the little man faced the rest of the room.

"Don't anyone move," he said.

The bartender and the waitress stopped smiling.

Harry could not believe this. This was the craziest thing he had ever seen. A four-inch Magnum in that pocket, maybe? The young Asian behind the bar slid slowly out of sight. The whole room was suddenly quiet, with only the sound from the TV.

Now the pocket was pointing toward Harry. "All them fancy words you've been tellin' my wife. You didn't think I knew what was going on?"

Rose looked truly alarmed now. "Roger! No! You wouldn't do *this!*"

The pocket turned toward Rose. "Making a fool of me, thinking you can get away with it because he's your boss?"

With his free hand, Roger Kribbs reached into his other pocket and pulled out a small leather-bound book. He tossed it to Harry. "Read it," he commanded.

Harry looked at the cover. *My Daily Thoughts*, it said. He looked at Rose.

"*Read* it!" Roger commanded. He swiveled his body to survey the room, the bulging right pocket pointing toward everyone in turn, then back to Harry again. Nobody moved.

Obediently Harry opened a page at random. It was blank so he thumbed back a dozen pages.

"'I can't live without her,' Harry wept, and clung to me after his wife's funeral. He had never opened up to me before.

'Yes, you can, and you will,' I said, as people started looking at us.

'My little dark lady,' he called me that day. 'You don't know how much

you've meant to me these past months, just knowing that you will be there when I get to work.'

'Oh, Harry, I'm glad! I'm glad!' I whispered. People were really staring then.

He wants me to let my hair come in natural again.

'Those big Italian eyes, like ripe olives,' he said. . . .'

"You wrote this?" Harry said incredulously, mindful of Roger's hand in the jacket.

She said nothing, her face pale.

"Keep reading," Roger ordered. Harry turned another page. If he wasn't sitting at a booth, he mused, he could leap forward and grab the guy, but the edge of the table was already touching his mid-section. "Aloud," said Roger.

Harry looked at the diary again. "*'Unlike some men I know, Harry says he adores the down on my arms.'*" he read.

Out of the corner of his eye, Harry could see the bartender slowly moving inch by inch, from behind the counter. There was a low murmur from the floor somewhere; the Asian man seemed to be giving a street address.

Rose started to cry. "Valentine's Day came and went, Roger, and you didn't even *say* anything! I didn't mind that we didn't go out on New Year's, and I don't care that you don't give me a present on my birthday, but you never even *say* something. How do I know you love me if you never talk?"

"You've always got to be hearing things, Rose. You know how I feel about you," Roger said. And then, to Harry: "Stand up."

His eyes traveling the room, Harry slowly began to edge himself out of the booth.

"Stand up and keep your hands up," Roger snapped, like a first sergeant. The bartender moved a little more. When Harry was on his feet, hands in the air, the little man said, "Take your pants off."

"What?" said Harry.

"Your pants. You're going to know how it feels to be humiliated."

Harry watched his eyes. Watched his hand. Slowly he unbuckled his belt and started to pull it through the loops of his trousers.

"Don't take the belt off, just unzip . . . "

The bartender lunged, tackling Rose's husband from behind, and a moment later Harry helped hold him down, fastening his ankles together with the belt.

"Check his pocket," the bartender said, and Harry did. Nothing there at all.

Everyone in the bar began talking at once, standing up to get a better view and breaking into laughter. Rose was standing too, clutching her purse, eyes huge. There was an acrid smell filling the air, however, and Harry turned to see the aqua negligee beginning to smoke where it had fallen over the candle on the table. He grabbed the garment and threw it to the floor, stamping on it.

"You want to fight this out?" Roger Kribbs yelled at Harry. "You want to go outside, I'll show you a thing or two."

"Relax. I don't want to fight, I don't want your wife, and I think you two have a lot to say to each other," Harry said.

Rose leaned over her husband. "It was the only way to tell you that I'm starving! I'm not just a part of the furniture, I have to know I'm loved."

"You think I'd put a roof over your head and food in your mouth if I didn't love you?"

A squad car pulled up, its lights flashing, and two officers came inside.

"What have we got?" one of them asked the bartender. He looked at the small man on the floor with a belt around his ankles.

"Got a gentleman who's having a little argument with his wife, and pretended he had a gun," said Harry.

The policeman knelt down beside Roger and wrote the particulars in a notebook. "Okay, we're taking him in," he said, getting to his feet again.

"Oh, Roger!" cried Rose. "See what you made me do?"

"You want to follow us to the Rockville Station, Ma'am, and file a complaint?" the other officer said to Rose.

She hesitated, then nodded.

Roger Kribbs glared at everyone in turn. As Harry put on his belt again, he told the man, "If Rose was getting fancy words, they weren't from me, and I don't think they were from Pavarotti either. But you and Rose need to have a little pillow talk, buddy. And for God's sake, remember her birthday!"

Harry moved toward the door after the policeman had left with Mr. Kribbs.

"Hey!" said the bartender.

He turned and put a ten dollar bill on the table, then followed Rose outside. She stood weeping beside her car. The Dodge Ram was parked at an angle nearby.

"You knew he was going to follow you here, tonight, didn't you?" Harry asked.

She sniffled, and wiped her nose with a tissue.

Harry waited. "What's been going on? You've been making up stories about me in your diary and leaving it around for him to read?"

She nodded, without meeting his gaze.

"You know, Rose, you've been causing me one heck of a lot of trouble. Tomato sauce on my pickup, a pizza in my face." She looked up, her mouth open in astonishment. "Your husband's been tailing me home, calling my number. He may not show it as much as you'd like, but by God he cares!"

She cried all the harder.

Harry touched her arm. "Okay. Follow the officer to the police station and take your husband home. And don't come back to work until you've told him everything. Understand?"

Nodding, she got in her car and drove away.

HARRY WAS BACK in his greenhouse the following morning when Wanda came to the door. "Rose isn't coming in today, Harry, she just called. She's quitting!"

"Imagine that," said Harry.

She studied him quizzically. "And she says she and her husband are going on a little trip to Florida to visit his cousin, and to thank you for all you've done for her." She waited. "Just out of curiosity, Mr. G., what *did* you do for her?"'

"Wanda, shut up," said Harry.

But word got out, and when Harry stopped by the barbershop a couple of days later to have a sandwich with Jim. Fred and Leroy were there too, waiting for the full story.

"What's this love triangle you've got going with some Italian woman at the garden center?" Fred asked, as Harry sat down at the card table.

"Just a little woman looking for more romance in her life," Harry said, opening his bag from the deli.

"Gee, Harry, women stick to you like fly paper!" Leroy said enviously. "They room in your house, hit on you at work, knock on your door. . . ."

"I heard he had a gun," said Fred.

Harry laughed. "A long index finger, maybe. I think maybe he's one slice short of a sandwich, but she loves him and they're off to Florida."

"She just asks you to meet her at Gallagher's and she's got this negligee in a bag?" said Leroy.

"The bartender was in for a haircut yesterday. The whole shop was listening," said Jim.

"I don't know how you do it, Harry." Leroy cast a forlorn look at the other men. "Don't know if I could begin again, with my prostate."

"I'll tell you, though," said Fred confidentially, "it's not so easy on the back."

Jim grunted. "It's when they wake you in the middle of the night, looking for action. Hell, our age, we've got to have a little lead time. Can't get Ginny to understand that."

"Get her to walk around in satin pants, put on some net stockings," said Leroy. "What do you think, Harry? Do these young women go for net stockings anymore?"

"Guess you'll have to find yourself a young woman, Leroy, and ask," said Harry.

IT BEGAN SNOWING on Sunday, Jodie's fifth birthday. Don had moved back home the day before, and was dishing up ice cream and blowing up balloons as needed. Harry went to the party, at which five little girls in ruffled dresses tried to see who could make the most disgusting noises at the table. Rosalind, a diminutive child with rakish eyes, won hands down.

Harry drove to the greenhouse later, and came home to find Don's car parked askew in the driveway. All day the snow had come down like feathers, decorating the yew bushes set out in buckets around the garden center, making high pointed caps on the fence posts. Like confectioner's sugar, it dusted every leaf, every bush, and gave the air on Old Forest Road such a clean fresh scent that Harry wondered why he'd favored spring.

Don got out as Harry pulled up.

"What's the problem?" Harry called.

"Elaine lost the snow shovel. How you can lose one of those things I don't know, but she thinks she used it to shovel leaves off the walk last October. Can you believe that? I checked around back, but couldn't find yours."

"It's inside the back door, Don. Come on in." Harry pulled the key from his pocket.

They stomped on the mat, leaving their frosty breath behind, and Harry walked to the kitchen counter. "How about some coffee? Warm you up."

"If you got it made."

"I keep it plugged in all day. Like a cup waiting for me when I get home." He reached for the mugs. "How are things?"

Don took off his cap and unbuttoned his down vest, then wedged himself into a chair, resting one arm on the table. "We're going to give it our best shot and see what happens."

Harry had hoped for more than that.

"Jodie doing all right?"

"She's glad to have me home, and I've missed her."

"Cream?"

"Naw." Don picked up the steaming cup, touched it to his lips, and lowered it again. "Let me ask you a question, Harry. Did you ever look at Beth and wonder why you'd married her?"

Harry tried to think. "I can remember a lot of times I looked at her and thought, 'This isn't the woman I married.'"

"So what did you do when that hit? I really want to know."

Harry took a swallow of coffee. "I guess I told myself I wasn't the same man either. We change, Don. But it's not all at once, and not both of us at the same time. It's not even all bad. Sometimes people change for the better. There would be weeks we weren't hitting it off, and then"—he smiled, remembering—"it was back to the way it was."

There were times, Harry realized, when it had seemed that he and Beth were moving on two separate planes—that their lives touched only occasionally. Some months it was a Redskins' game or an international crisis or a minor calamity with one of the children that suddenly drew them together, sharpened their focus, and held their attention to the same goal. And then, weeks later, he would find that the feeling had stuck. They had come back not because they had to but because they'd wanted. They'd *wanted*. It mattered.

"Yes," he repeated aloud, still smiling. "We always came back." And then he remembered the letter. It was always pulsing just at the edge of consciousness. He would have to live with the fact that there would be no knowing on that score, and he felt like a hypocrite, sitting here seemingly the model of marital bliss.

Don sat pondering awhile—a huge teddy bear of a man stuffed into a down vest. There was a hint of gray in his sideburns, but his cheeks were ruddy.

Harry felt obliged to say more. "I'm not asking you for details, but can you . . . are you able to put your finger on what the problem is?"

"Same as it's always been: I *like* a predictable life. I *like* going to the same job every day, coming home to my same chair at night. Elaine, though. . . ." Don sighed. "She wants to move things, change things, upset the old apple cart." He took a long slow sip of coffee without looking at the mug, then set it down again, eyes on the opposite wall. "She's like a horsefly, always biting at your hindquarters where you can't quite reach."

The kitchen clock seemed to have taken over the room, its loud ticking like a mechanical heart high on the wall.

"Yeah, I think that's it, Harry. She's a disturber of the peace. You've gotta march in time to Elaine's drum beat or you don't march at all. That's the way it's been, but maybe it'll be different now. Maybe in all the changing, Elaine'll decide to change herself. It could happen."

HARRY DID NOT want to make love again to Iris. He *desired* her, but he wanted her to want him, and she didn't feel the need. Now that she had rescued him a few times from his sadness, it seemed, he could be affectionately ignored.

So Harry spent his days in full concentration on the head of Max Bowen. His fingers, which were usually dry and cracked in winter, became soft and moist from their long immersion in the oil-based clay. Maybe he could do this thing—maybe he could really do it—a work all his own that would survive him, if only on Liz's mantel.

He was listening to public radio. Something of Tchaikovsky was playing, he'd forgotten what. He'd listen again for the name of the piece when it was over because it was something he would like to own. The longing in those notes! The haunting of the melody. Someone else had felt the sadness, the loneliness, the desolation, and survived—someone who had gone on to create music, giving voice to soul.

The quest to be unique, a human passion. Those thousands of personal web sites, Harry was thinking, each proclaiming, *I'm unusual! Look at me!* Those millions of homespun greetings on answering machines, including personal sound effects—the resident five year-old or the family dog.

Harry, too, wanted to anticipate more in life than the Publisher's Clearing House prize patrol. He wanted to be able to look at something and think, "I created this"—the way a woman, perhaps, looks at her children. And so he concentrated on the work before him, and tried to squeeze imagination and memory from his fingertips as they traversed the clay.

The sculptor's task, he knew, was not to create a true likeness, but to make it more than true. He might get the shape of the head exactly, the cheekbones, the chin, but it would have no vitality, no soul, unless he went a step further. A master sculptor had to create a deceit; he had to carve some of the details a little deeper, make the shadows more pronounced, in order to give the eyes a glint, for example. Harry sculpted and unsculpted so that the clay that was added one day might be subtracted the next. How could an old friend, whom he had cherished from across a card table, a living room, a patio, be so inscrutable now?

It was like Claude, he thought. After raising the boy to the age of twenty-four, the child he should have known best because he hadn't had to work quite so hard or so long when Claude came along, Harry knew least. If he were asked to fashion the head of his youngest son, Harry might even have found that more difficult still.

He closed his eyes as he cupped his hands over the clay and tried to envision his subject—to smooth the forehead, massage the cheek bones, stroke the heavy eyebrows and settle his fingers at last over the lids of those deep-set eyes. Was this what the stone carvers felt when they fashioned their gargoyles—eyes fierce, mouths open in a howl of defiance at the rain? If he didn't succeed in this project he could always turn Max into a gargoyle.

The nose, he was proud of. Harry felt he had captured Max's nose—the thinness of the bridge and the large oval of each nostril. But the eyebrows and eyes weren't right yet, and Harry worked with little regard for the time. He stopped only when Wanda told him that paperwork was piling up in the office, or that customers were complaining that he hadn't returned their calls.

So much of one's life work was not the job itself, Harry realized, but all the back-and-forthing of business, the jottings and scribblings, adding and subtracting, the sending and receiving and stamping and mailing and tying and drying and watering and seeding and trimming and moving that carried with it only the periphery of satisfaction, of envisioning a lawn well landscaped, a tree in bloom, or of holding in the palms of one's hands the facsimile of the head of an old friend.

He rose early in the mornings, fixing a thermos of coffee, and headed over the snow-packed streets to the greenhouse, his truck a small moving dot in the line of rush-hour traffic. When he passed Iris's old home, he saw that six inches of new snow covered everything in the yard, so that the clay terraces, the old car with the two flat tires, the row of house-shutter shelves holding long-dead plants were now refurbished with a soft coating of white, like plaster over a statue. Then he went to work in the greenhouse, cement dust around him like a reflection of the snow beyond the window—he and Max, dust to dust.

When his children needed to talk to him, they called the greenhouse and usually found him in. Claude, the dutiful son, called just to see how Harry was getting along.

"How is Sue these days?" Harry countered, tucking the phone between ear and shoulder, molding Max's lower jaw. "When's the baby due exactly?"

"I'm not sure," said Claude. "May or June."

"You're not sure?"

"She keeps track of things like this. The doctor will let us know."

Was Claude going to be a father to that child or not? Harry wondered. Nobody *commits* anymore. No one even *declares*. When was the last time the U.S. actually declared war, for example? We just rush in. We don't even commit to ourselves—don't know who we are. Harry could remember a time when, if asked what a man did for a living, he would say farmer or lawyer or priest or salesman. Ask somebody now and it would be "something to do with computers" or "something to do with finance." How did Claude ever explain to people that he was a designer of wrapping paper? What would he say when his child was born—that he did "something to do with fatherhood?"

Jack's calls, when he called at all, were more on the order of announcements. This man who owned the sports bar had agreed to take him on as a prospective partner, provided Jack put half of each month's salary back into the business. They'd work out some arrangement.

Thanks, Dad, Jack's tone implied, *for your lack of faith in me. Somebody trusts me, even if you don't.*

And then a call from Elaine.

"Jack and I had a long talk last night, Dad," she said. "He thinks you're being really hard on him."

"I didn't do a thing."

"That's my point. Mom used to give him almost anything he asked for, a lot more, I'll bet, than she'd admit. 'What else can I *do*?' she used to say. But *you* demand something of *us.* "

"And?"

"Well, maybe that's not so bad."

Harry thought about that as he made his way home on Thursday. He had no answers to give his children. He was a wall off which they bounced their ideas and, more often than not, got them right back again in their laps. Harry, the wall.

A Bach fugue was playing on the radio. That's what they said it was, anyway. It sounded more like a frantic conversation to Harry. Questions and answers. Then answers and more questions.

It was almost nine-thirty when he reached home. The driveway Harry had shoveled the night before had a new half inch of snow on it, so fine and dry he simply swept it off.

Inside, the house smelled like pizza. Harry was annoyed to find a cheese-encrusted pan in the sink untended. Music came from upstairs, but a textbook lay open on the kitchen table, and he knew that Kirsten, in her own way, was studying. He'd leave the pan in the sink another day and see how long it took her to realize it was hers to clean.

He skimmed the paper, put fresh food and water out for Zeke, then went to bed early, discontented that he could not seem to get Max's jawbone right. For a while he couldn't sleep—listened to bath water running upstairs, the sound of Iris's car pulling in about midnight. But at last he drifted off, and didn't wake until he heard Hahn come by for Kirsten the next morning.

Harry knew he should get up, that he was going to be late getting to work, really late, but he must not have slept as well as he thought because his head felt full of sleep. He dozed some more.

A half hour later he heard Iris leaving, the way she always gunned the motor, then sat there with it going full throttle. Hadn't he warned her about that?

For God's sake, let up! Harry thought. But the engine roared on and on, and finally the car blasted off from the curb.

When Harry roused himself to go to the kitchen, he once again found not only the cheese encrusted pan still taking up most of the sink, but muffin crumbs on the table and a half gallon of milk sitting out.

Goddammit!

Slowly he looked around him with Beth's eye—the way she would survey the house were she there. The stove top was splattered with the spray and drippings of a dozen sauces. The knobs on the control panel were gummy. The floor that used to be a beige pebble design seemed to have changed color entirely, and something crunched when Harry moved his foot.

He wandered into the other room and stood still, looking at the surroundings Beth had left behind, the house for which Harry Gill was steward. In the light from the window he could see cobwebs that had accumulated in one corner. Two corners. A long silvery strand reached from the top of one window to the ceiling fixture. Dust. Finger marks.

Worst of all, a coffee stain the shape of South America decorated the arm of the gold chair. Beth's chair. The tip of the continent extended down to the seat cushion, where it expanded once again.

Harry walked into the dining room, his chest feeling tighter. The ceramic jar sat in the bay window, empty now of Beth. The door of the china closet was dingy, unwashed for a year. One of the wine glasses was missing, broken. Iris had used it one night, broken it in her bedroom, and had told Harry she would buy another, but never did. Someone's loafers lay sprawled under one end of the table, Hahn's or Kirsten's, he didn't know whose.

Ha . . . rry.

His name again. He took a step, then stopped. The floor was squeaking. *Ha . . . rry,* it went.

And yet, standing there in the dining room, he heard soft footsteps on the floor above. He stood without breathing. Slowly, very slowly, as though there were weights attached to his ankles, Harry turned, picked up his feet, and made his way softly up the stairs.

The door of Iris's room was open, and when Harry reached the top of the staircase and crossed the hallway, he saw her unmade bed, her clothes scattered about. Shoes and magazines on the floor, a box of tampons, hair brush, tissues.

He went to Kirsten's bedroom—Elaine's—and slowly opened the door. Here too the bed was unmade, strewn with notebooks and clothes. Boots lay on the floor. A plate with a half-eaten pizza on it. Sweatshirts. A container of orange juice.

Harry listened again and heard nothing. The bathroom door was ajar and he crossed the hallway to push it open wide. Nothing but the smell of shampoo and a heap of towels that needed washing. Mold was beginning to grow along the crevice between wall and sink, and the soap dish had grown thick and gray with scum.

He turned toward Jack's room and listened again. Perhaps Jack had come home to live. Hadn't kept up the rent on his apartment, and had been locked out, so he just drove home in the middle of the night. Harry put his hand on the doorknob, then paused and tapped instead.

"Yeah?" came a voice from inside. Then, "Who is it?"

"Just me." Harry opened the door and stared at a man sitting on the edge of Jack's bed. It was not Jack. About his age, perhaps. Not Pete, the boyfriend, either. Yet someone Harry had seen before.

"Yeah?" the man said again, and added, "Good morning."

"And you are?" Harry asked.

"George, Iris's brother."

"I see." Actually, Harry didn't see at all.

"You didn't know?"

"Know what?"

"She said I could have this room." The man was in his undershirt and pants. "Said you never used it, didn't think you'd mind." He waited. "I thought she told you; she made me a key."

Something churned in Harry's chest that turned poker hot by the time his words spewed across his tongue. "Well, check-out time's nine o'clock," he said.

The man looked startled. Stared at Harry, then at the clothes and belongings heaped around the room, then back at Harry again. "You're kicking me out? What'd I do?"

"Unlawful entry, for starters," Harry said, and went downstairs.

The brother did not take his forty minutes. Harry heard sounds of banging and clunking, and fifteen minutes later, George came down with a large duffel bag and clothes over his arm. He headed for the front door.

"Key?" Harry said in the hallway, hand outstretched.

Iris's brother wordlessly dropped the key in his hand and left.

Harry went out to the shed and returned with a box of green vinyl leaf bags. Then he went up to Iris's room and removed everything from her drawers—underwear, pajamas, sweaters, face cream, Monistat 7, shoulder pads, T-shirts. . . . He felt like a Viking on a raid.

The gypsies had invaded his house, and he was returning the favor.

Everything went in the leaf bags. When he had filled one, he took another, then another. Harry looked under the bed, behind the door, on the shelves, in the medicine cabinet. Then he headed for Kirsten's room and raided that.

He carried them all downstairs, two at a time, set Iris's on one side of the hallway, Kirsten's on the other. Finally he took the sheets off the beds, pillow cases, the towels from the bathroom, and stuffed them all in the washing machine.

Wanda Sims phoned. "What's up, Harry?"

"I'm fine, Wanda."

"I was afraid you might be sick."

"No, actually I'm house cleaning."

"I don't believe it!"

"Believe it. I won't be in at all today."

When he hung up, he looked up cleaning services in the yellow pages, and set up a visit for the following week.

Iris came home over the lunch hour. Harry heard her car pull up in the driveway behind his pickup, and saw her sit for a moment, staring at the house, then get out and start tentatively up the outside steps. His heart gave the customary wistful twitch, but it couldn't change his resolve.

She opened the door. "Harry?"

"Iris?"

She took a few steps inside and stared at the leaf bags lining the hall.

"Yours," Harry said gently, pointing. "Kirsten's."

"What's the matter? George called me at work and said you kicked him out."

"Yes, I've decided to go out of the rooming-house business. I think you'll find everything in these bags. If I've missed anything, let me know."

"You went through my *stuff?* "

"As thoroughly as possible."

He could not tell if her expression was anger or surprise. "It's because of George, isn't it?" she said.

"George and Pete and Kirsten and Hahn. I didn't realize you were pregnant when I took you in, Iris, but you've filled my rooms faster than you cleaned them, and I decided I wanted the house to myself again."

"Well, *God*, Harry! All you had to do was say so. You didn't object when Kirsten took a room, so I figured—"

"You figured wrong. You never asked, you just multiplied. I'm sorry, Iris, but it just didn't work out."

"I offered to pay rent."

"I know you did. And I liked having you here, but now I want my privacy again, not the money. Can I help carry these bags to your car?"

She looked at him contemptuously. Then, grabbing up two of the bags, she muttered, "You bastard." And almost inaudibly, "You're all bastards, you know it?"

Down the steps she went, the leaf bags bouncing against her calves. Harry followed with more. By the time they had each made two more trips, however, the starch had gone out of her and she dug around in her bag for the house key.

"I'm sorry I said that, Harry. Thanks anyway for letting me stay as long as you did."

"You're welcome," he said as she dropped the key in his hand.

She got in her car but had no sooner started the engine than she turned it off again, got out, and came back up the steps.

"I forgot something." She marched past him as he held open the door. Going upstairs, she returned a minute later holding the painting of the sailboat at sunset. "I still owe thirty dollars on it, Harry, but it's mine," she said.

He smiled. "You don't know how happy I am to see you take it. Enjoy!"

He watched her leave as she walked around the car, the long

skinny look of her. He would miss her body, the curve of her back, the smell of her arms, the fullness of her lips. Her *self.* But at the same time, he wanted her gone. There had been passion on occasion, there had been tenderness, but the joy was missing, and Harry was hungry for joy.

By the time Hahn drove up with Kirsten at four, they had heard the news and had the key ready. Kirsten stayed in the car, too frightened, it seemed, to confront Harry, while Hahn took the bags. He spoke politely, deferentially to Harry, and when all the bags were in the car and Harry closed the front door, Hahn remembered a jacket of his hanging in the hall closet and came back for that.

The car pulled away at last, and Harry stood in the living room, in the quiet of his house, and waited for loneliness to move in. He braced himself, ready for it. Waiting.

But when it came, and it did come, it seemed only a shadow of its former self. It was not as deep or as cutting as he remembered. It had lost its punch, like the last gasp of a hurricane. Harry was still upright when it had passed. The wave had hit him from behind, spun him around and receded, and he was still standing.

He was not just Bereaved Harry, the Widower Gill. For thirty-four years he had been Beth's husband, longer than he had lived in his boyhood home, longer than he had been single. When he lost her, it was as though the looking glass had been taken away—his view of himself was missing. He had to find that again.

He walked over to the couch and sat down, a deep, resigned sigh on his lips, eyes closed. And then he felt the sofa cushion give, felt the nudge against his leg, and without opening his eyes, he put out one hand and rubbed the top of Zeke's head. The cat purred and nestled down against his thigh.

THE PHONE RANG, and when he answered, Liz said, "Harry, you sound strange."

"I *am* strange. I just kicked out all my roomers. I want the house to myself again, yet I hate to be alone. Is that nuts or what?"

"I've been there. I know exactly what you mean. But you know what it is now? Max is watching me when I undress. I can't go into the bedroom without feeling he's there. It's so creepy I've been taking my clothes off in the closet! I never undressed in the closet before. Is that certifiably insane or what?"

Maybe it was the time of year, Harry decided. With Easter approaching, the newspaper had a story on the Jerusalem Syndrome, as they called it. At Kfar Psychiatric Hospital in Jerusalem, it said, police sometimes bring two-hundred tourists a year for psychiatric intervention. The visitors come to Jerusalem to get in touch with their religious roots, and five days later they're wandering the streets claiming to be John the Baptist or the Virgin Mary. Weirdest of all, once the crisis has passed and they're themselves again, they remember the experience as "very pleasant." Maybe that's what was needed now. He and Liz could ship themselves to the Holy City and they'd fit right in.

"You still there?" asked Liz.

"Barely. Liz, listen. I need to ask you something, and no matter what you may have promised Beth, I need to know."

There was silence, and in that silence Harry felt sure she knew what he was about to ask: "I want to know if Beth ever had an affair."

"My gosh, Harry! What a question!"

"Whatever the answer, I can take it."

"Well, the answer is I don't know. It's not something we talked about over coffee, if that's what you think. I never asked if she had, and she never told me."

"Okay, but did she ever hint that she was thinking about it? Remember when the Madonna statue was crying, and you said it might be a sign Beth wanted to tell me something? Is that what you had in mind? Did you ever suspect?"

More silence. "There were times she was pretty mad at you, but she didn't run out and sleep with somebody. Not that I know of, anyway."

"Liz, this is something I can't ask anyone but you. As far as you know, are all my children mine?"

"My God! Whose else would they be?"

"That's what I want to know."

"You know what? I think you're up to Depression now. You're making progress, you really are. If you get through Depression, Harry, you've just got Apathy to work through and then you're on to Recovery."

"You didn't answer my question, Liz."

"Of *course* I think all your children are yours! I can see you in every single one of them, Harry. Now listen. I really called to find out how the sculpture is coming along."

Harry sighed. "It'll be a while," he said.

HE COULDN'T SEE the clock, but sometime in the night or early morning, the phone rang again. It went on ringing and ringing, and Harry heard next his own voice on the answering machine instructing the caller to leave a message after the beep. There was a click and the voice cut off.

Harry turned over in bed. Wrong number. He gave himself to sleep again, half conscious that it might be one of the Shaws, extracting revenge.

The phone rang again. This time Harry was awake enough to reach over and answer the one by his bed. "Hello?"

An explosive sob met his ear, and then hysterical crying. "H . . . Harry, they've almost killed him!"

Oh, my God! The voice was so high and tense that he could connect no face to it—only assume. Who was the girl Jack was dating now? Jennifer? No, the one after that. Lisa, he remembered. Was

Arlo on the prowl again? He had burned down Jack's laundry, for Christ's sake, what more did he want?

"Where is he?" Harry asked, his mouth dry, chest hurting.

"S . . . Sibley Hospital. In the . . . emergency room. Oh, God, Harry. . . !"

"Lisa, I'll be right there. Is anyone with you?"

There was almost a scream. "Harry, it's Sue! They've beaten up Claude. Hurry and come!"

FOURTEEN

The Music

DEMONS POSSESSED THE Cadillac.

Harry, with Dockers pulled on over his pajamas, shoes untied, careened out of the driveway. He was halfway down the block before he remembered to turn on the lights. He felt as though someone had pulled him feet first from his bed and was shaking the daylights out of him, upside down. His universe made no sense.

Arlo couldn't find Jack, maybe, so he took it out on his brother? Claude had been mugged, then beaten? He had copied another company's gift wrap and they'd sent thugs to teach him a lesson?

He had Old Forest Road to himself and made every light including the red ones. He could smell his own stale breath and imagined himself bursting through the doors of the emergency room, his foul-smelling odor clearing the way.

Don't let him die. Son or no son, don't let him die.

Did Sue know who attacked him? She had said "they." A gang must have broken in, Claude tried to fight them off, but they nailed him. Had Sue escaped completely? Had she been raped? The bastards! What if she lost the baby?

The gates were up in the visitor's lot, the spaces empty, and Harry had the door of the car open before he even turned off the engine. He tripped on a shoe lace and stopped long enough to tie it, one foot on the base of a lamp post.

As he rushed toward the glass doors of the emergency room, he could see Sue inside, sitting in a row of plastic chairs along one wall. Her gray coat was unbuttoned over the roundness of her belly, and she was wearing only a gown beneath. There was no one else in the waiting room, though he could see attendants moving here and there behind the doors to the examining area beyond.

Harry went immediately to her. She reached out wordlessly and hugged him.

"How is he?"

"I don't know yet. They took him right in, and the doctors are with him."

"What happened? Did someone break in, or—?"

She shook her head, pushing hard against her cheeks as she brushed back her uncombed hair. "No. It was outside a bar."

Harry squinted in confusion. "Outside a *bar*? I didn't even know Claude went to bars."

"He was with friends," Sue said. She reached over and touched his arm. "Harry, he's gay."

Now it wasn't just Harry who was upside down. The whole world was at a tilt. His mind played hopscotch. Sue's baby . . . their house . . . Claude's friends. What piece did he start with first? He kept blinking, as though there was sand on the underside of his eyelids. "But . . . why did they beat him up?"

"For no other reason than he's gay."

The outside door opened and Elaine came in, her face pale, without makeup.

"Oh, God! Dad, how is he?" She fell into Harry's arms, then crumpled onto a chair beside Sue.

Sue said, "When you didn't answer my first call, Harry, I called Elaine before I called you back." She turned to Elaine. "We don't know yet. The doctors are in there."

Elaine clasped her arms about her to stop shaking. "I called Jack like you said and left a message on his answering machine."

"I was afraid they might have to operate and need a relative to sign."

"How could *anyone* attack Claude?" Elaine cried. "Sweet, gentle Claude? Did the police catch them?"

"Some of them, I heard. But there were others. They said they were out to find some queers."

Elaine said, "Was David with him?"

Harry turned. "Who's David?"

"The one who called the police," Sue said.

"Have I met him?"

Sue nodded. "Do you remember the art show at Glen Echo? He was there."

A doctor came through the door beyond the desk. He walked to where the family was gathered. Harry stood up.

"Mrs. Gill?" the doctor asked, addressing Sue.

"Sue Merwin," she replied. "How is he?"

"We were concerned about a possible skull fracture, and he's got some bad lumps up there—twenty-two stitches to close up that forehead—but no fracture on the X-ray. The two broken ribs will heal."

Every bone, Harry could feel crack. Every imagined blow took his breath away.

"You're his father?" the doctor asked, turning to him.

"Yes."

The doctor squeezed his arm. "He took some pretty strong

blows to the back, but I think we have things under control. No internal bleeding that we can detect. He's conscious."

"Could we see him?" asked Sue.

"Of course."

"I'll be only a minute, Harry. I'll tell him you're here," Sue said, and followed the doctor through the double doors.

Harry sat down again beside Elaine.

"Dad, did Sue tell you?"

"That he's gay? Yes. Did you know?"

She nodded.

"You've always known?"

"For a long time."

"Why didn't you *tell* me? Why didn't *he*? " There was anger in Harry's voice. "What *is* it with you kids? People accept things like this now." He stopped, looking at the curtained cubicles beyond the inner door. *Well, maybe not.*

"I don't know. Claude and Sue just didn't want to tell you yet. Not after all you've been through with Mom. He was going to, several times, but Mother died, and then there was all that trouble with Jack. Claude figured it was just one more thing you'd have to grapple with. I don't even know when I first knew. It just grew on me."

Harry ran a hand through his hair. "Elaine, I don't get it. What's Sue doing living with him, then?"

"She's lesbian."

Jesus! He felt like a child who simply could not figure out an arithmetic problem.

"Then why do they—?"

"Live together? They're comfortable. That's the way Claude explained it to me."

"Comfortable? A gay and a lesbian have to live together to be *comfortable?* "

"Dad, Sue's in this high-profile job with a conservative company. They'd find some way to oust her if they knew, she feels sure. This way everyone accepts them and they each have their own friends."

"I just don't understand things anymore," Harry said wearily, leaning back and letting his head rest against the wall.

"They do care about each other. Really. They've been friends for a long time," Elaine said, putting one hand over his. "Oh, Dad, I hope he's all right." They both looked toward the glass doors.

"But . . . but is it Claude's baby?" Harry asked.

"Yes."

"Then how?"

"With a turkey baster."

Harry slid down further in his chair, closing his eyes. He did not want to live on a planet where gentle men were attacked by thugs and laundries were burned and fathers took off to live on houseboats and women conceived with turkey basters.

"You know this woman they're hiring to live in and take care of the baby while they work?" Elaine went on. "That's Sue's lover. Her name's Mary, and she's very nice. I think she was at the art show too." Elaine studied him, stroking the back of his hand. "Listen, Dad. When Sue comes out, why don't you go next?"

He did. The doors to the examining area opened by push-button, and Harry followed an attendant. His feet felt like sandbags hitting the floor.

They went past rooms A and B, with their white tile and sliding curtains, past the nursing station where doctors and technicians moved in and out in a buzz of voices, past room four where a woman was crying, to Claude, in room six, a regular room with a door. The attendant opened it for Harry and closed it again after him, leaving him alone with his son.

Claude lay on the examining table, but Harry did not recognize him at first. What he saw upon the pillow was head and hair that looked somehow familiar, but the face was puffy and red, the eyes half swollen shut. He seemed almost an infant again, the newborn in his hospital bassinet—fists clenched, mouth puckered, little slits for eyes.

There was no chair, so Harry leaned against the wall to steady himself. With each breath, Claude gave a soft moan. Harry felt the wetness on his own cheeks as Claude struggled to open his eyes.

Harry leaned lower. "Claude, it's Dad."

Slowly the sweaty head on the pillow turned in Harry's direction. "Dad?"

"Yes, I'm here," Harry said, and put his hand over Claude's.

"Well." Claude's lips stuck together. Like dough, the skin clung, pulling membrane from membrane, and the yeasty opening formed a sentence: "What . . . do you . . . think of me now?"

Harry replied, still holding his hand, "I never loved you more."

When Harry left the room, he met Jack, and was surprised when his son stopped in the narrow corridor and hugged him. They clung to each other for a moment, their hands spread wide over the other's back, fingers splayed, chin on the other's shoulder.

"It would have killed Mom," Jack said huskily. "She would have taken it personally, you know?" He pulled away and gave Harry's arm a little shake. "Think I should go in?" he asked.

Harry nodded. "He'll want to know you're in his corner."

CLAUDE WAS IN the bedroom when Harry drove to the little house in Glen Echo later that week. He had been napping, but sat up when he heard Harry's voice in the doorway. The swelling in his face had been replaced by large blue and purple bruises and the long track of stitches across his forehead.

Mary, Sue's friend, was also at the house, sharing the nursing duties. She was a friendly, open-faced woman who wore wool socks and spoke in a no-nonsense kind of voice. She also wore the same wide gold band on her ring finger as Sue's. Harry liked her, though try as he would, he could not erase the mental image of Mary and the turkey baster.

"The police were by today," Sue told him. "They think they caught all five of the men who did it."

Harry sat down on the edge of the bed. "You identified them?" he asked Claude.

"Not me. They came up from behind and got me first. Some of the other guys got a good look at them, though, and then one of the suspects named the rest."

"How many of your friends were there that night?"

"Nine of us, but they had the bats and chains. They had me on the ground, which is why I got hurt the worst."

Sue and Mary took a basket of laundry to the kitchen to sort, and soon a melody Harry recognized but couldn't name came from the stereo in the other room. Harry studied his son. "Do you *have* to go to bars, Clyde? You've got a home. I confess, I don't understand this arrangement, but—"

"Oh, I have friends in," Claude told him. "Especially David. He's my number one. But sometimes a bunch of us just like to party together. Go out—do things. Go to the theater. I think we should have the freedom to do that."

"Of course, but I'm worried about you. The world is full of crazies."

"That will never change."

"And now that I know—that you're gay—I worry on several counts."

"I'm careful."

Harry soundlessly let out his breath. He remembered his first night with Iris. Passions rise. Things happen. He was going on fifty-seven and he still acted on impulse.

Claude got up laboriously, holding his rib cage, and stood in his T-shirt and shorts, reaching for his trousers. Then he sat again and slowly pulled them on. "I wish I knew what you were really thinking," he said, his back to Harry.

"Lots of things," Harry replied truthfully.

"Let's hear them."

"Wondering why you felt you couldn't tell me before."

"I wasn't telling anybody, Dad. Didn't even admit it to myself until about five years ago." He reached for his sport shirt, and Harry handed it to him. "That's when I met Sue, and she was going through sort of the same thing. We understand each other, and in some ways, she's my best friend. So we live together, nobody questions. It's easy."

"But me?" Harry sat watching Claude's fingers fumble with the buttons of his shirt. "You couldn't tell me?"

"I don't think I would have had any trouble telling you, Dad. A couple times I did think about it, when David and I started getting serious about each other. But I *knew* how Mom felt about queers. And then she got sick, and it just seemed . . . plus the fact that you and Mom never accepted Uncle Wade."

Harry's mind leapfrogged into the past, then galloped forward again, back and forth. Wade just *was*. Acceptance was automatic. "I didn't realize you even knew about Wade."

"That's what I mean. You never talked about him. You swept it under the rug."

"I didn't feel we needed to discuss it."

"That's my point. Why would I want to go my whole life with people afraid to discuss me? As though I were a leper or something."

"Claude, we had Wade over for Thanksgiving and Christmas, all the holidays!"

"But did you ever invite his friends? Did he feel free to bring somebody?"

"He never mentioned it."

"And I'll bet you never asked."

"No." Harry shook his head. "No, we never did. It wasn't that. We didn't feel . . . We didn't mean . . ." But there was nothing to be said. Claude had said it all. "We've made mistakes, Claude," he said at last. "I hope I won't make them again with you."A long minute passed, memories stretching it out. "I'm curious. How did you know about Wade?"

"We all went to the mountains once, and Jack and I rode with him. Remember? We found a book under the back of the front seat. That's how we knew. We never told him we'd found it, but it had photos of men in it. He never went out with women, so we just figured."

Harry watched as his son stood before the mirror running the electric razor, raising his head and carefully maneuvering around the bruise on his chin. Beth had given the boy life, but Harry was witnessing another kind of birth. It was his job this time to see Claude off on the journey.

"Are you happy, Claude?" he asked when he'd finished shaving. He had to know.

"As happy as I've ever been—before the beating, I mean. I'm not that crazy about babies, but I know they'll be fun when they get to be around Jodie's age. Sue and Mary want a baby. So legally, I guess, I'll be the dad, but they'll do the raising. All three of us, maybe. Four, if David moves in. We haven't worked it out yet, but we will." He eased back down on the bed beside his father, both pondering the situation.

"You know," Claude said at last, "about being happy. One of the things Mom did—unconsciously, I'm sure—was to make Jack and Elaine and me feel that we were robbing her of happiness if we weren't happy ourselves. It was our *duty* to be happy for her. And this . . . it can get to be a burden, you know. Like you've got to press that old happiness button whenever you're around her or she'll be upset."

"I guess I can understand that."

Claude turned, hesitated a moment, then leaned over and gingerly hugged his father. "Thanks, Dad, for what you *haven't* done. It means more to me than anything else."

"Haven't done?"

Claude pulled away again. "Haven't suggested I see a psychiatrist. Haven't told me we'll ruin the baby. Haven't asked if I've been tested for AIDS. You didn't get out the old file box, either." He laughed. "Mom, bless her, would have wanted to 'cure' me. You're just letting me *be*. You'd be surprised how many of the guys don't have that."

"You're welcome," said Harry.

And then, as Claude reached for his shoes, he said, "I really think I'm comfortable with myself now. There was a time, way back, when I felt so different from everyone else in the family I was sure I was adopted and you'd never told me." He cast a wary smile in Harry's direction. "And then, when you and Mom were having some trouble—I won't ask, but I think you were involved with another woman—I was so mad at you—at what it was doing to Mom. I mean, when you started vacuuming the inside of your car before you went to work, wearing new shirts, the way you cut your hair and trimmed your nails—we knew."

What were his kids, porous? Harry was amazed at how much they'd absorbed. Even the most unremarkable details had reverberations he did not expect.

"Anyway," Claude went on, "I was so angry I wanted to hurt you like you were hurting Mom, or that I imagined you were, anyway. So I sent you a letter, but you never got it."

Harry felt as though every nerve on his scalp was coming alive, but Claude rambled on: "I was twelve. I wrote you that one of your children wasn't yours. *Me*, of course, who else? And I signed it, 'A friend.' I guess I just felt like I didn't belong in the family, and wanted to spread the hurt around. You gave me the excuse to do it."

Was it anger, relief, or shame that ballooned inside his chest? Harry wondered, feeling its pressure as a physical thing. He struggled to ask the right questions.

"What happened to it? The letter?"

"Mom got it. She said the type looked familiar and she realized it was from our own typewriter. She thought it was a self-addressed envelope you had enclosed with a customer's bill or something, and wondered why it was addressed to our house. Then she read the note, and knew it was from me."

"*How?* "

"I always hit the coma key instead of the period, and she saw that the coma after *Mr.* had been typed over."

The wild temptation to throttle his son gave way to an urgent need to protect Beth. If he told Claude what a torment the last few months had been, Harry would be admitting his own suspicions.

He couldn't speak. They were connected, this family. When one of them suffered, they all did.

"Dad?" Claude said tentatively, mindful of the silence.

Harry collected himself and cleared his throat. "What did your mom say?"

"Asked why I'd done it. Big scene. Tears from me. The works." Now it was Claude who lapsed into silence momentarily. Then, more softly: "After I told her how mad I was at you, she hugged me. Rocked me back and forth and said that what went on between you and her had nothing to do with me and I wasn't responsible for making things right again. That you'd work it out." Claude sighed. "That I was a sensitive kid who would make some girl a wonderful husband because I could understand how a woman feels."

Claude put one foot on the floor and picked up his other shoe. "I think it was right there I realized I could never tell her how different I felt. It would have been like a double betrayal. So I just . . . clammed up. Kept my worries to myself." He glanced over at Harry and waited. "What are *you* feeling?"

Sorrow that his younger son had felt so alienated. Relief that Beth had been faithful. Gratitude that the children with all their faults were his, and acceptance that, flawed as they were, he and Beth had produced these children. Strange. In his obsessive scrutiny to see who didn't belong, he had come to know them better than he ever had before.

"Dad?"

"That I could cheerfully choke you with my own two hands, and at the same time I'm glad you're mine. Wouldn't trade you for the world. What do you suppose your mom did with the letter?"

"Tossed it, I hope. Knowing her, though, she could have tucked it away somewhere—evidence of the depths of a son's love, you know. If she *did* keep it, I'll bet it's some place you'd never think to look. You're lucky she never told you about it—how upset I was. Would have made you feel guilty as hell. It means she really loved you, Dad."

"It means she forgave me," said Harry. "So she must have known how much I loved her." He raised his head as the music from the next room grew more familiar still. "Tchaikovsky?" he asked.

"Hey, yeah! Very good!" Claude smiled broadly. "He was gay, you know."

"Really!" said Harry.

"And he didn't die of cholera, the party line. He committed suicide. Grand old age of fifty-three."

"That true?"

"The real story is that he was caught with the nephew of a high-ranking official, and Tchaikovsky's colleagues were afraid that a scandal would look bad for them all. So they held a 'court-of-honor' and ordered him to commit suicide. Two days later, he took arsenic."

Wordlessly, Harry shook his head and went on listening. Finally, "All that unwritten music."

"Yes. Or, as Sue says, 'that only the angels can hear.'"

HARRY'S CHILDREN TOOK the news of Iris's ouster with some surprise.

"Well, it's your life, Dad," Claude told him. "Somehow I thought it was working out."

"Not really," said Harry.

"I'll bet it was hard to do," said Elaine.

"Yes and no," Harry answered.

It was Jack's reaction, however, that shook the ground under Harry's feet. After a silence that Harry found almost alarming, Jack said, "Dad, I'm so sorry."

"I think we all knew this was going to happen sooner or later," Harry said.

Over the phone, he heard Jack swallow. "No, Dad. I didn't plan it. Not really."

Harry hesitated. "What are we talking about here, Jack?"

"Why you kicked her out. Didn't she . . . tell you?"

And then Harry knew. "When, Jack?"

He heard him swallow again. "I was just so mad at you. The world was coming down around me, and you really pissed me off. It wasn't you. I mean, I was mad at myself mostly. But I knew how to hurt you, so I tried. I'm really, really sorry. There was no excuse."

"I asked you when."

"One of those Sundays you were working in the greenhouse. I came over to see you and Iris told me where you were. She was eating dinner, invited me to have some, and— I knew I shouldn't. I didn't even want her particularly. I just wanted to get back at you."

Harry dropped his chin on his chest and expelled all the air from his lungs. He felt he had to fill them completely again before any more words would come.

"God, you must hate my guts," Jack said.

"Tell me this: You didn't rape her, did you?"

"Christ, Dad!"

"Force her in any way?"

"Hell, no. She was easy." And then Jack added, "Not that easy. I didn't mean that. I think she probably wanted to stay on good terms with the family, that's all I can figure. I'm a louse. I know it, she knows it, and now you know it."

"It was one heck of a payback, Jack."

"I know. I'll just tell you this: Some day I hope I can do something I don't have to apologize for. I mean that."

"I'll hold you to it. The rest is water over the dam."

WITH THE FIRST anniversary of Beth's death looming ahead, Harry saw his house becoming the communication center for news reports. People began phoning with any excuse whatever to keep him connected, he guessed, to the world.

"Geth what, Grampa? I loth two teeth at wonth!" Jodie announced over the phone. "I can thitck my tongue all the way through to the other thide."

Don, who had shuttled the snow shovel back and forth between his and Harry's place, returned it on a Sunday when the sharp March air took on a sweetness not felt since October. Glistening rivulets of water raced excitedly along the curb in the street, carrying with them the dropping red buds of a box elder.

"So how are things?" Harry asked, meaning his daughter. How was her bitchiness? Her complaining? Her sarcasm? He left that part unsaid.

"Elaine wants another baby," Don said in answer.

"Oh?" Harry paused, rake in hand where he had been gathering up winter's discards.

"But I'm against it," Don said. "You don't have a kid just to be glue, you know—to hold something together."

"No," said Harry. "You don't do that."

"I'm not going to change Elaine and she's not going to change me. We either accept each other as we are or we go our separate ways. And right now, I don't know which it's going to be."

Harry wished the news had been more positive. But when he thought of the years Don had expressed no opinion at all, he could only think of this as progress, however it turned out.

"Whatever happens, Don, think of Jodie," was what he said.

"I will, and I do. And I'll say this much for Elaine: she's trying."

NEAR THE END of March, on the day Tracy got her braces removed and the load of Japanese maples came in, Jack called Harry in the greenhouse.

"Busy, Dad?"

"I'm packing up the weeping Madonna," Harry told him. "She's oozing from three or four separate locations now, and the owner decided not to have her recast. Pair of mermaids coming in tomorrow, so I'm trying to get this place cleaned out. How are things with you?"

"I decided not to get involved in that sports bar thing."

"Oh?"

"Too much stress. It's a whole lot different from laundries. People *have* to do their wash, but they don't have go out to drink. When they do, there are a hundred different places to choose from. I'm lucky I got out now before I sank any more money in it. Not that I had that much to sink."

"What are you going to do?"

"Believe it or not, I'm going to work in the bursar's office at the junior college. Figure it will help get me back on my feet, and it'll be a nine-to-five job. I'm going to look around, maybe take a few night school courses, figure out what it is I really want to do."

"Sounds sensible, Jack."

"Yeah, well. Sensible doesn't exactly turn me on, but it will look respectable on a resume. Who knows, I just might like having my weekends free."

No advice was asked and none offered, but at least Jack had called. There was still that tether to home. All Harry could provide was emotional support and the promise not to mess with his children's lives. It didn't exactly turn him on either, but maybe he too would like his weekends free.

SO HERE IT was again. Spring.

Once more, the goose was in her yellow raincoat—the goose and seven goslings, to be exact—and Harry had made it through the first year. His birthday came and went on April 2, with fanfare from the kids and a kiss from Jodie, but he did not welcome the rest of his life without Beth. After Iris, he was hesitant to try again. Singles didn't call it dating anymore, and how could you invite a woman out when you didn't even know what to call it?

He sat on the edge of his bed one Sunday morning, pulling on his socks and contemplating his golden years. He was at the age where his daughter gave him a stained glass window kit for his birthday to occupy him, and his sons gave him clothes to make him more attractive to the ladies, along with a subscription to *Travel and Leisure.* As he got older still, Harry knew, he would have, in addition to a free pass to the national parks, more funerals to attend. Every time he asked about a friend, he risked hearing about prostate surgery.

He got up and avoided looking at himself in the mirror. His body was like having another person to care for. If he did all the gum massaging, back-strengthening, heart-conditioning, muscle-toning exercises the health columns recommended, he would have to add another couple hours to his day.

"I hear you," he said to Zeke, and attended to the cat before he shaved. "Poor fella," he added, stroking the animal's head as it ate. "Poor ball-less, sexless, bag of fur. Eat up, Zeke! Eat, drink, and go back to sleep."

He straightened up and closed the cupboard door. *Ha . . . rry . . .* the hinges sang. He started down the hall. *Ha . . . rry* the floorboards crooned. He knew that while Beth was gone, her whispers were in every room, the yard, his truck, the greenhouse, as surely as the photograph he carried in his wallet. She had left behind a memory as warm, irritating, funny, practical, soft, maddening, provocative, mundane, irrational, tender and complex as she had been in life. She hadn't been trying to tell him a thing because, in their life together, they'd said it all.

He drove to the garden center after breakfast, glad for the slower pace of Sunday drivers on Old Forest Road. The greenhouse was both his salvation and the ultimate testing of himself. It was only when he pulled up to the door that he remembered why he had been avoiding it lately: there was no other work to be done except Max. The swan, the dolphin, the Apostle Paul and Venus had all been cast and shipped back to their owners. The leaky Madonna had gone to rehab to dry out, the mermaids were done except for sanding, and only Max sat waiting, his lidless eyes staring lifeless and cold, even a little crooked, from their sockets.

Maybe that was what was wrong, Harry thought, studying his sculpture now. Maybe the lids were too narrow; you hardly knew they were there. He left the door open to bring the April fragrance into the shop, but it did nothing for his spirits; the real Max was as elusive as ever. Each day that Harry stepped up to his workbench, he waited for the recognition to hit that this was indeed his friend of thirty-some years. But each time his brain had to be told. Each time the ears seemed to be wrong, or the mouth, and if not the mouth, the chin, the eyes, the jaw. Was there ever an artist content with his work? Did a master sculptor even, ever step back from his creation to say, "This is more than I ever dreamed?"

Probably not. And so Harry labored on. A pinch off the left ear, more fullness about the neck. Raise the forehead, maybe? No. Hell, *lower* the forehead; Max looked like an alien. Perhaps Harry was being too exact and it was better than he thought.

It was partly because he was playing Rachmaninoff that he did not hear the car pull up outside the greenhouse. He had bought the tape on sale, and did not know where this Russian belonged in the eclectic collection of tapes he had purchased so far. But no sooner had he begun to listen than he thought of Tchaikovsky and Rimsky-Korsakov, and sensed how they all fit together—the structure of things, their music. It was new and yet familiar. He delighted in it. And as Harry reached out to turn up the volume, Liz Bowen stepped through the door.

It was too late to hide Max, but Harry did not want her to see it. He needed another month at least, yet there she was, standing in the doorway in one of Max's suit coats.

"I thought I'd find you here," she said. "It's a beautiful morning so I guessed you'd be in your shop. You don't get out enough, Harry. You're working too hard."

He hastily draped a towel over the sculpture and moved between Liz and the workbench. "I had the same thought," he said. "In fact, I'm closing up." He reached for the light and pulled the string, then realized he hadn't turned it on. Sunlight flooded through the green opaque windows and seemed to dance along with the music.

"I wanted to see how Max is coming," Liz said, slipping off the suit jacket and flopping it over the work stool. "I haven't been here for a long time." She was wearing her own slacks and sandals, but one of Max's shirts, sleeves rolled up to the elbows.

"Stop by next week," Harry pleaded. "I'll let you see it then." But Liz edged around him. "Come on, Liz."

Harry waited by the door, jingling the keys in his hand, watching her face. Her hair definitely *did* have more silver, and he wondered if this was about the time brunettes turned blond. He'd always hated that. You remembered a girl from high school, perhaps, as a dark brunette, and then one day you saw her on the street, wrinkles and all, and she was blond. You tried to remember how she'd looked in chemistry, and wondered if she bleached her bush now too, or didn't mind the incongruity.

Liz reached forward and removed the towel, placing it to one side. Then, both hands on the revolving base, she moved the bust of her husband around slowly so as to see it from all angles.

She was not smiling. For a moment Harry wondered if she were even breathing, and he began to hope. The shock of recognition? Had he done it, then? Had his hands, which had spent their life copying the masters, accomplished more than his eye could see?

He wished she would speak. She seemed to have become a statue herself, arms out in front of her, fingers resting lightly on the base.

Something was happening to her face, however. Harry couldn't tell what. Her chin seemed to be rising, the eyes growing more narrow, and suddenly her jaw began to tremble. She was crying.

"God, Harry!" she wept, as her hands fell to her sides and her face began to crumble. "It doesn't look like him at all!"

Harry stood with his fingers on the doorknob, unable to go in or out. The moment of truth, and he wasn't ready.

"Not at *all!*" she wept bitterly. "I'm s . . . sorry, but the head doesn't even look the way it did when I brought it over. The forehead's . . . too high, and the. . . . Oh, Harry!"

It was not a cry of anger but of anguish. She fumbled in the pocket of her slacks and produced a tissue, then suddenly burst into loud sobs.

Harry watched helplessly as she flailed about, finding the one tissue inadequate and stopping to search the pockets of Max's suit coat until she found another. Her face looked contorted as she lifted her arms to blow her nose, but then, like a conductor who has lost control of the orchestra, let them drop. Whenever she tried to speak, the words seemed caught in her throat. Finally:

"It was so stupid of me, so idiotic, all this Max business. Max this and Max that. As though somehow the smell of his clothes or the crease of his trousers or this . . . sculpture—*anything*—would make him real to me, and nothing works, Harry! *Nothing works!*"

She turned to him, her face wet, and in the only gentlemanly thing he could think of to do, Harry put his arms around her and patted her back.

Liz went on sobbing, her hands tightly clasping his shoulders, and he felt her weight press even more heavily against him. She said nothing, but poured out all the grief of the past two years onto his chest.

He was waiting for the realization that he had failed—that not even here in his own shop was he the creator. He would be an enabler, one who takes something second-hand and keeps it going—the house, his children. Yet the sadness which had haunted him so relentlessly in the past hung back. Any moment, Harry thought, he would feel it seize him by the throat. Any moment it would fill his being.

The only thing he could feel, however, was the softness of Liz's body against his. Her hands found their way behind him and encircled his back. Harry could smell the scent of her hair.

Perhaps. . . . He watched as the sun, moving in and out of the clouds, lighted up the windows of the greenhouse, turning the green of the glass almost white. Perhaps it was not creation after all that would fulfill him. The critical part, maybe, was the nurturing of a thing—a person—once it was born.

Instead of depression, Harry was conscious of a feeling of familiarity here with Liz. Hers was not Beth's body, but it had the roundness, the softness of middle age, the slight puffiness to her back above her bra, the fullness of her hips, the ease with which she nestled against him, that made him feel as though she belonged. She *belonged.*

She had stopped crying now, aloud anyway, and seemed to become more pliable in his arms. Relaxed. Secure. Rachmaninoff played on, magnificent and determined, and Harry almost wanted to tap out the rhythm on Liz's back with his fingers. Then he realized that these same fingers were caressing gently behind her ear.

"Harry?" she said softly.

He leaned down and kissed the top of her head. Was he crazy?

"What are we doing?"

"I don't know," he answered, "but I like it."

"I don't think I want a bust of Max even if it looked like him," she said into the crook of his arm. "Because I don't think it would help." She straightened, still holding onto him, and met his eyes. "And you know what? It doesn't matter. What we had, Max and I, is mine to keep, so all the rest—his clothes, this bust—they just don't matter."

The phrase seemed part of a melody that came back again and again in subtle variations. He looked down at her, cupping her face in his hands—the face of a woman who had confronted the dark abyss and climbed out the other side. Maybe she would show him the way.

"Tell me something, Liz. Do you think we'll ever get over it?"

"No. We just get more used to it, that's all." She put her arms around his neck, leaning backward so she could study his face. "It's been two years since Max died, and I still show his picture to perfect strangers. Isn't that a little nuts?"

"Would you believe I haven't thrown out Beth's cereal? It's right there in the cupboard."

"I sleep with his pajamas, and I've *never washed them*, Harry!"

"I've kept all her perfume."

The haunting melody that had moved in and out of the Rachmaninoff piece ended in passionate grandeur and the cassette player fell silent.

Harry slowly released her and grinned. "Look. Why don't we go to a movie this afternoon, buy some popcorn, and start from the beginning."

She smiled the way she used to smile for the thirty-three years Harry and Beth had known her.

"All right," she said, picking up her handbag. "Don't forget to turn off the cassette player."

"Max's coat," he said, pointing.

"You've still got plaster dust on your pants, Harry."

He turned so she could brush off the backs of his legs and then, one arm around her shoulder, he guided her outside and closed the door behind them.